Eddie

The Freshman Year

2017

Eddie
The Freshman Year

Robert E. Zee

ISBN-13: 978-1987451726
ISBN-10: 1987451724

Disclaimer

This is purely a work of fiction and fantasy. Any names, characters, schools, businesses, places, events and/or incidents are either the products of the author's imagination or used in a fictitious manner. Any resemblance to actual persons, living or dead, or actual events is purely coincidental.

Please Note

This book is the first in the Eddie the Mechanic series. To find out the rest of the story, please read Eddie - The Sophomore Year, Eddie - The Junior Year, and Eddie - The Senior Year. After the high school years, the story continues into the college years and beyond.

Contents

The Early Years

Eddie was born into a family of second generation Americans. His grandparents came over from Eastern Europe with little more than a suitcase and the clothes on their back. Although they work hard, they have very little to show for it. Eddie's father also works hard and has a little bit more to show for his labor. There is always good food on the table, and time for Eddie's parents and grandparents to spend with Eddie. Since Eddie's family doesn't have much, anything that Eddie has is highly valued.

Eddie's father, Dominik, is employed as a jobber. A jobber is someone who can do just about anything having to deal with construction or mechanical things. Simply put, a jobber is someone who is hired to do a specific job, completes it, and moves onto the next job. Although Dominik does not have a fancy job title, he is very much in demand for his broad range of skills. Having work lined up for weeks in advance, he always has enough to keep him busy.

Since Eddie does not have a lot of "stuff," he spends much of his time in other ways. Eddie likes riding his bicycle, playing football with the older kids, or swimming in the county pool. Eddie can run faster than most of the older kids, so they let him join their football games after school. They all play on a field that is a few blocks over, so getting there is easy for Eddie. When they throw the ball to Eddie, he takes off like a lightning bolt toward the goal line. At ten years old, Eddie was able to outrun his father. At twelve years old, Eddie was pushing a lawnmower, cutting the neighbor's lawns for exercise and profit. Now, at fourteen years old, Eddie is the middle school track star.

After school, while the other kids are watching TV or just hanging out, Eddie is usually found riding his bicycle. Riding with one or two of his friends who are able to keep up for the ten or fifteen miles, Eddie gets quite a bit of exercise. On the weekends, Eddie rides quite a bit farther, perhaps to the beach, the mall, or just around town. On a rainy day, Eddie typically works on his bicycle and works out. He would repack the wheel bearings, true up the wheels, or perform other maintenance, fine tuning his mechanical masterpiece that he built from scratch. While he is thinking of other ways to improve his bicycle, Eddie works out with weights, which are set up next to the workbench in the basement. Occasionally, some homework might even get done between exercises.

Eddie is highly mechanically inclined. If it were mechanical, and broken, Eddie is somehow able to fix it. He often makes improvements to anything mechanical whenever he can. At fourteen, Eddie is already able to change the oil in his father's car. Learning from his uncle, who lived down the street, and from his father, Eddie is also able to tune up an automobile. Eddie's uncle, who is employed as an airplane mechanic, would watch as Eddie works on a car, giving Eddie as little supervision as he could. His uncle always encourages Eddie to figure things out for himself. Giving Eddie some words of wisdom, his uncle repeatedly says, "if you can't fix it, you'll have to pay somebody to fix it."

Eddie is the fastest guy in the middle school, well, except for a guy named Mark. Both Eddie and Mark train equally hard, but are totally unaware they are even training. Their training consists of activities they enjoy doing. Both eat well, primarily because their parents grow much of their own food and shop at the farmers market instead of grocery stores. Eddie and Mark both always give the proverbial 110 percent, if more than 100 percent is even possible, all in the spirit of having fun. Eddie and Mark excel at just about any sport they venture to play. Although they are teammates, some sort of synergistic competition always exists between Mark and Eddie.

Mark, like Eddie, cannot be found anywhere near a television. This is because a television can't be found anywhere in Mark's home. Having no television gives Mark much more time to do other things, such as working out and running. Mark proudly wears a T-shirt in gym class, quite fitting with the words "Muscle Man of the Year," which he had made at a local T-shirt shop. Unlike Eddie, who bicycles everywhere, Mark prefers to walk or run anywhere he goes. The good news is that the county pool is only a mile away from his home. The short run is a small price to pay to cool down on a hot Summer's day. Although swimming laps in the pool is yet another way to work out, Mark thinks of it more as having fun rather than a workout.

Mark has a slight bit of an advantage in the sports arena. He is a year older than everyone else in the eighth grade. Mark's mother missed the deadline for kindergarten registration years back. Mark's parents, originally from Czechoslovakia, are first generation Americans. English is not Mark's mother's first language, so something must have gotten lost in the translation regarding the registration date. The year delay gave Mark an extra year of riding his bicycle, running around, and playing in the woods. Sitting in a classroom, drawing pictures destined to decorate the refrigerator, was delayed for a year.

Mark's father, Joseph, is also employed as a jobber. Mark's and Eddie's fathers occasionally work on jobs together. While Eddie's father works mostly on mechanical items, Mark's father works mostly on construction. Mark, learning from his father, is on his way to becoming a master of home repair at the age of fifteen. Mark is able to replace siding, frame a structure, do electrical and plumbing repairs, and even paint without making a mess. During Summer vacation, Mark's father occasionally takes Mark along on a job, giving him the heavy work to do. Even when carrying a tool box, Mark will often do curls to build up his biceps, or shrugs to build up his Trapezius muscles. Mark's father pays Mark for the work he actually does, not by the number of hours he put in.

Mark and Eddie are, at best, average in school. Not surprisingly, gym class is their best subject. They are always picked at the top when choosing teams. Occasionally, they will be on the same team, which usually meant a disaster for the opponents. In eighth grade, there is a period known as study hall, where the students go to the library and study, or sit and do homework in the lunch room. During eight grade study hall, not surprisingly, Mark and Eddie return to the gym for an extra period of gym class.

Eddie and Mark already have the skills that could earn them a living in the marketplace. School is the prescribed path to get a better job someday. That is the hope and dream of immigrants, to get a better life through a better job. A better life comes through hard work, both in school and at work. Sitting around and being lazy is not an option in Mark's and Eddie's homes.

At lunchtime, Mark and Eddie are seemingly the CEO and CFO of the daily game of Kill the Man with the Ball. Played by the usual 40 or so mixture of sixth, seventh and eighth graders, only the fast and tough guys survive. Others will quickly become part of the turf should they dare to stray from the library or lunchroom. Being in eighth grade, and proudly at top the middle school food chain, Eddie and Mark are untouchable.

The story line usually follows the same script. Mark, being chased down by the pack, throws the ball to Eddie, who runs for a while, only to return the favor once the pack gets close. Just to keep things interesting, occasionally Mark or Eddie will throw the ball to some unsuspecting newcomer to the game. Without a moment's notice, the new guy on the block gets a quick lesson in Rugby etiquette. Not surprisingly, a few of the other track team members also excel at this game. A vague rule seems to exist among the track team not to take down another team member.

Today, there is no game of Kill the Man with the Ball for either Mark or Eddie. After school today is the last track meet of the year and Mr. Harris, the coach, does not want the team expending any unnecessary energy on such meaningless lunchtime endeavors. Mr. Harris also has a habit of frequenting the lunchroom on the day of a meet. He makes sure the team is not eating anything that will later interfere with their performance. If Mr. Harris sees French Fries on a track team member's lunch tray, he will take them back to the lunch line and bring them something more healthy to eat. Occasionally, Mr. Harris will stand behind the lunch line and, when a team member moves through the line, he will make sure they chose a healthy lunch. With Mr. Harris, losing a meet is not an option.

Hanging out against the brick wall, Mark, Eddie, and a few other track buddies watch today's session of Kill the Man with the Ball. "It looks like Tim's having a good run," expresses Mark, with great surprise. After a long pause, Eddie replies, "Gump's going to blind side him. Watch this." Tim takes a wide right turn, and coming around the side of the pack to cut him off is Daniel Gaspari. Daniel, also known as Gump, is an outside linebacker on the football team and a wrestler. Gump is not exactly the guy you'd want to take you down. Gump, seemingly out of nowhere, plows into Tim like fully loaded dump truck running into a shopping cart. As the ball comes lose, Gump wrestles for it and takes off. The pack takes off chasing Gump, leaving Tim mangled and face down in the grass to meditate for a while. "That didn't end too well for Tim," says Mark, laughing along with Eddie. Neither Mark nor Eddie would ever go down like that, for they are too fast for anyone to catch. If it ever looked like they were going down, they quickly toss the ball to someone else, and let them take the hit.

With the meet three hours away, it's back to class for Mark and Eddie. Neither will too pay much attention to anything said in the classroom for the rest of the day. Their mind is on the meet, where it perhaps should be. Health class is right after lunch, so it is a class that Eddie and Mark can coast through. Mark and Eddie stop by their lockers to pick up a few books before they head to class. Sitting in class will give them some well needed rest before today's track meet later in the afternoon.

In health class today, the topic is illicit drugs, and why you should not take them. The topic of drugs is in the syllabus by no accident. Next year, the class will be in high school where drugs are commonplace. Mr. Coleman, the instructor, is describing the types of illicit drugs, the effects of each drug, the dangers, and why you should not take them. In his lecture, Mr. Coleman mentions, "by the time you graduate from high school, statistically 25 percent of you will have tried marijuana at least once." Mr. Coleman's job is to discourage such activity among the students.

Eddie, rarely participating in class discussions, thinks about what Mr. Coleman said for a moment, and raises his hand. Mr. Coleman is quite surprised to see that Eddie is actually participating in class. Mr. Coleman also displays some enthusiasm that anyone is even paying attention to his lecture. Pointing to Eddie, Mr. Coleman asks, "yes, Eddie. Do you have a question?" "Yeah," Eddie responds, "if 25 percent of us are going to try pot, does that mean 25 percent of the teachers in this school have tried it too?" The class bursts out laughing, quickly followed by an uproar of typical student chatter.

While Mr. Coleman hopelessly tries to get the class under control, students are commenting to each other, "how about Mr. Otto?" "Miss Brown, I bet she's tried it!" "Oh, yeah! And, Miss Knox," comments one student, with another responding, "oh, for sure! You know she's done it!" After about ten minutes, order is somewhat restored but, by then, the class is over. The bell rings, and the students move on to the next class. The rest of the school day is less eventful, except for, perhaps, the story Eddie gave Mr. Coleman to tell later today in the teacher's lounge.

Mark and Eddie both know that Mr. George Frazier, the high school track coach, will be at today's meet. Mr. Frazier will be scouting the talent that he will inherit for next year's track season. Today's meet will be held on the track that encircles the Kill the Man with the Ball field, commonly known as the football field. This is Mark and Eddie's field. No one comes anywhere near Mark and Eddie's field and wins. It is also well known that, with Mr. Frazier, the person coming in second place is the first loser. Today, with Mr. Frazier standing aside Mr. Harris, winning, and winning big, is the only thing that matters. Centerville Middle School, the opposing team, is a formidable opponent. If the pressure was ever on, it is today.

As the final bell rings, classrooms empty into the halls, lockers slam shut, and many students are headed to the doors. Some students get on their busses to go home. A few students walk home. Others stay around for some after school activities. Today, however, is a little different. A large group of students, mostly the athletic guys and girls, is headed out to the track to watch today's meet.

Some parents are already standing around the track, waiting for the competition to begin. Everyone knows what is going down on the track this afternoon. Eddie and Mark will be competing head to head in the 100-yard dash. They will not only be racing head to head, but they will be up against one of the fastest guys in middle school in the county. And, knowing that Mr. Frazier will be at the meet, everyone expects a highly competitive afternoon.

Mark, Eddie, and a few of their track buddies, head down the hall to the locker room. Many members of the team are excited about the meet, while others are nervous and apprehensive. If Mr. Frazier was not attending the meet, a more relaxed atmosphere would be felt, especially among the students who are entering high school next year. Mr. Frazier's presence, however, will probably motivate the team to run faster than they normally would.

Gary Mitchell, the school's five-star distance runner, appears to be a little nervous today. Gary will be running the mile in today's meet. He will be competing against some twig of a guy who looks like his lower body was stretched on a rack or something. The twig slightly edged out Gary in a cross country meet this past Autumn. Gary is not about to let that guy beat him a second time. Standing about five feet, eight inches, Gary has a body fat measurement in the single digit numbers. By not carrying any extra weight at all, he is able to move his body the entire mile with great speed and efficiency.

Eric Johnson, running the 220-yard dash today, is acting like he already has his race wrapped up. Johnson, who may not have delivered the best times this year on the track, is nevertheless a brilliant runner. He will typically run only as fast as he needs in order to win the race. Running distances from short sprints to 440 yards, Johnson is not someone to underestimate. Johnson's greatest strength is the ability to sprint for 110 yards at nearly his top speed at the end of a race. This makes him well suited for the 220-yard dash, the 440-yard run, or the half mile.

Axel Braden, with his usual optimism, reassures the group, "we are gonna kick ass! Kick ass! That's what we're gonna do! Kick their ass!" Braden, who will be running the 440-yard run today, has great cause for optimism. Braden's consistent sub-60 second quarter mile is virtually a one man race. No one seems to know Braden's limits. It is not even known whether Braden knows his own limits. It seems that, when Braden's brain commands his body to perform, it performs, and performs well.

Robert Bradshaw, the doctor of the shot-put, is not worried at all. Standing about six feet tall, and weighing more than 200 pounds, Bradshaw tosses the shot-put around as easily as most people would toss around a baseball. It's rarely a discussion of whether Bobby B. will win the shot-put event. The real question is by how much he wins. Bradshaw has not lost his event all year, and is not about to start today.

Mark and Eddie are eerily and unusually quiet today. They will be up against some square-jawed guy who looks like an old Rock 'em Sock 'em Robot from the early 1970s. The robot, who gave them a run for their money last year, had to settle for third place, and is not about to let that happen again. It's a sure bet he's not going to settle for anything less than first place today. Eddie will also not settle anything less than first place either. Neither will Mark. The competition between these three runners is what will make the 100-yard dash the main event at this afternoon's meet.

Before the meet, the team members congregate in the hallway near the door to the locker room. One guy mentions something about perfect weather. That is encouraging, since no one wants to run in extreme heat or cold, or in the rain. Eric Johnson pulls out an apple, and starts eating it to get his carbohydrate levels up. Since everyone was sitting in class all day, a few of the athletes begin stretching. The chit chat eventually dies down, and the team heads into the locker room.

While they are dressing, some guy named Jimmy O'Brien, informs Mark, "I hear their fast guy runs a 10.5." "Shut up, junior," replies Mark. Mark is not interested in listening to that kind of encouraging bullshit right now. Jimmy O'Brien is only on the track team because his father is a teacher in the high school. The team would be better off without O'Brien, who hasn't won a race all year, and probably never will.

Quite the opposite of Jimmy O'Brien is Axel Braden. With his one-track mind, Braden continues reassuring everyone, "we're gonna kick ass today!" Braden, who is always very optimistic, could easily double as a one man cheerleader for the team. If you ask Braden, he will tell you that he has already won his events, and that the team has already won the meet.

"Listen up," coach Harris yells through the locker room, "everyone in the gym in five minutes." In five minutes, the coach will announce the lineup and give the team any inside information he may know about the opponent. Any inside information doesn't matter much to Mark or Eddie. They already know who they are up against. And, as for Gary Mitchell, he's not about to let that six-foot six-inch tooth pick beat him again.

Almost like an afterthought, Coach Harris reminds the team, "and please remember to take your spikes off before you walk into the gym. Spikes on a wooden gym floor don't mix." The team knows this quite well, for they are reminded to take their spikes off when entering the gym before every practice and every meet. A few years ago, several sprinters walked across the gym floor wearing spikes. This made the gym appear like someone drove a lawn aerator across the floor in circles. For some odd reason, the damage done to the gym floor irritated the basketball coach.

The team, seated on the bleachers, looks to the left as Mr. Harris walks in. "This is the most important meet of the year," the coach declares to the team for at least the fifth time today. Reading from his clipboard, he announces the line up. Everyone has two events, their main event, and another event that may change from meet to meet. "Mitchell, Livingston, and Ford, you're running the mile," announces Mr. Harris with obvious pride. "Braden, Hill, and O'Brien, the 440," Mr. Harris notifies the team. The pontification drags on, with everyone in a daze of sorts until they hear their own name. "Mark, Eddie, and Hoffer, the 100-yard dash," announces Mr. Harris, which is no surprise to anyone. Next year, Hoffer, who looks very promising, will be on his own in the 100-yard dash.

Staring out into space, Mark and Eddie hear their name again a minute or so later, both missing entirely the event that was announced. Eddie, still in a daze, pipes up and says, "who?" "You, and the same 4 by 440 relay team as the last meet, and every one before that," replies Mr. Harris, who didn't seem too annoyed, understanding the pressure the team is under. "OK, everyone up, and we all walk out together," insists Mr. Harris, smiling as if he knows something the team does not.

Moving out from the gym into the hall, the team heads out the door. The sprinters sit on the retaining wall, and put on their spikes. They will be the last ones to get out to the field. Mark and Eddie will be up in the 100-yard dash, which is right after the 100-yard hurdles. The first event, the 100-yard hurdles, is an event that does not interest them at all. No one really wants to run the hurdles. A race that is usually reserved for newbies, the 100-yard hurdles is some sort of rite of initiation to join the team. Once they get their shoes on, Mark, Eddie, and Hoffer head to the starting line, standing aside as the hurdlers fumble with the starting blocks as if they've never seen them before.

Since this is a middle school track meet, today's meet is managed by five Timekeepers and one Field Judge. A track meet is usually coordinated by several officials, who are the Meet Director, Meet Announcer, Starter, Lane Judges, Field Judges, and Timekeepers[1]. Running today's meet, the Head Timekeeper gets the awesome responsibility of serving as Meet Director, Meet Announcer, and Timekeeper. The Head Timekeeper meets with the coaches to go over the schedule of events. This only takes a minute or two, as everyone has been through the same procedure all season. Wasting no time, the Head Timekeeper then instructs the coaches to have their teams prepare to run the 100-yard hurdles.

Mark spots the square-jawed Rock 'em Sock 'em Robot standing off to the side of the track, walking back and forth nervously looking at the ground. "There he is. He looks worried," Mark whispers to Eddie. "Good," Eddie replies confidently. Eddie, who spotted him a little earlier, tells Mark, "he'll burn himself out worrying before the race. He's already checked his laces at least a dozen times." After hearing Eddie's comment, a big grin comes across Mark's face. Mark is now thinking of a plan to throw the square-jawed nervous wreck off base right before the race.

The hurdlers are set and ready to run, but Mark and Eddie pay no attention. As the gun goes off, the sound of spikes grinding into gravel announces the beginning of today's track meet. The hurdlers are gone. Now it's down to the real business.

Paying absolutely no attention, to who won the hurdles, Mark and Eddie walk onto the track. Eddie, checking the roster posted on the music stand borrowed from the band room, is in lane three. Next to him, in lane four, is Mark. The square-jawed guy, still checking his laces every minute or so, is in lane five. Mark points to square-jawed's shoes, and says to Eddie, "let's psych him

---

[1] See Appendix I.

before the race." Eddie replies laughing, "yeah, tell him that his shoe laces are untied right before the gun." Mark, who will have to do the dirty work since square-jaw is the lane next to him, agrees.

Mark and Eddie adjust their blocks, which takes them just a few seconds. After doing some last minute stretching, Mark and Eddie are as ready as ever for the race to begin. The squared-jawed guy, in the mean time, is endlessly checking his shoe laces, and adjusting his blocks. Looking down the track, Eddie sees the track lined with a few dozen people on each side, with more headed toward the area. Eddie wonders where they all came from. After all, this is a middle school track meet, not the Olympics. Eddie looks over at Mark who, like Eddie, appears quite confident. Eddie tells Mark, "it looks like we have an audience."

"On your marks," announces the Starter. This is it, the big moment. Time appears to slow down, as Mark, Eddie, and the others, walk up from behind their blocks and position themselves as they have many times before. After getting positioned in the blocks, Mark looks over at the squared-jaw guy positioning himself in the blocks. Mark motions vaguely to the blocks and his shoes, and says to the square-jawed guy, "you may want to fix that," leaving incredible uncertainty as to what may be the problem. Eddie laughs under his breath, thinking to himself, "that was a really good one." No one else has a clue about what just transpired.

"Set," the magic word from the Starter that gets the adrenaline flowing, is heard by all. The square-jawed guy, still examining his shoes and blocks, is thrown a little off base. The goal was accomplished by Mark in the distraction department. Time appears to stand still to the runners, as dead silence surrounds the track. The runners all get set. Once they are motionless and ready, the Starter will pull the trigger. Everyone, including the spectators, is ready. Mr. Frazier, the high school track coach, is also ready at the finish line with his own stopwatch. Mr. Frazier, who almost qualified for the Olympics in the 100-meter dash about a decade ago, not only looks at how fast you run, but also looks at how you run. He is every bit as set as the runners.

About ten yards in front of the runners, the Starter raises the gun into the air with his finger on the trigger. Another official, with his own gun, is lined up with the runners and will be checking for any false start. No one wants to hear the sound of the second gun, signifying a false start. With their heads facing forward, Mark and Eddie have their eyes to the left on the Starter's finger. Mark and Eddie are not stupid. They are masters at anticipating the gun. They both know that the Starter should have the gun out of view behind his back. When the Starter's finger shows the slightest movement, they will set their eyes forward and take off.

When the Starter's finger on the trigger begins to move, Mark and Eddie fix their gaze forward. Just as the sound of the gun startles everyone, Mark and Eddie are off a split second before anyone else. Mark and Eddie are already leading the pack ten yards into the race. The square-jawed Rock 'em Sock 'em Robot is embarrassingly in fourth place shortly after leaving the blocks. Perhaps Mark's comment caused more distress than expected.

Eddie, pouring on the power, takes a slight lead over Mark. At about 40 yards into the race, two groups clearly emerge. Mark and Eddie are in the first group. The others, who are five yards behind, are in the second group. The second group is now marginally being lead by square-jaw. By 60 yards, barring some unforseen circumstances, first and second place are already locked in. Now in a two-man race, Mark and Eddie are head to head. No one else stands a chance to catch them. The spectators are all watching intently. They cannot tell whether Mark or Eddie is ahead. Neither can the two runners, who, by now, are running faster than they ever have before.

With 20 yards left, Mark and Eddie are still head to head. Neither Mark nor Eddie exhibits any signs of slowing their pace. As the cheering gets louder, the finish line draws nearer and nearer. With ten yards remaining, Mark may have a quarter step advantage, which is quickly eroded away as the two runners approach the finish line. Both begin the lean forward two or three yards before the finish. In a flash, they both cross the finish line. A second later, the Rock 'em Sock 'em Robot crosses the line. The robot is quickly followed by Hoffer, then the rest of the pack.

The words, "Mark or Eddie," can be heard everywhere in the crowd. "Eddie won," is heard from some, yet others say, "no, Mark won!" One of the football players watching the race was heard boasting, "those two guys run like machines!" Mr. Frazier, the high school coach, did not care who won. Mr. Frazier cannot contain his excitement. He keeps repeating, with a big grin on his face, "that was a 10.1 hundred, a 10.1! Can you believe it?"

This race was not a bad performance for a fourteen and fifteen-year-old. The Timekeepers and the coaches could not discern a clear winner of the race. All watches recorded the same time, which is 10.1 seconds. Silence emerges, as the officials walk off to the side, and have a discussion. Everyone wonders what the officials may be discussing that could be taking so long.

Wandering away from the crowd, Eddie is more intent on finding a bottle of water or some Gatorade than listening to the results. Eddie makes his way to the refreshment table, which is set up near the field events. Eddie downs a few cups of water and a cup of Gatorade. He talks briefly with Robert Bradshaw, also known as Bobby B., the doctor of the shot-put. True to form, it looks like Bobby B. has already locked up first place with his first attempt today. The shot doc asks Eddie, "who won the 100-yard dash?" "I don't know," replies Eddie. Bobby B. asks, "you don't know? How can you not know?" "It was close, really close. They're talking about it now," says Eddie, giving the best answer he has. Eddie then wanders back to the crowd, telling the shot doc, "I'll let you know. I'm going to go and find out now."

After cooling down by walking out in the field, Mark stands near the finish line waiting for the news of who won. Mark is exuberant by his 10.1 second time, of which he was informed by Mr. Harris. He has reason for celebration because a 10.4 was his previous best time in competition. Mark, like everyone else, does not know whether he won or Eddie won.

At the finish line, the announcement finally comes. "In third place, with a time of 11.3 seconds, Todd McCutchen," announces the Head Timekeeper, which is a surprise to everyone. That time represents McCutchen's worst official run of the season. The Head Timekeeper, announcing to the crowd, says, "and we have a tie for first place. With a time of 10.1 seconds, the winners are Mark Svoboda and Edward Bogenskaya." A lot of cheering is heard, amongst some heated discussion between some who think Eddie won, and some who think Mark won.

Mr. Frazier instructs his assistant, a blonde haired athletic-looking high school girl, to write the names of the winners on her clipboard. He also instructs her to write down their times. Mr. Frazier is taking notes, or rather the high school student helping him today is taking notes. He will find Mark and Eddie next year when they are in high school one way or another. Mr. Frazier is unwilling to let any potential talent escape.

While the runners get ready for the 4 by 220 relay, Eddie makes his way back to the finish line. He is totally unaware of his official time and that there was a tie. Before Eddie gets back to the crowd, he gets the news from a 25-year-old guy in a mechanic's uniform. The mechanic looks as if he just left the garage, spending the day rebuilding an engine. Eddie is fairly certain that he's never seen him before. The mechanic tells Eddie, "it was a tie. You ran a 10.1. Great job!" With his mind elsewhere, Eddie replies, "hey, thanks!" Eddie wonders why a mechanic showed up for the meet, thinking that he is probably somebody's friend. The mechanic looks over at Mr. Frazier and his student assistant, and then walks away.

Walking up to the crowd, Eddie gives Mark and a few others a high-five. Mr. Harris and Mr. Frazier, congratulate Eddie. Unable to contain his excitement, Mr. Frazier exclaims, "that was a 10.1! Good job! Good Job!" Eddie replies to Mr. Frazier, "awesome!" After thinking for a second, Eddie finally realizes his accomplishment. Eddie exclaims, "wait, a 10.1? Wow, super awesome!" Eddie doesn't want to get too excited. He still has to run in the 4 by 440 relay, which is the last event of today's meet. Eddie talks with a few of his friends, as the focus shifts to the 4 by 220 relay.

Off in a distance, in the middle of the Kill the Man with the Ball field, is the square-jawed guy. The square-jawed guy now has a name, Todd McCutchen. Mark and Eddie have a tendency to make up a name or mispronounce the name of anyone they don't like. To Mark and Eddie, he will now be known as McCrutchen instead of Rock 'em Sock 'em, square-jaw, or his real name, Todd McCutchen. McCutchen, kicking rocks, making a fist, and throwing his hands in the air, is obviously not a happy camper. Eddie is amused, watching McCutchen expend energy on a childish meltdown. McCutchen should be conserving his energy for the upcoming 4 by 440 relay. Mark and McCutchen will be the anchormen in the relay. Eddie will be passing the baton to Mark, hopefully long before McCutchen receives his.

Mark and Eddie move with the crowd from event to event. They catch up with Braden, who just ran a 65-second quarter mile. Braden lets Mark and Eddie know that he could have done better. "I ran just fast enough to win," Braden assures them as he catches his breath. Eddie replies, "that's OK, bro. You won. That's all that matters." Braden, who conserved as much energy as he could, will have to run 440 yards again in just a few moments. Braden will be first off in the 4 by 440 relay, followed by Eric Johnson, who won the 220-yard dash earlier today, then Eddie and Mark.

Eddie wanders over to the field event area, and catches up with Bobby B. again. The track events and field events occur simultaneously, so the athletes rarely get a chance to mix during a meet. Eddie and the shot doc fill each other in on how the events are going. Both deliver good news to each other.

Since Bobby B. and Gary Mitchell are good friends, Eddie mentions to Bobby B. that Mitchell beat the walking toothpick in the mile.

The shot doc tells Eddie that he came in first place in the shot-put, beating out the opposition by 16 feet, which is no surprise to Eddie. Joking with Bobby B., Eddie asks, "that's it? Only 16 feet?" Bobby B. replies, "I'm having a bad day. I only broke my old record by two feet." They both have a good laugh, and Eddie tells the shot doc to come watch the relay. The shot doc's job is frequently done quickly, so he usually hangs around the field events encouraging the rest of the field athletes. But, because of all the excitement today, the 4 by 440 relay is one race the shot doc does not want to miss.

Eddie and Bobby B. meander back to the starting line for the relay race. The shot doc mixes with the crowd as Eddie meets up with Mark, Braden and Johnson. They casually look around to see if they can find who they are up against, knowing for sure that McCutchen is Centerville's anchorman. They spot McCutchen, who finally got over his meltdown, with two others. One of the guys standing with McCutchen just lost to Braden. Not much is known about the other guy who is standing with them. With the race just a few minutes away, there is still no sign of Centerville's fourth runner. But, Eddie and his teammates don't care. Their confidence level is better now than at the start of the meet. McCutchen, and his team, seem to be more concerned with Mark and Eddie's team, pointing in their direction several times. Jogging over from the field event area is Centerville's high-jumper, who will fill the remaining position in the relay event.

The announcement comes from one of the officials to prepare for the final event. Braden moves into position, next to the guy he beat out in the quarter mile earlier today. The guy is probably not too happy to see Braden again. Braden, running in place, is yelling, "I'm hot! I'm hot today! I'm kicking your flimsy ass again! Once just wasn't enough! We're all kicking ass today!" Braden has this uncanny ability to suck any optimism and confidence out of his opponent, albeit quite unintentionally.

A few yards behind Braden, the other legs of the relay race are standing to the inside of the track near the handoff zone. As a formality, a Timekeeper points out the handoff zone to the teams and describes the penalty for handing off outside the zone. Handing off the baton outside of the transition zone results in an immediate disqualification. A disqualification means you lose the race by default, which is not something that anyone would want to be responsible for. The Timekeeper again motions for the teams to get ready, and instructs the teams, "run a fair race." No one really knows why officials occasionally say "run a fair race." It's not likely that a runner is going to pull out a can of mace and spray the other runner on the other side of the track while no one is watching.

"On your marks," announces the Starter in a Robotic monotone voice. The runners get ready. "Set," he proclaims, two or three seconds later, but the anxious runners were already in the process of getting set. Waiting for at least two seconds of stillness, the Starter fires his gun, and the runners take off.

Braden leaves the starting line with enough speed to convince anyone he is running a 40-yard dash. His opponent again struggles to keep up, remembering that, just 20 minutes ago, Braden kicked his butt in the quarter mile. A quarter ways around the 440-yard track, Braden begins to slow his pace slightly. Judging the distance of the runner behind him by the sound of the runner's feet, Braden stays a comfortable ten to fifteen yards ahead. Braden keeps this pace for the next 200 yards or so, and then begins to make his move. Sprinting the last 100 yards, the gap begins to widen. His opponent closes the gap to some degree, but has lost any opportunity to win this leg. Watching Braden approaching the transition zone, Johnson takes off cautiously. Johnson times the transition well, and the handoff goes perfectly.

At the beginning of Johnson's leg, his opponent is 30 yards behind. Johnson's opponent, the high jumper, is gaining ground and was apparently underestimated. Passing Johnson about halfway around the track, the high jumper shows no sign of fatigue or slowing down. Mark, who looks over at Eddie, exclaims, "shit!" Eddie yells, "where the hell did they get that guy from?" Just then, McCutchen mumbles something in the direction of Mark and Eddie, but they ignore him.

Eddie takes to the track. There is now real work to do. Mark and Eddie will not be happy with second place, especially since there are only two teams in the race. The high jumper comes in ten yards ahead of Johnson, and hands off the baton first. Impatiently waiting for Johnson, Eddie feels as if 30 seconds have elapsed since the opponent passed his baton. In reality, however, less than two seconds have elapsed. Receiving the baton from Johnson, Eddie takes off like a wild man.

Eddie begins to gain ground on his opponent during his leg. It is difficult to see whether Eddie is speeding up or the opponent is dropping his pace. At the halfway mark, Eddie passes the opponent, who is struggling to speed up in order to catch Eddie. Eddie, however, will not allow himself to be caught. Eddie remembers that, according to Mr. Frazier, second place gets the grand title of being the first loser. Knowing that Mr. Frazier is watching, Eddie will not be beaten.

Meanwhile, back at the starting line, Mark and McCutchen take to the track. Because Eddie is ahead, the Timekeeper assigns Mark the inside position. McCutchen remembers well Mark's comment just before the gun went off in the 100-yard dash. In an attempt to even the score, McCutchen says to Mark, "your laces aren't tied right." Looking at Mark with obviously fake deep concern, McCutchen adds, "one loop is too long, and you're going to trip." Without even looking down, Mark authoritatively declares to McCutchen, "shut up, junior." That certainly backfired on McCutchen. Mark two, McCutchen zero.

For the last 100 yards of his leg, Eddie sprints as fast as he can, knowing that Mark will be up against McCutchen. Eddie's opponent was left in the dust, and burned out three-quarters of the way around the track. This is the nature of a relay race. The team in the lead often changes throughout the race. Eddie enters the transition zone, and passes off the baton flawlessly to Mark. McCutchen, if he is going to win, has more than 30 yards to make up. He has made up this yardage in the past, which is why he is their anchorman. McCutchen grabs his baton, and chases down Mark.

Mark maintains his 30-yard lead for the first 100 or so yards. McCutchen, giving it all he has, is just unable to catch Mark. Perhaps McCutchen spent too much energy on his temper tantrum earlier after he lost the 100-yard dash. Mark, now with about 200 yards to go, knows he has the race wrapped up. Instead of slowing his pace and taking it a little easy, Mark speeds up. The gap begins to widen between the two runners. With 100 yards to go, Mark now has almost a 60-yard lead, which equates to about six seconds at this pace. As Mark gets closer, he can hear the rest of the team members cheering him on. This gives him even more motivation to keep the speed up, even though he's already won the race. Mark cruises across the finish line, leaving McCutchen far behind, almost in a different zip code.

Mr. Frazier, the high school coach, again unable to contain his excitement, is exclaiming, "that was a 56 quarter, 56!" Mr. Harris, who is usually a little reserved, also shows his excitement, telling the team, "that was your best run of the year!" And it was their last run of the year. That phenomenal finish was the close of this year's track season.

With the team winning the meet, Mr. Harris is quite exhilarated, partially because he has a team that impressed Mr. Frazier. The flip side of it is that Mark, Eddie, Axel Braden, Eric Johnson, Gary Mitchell, Robert Bradshaw, and a few others, will move on to high school next year. Mr. Harris will have to develop new talent for next year's season. As the team heads to the locker room, they share notes on each event, and congratulate each other on a season that could not have ended better.

It's a sure bet that Eddie and Mark will be training hard this Summer. After all, next year is high school, and they both will be competing for a place on the varsity track team. In high school, there is indoor track during the Winter, and the usual Spring track season. Eddie and Mark will both have to step up their game. After all, next year will be high school, where the competition is real. They both look forward to being part of the Northside High Eagles.

Summer Begins

On a sunny Summer's day, Mark's mother, Mariana, runs into Eddie's mother, Nina, at the local farmers market, which is quite a frequent occurrence. Nina and Mariana both shop on Friday afternoon, right after the new shipments arrive, and at least one other time during the week. By Saturday morning, the food has been picked over, and neither want to put second rate food on the table for their families. Two or three trips per week assure that the food is always fresh.

Nina mentions to Mariana, "the blueberries look good today." Mariana replies, "be sure to get a cantaloupe. They have the better fresh ones this week." After comparing notes about what is fresh or a good deal, they continue shopping on their own. Nina and Mariana also have their own gardens at home. Their gardens produce more than their families can eat, so they exchange the fruits of their labor with each other as well. Occasionally, Nina will bring Mariana a fresh chicken. Nina's parents live a few miles away, and have a small chicken farm and grow their own vegetables.

Meeting up again a few minutes later, Mariana asks Nina, "how's Eddie been doing?" Nina replies, "he's always out riding his bicycle or at the pool swimming laps. He's also cutting a few lawns, cleaning pools, and doing some odd jobs for money this Summer." Nina asks, "and Mark, how has he been doing?" Mariana replies, "oh, he's lifting weights every day and running down the path along the parkway. He says he has to get stronger and in better shape." This is no surprise to Nina, since Eddie has the same goals. "If he wants to get stronger, I'll show him what work is," Mariana chuckles.

Just then, walks up Kathryn Black, the mother of one of Mark and Eddie's classmates, Charles, also known as Chuckie. Announcing her unwanted entrance into the conversation, Kathryn sarcastically greets them, saying, "well, well, well, if it isn't Mariana Svoboda and Nina Bogenskaya." In the same sarcastic tone, Nina replies, "well, if it isn't the Kathryn Black," adding an obviously fake smile. Nina always refers to Mrs. Black as an inanimate object, adding, quite intentionally, the title "the" in front of her name.

Nina, not that she really cares, asks Kathryn, "how is your little Chuckie doing?" Kathryn replies, "he's doing well, very well." Kathryn sarcastically asks Nina, "and your son, what is his name?" Nina replies, "Eddie is doing awesome. He had a very good year in track. Thank you very much for asking." Turning to Mariana, Kathryn, raising the sarcastic tone a notch or two, asks, "and Mark? Did he pass school this year?" "He's still alive," replies Mariana, trying to end the conversation and get rid of the highly toxic unwanted intruder.

Pretending to have deep concern regarding Kathryn's health, Nina informs her, "the lard is on sale today. You should check it out. Pick up a few tubs while you still can." Kathryn moves on, feeling once again like she's been run over by a freight train just seeing Nina and Mariana. Nina and Mariana have a good laugh, and go on their way again. They'll meet up again in a few days, hoping not to see Kathryn again anytime soon.

Chuckie, Kathryn's son, used to be the school bully a few years ago. Eddie, for some reason, appeared to be Chuckie's prime target. Eddie simply ignored Chuckie, which fueled Chuckie even more. The proverbial apple, in this case, did not fall far from the tree. Chuckie is just like his mother, both bullies of sorts, but each in their own way. Chuckie once started a fight with Eddie, which proved to be a very big mistake. While other kids are getting taller and stronger, Chuckie is increasing the girth around his mid-section. For some reason, Kathryn blames all of Chuckie's problems on Eddie. Kathryn, even though her family is well off financially, has a deep resentment of Nina and Mariana. Nina and Mariana have something that Kathryn, with all her money, could not buy - happiness.

Kathryn, pretending not to know Eddie's name, knows his name really well. Last Spring, Chuckie tried to get a whole Summers' tan in one day. All Chuckie got out of that deal were a really bad sunburn, and the nickname "pinkie" for a while. In the locker room, after gym class, Chuckie was asking if anyone had any advice for sunburn pain. Eddie piped up with some advice, and told Chuckie, "put some BENGAY on it, and take a really hot shower." "Here, use mine," insisted Eddie, trying not to laugh as he tossed the tube to Chuckie. Chuckie put the cream on his shoulders, arms, and legs, and headed for the shower. About two minutes later, Chuckie let out the loudest scream imaginable, echoing through the locker room, and heard all the way down the hall in the school lobby. Eddie, as he headed out of the locker room to class, yelled back to Chuckie, "keep the tube, junior. It's yours!" Later that night, Kathryn phoned Nina, giving Nina a piece of her mind. Kathryn tried to convey how bad Eddie was in pulling that stunt. Nina also had something to convey to Kathryn, which is how stupid Chuckie must have been to even try that.

For a while, Mark was also a prime target of Chuckie's bullying. Mark would bring his lunch to school, which was usually yogurt, lean meats, vegetables and fresh fruit. Chuckie was always bugging Mark, offering him advice like, "why don't you just get a burger and fries like everyone else." Mark started replying, "because I don't want to look like you," or, "get that chicken fat back to the chicken, junior." No longer effective in badgering Mark, Chuckie quickly moved on, harassing anyone who looked vulnerable. Mark and Eddie became too formidable a target for Chuckie's moronic mind games.

Neither Nina nor Mariana fully understands the athletic abilities of their sons. They also do not understand the part that they each played over the years in Eddie's and Mark's physical development by feeding them a good diet and encouraging them to exercise. The thought of fast food or eating a school lunch is not on their list of things to consider. By allowing them to play outside, ride their bicycles, and get exercise, Eddie's and Mark's parents paved the way for their sons to become good athletes. But, this is what is normal and natural to them. The results of their clean natural diet, coupled with exercise, will be evident in the upcoming years.

Meanwhile, while the parental units are off shopping at the markets or at work, Eddie is usually working himself, working out, or out riding his bicycle. Eddie typically rides 20 or 30 miles per day a few times during the week, sometimes with friends, and sometimes alone. He would often ride along the paved path along the parkway, which ultimately takes him to the beach. The beach is eleven miles away, which is a very easy ride for Eddie. Eddie would occasionally catch up with Mark on the path, who uses the path for running. Eddie would drop his pace to Mark's running speed, and they would talk for a while. Shifting gears, Eddie would then head down to the beach.

On a hot day, Eddie typically rides his bicycle to the county pool. Eddie is not a fan of the heat. Anything above 90 degrees is a prescription for swimming rather than cycling. Swimming laps in cool water always sounds a lot better than riding in the heat. On rainy days, Eddie could be found tuning up his bicycle between sets of lifting weights. Eddie has about 250 pounds of weights and a bench, which was given to him by a neighbor. His neighbor moved across country and, since the weights were too expensive to move, he gave them to Eddie. Eddie also does some Summer reading, studying books on working out, not reading Nancy Drew mysteries.

The Fourth of July brings Eddie and his date, Claudia, to a local park, along with Mark and his date, Sharon, to watch the fireworks. They all bicycle together to the park, find a place to lock their bicycles, and walk to the festivities. Mark and Eddie each carry with them a duffel bag, with a few beach towels to lie on the ground, and a small cooler with a few drinks.

On the way, they stop at a restroom since they all keep themselves well-hydrated. Claudia and Sharon get into the line for the ladies' room, which is about 20 women long and growing. Eddie and Mark walk right into the men's room. Out in a minute or two, Eddie walks up to Claudia and Sharon and whispers to them, "when we wave to you, run up and use the men's room." Claudia whispers, "what are you guys up to now?" Eddie whispers back to Claudia, "just trust me." Eddie then runs back to join Mark.

Meanwhile, Mark counts the number of men currently occupying the men's room. "How many?" inquires Eddie when he returns. Mark replies, "three." To keep track of the occupancy, Mark tells Eddie, "I'll count up, and you count down." Mark and Eddie have it all planned out. When someone walks in, the count goes up. When someone walks out, the count goes down. "Four," Mark says to Eddie, as someone walks in. "Two," replies Eddie, as a father and son walk out, followed quickly by "one," as someone else leaves.

Some guy stops and asks Mark and Eddie, "what are you guys counting?" Eddie replies, "we work for the park department, and we're monitoring peak restroom demand." The guy actually believes Eddie, and moves on. The process of counting up and down continues for a few more minutes. A few others wonder why Eddie and Mark are counting the number of visitors to the restroom. Eddie finally announces the long awaited "zero."

Mark and Eddie wave to their dates, who run quickly from their line into the men's room. Half of the 30 or so women now waiting in the women's line, figuring out what just happened, also rush to the men's room. Eddie and Mark have a good laugh as they see ten women now lined up in front of the men's room. While they wait for the girls, Eddie and Mark are amused by the men who walk up, and find no facility to use. In a few minutes, the group moves on, leaving the crowd with two ladies' rooms and no men's room.

The group walks through the crowd, looking for a place to sit and chill. They catch a glimpse of Axel Braden with another girl from school, Wendy. Eddie, already pulling the towels out of his duffel bag, asks Braden, "do you got room for a few more?" Braden replies, "sure, pull up a towel," as he is laying on a towel himself, staring at the sky. Mark casually mentions to Braden, "if you're working on your suntan, bro, you got to do that during the day when the sun is up." Braden, who is African American, replies jokingly, "you're looking a little pale, Mark. Are you sick or something?" Wendy comments, "you guys are too funny." Wendy is as light skinned as one can be, with blonde hair that has seen a couple bottles of Sun-In this Summer.

The group is quite chilled out, with a very different energy level than during the last track meet of the season. Not much conversation goes on, just relaxation, and watching fireworks. Eddie asks Braden, "what have you been up to this Summer?" Braden replies, "working out. I bought a barbell set and a bench." Braden is already built like a tank and has chest muscles bigger than most of the girls' breasts. A few minutes later, Braden asks Eddie, "so, what you been doing?" Eddie pauses to think for a while, since his brain has checked out a while ago. Eddie finally replies, "working out, riding my bicycle, cutting a few lawns, and cleaning a few pools." Braden tells Eddie, "wow, you're busy." As the finale goes off, a little more life comes into the chilled-out group as they slowly drift back to reality.

After the finale, everyone stands up to say goodbye. "See you later, bro," Eddie utters to Braden, as if he had just awakened. Braden replies, "catch you later." Mark tells Braden, "good seeing you," as he gives Braden a fist bump after picking up his towel. Claudia and Sharon, who are a little less vocal, give Wendy a hug. Braden and Wendy then head off in the other direction. Eddie and Mark, along with their dates, walk back to where they locked up their bicycles. On the way home, they decide to take the long way, just to get more exercise.

Mark, Eddie, and their dates ride around town for a while to see if there is anyone to catch up with. At 11:00 p.m., there is not much action around. Everyone is just getting home from any fireworks they were out watching earlier. Anyone that was watching fireworks on TV is probably in bed already. As they pass Angelo's Service Station on the corner, Eddie and Claudia go straight, Mark and Sharon hang a right. "Catch you in a few," Mark yells out to Eddie. "It's been fun," Eddie replies. The girls also exchange goodbyes and everyone is on their way.

The next morning, on Monday, Eddie wakes up early to beat the heat because he has the usual three or four lawns to cut. Eddie cuts lawns and cleans a few pools two or three days a week, giving him the remaining four or five days to himself. What Eddie doesn't finish today, he'll finish on Wednesday or Thursday, depending on the weather.

Walking down the street to a lawn a few doors down with the mower, with some other equipment stacked on it, Eddie runs into Larry, a guy from his class. Totally missing the obvious, Larry asks Eddie, "what are you doing?" Eddie replies, "cutting lawns." With a puzzled look on his face, Larry asks, "why?" Eddie replies firmly, "to make money. That's why." Giving Eddie some words of wisdom, Larry responds, "it's hard work. You'll get all dirty and sweaty." Coming from a family with a history of desk jobs, Larry will probably follow in their footsteps. The conversation goes nowhere. Fortunately, Eddie has arrived at the lawn he needs to cut, and says to Larry, "I got to go."

Starting the lawnmower with one strong pull, Eddie goes to work. Eddie's lawnmower is not self-propelled. He has to push it, giving him a good workout as he mows. When he finishes the job, Eddie knocks on the door, collects his money from Mrs. Lacy, and heads off to the next lawn on today's list. At the end of the workday, which is 1:00 p.m. today, Eddie heads home for lunch.

After lunch, Eddie gets on his bicycle, and heads to the pool. The temperature is approaching 90 degrees, so the pool will be a welcome relief from the heat. Upon arriving, Eddie notices the pool is crowded, which is not exactly ideal for swimming laps. But, that doesn't stop him. Diving into the pool at the sparsely populated deep end, Eddie begins swimming his laps. Navigating through the kids playing at the shallow end, he spots a vacant spot along the wall, does his flip turn, and swims back to the deep end. After a while, the deep end clears out and Eddie swims his laps across the pool along the short dimension. After an hour of swimming laps, with only one short break, Eddie is now all cooled off, and heads home.

Later that week, Eddie's sees one of his friends, Peter, riding up on a new bicycle. Eddie comments, "wow! This is very impressive," as he is looking over the bicycle that is equipped with Campagnolo components and high performance tires. Peter is one of the few who can keep pace with Eddie. With Peter's new bicycle, Eddie might now be the one trying to keep up with Peter. With state of the art components, and a few pounds lighter, Peter's new bicycle gives him a distinct advantage. They go for a quick ride together, and Eddie can see an immediate difference in Peter's performance.

Later that evening, Eddie contemplates that, in order to get in better shape and stronger, a different bicycle might be better alternative. Eddie remembers that there is a used track bicycle on display in the window at the bicycle shop downtown. With fixed gearing, the track bicycle would force Eddie to work harder when going up hills. There would be no more down shifting to make the ride easier. To Eddie, any money spent on physical fitness is money well spent. Eddie decides that he will check it out tomorrow.

The next morning, Eddie arrives at Vito's Bicycle Shop at 10:00 a.m. sharp, when it is supposed to open. The shop owner, Vito, is nowhere to be found. With the door locked, Eddie looks over the track bicycle through the window. Eddie has seen this bicycle many times, but never really got a good look at it. The bicycle looks like it is in great shape, with not a scratch on it. Even the tires on the bicycle even appear to be new.

A few minutes later, Vito, a 60-year-old bicycle enthusiast, arrives on his bicycle, and opens the shop. Vito asks, "do you need a few parts, Eddie?" Eddie enthusiastically replies, "no. I'm just looking at the track bike." Vito asks Eddie, "do you want to take it for a spin?" Eddie replies, "sure." Vito has known Eddie for a few years. Whenever Eddie makes an improvement to his bicycle, Vito is Eddie's source for parts and advice.

Before Eddie takes the bicycle out on the road, Vito explains a few things to Eddie about a track bicycle. Giving Eddie the rundown, Vito explains, "this bike has been modified for road use. It has a front brake, but no rear brake, so you have to be careful. And most track bikes have only one rear gear. This one has two. It has a 13-tooth and a 17-tooth, one on each side of the hub. You'd use the 17-tooth gear in hilly areas and the 13-tooth on flat areas. The 17-tooth is free wheeling, and the 13-tooth is fixed. If you want to change gears, you'll have to flip the wheel around. The front chainwheel is a 48-tooth. It also comes with a 54-tooth that I have somewhere in the back." Vito also mentions, "two water bottle mounts and a pump peg have been brazed onto the frame." Eddie is now ready to take the bicycle on a test ride.

Without hesitation, Eddie gets on the bicycle and takes off down the busy street. The bicycle feels solid, smooth, and very responsive. Eddie notices that starting from a standstill is a lot more work than his ten-speed. This is partly due to the current set up using the 13-tooth rear sprocket. Going around corners is tricky, since the pedals are always in motion on a track bicycle. Eddie, however, quickly gets the hang of it. Getting up to speed takes a little longer, but Eddie quickly realizes he can ride faster with less effort on the track bicycle.

About ten minutes later, Eddie arrives back at the shop. All excited, Eddie informs Vito, "it rides great!" Vito already knows that. Eddie asks Vito, "how much is it?" Offering Eddie a great deal, Vito puts a generous offer out on the table, "for you, two hundred dollars. I can also sell your bicycle if you'd like." Eddie replies, "let me see what I can come up with." Before he leaves, Eddie asks Vito, "how much can you get for mine?" Vito responds, "the way you have it built out, probably two hundred fifty, maybe more." Vito's answer surprises Eddie in a positive way. Examining the track bicycle one more time, Eddie searches for that one little flaw that just cannot be found. Eddie lets Vito know he'll be back tomorrow, and heads home.

Later that night, Eddie thinks over the deal that Vito proposed. Eddie reasons to himself that North of the turnpike is hilly, where the 17-tooth rear sprocket should be fine. South of the turnpike the roads are flat, and the 13-tooth will provide a good gear ratio. Eddie also reasons that the 13-tooth sprocket will get him to the beach on the South shore even faster, since it is all flat level ground to the South. At that time, Eddie realizes that he only uses about four speeds of the ten that are available on his bicycle. That about decides it, Eddie is going to take Vito's deal.

The next morning, Eddie heads over to Vito's again, with a little over two-hundred dollars. Looking over the bicycle again as Vito walks up, Eddie tells Vito, "I'll take it." Vito replies, asking, "OK, what do you want me to do with yours?" Eddie asks, "can you sell it for me?" Vito replies, "let me make a quick phone call. I'll be back in a sec."

While Eddie looks over the bicycle in greater detail, Vito walks to the back of the shop to call a prospective buyer. Being in the bicycle business for 40 years, Vito knows who is in the market for what. In five minutes, Vito returns with some good news. Vito exclaims to Eddie, "I can get you two-hundred-seventy-five dollars for yours!" He asks Eddie, "I got him on hold. What should I tell him?" Taking no time to deliberate, Eddie tells Vito, "go for it! I'll take it." Eddie lifts the 18-pound bicycle out of the window display, as Vito goes to the back of the shop to set up the deal.

When Vito returns, he informs Eddie, "he's on his way. He'll be here in an hour or so." Eddie replies, "wow, that was fast!" Vito tells Eddie, "it was fast. He's admired your bicycle for a while. He's been riding around on a bike that looks like it's been made out of old plumbing tubing." The buyer, like Eddie, frequents Vito's shop. Eddie and Vito walk up to the vintage cash register, and they make the exchange. Vito tells Eddie, "that's two-hundred dollars with the tax." Not wanting to be bothered with details, Vito hates to figure out tax. Every price he quotes is a round number and always includes the tax. No sane person would ever want to be Vito's accountant.

After the transaction, Eddie transfers his water bottle and his tool kit to his new bicycle. Eddie asks Vito, "what do you want me to do with mine?" Vito tells him, "I'll put it in the back. Come back later and pick up your money." Vito then mentions, "oh, and I'll find that 54-tooth front sprocket for you. And, there are a few more links to the chain for when you use the 54. I'll find those too." Eddie thanks Vito, and rides home on his new bicycle.

The bicycle Eddie just bought was custom made for a guy named Danny, who also owns a bicycle shop. Danny used to race bicycles, but he broke his ankle last year in a crash, and has been unable to race since. Danny's bicycle shop is primarily oriented toward kids rather than serious riders, so Danny asked Vito to sell the bicycle in his shop. The bicycle Eddie just purchased is a brand new custom-built track cycle made for Danny. There is not a great demand for track bicycles. Eddie got a great deal because the bicycle has been in the window for more than a year. Eddie paid less than a quarter of what Danny paid for it when it was new.

Later in the afternoon, Eddie arrives again at Vito's shop, riding his new track bicycle. Vito asks, "so, how do you like it?" Eddie replies, "awesome! I should have bought this a long time ago. I can already tell I'm going to get a better workout." Looking around, and not seeing his old bicycle, Eddie exclaims, "he bought it!" Vito smiles and replies, "that he did! And he's as happy as you are. And, I have your money. Two-hundred-seventy-five dollars, just like we said." While Vito walks over to the cash register, Eddie asks Vito, "how much do I owe you for selling it?" "Aw, nothing, Eddie," Vito chuckles, "I was just glad to get that out of my window. You're happy. He's happy. Danny's happy. We're all happy." Eddie uses part of his $275.00 to buy a rear brake for the bicycle, a light, and a few spare tubes. Vito puts Eddie's purchases in a bag, along with the 54-tooth sprocket and the extra links to the chain that he found in the shop. Eddie thanks Vito, and heads home to install the rear brake.

Installing the rear brake and making a few adjustments to the seat and handlebars, Eddie gets his bicycle in good shape for long rides. The only major difference is that, with the high performance tires, Eddie will now have to carry two spare tubes instead of just one. High performance tires are quite a bit lighter and thinner, and are more prone to being punctured when compared with the thicker road tires. Carrying several spare tubes is a necessity. The water bottles, pump, and tool kit all fit nicely on the frame of Eddie's new bicycle. The spare tubes also fold up nicely, and fit snugly into the tool bag.

For the next few days, Eddie rides around town on his new bicycle, thoroughly convinced that he made the right decision to buy it. With the fixed gearing, a standing start is more work, but also gives a better workout. Once Eddie is up to speed, less pedal effort is required, allowing him to ride faster. This translates into a longer ride for the same amount of energy. It also translates into getting to the beach faster. On the hills, Eddie gets a better leg workout than he ever thought possible on a bicycle.

Leaving early one morning for the beach, Eddie takes the usual route on the path along the expressway. Halfway to the beach, Eddie encounters Mark, who is out on an early morning run. Slowing to Mark's running pace, Eddie pulls alongside Mark. Mark immediately notices Eddie's new bicycle. Mark asks, "hey, is that a new bike?" Eddie replies, "yeah. I picked it up a few weeks ago."

The two buddies stop in order to take a break, and talk for a while. Mark and Eddie talk about what they have been doing this Summer. Mark, who has been stepping up his game, boasts to Eddie, "my bench press is up to 200 pounds." Eddie replies, "wow, you must be working out hard." Bringing up the subject of track, specifically the 100-yard dash, Mark informs Eddie, "I hear a rumor that a guy named Paul Mahoney, who is a senior this year, runs a 10.4 consistently. That's the best they got up there. Everyone else's best is like in the upper 10-second range. The other thing I heard is that the best guy they have runs the 440 in just under 60 seconds. All the better runners graduated last year, so I hear." Eddie, amazed by what Mark just said, exclaims, "wow! Then it looks like we're all in!"

Mark is fully determined to steal the show during Winter track tryouts. Not wanting to cool down too much, Mark and Eddie continue on their way, with even more motivation just knowing that they will be serious contenders for the track team next year. For the remainder of Eddie's ride to the beach, Eddie contemplates what Mark just told him. Eddie and Mark can both beat Paul

Mahoney's 10.4 second 100-yard dash time. And, Eddie, Mark, Braden, and Johnson can all easily break 60 seconds in the quarter mile.

The next weekend, Eddie is downstairs working out with weights, looking at a bicycle that does not need much work. Looking even closer, there is not even much room for improving the bicycle. Working out, however, is taking more of a priority as the Summer moves along. Eddie can only bench press 185 pounds, whereas Mark can bench press 200 pounds. Eddie feels that he has to keep up, or at least try.

While working out, Eddie has the radio cranked up, listening to the song Layla, by Derek and the Dominos. Songs like Layla have a lot of energy to them, and are perfect when working out. Between sets, Eddie decides to install the light on his bicycle that he picked up at Vito's a while ago. The light will extend the time he can ride, since the days will become shorter as Autumn arrives. After his workout, Eddie heads upstairs for dinner.

Eddie is greeted by his grandmother, who is over for dinner tonight. As Eddie walks into the room, his grandmother's finger goes up in the air slowly, shaking back and forth. She sternly warns Eddie, in her Eastern European accent, "you should not listen to dat music! You're gonna take a da dope!" The advice comes across as if Eddie's grandmother has extensive medical research indicating that listening to Derek and the Dominos causes a person to take dope. Eddie's younger brother, John, listens as his grandmother gives Eddie some wisdom and advice, laughing under his breath. While Eddie's grandmother has a great concern, it is unfounded. Eddie is not taking dope. Eddie's grandmother also once told Eddie he should not lift weights, because it was going to give him a heart attack.

The dinner menu tonight is two freshly prepared chickens that Eddie's grandfather slaughtered earlier today, and fresh vegetables from the garden. Eddie's mother and grandmother both prepared the meal. Eddie's father and grandfather went outside earlier, looking through the garden for anything that might be ripe that might make a good addition to the meal. When dinner is put on the table, Eddie eats a half chicken all by himself. He has been consuming more protein, trying to gain more muscle mass. For dessert, there is apple pie, made from apples picked earlier today by Eddie's grandfather. After dinner, Eddie takes the glass pie dish, scrapes the leftovers with his fork, not wanting anything to go to waste.

As the Summer moves along, Eddie continues to cut lawns, clean pools, swim at the county pool, and ride his bicycle. Since buying his new track bicycle, bicycling has become Eddie's favorite sport. Organized bicycle racing, however, is difficult to come by. Eddie and his friend, Peter, often take their bicycles to the high school parking lot of a nearby town, which has distance markings that are used for indoor track practice. Indoor tracks, which are rubber or wooden tracks, are difficult to find. That particular school's team practices in their parking lot. Eddie and Peter time each other over various distances, using each other's bicycles. Eddie and Peter determine that Eddie's track bicycle, in every case, allows them to attain greater speed at any distance. This, however, is over flat level ground. If the time trials were on hills, Peter's newly acquired ten-speed bicycle would probably be the clear winner.

Over the rest of the Summer, Eddie runs into Mark a few more times along the path next to the parkway. One morning, when Mark and Eddie meet on the path, Eddie makes an offer to Mark, asking, "do you want to try out the bike?" Mark replies, "sure, I'll give it a whirl." Eddie has the bicycle configured with the 54-tooth front sprocket and the 17-tooth rear sprocket, which gives a good gear ratio on level ground. Getting on the bicycle, Mark heads down the concrete path along the parkway, yelling back to Eddie, "I'll be back in a bit." Eddie heads over to the shade, since he doesn't like the heat. He sits on a large boulder under a tree, waiting for Mark to return.

Riding along the path, Mark picks up considerable speed. It doesn't take Mark long to realize that, on Eddie's bicycle, he can ride very fast. Mark realizes he can ride faster than he's ever ridden before. Mark thinks to himself, "so this is why Eddie rides all the time." It also did not take Mark long to realize that he does not get as hot, as compared with running, while riding the bicycle. The increased speed cools him off as he rides. As Mark comes to the bridge abutment three miles down the path, he turns around. On the way back, he decides to give it all he has. Mark, turning the cranks with all the energy he could muster up, rides back faster than he ever thought possible on a bicycle.

Sitting on the boulder, Eddie sees Mark approaching. Eddie gets up, and walks back to the concrete path. Already knowing what Mark thinks by the expression on his face, Eddie asks, "so, how does it ride?" With no hesitation, Mark replies, "I want one! It rides really nice," as he catches his breath. Mark asks, "where'd you get it?" Eddie responds, "Vito's Bicycle Shop. It's the one that was in the window for more than a year." Mark tells Eddie, "I definitely have to check it out." They talk for a while longer as Mark looks over Eddie's bicycle in more detail. Eddie then gets back on his bicycle, and rides toward the beach. As Eddie rides off, Mark continues with his run, having something more to think about.

Eddie - The Freshman Year

The Portal

With two more weeks of freedom before school starts again, Eddie decides to hit the beach one more time. In a few weeks, good beach weather will be hard to come by, so Eddie takes advantage of a warm and sunny Wednesday afternoon. Everyone else is out doing some last minute school shopping with their parents, so Eddie will have to go it alone this time. Packing a lunch, some Gatorade, and a rolled-up towel in his duffel bag, Eddie is off to the beach.

The ride to the beach usually takes Eddie past Mark's house. Seeing Mark in his front yard raking dirt, Eddie stops to say hello. Eddie asks Mark, "what are you up to?" Mark, who is sweating profusely, replies, "the septic tank was pumped. My dad told me to straighten up the yard. I'm going to head to the pool after I get finished with this. I'm almost done." Mark looks at raking dirt and repairing the yard as just another opportunity to work out, not as some task to get through as quickly and easily as possible. Eddie heads to the beach, letting Mark get back to his workout.

Riding down the road for about a half mile, Eddie enters the path along the parkway. After about a mile, Eddie suddenly notices it is becoming more difficult to pedal. When a bicycle suddenly gets harder to pedal, it usually means a flat tire. Eddie has experienced this many times before. Getting off of his bicycle, Eddie takes a look at the tires. Pressing his thumb into the front tire, the pressure in the tire seems to be fine. Pressing his thumb into the rear tire reveals quite a different story. The tire is flat. Eddie removes his frame-mounted pump, and pumps up the tire. Eddie hears the air leak out of the tire as he pumps it up, which means only one thing. He heads off into the shade to change the flat tire.

Walking off the path, Eddie quickly finds the perfect shady place to change the tire. He finds the boulder on which he sat when Mark tried his bicycle a while ago. In that area, there are actually three large boulders, about ten feet apart. The boulders make for a nice workshop for his emergency repair.

Removing some tools and a new tube from his tool bag mounted behind the seat, Eddie places the tools he'll need on top of one of the boulders. Eddie removes the rear wheel, which takes less than a minute. He leans the bicycle on the second boulder, being careful to not let the chain sit in the dirt. The third boulder provides a convenient place to sit, as he removes the tire from the wheel. Removing the flat tube and tire only takes a few minutes. Eddie installs the new tube, replaces the tire, and begins pumping up the tire. After obtaining the requisite 90 pounds of pressure, he reinstalls the wheel on the bicycle. Eddie is now ready to get back on the road.

Before getting on his bicycle, in the midst of the three boulders, Eddie stretches his hamstring muscles, as he has done many times in the past. After a minute or so, Eddie stretches his shoulders, raising his arms up to the sky, then raising them one at a time. Raising his right arm, he says to himself, "I wish it were ten years from now," thinking that, by then, they will have bicycle tires that do not go flat.

As Eddie goes on his way, the background noise from the parkway changes abruptly, and clouds appear in the sky, as if a storm is about ready to roll in from the South. The temperature also drops by a few degrees, a definite sign that an abrupt weather change is about to occur. Eddie checked the weather earlier today, which was supposed to be upper 80-degree range and sunny. Still optimistic about the weather, Eddie continues his ride to the beach.

A minute or two later, it appears that a significant thunderstorm is rolling in from the South. This is not good news for Eddie, since the beach is now seven miles away, and in that direction. That would mean the storm is over the right beach. Eddie decides to turn around, and call it a day. With a good tail wind, Eddie makes good time up the path next to the parkway. Leaving the path, and riding onto the side street, something looks eerily different to Eddie. Eddie thinks to himself that the difference he perceives is due to the darkened sky from the bad thunderstorm rolling in.

As Eddie rides up the road, the wind begins to pick up. The flashes of lightning and sounds of thunder get closer together, meaning the storm is about to hit. Almost to the intersection where Angelo's Service Station is, Eddie thinks to himself that he might stop at Angelo's and wait for the storm pass. As Eddie approaches Angelo's he looks up, and is surprised to see that Angelo's sign is gone. The sign has been replaced by one that says "Eddie's Service Station." Thinking this is quite odd, Eddie surmises that perhaps Angelo sold the station. Eddie decides to pull in the station anyway.

Eddie, and a lot of the other kids in the area, know Angelo well. Angelo is always very helpful to the high school kids, giving them advice about fixing problems they may encounter with their first car. Angelo also guides the younger kids on making basic bicycle repairs, teaching them how to do the repair, rather than repairing it for them. If it is something beyond their ability, Angelo sends them downtown to Vito's Bicycle Shop. Angelo runs the service station almost all by himself, with occasional help from his wife. Hiring a high school or college student from time to time, Angelo is happy to help them out when they need a job.

Eddie rides into the station, through an open garage door, looking for Angelo. Not seeing any sign of Angelo, Eddie peeks through the glass door to the office, and sees no one inside. "I've been waiting for you," announces a mechanic looking out from behind an open hood. The mechanic, who looks like he is training for the Mr. Universe contest, walks up from the back of the shop.

Eddie asks, "hey, where's Angelo?" Realizing that this is Eddie's first trip through the portal, the mechanic replies, "yeah, well, um, about Angelo. We've got a few things to talk about." Eddie thought the mechanic had some news about Angelo, which he did. But, the news about Angelo is a drop in the bucket compared to what Eddie is about to learn. The mechanic instructs Eddie, "step into the office with me," as he closes the garage doors. As they both walk into the office, the mechanic puts a sign in the window that says Closed. He then walks up to an electrical panel and flips the switch to shut off the pumps, knowing that the talk with Eddie is more important than customers at the moment.

The mechanic curiously asks Eddie, "have you ever seen me before?" Thinking for a moment, Eddie replies, "no." After a short pause, Eddie changes his answer, and exclaims, "wait! Yeah! At the track meet! You were there when I ran the 10.1 in the 100-yard dash! You're the guy who came up and told me my time!" The mechanic replies, "yeah, that was me." Changing the subject, Eddie asks, "where's Angelo?" Eddie thinks that perhaps Angelo took the day off. Evading the subject, the mechanic answers, "he's not here right now." Reconsidering the answer he gave Eddie, the mechanic adds, "I bought the station from Angelo." Since Eddie is going to find out anyway, the mechanic figured he might as well tell him now. The mechanic tells Eddie that Angelo moved back to Greece, from where he immigrated many years ago.

As the storm outside gets fierce, the mechanic tells Eddie, "let's get down to business." The mechanic repeats Eddie's day verbatim to him, describing in vivid detail, "you were riding to the beach and, on the way there, you got a flat tire. Then you stopped in the middle of three large rocks to fix it. After fixing the flat tire, you raised your right arm and wished it was ten years from now. Oh, and by the way, in ten years, we still don't have a bicycle tire that won't go flat. Then, you headed to the beach but, because a storm was rolling in, you decided to ride home." Eddie is amazed that the mechanic knows this, since no one was around when Eddie got the flat tire. The mechanic tells Eddie, "and, when the storm got bad, you decided to stop in here." Eddie asks, "OK, now how do you know all this?" The mechanic replies Eddie, "I'll explain."

Handing Eddie a newspaper, the mechanic tells Eddie to have a seat. The mechanic asks Eddie to look at the date. Thinking that he is dreaming, Eddie sees a date ten years into the future. Eddie exclaims to the mechanic, "tell me this isn't real!" Getting right to the point, the mechanic replies, "no, this is very real. You moved through a time portal. But, don't worry. You'll be back home in two hours." Not knowing how to respond, Eddie exclaims, "what!" The mechanic explains, "time portals and parallel universes, they're real." Repeating himself, the mechanic says, "the area among the three rocks where you fixed the flat is a time portal. You raised your right arm, stated when you wanted it to be, and you got here. If you walk into the portal again, you'll be back in your time, ten years ago. I promise. And not only that, the weather will be a lot better."

Eddie is still highly skeptical, still thinking he is dreaming or something. Repeating what the mechanic said, Eddie asks, "so, time portals really exist?" The mechanic tells Eddie, "listen to the radio. Here, let me turn it up." Turning up the volume on the radio, which is tuned to a local radio station, the mechanic asks, "when have you ever heard any of this stuff before?" Answering for Eddie, the mechanic says, "never." Showing Eddie more evidence, the mechanic tells Eddie, "and take a look at this office. Have you ever seen it so clean when Angelo is here? And look outside. The junkyard in the back is gone. There are grass, trees, and a picnic table out there now." Walking to the window, Eddie and the mechanic take a look. Pointing out some more changes, the mechanic shows Eddie the back of the station, telling him, "I put that wall up around the back, and that brick storage building." Eddie confesses, "well, you certainly have some good points."

Eddie finally composes himself. After all, it's not every day you go through a time portal. The mechanic reassures Eddie that everything is going to be fine. There is a lot of talk about time portals and parallel universes in movies and books, but this one is for real. Finally, getting some semblance of reality, Eddie notices the name tag on the mechanic's shirt. The shirt is embroidered with the name Eddie. Still not putting all the pieces of the puzzle together, Eddie asks the mechanic, "so, your name's Eddie too?" Dropping the bombshell, the mechanic replies, "yeah, it is. I am you. You in the future."

Eddie, astounded by what he just heard, nevertheless, begins to make sense out of the whole experience. Eddie asks the mechanic, "so, I'm going to be a mechanic?" The mechanic smiles, and replies, "it sure looks that way." Telling Eddie what he already knows, the mechanic explains to Eddie, "look, you've always worked on mechanical things. No one is better at it than you. This is the best job in the world. And, you'll be known around town as 'Eddie the Mechanic', the best mechanic around." Eddie takes a deep breath, and exclaims, "wow!"

After learning that the mechanic is Eddie in the future, Eddie notices some resemblance of himself to the mechanic. The resemblance, however, is somewhat vague. At six feet, five inches tall, the mechanic is a good eight inches taller than Eddie. The mechanic's hair is short, but Eddie's is down to his shoulders. Although Eddie has a well-built physique, the mechanic's appearance suggests that he works out several hours a day.

As the storm passes, the mechanic stands up and invites Eddie to walk back into the three-bay repair shop. Showing Eddie the repair bays, the mechanic tells Eddie, "I've cleaned up around here. Take a good look. Everything is in its place." Eddie looks around the shop, which looks meticulously in order. The mechanic opens the garage doors, and they walk outside. The mechanic tells Eddie, "if you still have any doubts, look at the cars driving around. You've never seen a lot of these. There's a new 'Vette over there." The mechanic points out a new red Chevrolet Corvette as it drives down the road. Eddie responds, "wow, it looks cool." The mechanic adds, "and a lot of these cars that you see driving down the street, well, they're imports. And, that green MGB over there is mine, but more about that later."

Eddie and the mechanic walk back into the office. They sit and talk some more. Recalling the 100-yard dash during the last meet in middle school, the mechanic explains to Eddie that the portal is how he was able to go back in time and watch. The mechanic goes on to explain, "it is you who wanted to watch the race. You wanted to see who won." The mechanic carefully explains to Eddie, "at some time in your future, you will go back to watch that race, and there you will be, watching yourself run. It was as close as you could get. It was definitely a tie."

Eddie thinks about all that the mechanic has said, and asks, "where's Mark?" Giving Eddie some reassurance, the mechanic replies, "Mark is doing good. He's got his own business, doing what his father does. He helped me with a lot of the clean up around this place. He built the storage building in the back for me. We've done a lot of work together." Eddie replies, "wow, it sounds like to me that everything is good." The mechanic replies, "life is good."

Eddie asks the mechanic, "so, you bought the station from Angelo?" The mechanic, spilling the beans, tells Eddie, "yeah. About two years ago. I bought the land, the building, and all the tools. I paid for it with cash and gold." The mechanic, explaining improvements he has made, tells Eddie, "I put a small parking lot in the back for overflow. I also bought the old house in the back, knocked it down, and put in some greenery. You know, a nice place where I can sit when I eat lunch. Sometimes Mark will make it over for lunch. We sit out back in the shade, and we talk." The mechanic stands up, and tells Eddie, "let's go outside and take a look out back." Eddie and the mechanic walk to the back door, and into the beautifully landscaped back yard of the shop.

Eddie looks around at the eight-foot brick wall surrounding the land behind the shop, and the brick storage building. The shop is even brick on all four sides. Eddie sees a nice large grassy area with a few trees off to the left of the storage building. In the center of the lawn is a picnic table set on a concrete pad. The back of the shop looks like an oasis compared to the busy intersection in the front. The mechanic mentions, "here's all your landscaping skills put to work." Taking a closer look, Eddie sees artistic metal sculptures mounted on the brick wall, some nice yard ornaments, and an automatic sprinkler system. This is clearly not your average service station.

Eddie inquisitively asks, "OK, where did all the money come from for all this?" Getting down to business, the mechanic replies, "the time portal. Well, that and gold." Eddie, trying to piece together the puzzle, asks, "gold? How gold?" The mechanic explains, "yeah, gold and the stock market. In your time, the price of gold is about $65.00 per ounce. In August of 1980, the price of gold is $850.00 per ounce. Now follow me here. If you buy gold in your time, and bring it through the time portal forward to 1980, you make almost $700.00 per ounce. That's after the buying and selling commission."

Eddie takes a little bit of time to fully comprehend the mechanic's explanation, but he eventually sees where this is going. Eddie, in amazement, answers the mechanic's explanation with words of undeniable wisdom, "so, you can get as much money as you want." The mechanic explains, "yes, it would sure seem that way. But, I use it to help other people too. If someone can't afford their car repair, I'll give them a break on the price." Eddie now has a good understanding of how the mechanic owns his own shop, land, and tools, all at the age of 24.

The mechanic explains to Eddie that there is one catch. When you go back in time, you can't take back anything that has not already been created. In other words, you can't take a $100.00 bill from 1980 and bring it back to a time before it was printed and expect to use it. No one would have seen a $100.00 from 1980 ten years in the past. It would not be recognized or accepted. The mechanic, therefore, is an avid collector of older currency that would be accepted at an earlier time. Newer currency would be deemed counterfeit.

The mechanic instructs Eddie, "I'll give you $300.00 before you go back. Take it back to your time and buy four ounces of gold. Then, bring the gold back here to me. Just go through the time portal to August of 1980. We'll sell it for about three grand when you return." The mechanic tells Eddie, "then you bring the money back with you to your time, and buy more gold. Later, you'll invest the money in the stock market. You'll know which stock to invest in by looking at today's newspaper, and comparing it with the paper in your time when you get back home. You'll make millions. You're going to be a mechanic who looks like a really good investor." With nothing to lose, Eddie agrees to give it a try. After all, he's really not out anything if it doesn't work. Eddie did have one question, and asks, "if this is all true, then why the mechanic's shop?" The mechanic answers, "it's simple. If you got to do something, you might as well do what you love to do."

Eddie asks the mechanic, "what about the portal? How does it work?" The mechanic replies, "I don't know any more than you do." "But," the mechanic adds, "when you get back, make a careful drawing of the rocks, angles, and distances that make up the portal. Try to figure it out." Eddie, somewhat mentally fatigued, says, "this is a lot to think about." The mechanic explains to Eddie, "just remember that everything you see here, in the future, will happen. Why the shop is here is because of what you did back in your time.

You decide what kind of life you want. Where you will be in the future is based upon all the day to day decisions you make. If you don't act, you may end up living on Second Street."

The time draws near for Eddie to return to his time. Eddie tells the mechanic, "I guess I'd better get back," as they walk back into the shop. The mechanic instructs Eddie, "just ride back to where the portal is, and walk back into it. You will immediately return you to your time." Walking back to his safe, the mechanic takes out $300.00 cash, in old bills. Handing the money to Eddie, the mechanic reminds him to buy four ounces of gold. The mechanic instructs Eddie, "buy the gold in the coin shop near the mall, next to the stereo shop. Jimmy is the owner. He will treat you right."

Eddie puts the money in his pocket, as he and the mechanic walk toward his bicycle, which Eddie had propped up against a tool chest earlier. Eddie repeats to the mechanic, "August 1980," and repeats it to himself several times. The mechanic bids Eddie farewell, telling him, "see you later." Eddie gets on his bicycle, and rides off in the direction of the beach. The mechanic walks back into the office, removing the Closed sign he placed in the window earlier. After turning the pumps back on, he walks back into the shop area and continues working on the engine.

As Eddie rides down the road, he notices the different cars, and how the appearance many of the homes have changed. He takes the turn to enter the path along the parkway, and heads South toward the beach. As he approaches the portal, he slows down, and gets off of his bicycle. Walking toward the portal, he skeptically thinks to himself, "why am I doing this? This can't be real." Eddie walks into the space among the three boulders, and walks out the other side. "Well, I did it," he says to himself.

Eddie gets on his bicycle again, and heads home. Leaving the parkway path, he takes the same side streets as earlier today. Passing by Mark's house, Eddie sees Mark has completed the work in the front yard, and must have headed to the pool. Eddie also notices the dirt in Mark's front yard is dry as a bone. It's obvious that no rain has fallen at Mark's house this afternoon. As he comes up to the intersection where the service station is, he looks up and sees the sign that reads "Angelo's Service Station." This gave Eddie quite a comforting feeling. Everything seems like it is back to normal.

When he gets to the intersection, Eddie decides to stop in and see Angelo. Riding into the service station, Eddie sees all three garage doors open. Angelo yells out to Eddie over the sound of a loud engine he is working on, asking, "hey, Eddie! How come you're not at the pool or beach or something?" Eddie yells back, "I didn't make it there today. I'm just riding around today." Stepping out from behind the hood, Angelo asks Eddie, "do you need anything?" Eddie replies, "no. I just stopped by to say hey." Angelo and Eddie talk for a while, but Eddie's mind is elsewhere. Looking around the station, as he is absent-mindedly talking to Angelo, Eddie notices what a messy condition the station is in, both inside and out. Angelo asks, "are you OK?" Eddie responds, "yeah. I just had a long day, and it's hot out." After they talk a little more, Eddie then heads home, as Angelo returns to working on the engine.

Eddie arrives home, which is not far from Angelo's Service Station. After putting his bicycle away, he goes into his room to take a nap. But first, he stashes away the $300.00 along with the other money he earned from cutting lawns. Before he drifts off to sleep, he wonders if he should tell anyone about the portal. He quickly comes to the conclusion that if he tells anyone, they will not believe him, or worse. They will think he is crazy.

An hour later, Eddie's mother yell upstairs, "Eddie, it's dinner time!" Eddie wakes up from his nap, and stumbles downstairs to dinner. During dinner, Eddie doesn't say much. His mother asks him, "Eddie, are you feeling OK?" Eddie tells her, "yeah. I just had a hard workout. I went for a long ride, and it's hot out." Eddie's mother tells him, "eat, eat, you have to cut lawns tomorrow!" Tomorrow is Thursday, so Eddie has to get up early to cut the lawns he did not cut on Monday.

After dinner, Eddie goes back to his room, and thinks about what he discussed with the mechanic. He decides to get up early and finish cutting the lawns before lunch, so that he can go buy the gold. If there is enough time, he thought that he would go to the portal, and make a drawing, as he was instructed by the mechanic. After all, school starts in two weeks, and time will be limited. Going downstairs to the workbench, Eddie finds a tape measure, some string, and looks around for a protractor to measure the angles. Finding the necessary tools, he places the equipment in the tool bag on his bicycle, along with paper and a pencil. After the long day, Eddie goes back upstairs, takes a shower, and goes to bed.

The next morning, Eddie wakes up early to get his lawn duties done as fast as possible. He has other things on his agenda for today, and dilly dallying is not one of them. He eats breakfast, and is off to cut lawns. While cutting the lawns, Eddie contemplates the remainder of the day, rehearsing his plans in his mind. There are only two things on his list. One is to buy the gold, and the other is to draw a diagram of the portal. While this is simple enough, the two tasks consume his thoughts for the entire morning. One thought, however, could not escape from his mind. Eddie thought that, if he can bring $300.00 into the future, and then bring $3,000.00 back to the present, he may not have to work so hard.

After cutting the lawns, Eddie eats lunch, and tells his mother he is going out for a ride. Eddie's mom reminds him to be home on time for dinner. Eddie is often late for dinner. His afternoon bicycle rides will occasionally take a little longer than expected, especially in the heat.

Eddie rides to the coin store near the mall, as the mechanic instructed. The coin store is not too far from the portal, about two miles away. Locking his bicycle outside, he enters the store, which is now occupied by two people, Jimmy, the proprietor, and Eddie. Jimmy asks the young customer, "what can I do for you today?" With some hesitation, Eddie responds, "I want to buy some gold." Jimmy replies, "gold is a good investment. It's only going to go up." Eddie asks Jimmy, "how much is four ounces?" Punching a couple numbers into his adding machine, Jimmy comes up with the price. He tells Eddie, "$289.50, which includes my commission." Eddie responds, "OK, I'll take it."

Jimmy then inquires of the fourteen-year-old, "what kind of business are you in?" After all, it is not every day that someone Eddie's age comes in and buys four ounces of gold. Eddie replies, "I cut about eight lawns a week, clean pools, and do a lot of odd jobs. A mechanic told me I should invest in gold." Jimmy responds, "he's a very wise man." Looking over the gold, Eddie hands over the $300.00 cash. Eddie says to the proprietor, "I'll be back for some more, OK?" which seems like half question, and half statement. Jimmy responds, "you can come back for as much as you want. It's a better investment than the bank." Eddie replies, "awesome," and then gives Jimmy a fist bump. The fist bump goes a little awkward for the middle-aged owner of the coin store, but Jimmy now understands the gesture.

After placing the gold in the tool bag behind the seat, Eddie unlocks his bicycle. He rides in the direction of the portal to draw the diagram. The portal is only about two miles away, which takes Eddie less than ten minutes, even in traffic. On the way, he replays in his mind what the mechanic told him, that, while in the portal, you raise your right arm, state when you wanted it to be,

Eddie - The Freshman Year

and you will get there. Eddie was in the portal once before, waiting for Mark while he was on a test ride of Eddie's bicycle. There was no time travel that time. Eddie figures he's safe, and won't be transported in time just by drawing a diagram.

Arriving at the portal, Eddie leans his bicycle against one of the boulders. Looking over the boulders, which appear to be light grey, Eddie notices a dark spot near the center of one of the boulders. Looking at the other two boulders, similar spots are seen. Scraping away some dirt with his foot, it appears there is also rock between two of the boulders underground. The boulders do not appear to be just large rocks, but rather part of a larger rock hidden beneath the surface. Eddie, being no geologist, is not sure what type of rock the boulders are made of.

Using the tape measure, Eddie measures the distance between the base of the boulders. Coming up with three different measurements, six feet, ten inches; seven feet, eight inches; and, seven feet, eleven inches, he records them on his paper. Measuring the distance from one dark spot to another, Eddie records the distance of ten feet, three-and-one-half inches. To the other dark spot, the same distance is measured, ten feet, three-and-one-half inches. Eddie then takes the tape and measures between the other remaining points, and comes up with the same distance, ten feet, three-and-one-half inches. That, Eddie thinks to himself, is interesting. He then records the distances on his paper.

Eddie also remembered the mechanic told him to also measure the angles. Tying a string to a wrench, he places the wrench on the boulder, and lines the string over the dark spot. Placing the string across the dark spot on the second boulder, Eddie uses a small rock to hold the string in place. He repeats the procedure with all three dark spots, using anything he can find to anchor the three strings. Making sure everything is lined up perfectly, Eddie gets his protractor, and measures the three angles. Eddie measured the first angle to be slightly more than 52 degrees. The second and third angle all measured the same as the first angle, somewhere between 52 and 53 degrees. He then creates a drawing of the boulders, with the distances and angles he measured. He collects his tools, puts everything in his tool bag, and heads back home.

When Eddie arrives home, his mother asks him, "did you have a short ride today?" Eddie replies, "yeah. I got a few things to do before school starts again." Eddie's mother asks, "like what?" Eddie replies, "I have to work on my bicycle." Eddie's mother responds, almost prophetically, telling him, "oh, Eddie. You're always working on something. You're going to be a mechanic someday." Eddie tells her, "well, I have to buy some better tires. The lighter tires get a lot of flats." The tires that came with the track bicycle are of a lighter weight and thinner, and are designed for track use. With Autumn and Winter just around the corner, Eddie does not want to get stuck fixing flats in the cold weather. He tells his mother that he is going to Vito's in a few minutes.

Eddie makes the trip to Vito's and picks up two new tires that are more appropriate for road use. He also buys a small cloth bag to fit on the handlebars. When he gets home, he spends the rest of the afternoon replacing the tires and tuning up his bicycle, working a lot slower than usual. He installs the cloth bag on the handlebars, which he bought for carrying food. While he is working, Eddie contemplates the portal and where this could lead. Occasionally looking at the gold, which is still in the tool bag, he realizes this is real.

The Return Trip

With Summer break nearing its end, Eddie contemplates making one more trip through the portal sometime before school starts. The first trip was purely an accident. The next trip, however, will be purposeful. After all, he has the gold, so he might as well see if he can sell it for a profit. The second trip, if it is even possible, would be more of an adventure rather than a surprise.

Hoping to get some answers, Eddie decides to take the drawing of the portal, with the distances and angles, to a high school honor student, Ralph, who lives down the street. Barely knowing Ralph at all, Eddie is hopeful that a future fellow high school student can help him understand the diagram. Ralph's father is an account, and has always stressed the value of education. Eddie is hopeful that Ralph, who will be a senior this year, could shed some light on his drawing.

Eddie walks to Ralph's house, since it is not far. When he arrives, he knocks on the door. Ralph's mother answers the door, prompting Eddie to ask, "is Ralph here?" "Whom may I say is calling?" Ralph's mother responds in perfect English. "Eddie, from down the street," he replies. She tells Eddie, "I shall retrieve him for you," speaking to the visitor as if she were born on a different planet.

Ralph comes to the door, and invites Eddie in. The two, who have met once or twice before, reintroduce themselves. After they talk for a moment, Eddie tells Ralph that he has a geometry problem that he is trying to understand. Eddie asks Ralph, "can you take a look at this and see what you think?" "Sure, let me see it," responds Ralph. The honor student takes a look at Eddie's drawing, and asks, "where did you get this?" Eddie responds, "I drew it myself." Ralph sternly tells Eddie, "the only thing this will get you is an F in geometry class." Eddie, who is dumbfounded, responds, "what do you mean?" Ralph explains to Eddie, "this is an equilateral triangle. The inside angles must be 60 degrees. You have them labeled as 52 degrees." With firmness, Ralph adds, "this is not even possible." Reassuring Ralph of the accuracy of the diagram, Eddie replies, "but, I measured it myself." Ralph, in a curt tone, tells Eddie, "maybe you should just stick to cutting lawns." Eddie, figuring he is not going to get any help from Ralph, thanks him for taking a look at it, and heads home.

Eddie's first academic experience with a high school student was not at all a good one. The encounter with Ralph was all Eddie needed to motivate himself to go home, get his bicycle, and ride to the portal right now instead of in a few days. On his way home, Eddie is hoping that everyone in high school is not like Ralph. Ralph cut into Eddie like a shark at feeding time. In a purely academic way, Ralph beat Eddie to a bloody pulp. Eddie is used to people pointing out his academic deficiencies, so he just moves on.

Getting on his bicycle, Eddie checks that everything he needs is in his tool bag. He has the gold, the drawing, his tools, two spare tubes, and is ready to go. On his bicycle, he sprints down the road, and heads toward the portal. Eddie seems to have a little excess adrenaline after his encounter with Ralph. He passes Angelo's Service Station and Mark's house, and gets to the path next to the parkway in record time. As he approaches the portal, he slows down. Getting off of the bicycle, Eddie walks toward the portal.

Eddie briskly walks into the midst of the three boulders with his bicycle. As the mechanic instructed him, Eddie raises his right arm into the air and says, "August 1980." The sound coming from the parkway, as before, changes. This time, however, the weather is better than the last trip. Eddie walks over to the path, and rides back in the direction from which he came. Passing Mark's house again, he takes a good look and notices it does not look too different from before. As Eddie rides farther down the road, Angelo's Service Station slowly comes into view. Eddie looks up, and the sign in front of the service station has Angelo's name on it.

Somewhat apprehensive, Eddie peers into the service station from across the street. The station appears to be deserted, with just a few cars parked off to the side. From a distance, Eddie sees someone inside. He then rides toward the station, which has all three bay doors open. As Eddie gets closer, he sees the mechanic inside, pressure washing the floor. Getting off of his bicycle, Eddie walks into the service area. The mechanic waves, which is a relief to Eddie.

Yelling over the sound of the pressure washer, the mechanic asks Eddie, "do you have any gold?" This question gave Eddie even more confidence, but confidence in what is the question. Eddie replies, "I sure do." The mechanic walks over to the pressure washer, which is on the side of the building, and turns it off. Eddie asks, "is Angelo here?" The mechanic replies, "no. He just moved back to Greece. I just bought the station from him a few weeks ago." Stating the obvious, the mechanic tells Eddie, "I'm cleaning it up a bit. This place was a mess, but it's getting there." Looking around, Eddie remembers how organized the station appeared last time he saw the mechanic.

The mechanic tells Eddie to bring his bicycle inside, and closes the garage doors to the shop area. They both go into the office and talk for a while. The mechanic explains to Eddie that the shop has been closed for three weeks in order to clean it up. The mechanic proudly tells Eddie that he ordered a new sign, which says Eddie's Service Station, which will be installed next week. Pressure washing the station, inside and out, is the last thing on the list to be completed. After the pressure washing is completed, the station will be ready to reopen. The mechanic asks Eddie, "well, are you ready to go to the coin store?" "Sure," replies Eddie. After locking up the station, the mechanic and Eddie leave, and walk over to the mechanic's car.

The mechanic's car, a British Racing Green 1969 MGB, with factory wire wheels, looks immaculate. "Nice set of wheels," Eddie compliments the mechanic. Giving Eddie a hint of his future, the mechanic replies, "the next time you drive by Angelo's, it's going to be sitting over there in the corner, next to the fence." The mechanic tells Eddie the story behind the car, "when I was in high school, taking auto shop, Angelo told me I could have it. He said a customer had it towed in, and never wanted it back after hearing what it would cost to fix. After Angelo told him how much it would cost to fix, he sold it to Angelo for next to nothing. The customer was so frustrated with it. He just wanted to get rid of it."

Eddie, curious for knowledge, asks, "what was wrong with it?" Going into detail, the mechanic replies, "the overdrive box needed to be rebuilt. It needed a valve job, and a few other minor things. But, I wanted to do things right. The engine block was bored out. I put in oversized pistons, oversized stainless steel valves, a balanced crankshaft and a balanced camshaft. Then I added a stainless steel exhaust. The suspension was totally reworked, and an anti-sway bar was added. It runs really good now. Actually, it runs and performs better than when it left the factory."

Eddie and the mechanic get into the car, which fittingly has the top down on such a beautiful day. The car starts flawlessly, and the engine sounds better than the day it left the factory. They head down the road toward the coin shop, which is in the same direction as the parkway. Driving under the bridge to the parkway, the echo of the engine off the wall sounds like a well-tuned racing machine.

Pulling into the parking lot of a small shopping center near the mall, the mechanic finds a parking place far from the storefront. The mechanic explains to Eddie, "you'll have to wait here." Eddie responds, in disappointment, "why?" The mechanic explains, "you bought the coins last week. You've seen Jimmy once before but, by August 1980, he will have seen you many times." Eddie, gaining wisdom, sees the mechanic's point, and responds, "oooooh, I get it." The mechanic tells Eddie, "I'll be back in a sec." Giving Eddie something to do while he is away, the mechanic tells him, "pop the hood and take a look underneath."

While the mechanic is selling the gold in the coin store, Eddie looks over the MGB. Inside, the car is in showroom condition. Eddie gets out of the car and reenters on the driver's side. He opens the hood, and gets out to take a look. The engine compartment is clearly not the original factory design. Looking around, it appears that the Lucas electrical system has been extensively re-engineered to something that will not catch on fire. The rubber gas lines going to the twin SU carburetors have been replaced with higher quality braided metal lines. And the puny little stock fuel filter mounted in the engine compartment has been replaced with two larger filters, one for each carburetor. All of the nuts, bolts, and fasteners have been upgraded to stainless steel. Eddie, needless to say, is impressed by the work.

The mechanic returns, with $3,150.00 in cash. Eddie closes the hood, and they both get into the car. Handing the cash to Eddie, the mechanic tells him, "go ahead and put it in the glove box." The mechanic explains to Eddie, "when we get back to the shop, we'll have to separate out the bills that are later than the date you came here from. The older ones you can take back with you, but the newer ones you can't. But, I have some older bills at the shop in the safe that we can swap for the newer ones."

When Eddie and the mechanic get back to the shop, they go into the office to sort the money. Quite different from the way it looked three weeks ago, when Angelo owned the station, the newly renovated office is immaculate. The mechanic goes back to the safe and gets some older bills. Hidden in a private restroom, the safe is concealed behind a wall that raises up into the ceiling on a track. Vertical molding attached only to the adjacent walls hide any hint that the wall may be movable. No one would ever suspect that the safe is hidden behind the wall. They swap the newer bills for some older ones. Eddie now has $3,150.00 in old bills, mostly hundreds and fifties. Eddie thinks to himself that amount represents a profit of $2,850.00.

After sorting the money, Eddie asks the mechanic, "can I show you something?" The mechanic replies, "sure. What do you have?" Going into the shop to get the drawing he made of the portal, Eddie brings it back to the office. Laying the drawing on the desk, Eddie tells the mechanic, "here's the drawing." Eddie explains, "I showed it to Ralph, this honor student down the street, and he told me it's not possible." Looking at the drawing, the mechanic explains the portal to Eddie, "ten feet, three-and-one-half inches is 3.14 meters. That number, 3.14, is pi. You'll learn about it in tenth grade in geometry class. The angles should be 60 degrees, but they are about 52 degrees, which you did, by the way, measure correctly. That is why it is a portal. It doesn't follow the rules of the universe." The mechanic adds, "the angle of the hydrogen atoms in a water molecule is 104.5 degrees. The 52-degree angle that you measured is about half that angle." The mechanic humbly admits, "beyond that, I don't know. Maybe you'll run across someone who can figure it out." Eddie, who was somewhat confused earlier, now has a better understanding about something that makes not sense at all.

Changing the subject, the mechanic tells Eddie, "next time, bring the gold forward to September 2011. The price will be somewhere around $1,750.00 per ounce." "Wow," exclaims Eddie. Eddie asks the mechanic, "how much should I bring with me?" The mechanic replies, "as much as you want." The mechanic suggests to Eddie, "buy the gold in small amounts, not all at once. Get some from the shop down on Sunrise Highway too." After all, a 14-year-old buying thousands of dollars of gold might attract the wrong kind of attention.

Before Eddie leaves, the mechanic gives Eddie some wisdom regarding money. The mechanic tells Eddie, "money is just a way to buy your way into an unobtainable destination even faster." The mechanic, explaining himself, continues, "with the money, all of this can be built, but it means nothing if you aren't happy. When you get back, focus on school and sports. Fun in school, competition in sports, enjoyment from working on cars, that's the kind of stuff that matters." The mechanic says to Eddie, "oh, and one last thing. Ralph will someday be your accountant, but keep that a secret." To that, Eddie could only reply, "seriously?" How that will unfold will be a future mystery.

Eddie packs the tool bag with the cash, as the mechanic reminds him, "September 2011." As they say goodbye, Eddie repeats to the mechanic, "September 2011, got it." So that he does not forget, Eddie writes the date on his drawing of the portal. Eddie gets on his bicycle and rides toward the portal.

On the way back to the portal, he notices Mark's parents getting out of their car. Eddie thinks to himself, "good, Mark's parents still live here." They do, however, look a little older. That leaves Eddie to wonder where Mark is at this place in time. He decided that will be a question to investigate during another trip. Arriving back at the portal, Eddie walks in, and is immediately transported back to his time, with $3,150.00 in his tool bag.

For the remainder of the Summer, Eddie continues to cut lawns, clean pools, and go on a few rides. During each ride, he stops by the coin store and picks up a little gold, which Jimmy is glad to sell to him. He also frequents the coin store on Sunrise Highway, which is a considerable distance away. Taking the mechanic's advice, Eddie does not want to buy too much gold at once and bring attention to himself. Eddie decided he would accumulate gold, which is in the $65.00 per ounce range, until the money ran out. He would then go back to the portal, and redeem it at a date in the future.

The First Weeks

With the Summer coming to a close, and school about ready to start, Eddie will soon meet up again with his friends. The talk during first day of school will invariably be the usual, "what did you do over the Summer," type of gibberish. All the students will be checking out everyone else's wardrobes. The seniors will be watching carefully to see who now drives to school instead of taking the bus. The upperclassmen will be checking out the freshmen, and vice versa. Some of the track team members, particularly some guy named Paul Mahoney, will be looking for two guys named Eddie and Mark. Mahoney has heard rumors of their speed, which he has a hard time believing. None of this, however, concerns Eddie, who lives in his own world.

Last year, Paul Mahoney was the star of the high school track team. Mahoney is on his way to getting a scholarship in track, which he hopes to procure early in the season. Mahoney's primary events are the short sprints, and the 4 by 440 relay. Last year, Mahoney and his track buddy, Darryl Bell, were accompanied by two seniors in 4 by 440 relay, both of who were faster than Mahoney or Bell. This year, Mahoney feels that he is entitled to run whatever race he chooses simply because he is the senior member of the team. Anyone who comes along to threaten that entitlement will certainly not be Mahoney's friend.

On the day before school starts, while out on a ride, Eddie encounters Mark running along the road. Mark, who had a good run up the path along the parkway, is now on his way home. With less than a quarter of a mile left to go, Mark starts to walk and Eddie gets off of his bicycle and walks with him. The two friends talk, mostly about what they've done over the Summer. Mark, whose father had taken him out on quite a few jobs, tells Eddie he made a lot of money this Summer. Mark also tells Eddie he is saving up for a good bicycle. Eddie tells Mark that it would be easier to get to the beach if he had a good bicycle. Eddie's comment provided Mark even more incentive to buy one before next Spring. When they arrive at Mark's house, they talk for a little while longer, and Eddie heads home.

When Eddie gets home, his mother asks him, "hey, Eddie. Are you ready for school tomorrow?" Eddie, not knowing whether he is ready or not, tells her, "I guess so." She asks, "do you need anything?" Eddie answers her, "I guess I'll find out tomorrow." Eddie's mother is not too concerned with Eddie being prepared for the first day. Nothing happens for the first few days of school anyway. Everyone knows that but, nevertheless, people get stressed about it anyway.

The big day finally arrives. Eddie's mother proudly wakes him up herself because this is her son's first day of high school. Slow to get moving, Eddie has been waking up at 8:00 or 9:00 a.m. over the Summer, not 6:00 a.m. like he does today. Eddie's mother serves him a good breakfast, which he eats while she makes him a healthy lunch. As she makes him a sandwich on homemade whole grain bread, she asks if he wants anything special. Eddie asks for some cantaloupe, cut up, and placed in Tupperware, because it is easier to eat that way. Also asking for a bag of sunflower seeds and pumpkin seeds, Eddie is clearly not your typical fourteen-year-old.

Eddie heads out to the bus stop, where the upperclassmen and freshmen congregate in two separate groups. This is not too unusual to see during the first week of school. The division will break down in a week or two. Since the school is only a little more than one mile away, Eddie could have just as easily walked. At the bus stop, the typical conversation ensues. The students secretly check out what everyone is wearing, and looking over the new guys. A few of the seniors are absent from the bus stop today, such as Ralph, and will be for the rest of the year. They are driving their cars to school, which is not very far away, just because they can.

The bus arrives, and everyone gets on. The upperclassmen get on the bus first, claiming the better seats, not that any seat on a school bus is really good. At each bus stop, everyone entering the bus is carefully checked out, which is typical for the first few days of school. When the bus finally arrives at school, everyone gets off the bus as if it were a fire drill. In the front of the school, some small groups of friends, who haven't seen each other all Summer, meet together. Some students go inside, and others wander around aimlessly, trying to figure out where to go.

As Eddie enters the school, he walks up to Mark and Bobby B., who are standing around looking for someone they might know. The three guys compare their schedules, and it looks like they have some of the same classes together. One realization that is immediately evident is that they all have gym class during eighth period, which prompts for immediate celebration and high-fives. They also all have the first period class together, which is English. The teacher is Miss Kristen Starr, one of the most liked teachers in the school. First period also doubles as the home room class, where attendance is also taken. The big challenge of the morning is to find room 117, which should not be too hard. They walk around the halls for a while, and eventually find the room.

Eddie and his friends walk into the classroom, and immediately see Axel Braden sitting near the window with Wendy. Mark yells out, "yo bro," as he is looking at Braden across the room. Braden immediately responds, "this is high school. Who let you guys in?" Eddie yells back to Braden, "I tried to sign up for eight periods of gym class, but they wouldn't let me. So here I am." They all have a good laugh, while the rest of the class is marginally entertained. They all sit together, leaving no doubt which side of the classroom will be the center of attention.

The background noise in the classroom immediately comes to a halt when the English teacher, Miss Starr, enters the room. The twenty-five-year-old teacher, who looks like her wardrobe is from Saks Fifth Avenue, seems to command immediate attention just by her presence. Miss Starr informs the class, "this is ninth grade English slash home room. Please check your schedules and make sure you are in the right place."

Just then, a student in the back mutters something unintelligible, prompting Miss Starr to respond firmly, "let's get something straight. When I am speaking, you are to listen." Miss Starr, looking at the offender, continues, "if that is too difficult, I will arrange a meeting for you after school, commonly known as detention." That incident put an immediate end to any misbehavior in Miss Starr's English class.

Miss Starr, while taking attendance, is probably the first teacher to pronounce Mark's and Eddie's last names correctly. After all, she is an English teacher. The rest of the class goes very well and, by the end of the class, everyone is convinced that Miss Starr is a very amiable person. The bell rings, and it's off to the next class.

For Eddie, and some of his friends, the final class of the day is gym class. On the first day, the class meets in the gym. A mixture of freshmen and sophomores, the students are sitting on the bleachers with others in their grade. The instructor, Mr. Frazier walks in and introduces himself. Mr. Frazier gets down to business and begins lecturing the class. His lecture begins, "you have to be at work on time, and the train leaves in six minutes. You live one mile from the train station. Your car doesn't start. Are you going to make it to work that day?" Raising another hypothetical question, Mr. Frazier asks, "there's a 100-pound rock blocking your driveway. Are you strong enough to move it, or will you get a hernia trying to lift it?" Mr. Frazier comically adds, "or maybe you'll have to call me to move it for you! And, I'll charge you to do it!"

Explaining his ultimate goal to the class, Mr. Frazier explains, "my goal is to get you to the station on time and make sure you can move that rock! If I can get you to the station on time, and get you to move that rock, you will get a passing grade. If I cannot get you to the station on time, or you cannot move that rock, then I have failed. But, if I fail, you are the one that will receive the failing grade, not me!" This is not exactly what the students were expecting to hear on the first day of gym class.

While Mr. Frazier is lecturing the class on the benefits of physical fitness, the sophomores look around the room, checking out the freshmen. The sophomores are aware that Mr. Frazier will coordinate the introductory freshmen versus sophomores football game during the next gym class later this week. This match up will catch the freshmen by surprise. The sophomores fully intend to let the freshmen know who's boss once the competition starts.

Eddie, Mark, Bobby B., and Braden, all sitting together, somehow landed in the same gym class. Daniel Gaspari, also known as Gump, sits with Eddie and his friends. Gump is a football player and a wrestler, with good all-around athletic ability. Some of the sophomores, looking in the direction of Eddie and his crew, wonder how some of the freshmen have more than their fair share of muscle. The sophomores, however, will find out later whether Eddie and his crew have what it takes to complete with upperclassmen.

At the end of the school day, Eddie decides to walk home with Bobby B., the doctor of the shot-put, rather than take the bus. After crossing the four-lane road, the trip to Eddie's house will be on all side streets. Bobby B. lives less than a half mile from the school, so walking will be his usual regimen. On the way home, they talk mostly about the day, and that high school doesn't seem like it will be too difficult.

As they turn the corner, they see Gary Mitchell, their track teammate, being harassed by two upperclassmen. There are a few bystanders, who are secretly hoping and waiting for a fight to break out. The high school is known for its hazing of freshmen, which Eddie and Bobby B. just walked into, witnessing it first hand. It appears that Gary is today's target. They quickly figure out what's going on, and come up to Gary and his presumed adversaries.

Eddie asks Gary, "what's going on here?" Before Gary could answer, one of the thugs takes control of the conversation. With a threatening tone of voice, one of the troublemakers asks Eddie and Bobby B., "you two freshmen?" Eddie replies, "yeah, junior. What are you going to do about it?" The thug comes up to Eddie, and attempts to deliver a punch to his mid-section. The shot doc is standing with his arms crossed, ready to intervene if necessary. Eddie quickly grabs the aggressor's arm, turns him around, placing him in an arm bar. Giving the instigator a swift kick to the back of his knee, Eddie pushes his locked arm forward. This lands the thug face down on the pavement.

Gary, Bobby B., and Eddie all stand together as the thug gets up. Eddie questions those standing around, asking, "who's next?" With no one stepping to challenge Eddie, Bobby B. comments, "it looks like they've turned into chickens." Wisely, there are no other challengers today. The crowd disperses, walking away with the knowledge that there are a few in the freshman class who are best not antagonized. Eddie, Gary, and Bobby B. all walk home together, knowing tomorrow will be a better day.

Two days later, in gym class, is the match-up between freshmen and sophomores. As the students dress for class in the locker room, Mr. Frazier, the gym teacher, announces today's grand activity. "Today we are playing football," announces Mr. Frazier, in an energetic upbeat tone. Mr. Frazier informs everyone, "the freshmen will compete against the sophomores! Get ready, and be out on the field in five minutes, and have your team captain picked before you get on the field."

A lot of chatter rises in the locker room. The sophomores are all discussing how they are going to destroy the freshmen. Some of the freshmen, somewhat discouraged, are talking amongst themselves about how the match up is not fair. Not all freshmen, however, are discouraged. Braden, with his usual enthusiasm, rants, "we're gonna kick ass! We're gonna kick a lot of sophomore ass today! Something is finally going my way!" Braden's exuberance fires up Mark, Bobby B., Eddie, and Danny, who is also known as

Gump. Some of the sophomores, looking over at Braden and his 42-inch chest, are already beginning to feel as if they've been beaten.

On the field, Mr. Frazier quickly instructs the team captains to pick eleven men to start, and the rest will substitute. Mr. Frazier also makes the executive decision that the sophomores will get the ball first. Disappointing to some, Mr. Frazier also announces, "this is touch football, not a game of tackle." And, as a final note, Mr. Frazier tells the teams, "there will not be a kickoff, but you will start your possession on the 20-yard line. And, there will be no point after attempts." After all, this is gym class, not a varsity football game.

Gump has been chosen by the freshmen to be the team captain, since he is on the football team. Although Gump is an outside linebacker, he is more or less an all-around athlete. Gump is also a wrestler, competing in the 182-pound weight class. During the football season he weighs in at about 190 to 200 pounds. Gump could earn a spot on just about any team the school has to offer, but he primarily sticks to his strengths, which are football and wrestling.

The sophomore's team captain is Anthony Ambrosini, who is also on the football team. Playing running back and occasionally wide receiver, Ambrosini looks like a throw back from the sixties. With his long dark hair, if dressed in a tank top and leather jacket, he'd appear to belong to the Grease cast. Although he is second string in football this year, Ambrosini has the potential to be a good athlete. Ambrosini's big hindrance is that he occasionally cannot keep his emotions under control on the sports field.

Gump, well aware of Eddie and Mark's speed and agility from the Kill the Man with the Ball games, announces, "Eddie and Mark, you both play safety." Gump continues, "Bobby, you play middle linebacker, and bury their quarterback. Me and Braden will be the cornerbacks. I'll take the right side. Everyone else, get on the line." Some of the students were looking at Gump as if he were speaking a foreign language. The core team, to whom Gump assigned positions, understood their assignments well. Gump instructs two or three of the less athletic students as to where they should be positioned. The sophomore offense gets set and everyone is ready to play.

Mr. Frazier blows the whistle, and instructs the teams to begin play. The ball is snapped, and Ambrosini, the sophomore quarterback, throws a quick screen pass to the tight end. Gump is right there to knock the ball down, resulting in no gain. Ambrosini quickly recognizes that Gump and Braden pose a slight problem.

For the next play, Ambrosini calls for a long pass. The ball is quickly snapped again, with the sophomores trying to catch the defense off guard and show them who is boss. With Bobby B. putting pressure on the quarterback, the ball is haphazardly thrown to a receiver running deep to the left. Mark chases the receiver down, jumps in front of him, and intercepts the ball. With no hesitation, Mark is headed straight to the end zone, encountering a crowd headed his way. Mark quickly breaks to the right, where Eddie and Gump are blocking the defenders, leaving clear a path for him to the end zone. Mark scores a touchdown and, after two plays, the freshmen are ahead six to nothing.

Mr. Frazier tells the sophomore offense, in an attempt to raise their energy level, "you're the offense! You're supposed to be scoring points, not playing defense!" The sophomores line up again at the 20-yard line for their second attempt at embarrassing the freshmen, just as they have promised. The freshmen are ready, but the sophomores are taking a little more time planning for their second possession. As the sophomores line up, Ambrosini, their quarterback, surveys the field. Ambrosini snaps the ball, looking for an open receiver. Just then, Bobby B. breaks through the offensive line, buries Ambrosini, and shuts the play down for a loss. Bobby B. apparently forgot that this is a game of touch football, and tells Ambrosini, "sorry, dude."

The offense, calling the same play, lines up, and quickly snaps the ball in order to catch the defense off guard. Ambrosini throws a long pass to the left wide receiver who is open but, in a split second, is now tightly covered by Eddie. Eddie intercepts the ball, and immediately runs to a vacant area of the field. Looking for a path to the end zone, Eddie drops back a few yards. Being chased by the sophomore offense, Eddie traverses the field as if he was playing a game of Kill the Man with the Ball. Eddie, scrambling and running back and forth and in circles, has worn out some of the less athletic players who have given up chasing him down. Seeing an opening, Eddie makes a clean break from the pack, running straight toward Ambrosini, who is now protecting the end zone. Ambrosini, who is dumbfounded, runs straight on for Eddie. Eddie quickly breaks to the right, and scores the second touchdown of the game. Eddie ran more than 300 yards to score his touchdown. Only 40 of the 300 yards, however, were in the direction of the goal line.

Quite amused by the last play, Mr. Frazier, looking at Ambrosini, yells to the sophomores, "they're creaming you!" Mr. Frazier runs up to join the sophomores in their huddle. This is their third possession of the game, and they have nothing to show thus far. Mr. Frazier instructs them to run the ball, thinking that, at least, they won't lose it as easily. The sophomores line up again, this time with an unbalanced line to the right. Gump, playing right cornerback, signals to Braden, who is on the left, to watch for the run. The ball is snapped, and Ambrosini hands off to his running back, who runs to the right. Braden, plowing through a few offensive blockers as if they weren't even there, stops the run for a small gain. The sophomores try running a few more times, but the speed of Braden, Mark, and Eddie is too much for them to overcome. With the sophomores surrendering the ball on downs, the freshmen finally get to play offense.

Gump, the team's captain, tells the team that he'll play quarterback unless someone else wants to give it a try. There are no volunteers, so Gump will be the quarterback. Gump, who played Kill the Man with the Ball with the group last year, knows that Eddie, Mark, Braden, and Bobby B. can all catch the ball well. Not wanting to leave anyone out of the game plan, Gump asks, "does anyone have any ideas?" Mark quickly volunteers, saying, "throw me a short pass, and I'll see what I can do." Mark's response was an understatement, and everyone knows it.

The players get set, with Mark and Eddie playing wide receivers on opposite sides. Before the ball is snapped, the sophomore defense is nervously looking around. Gump takes the snap, and within two seconds, throws the ball to Mark. Knowing Mark's speed, Gump aims a few yards in front of Mark, who is already 15 yards down the field. Mark, who has already left the sophomore's safety in the dust, has a clear shot to the end zone. Mark catches the ball and, with no one remotely close to him, sprints into the end zone, untouched.

With the score at 18-0 in the first ten minutes, the sophomores are looking kind of ragged. Mr. Frazier tells the worn out sophomore team captain to substitute some fresher players for tired ones. Pulling Eddie, Mark, and Braden from the freshman lineup, Mr. Frazier also calls for substitutions for the three freshmen players. He then tells the teams to continue to play.

Taking Eddie, Mark, and Braden to the oval track on the other side of the schoolyard, Mr. Frazier tells the three track stars, "you're going to run a 440-yard dash for time." Mark pipes up and mentions, "I thought we were playing football." Mr. Frazier responds, "you'll get back to the game in a few minutes." Recognizing Eddie, Mark, and Braden from last year's middle school track meet, Mr. Frazier wants to see how well they perform. As he inspects his stopwatch, Mr. Frazier firmly tells them, "I want the best run you can do."

Although Mr. Frazier has many stopwatches, his Tag Heuer vintage timepiece accurate to 1/100 second, and his Swiss-made Leonidas stopwatch are hanging around his neck today on sterling silver chains. They say that Mr. Frazier has two wives, one is named Dawn, and the other one is his stopwatch. Some of the students even say that Mr. Frazier is the reincarnation of the Greek god Chronos, for he is always timing something.

Rarely do Eddie, Mark, and Braden race each other outside of formal competition, so this race will prove interesting. Eddie, Mark, and Braden are lined up, and ready to go. Mr. Frazier, with his stopwatch in his hand, announces, "on your marks, set," and, after a short pause, announces, "go." The three freshmen are off, as the football players gaze over at the three runners, wondering what is going on. Unknown to anyone in the gym class, many bored students sitting in their classrooms are also watching the activities out on the field.

The three runners leave the starting line as if they are running a 100-yard dash. At 100 yards, Mark and Eddie take a slight lead, with Braden two steps behind them. The 440-yard run is Braden's race so, although he is slightly behind, it is best not to underestimate him. At 150 yards, the runners slow their pace a bit, as to not burn themselves out. Halfway around the track, it is Mark, Eddie, and Braden, in that order. Barely two steps separate any two of them. Mr. Frazier looks down at his stopwatch at the halfway mark, already knowing that this is going to be a good run. Passing the 220-yard mark, Braden makes a move, passing Eddie, and comes up behind Mark. Eddie is not about to finish last, so he turns on the juice, and passes Mark. Mark, likewise, is not about to lose, so he catches up with Eddie and Braden. Eddie, Mark, and Braden, coming around the curve into the final straightaway, are all head to head. Each one wants to win, and each one refuses to lose.

The final 100 yards is a sprint to the finish. Still head to head with 50 yards to go, there no clear sign of a winner yet. With 25 yards left, Braden slowly takes the lead by about two steps. Eddie and Mark are still head to head, neither showing any weakness. Braden crosses the finish line first, as Mr. Frazier presses the button on his stopwatch. Braden is followed by Eddie and Mark, who were barely two steps behind, which is only a tenth of a second or so. Mr. Frazier looks at his stopwatch, exclaiming over and over, "that was a 54 quarter, a 54 quarter!" And, the three guys who delivered the performance are all freshmen.

While Eddie, Mark, and Braden ran the 440-yard dash, the football game had stopped, and both teams turned their focus toward the race. The girls, playing soccer on the adjacent field, were also distracted by the race. As the runners walk to cool down, Mr. Frazier jogs up to them, repeating their time, "that was a 54 second quarter mile! A 54 second quarter mile!" Eddie, Mark, and Braden exchange high-fives and fist bumps. Mr. Frazier tells Eddie, Mark, and Braden they can return to the football game after the next play.

During the next play, on the sidelines, Mr. Frazier again conveys to Eddie, Mark, and Braden how impressed he is with their performance on the track. After the play is over, Mr. Frazier yells out to the sophomores, "these guys just ran a 54 second quarter mile! They're worn out now, so maybe now you can score a few points!"

Eddie, Mark, and Braden go in, not quite fully recovered from the quarter mile race they just ran. The score is still 18-0, and the sophomores have the ball. Ambrosini snaps the ball, and throws a deep pass to a receiver in the vicinity of Eddie. Fatigued from the race, Eddie runs up behind the receiver and punches the ball into the air with his fist. Eddie made no effort to catch the ball. Still not fully recovered from the race, he just wanted to shut down the play. Mark, who is also in the area, catches the airborne ball and just stands there for a second or two. Mark, quickly approached by an offense that has now reverted into defensive mode, laterals the ball back to Eddie. Eddie, who is now alone on his side of the field, catches the ball and sprints to the end zone for another touchdown. The score is now 24-0.

The last interception did not sit well with the sophomore's quarterback, Anthony Ambrosini. Ambrosini, quite disgusted, looks over at Eddie as he returns from the end zone, and asks, "what kind of tribe are you running?" Eddie grins, and replies emphatically, "that's my tribe, junior! Don't mess with 'em." When Eddie calls someone "junior," it is his way of telling them they really need to step up their game. From then on, Eddie, Mark, Axel Braden, Robert Bradshaw, Gary Mitchell, and Eric Johnson will be known as Eddie's Tribe, or just The Tribe.

The remainder of the game was pretty much the same story. The sophomores didn't score a single touchdown that day, with the final score being 42-0. Mr. Frazier was too self-absorbed with Eddie, Mark, and Braden's phenomenal 54 second quarter mile to care about the outcome of the game. On the way back to the locker room, the sophomores did not have much to say to the freshmen. The freshmen, however, had cause for celebration, for they were supposed to lose this game, and lose it in a big way. One person, however, has a score to settle. Anthony Ambrosini, the team's captain and quarterback, is quite embarrassed by the loss. He is determined to redeem himself in a future competition against Eddie and his tribe.

The next day, word got around the school about the football game and the 54-second quarter mile. The game proved quite entertaining to all who had a view from the school building. Mr. Moreno, the football coach, who teaches history, had a good view of the game from his classroom window. While attempting to teach, Mr. Moreno was quite distracted by the game. The play of the game was Eddie's 300-yard run all over the field to score a touchdown. What Eddie, Mr. Frazier, and the rest of the gym class did not know was that, in a few of the classrooms, the teachers and students came up to the window and watched them play. There is no doubt there was a discussion about that game in the teacher's lounge after that class.

The first few days of the school week went a little rough, but the days eventually got a lot better, with the rest of the week going very well. Since it was the first week of school, not too much was expected academically from any of the students. By the end of the week everyone had their schedules all sorted out and extracurricular activities were in full swing. Best of all, Eddie, Mark, Bobby B., Braden, and Gump all undoubtably locked in an A in gym class.

Eddie takes advantage of the time after school to continue buying gold. With the money he brought back from the future, he could buy about 48 ounces of gold. Over the past few weeks, Eddie noticed the price was inching up very slowly. While out riding one day, Eddie found a third place to buy gold. In a local department store, there is a coin and stamp counter. The prices in the department store are a bit higher, but gave the advantage that he would not be frequenting the same places every time he buys gold. In the department store, there is also the advantage that a different clerk is on duty each day.

After school one day, Eddie returns to the school on his bicycle to check out the Autumn sports teams. Eddie was not interested in either football or soccer but, since Gary Mitchell is on the cross country team, he thought he'd check it out. The cross country team usually runs along a three-mile loop on the roads behind the school. Eddie is not a distance runner, and would rather ride his bicycle for 50 miles as opposed to running three miles. With no sign of the team on the school grounds, Eddie rides along the three-mile loop.

Halfway around the loop is a small pond, which Eddie has passed many times in the past on his bicycle. As Eddie approaches the pond, he can see the runners across the water. As Eddie gets closer, he notices there are about six runners in the pack. There is, however, no sign of Mitchell. Catching up to the pack, Eddie sees another group of four runners a little farther ahead. And there is Mitchell, in the middle of the front pack. Passing the trailing group of runners, Eddie approaches the four runners in front. As he passes Mitchell, Eddie yells out to him, "hey Mitchell! When are you going to start running?" That was all Mitchell needed to pour on a little more speed and press the pack to run faster. Eddie rides his bicycle back to the school, to see what else may be going on.

When Eddie gets back to the school, he turns into the parking lot through a narrow walking path that serves as a short cut for students who walk to school. This is the same path Eddie takes when he walks home. At the far side of the lot, where the students are allowed to park, he sees Ralph, the honor student. Ralph and another guy appear to be looking at the tires on Ralph's Volkswagen Beetle. Eddie thinks to himself, "wow, Ralph got himself a VW Bug."

As Eddie gets a little closer, he quickly realizes the guy with Ralph is not admiring the tires or workmanship of Ralph's vehicle, but letting the air out of one of the rear tires. Deflating the tires is some moron named Steven Wagner. Wagner, at five feet, seven inches and 125 pounds is too much of an opponent for Ralph, who is five feet, eight inches and weighs about 105 pounds. Wagner, being kind of scrawny, is limited to picking on the low hanging fruit. Ralph is telling Wagner to stop, but Wagner pushes him away, and continues with his nasty deed.

Riding up, Eddie gets off of his bicycle, and props it up against the fence. Eddie, walking up to the car, asks, "do you need any help?" Wagner replies, "yeah. You can start letting the air out of the other tires." Eddie responds authoritatively, "not you, pinion head. I was talking to Ralph!" Standing behind the pinion head, Eddie tells him to stand up. Putting Wagner into an arm lock. Eddie firmly tells the pinion head, "this is an automobile. You don't let the air out of the tires unless you are going to pop the tire off the rim and put on a new one. Got it?" Wagner, struggling to escape from the arm lock, responds, "who the hell are you?" Eddie replies, "I am Eddie, the Mechanic, and don't you forget it."

Eddie tells Ralph to get the pump from his bicycle. Ralph hands Eddie the pump. Eddie, pushing Wagner to the ground, tells him, "sit down, junior, and don't even think about moving." Eddie fastens the pump to the tire, and tells Wagner, "start pumping, pinion head!" Wagner, beginning to speak, says, "I'm going to." Before Wagner could finish the sentence, Eddie interrupts, and exclaims, "I said start pumping!" Looking up at Eddie, and his five-foot-nine-inch, 170-pound muscular frame, Wagner is left with little choice. Wagner starts re-inflating the tire that he was caught maliciously deflating.

Eddie stands along side Ralph, with his arms crossed, watching Wagner pump up the tire. Ralph thanks Eddie for helping him out. Ralph also apologizes for treating Eddie so rudely when Eddie asked about the math problem over the Summer. While Wagner is pumping up the tire, Eddie mentions to Ralph that it should take him a good half an hour or more. Eddie asks Ralph, "what's the matter with this guy anyway?" Ralph responds, "he's just basically a jerk." Wagner, who is quite angry, begins to yell out, "just shut." Wagner is quickly interrupted by Eddie, who sternly tells Wagner, "shut up and pump, junior!"

After fifteen minutes goes by, Wagner is still not finished, and is showing signs of fatigue. Wagner, whining like a baby, tells Eddie, "I can't pump anymore! My arm's giving out!" Fed up with Wagner's poor conditioning, Eddie tells Wagner, "you got another arm. Use it, junior." Eddie then asks Ralph if he has a tire gauge. Ralph gets the tire gauge out of the glove box, and hands it to Eddie. Removing the pump from the tire, Eddie checks the pressure. Eddie announces, "twenty-two pounds. Only five more to go." Full of compassion, Eddie fastens the pump to the left side of the tire valve, so Wagner can use his left arm to pump. Wagner continues pumping for another ten minutes.

Anyone who's tried to pump up an automobile tire with a frame-mounted bicycle pump knows that it is faster to roll the tire to the closest service station, fill it up, and roll it back. Eddie tells Ralph, "let's check the pressure again." Wagner moves over, Eddie removes the pump and Ralph checks the pressure. Wagner nearly panics, hearing a little precious air escape while Ralph checks the pressure. Ralph announces, "twenty-eight pounds. It should be twenty-seven." Eddie instructs Ralph, "let a little out." Eddie looks over to Wagner, telling him, "shut up," before he even has a chance to speak. If Ralph accidently lets out too much air, it's a sure bet Wagner will be pumping again. Ralph gets the pressure set at exactly twenty-seven pounds. Eddie tells Ralph to check the other three tires. Still being obstinate, Wagner begins to say, "I'm not pumping," again interrupted by Eddie, who responds, "oh yeah, you will be!"

Ralph verifies the tires are all at the correct pressure. Wagner, who will probably not be able to move his arms for a few days, is relieved to some degree. Grabbing Wagner by the arm again, Eddie warns him, "if I ever catch you touching this car again, you are going to wish it ran over you compared to what I'm going to do to you! Got it?" Wagner, in pain from the arm lock, responds, "yeah, yeah, I got it! I got it!" Eddie tells Wagner, "good!" Eddie gives Wagner a firm shove, and Wagner leaves the scene as fast as possible.

Eddie tells Ralph, "I bet he won't be letting air out of tires anymore." Ralph again thanks Eddie for helping him. Eddie reassures Ralph, "if he bothers you again, let me know." Ralph gets in his car and drives home. Eddie, riding home on his bicycle, passes Ralph on the road. From that day on, Eddie has been known as Eddie the Mechanic.

Wagner's nasty deed earned for him an interesting nickname at school. Pumping the tire up for more than a half hour with the bicycle pump, Wagner's biceps and elbows were so sore and inflamed that he could not fully extend his arms. Walking around school with his arms bent at a 90-degree angle, Wagner's arms looked like the front legs of a Tyrannosaurus Rex. For the rest of the school year, Wagner was known as "T-Rex."

The Turn of Events

Two weeks into the school year, Eddie has accumulated 48 ounces of gold, and figures that he must redeem it soon. With the weekend finally arriving, he figures that now is the perfect time. Eddie still has his lawn duties, which he is now confined to do on the weekends. Since it is the end of the mowing season, each lawn is on two week schedule, so he has only four lawns to cut each week instead of the usual eight. His lawn maintenance business will end in about two months, when the weather gets colder.

Waking up a little late, Eddie comes downstairs and makes himself his own breakfast. Eddie's mother is doing a few Saturday morning chores around the house, while his father is at the Italian delicatessen picking up a few items that he cannot get elsewhere, such as fresh pickles and Capocollo. Eddie makes a plate of fresh blueberries, cantaloupe, skim cheese, yogurt, and an English muffin with homemade strawberry jam. Eddie's mother, looking at the plate, asks him, "are you a little hungry already?" Eddie tells her, "I have four lawns to cut this morning. I want to get them done early so I can go out on a ride." Eddie's mother asks him, "isn't cutting four lawns enough exercise?" Eddie replies, "well, maybe a short ride then." After finishing his breakfast, Eddie gets ready to go to work.

Before cutting the lawns, Eddie prepares for his afternoon ride, giving his breakfast a little time to digest. He checks his tool bag to see if he has all that he needs. He loads the gold into the handlebar bag he bought a while ago, which is getting a bit on the heavy side. Eddie takes a quick look at the drawing he made of the portal, on which he wrote the date, September 2011. After double checking everything, Eddie is ready for his ride later this afternoon.

Eddie heads out to cut the lawns, which are all clustered in the same area of his neighborhood. With the cooler weather, he is able to get four lawns cut in the time it usually takes to cut five. While Eddie is cutting lawns, he thinks about the freshmen versus sophomore football game played the first week of school. Football, he thought, seemed like it was fun, more fun than the pick up games after school. Thinking a little deeper, he figured the varsity football team would be a lot more serious competition than gym class. Eddie reasoned to himself that football is just a game of Kill the Man with the Ball with strict rules. Eddie's assessment is not far from the truth.

After cutting the lawns, Eddie heads home for lunch. As he is putting the equipment away, he notices that he is less tired than usual after working in the cooler weather. Thinking back to the day Mr. Frazier made him run the quarter mile, along with Mark and Braden, it occurred to him that a 54 second quarter mile is his personal record. This news sounded even more encouraging to Eddie for the Winter track season. Eddie will be running indoors, and not in the heat, which may translate into increased performance and better times.

Lunch is usually eaten together in Eddie's home. Today, however, Eddie's father is absent because he has to finish a job that will have to be completed by Monday. Eddie's father returned earlier today from the delicatessen, with fresh food in hand. Eddie's father made his lunch, and immediately headed out to work. For lunch today, Eddie has a ham and Capocollo sandwich made on homemade whole grain bread. A generous serving of pumpkin seeds and sunflower seeds completes the midday meal. While eating lunch, Eddie wonders what kind of food the mechanic has to eat in 2011.

After lunch, Eddie goes to the basement and gets his bicycle. Since he just ate lunch, he rides a lot slower than normal toward the portal. Today, Eddie is in no rush. He has nothing planned for the rest of the weekend, other than a little bit of homework that will not take too long. Passing Angelo's Service Station, Eddie notices that the station is very busy on Saturdays. It occurs to Eddie that Angelo works six days a week. A little farther down the road, Eddie gets on the path to the portal. While approaching the portal, he looks at the parkway, noticing that there is not a lot of traffic today. Not as many people are headed to the beach now that the weather is getting cooler.

Entering the portal, Eddie raises his right hand, and says, "September 10, 2011." He picked the tenth because it was on a Saturday. The sound on the parkway gets very quiet, and the air suddenly appears a lot cleaner. Looking over at the parkway, there are now more cars than a minute ago. Eddie also notices that the cars are quieter. Eddie rides down the path toward the service station, which is unfortunately away from the beach since the weather is nice. Turning off the parkway path, Eddie enters the side streets. The first thing he notices is that all the cars look very different. The second thing he notices is that the roadway does not smell like car exhaust. Continuing to the service station, Eddie marvels at all the changes he sees in the homes and shopping centers.

As Eddie approaches the service station, he notices that all the bay doors are closed. Eddie rides in, and sees the mechanic sitting behind his desk working on something that he does not recognize. After getting off his bicycle, Eddie opens the door, and walks in. He is careful not to leave the bicycle outside because the gold is in the handlebar bag. Eddie sees the mechanic sitting at his desk, who appears worn out and fatigued. The mechanic is older now. His once twenty-one inch arms are now fifteen inches, and it appears he's lost a lot of weight. Although the station is open, it seems the mechanic has taken a day off.

The mechanic greets Eddie, "oh good, you're here." Eddie asks the mechanic, "are you not busy today?" The mechanic tells Eddie, "no, I'm just pumping gas and looking up some stuff on the internet." Never hearing the word "internet" before, Eddie replies, "on the what?" The mechanic replies, "the internet." Thinking for a moment, the mechanic tells Eddie, "oh, yeah. There is no internet in your world yet." Eddie walks to the other side of the desk to take a look. This is Eddie's first look at a laptop computer, which has Google search results on the screen. Eddie has no idea what he is looking at, nor the power that is at the mechanic's hands.

Eddie wants to take a look, and see how this internet thing works. However, the mechanic has something much more important to discuss with Eddie. The mechanic tells Eddie, "we have something more important to talk about right now." Seeing a look of concern on the mechanic's face, Eddie responds, "like what?" As he closes the laptop, the mechanic tells Eddie to have a seat. Eddie pulls up a chair on the other side of the desk.

Eddie asks the mechanic, "what's up?" The mechanic, who has always been frank with Eddie, tells him, "you're sick." Eddie responds, "what do you mean, I'm sick? I just ran a 54 second quarter mile in gym class. I feel great!" The mechanic explains, "no, it's not that kind of sick. You have a genetic disorder. It's called MTHFR. No one has ever heard about it in your time. It was discovered just a short time ago."

Eddie, not knowing how to respond, inquisitively asks, "well, what is it?" The mechanic explains to Eddie, "it means that your body can't process the vitamin called folic acid properly. You need the active form of the vitamin, which is methylfolate, which you can't buy at your time. This is a lot to understand, but it causes something called homocysteine to build up and that will cause arteries to clog." Eddie, a bit startled, asks, "what? How did you find out about this?" The mechanic tells Eddie, "I hurt my back lifting a transmission a few years ago, and I went to a chiropractor. Just recently, I told him I was getting tired. He suggested I get a genetic test. That's how we found it."

The mechanic spells out to Eddie that he needs to take methylfolate, and other B vitamins, especially B12, otherwise he is going to have a lot of problems when he gets older. The MTHFR genetic defect was not known during Eddie's time, and the vitamins he needs to take are not readily available at his time. Eddie will have to go through the portal, buy them in the future, and take them back with him when he returns to his time. Reminded that the mechanic is Eddie, but in the future, he sees that the mechanic, now in his early 50s, is not well. Realizing that, if this is his destiny, Eddie has the power to change it.

The mechanic tells Eddie, "let me make a phone call." Pulling out his iPhone, the mechanic begins to call his chiropractor. Eddie stops him, asking, "what in the world is that thing?" The mechanic replies, "it's my cell phone," showing it to Eddie. The mechanic tells Eddie, "oh, yeah. They don't have those either where you come from." Eddie is amazed that a small plastic box with a plethora of interesting pictures on it is actually a telephone. To Eddie, a telephone is a large cumbersome black box with a receiver and a dial, or, if you're really lucky, pushbuttons. As the mechanic is calling his chiropractor, Eddie is listening to the radio playing in the background. The song he hears is Need You Now by Lady Antebellum, which he really likes.

The mechanic calls his chiropractor, Dr. Bobin. The doctor is usually not in the office on Saturday. He figures he'd check anyway. Fortunately, the doctor answers his cell phone, and the mechanic asks, "hey, are you in today?" Dr. Bobin informs the mechanic that he is not, but asks him what he needs. The mechanic tells the chiropractor, "I need to pick up some of the vitamins and some of the methylfolate." The chiropractor informs the mechanic he can meet him at the office in thirty minutes, if he wants. The mechanic agrees, telling him, "sure, thirty minutes. Thank you very much."

The mechanic instructs Eddie, "put your bike in the back. We're going to the chiropractor." Just to check, the mechanic asks Eddie, "did you bring any gold?" Eddie replies, "yeah. Forty-eight ounces. It's in my handlebar bag." Doing some quick math in his head, the mechanic realizes that amount of gold represents about $85,000.00. It's not going to be possible to sell that much gold all at once for cash anywhere. The mechanic informs Eddie, "that's about eighty-five thousand dollars of gold. We can't sell all of that right now." The mechanic directs Eddie, "go and get five ounces out of your tool bag." Eddie walks into the shop and gets the gold out of the handlebar bag. While Eddie gets the gold, the mechanic shuts off the pumps and turns the outside signs off. They walk to the mechanic's car, which is still the 1969 MGB he got from Angelo years ago when he was in high school. The mechanic tells Eddie he has another car, which also seats two, but drives the MGB on weekends and when the weather is nice.

The mechanic is known around town to everyone as "The Mechanic." Representing the skill of the mechanic, the MGB is an icon many are familiar with. Cars like the MGB should have been retired years ago, but this one is running better than the day it left the factory. When the British Racing Green MGB drives down the road, everyone knows who is driving it. It would be easier for the mechanic to keep the car running and drive it that it would be to explain to everyone that he no longer has it. For this reason, the mechanic will always have the MGB. Whenever anything goes wrong with the MGB, no matter how small, the mechanic is quick to repair it. After all, the condition of the mechanic's car is a testimony of his skill.

The mechanic and Eddie drive down the road, and under the bridge to the parkway. Past the bridge, the area has gone commercial. Eddie barely recognizes the road. The coin store is in the same place it has been for years, but the area around it is more built up now. They pull into the parking lot, and the mechanic reminds Eddie that he has to either wait in the car, or walk around. Eddie knows that he cannot enter the coin shop with the mechanic, because Jimmy, the proprietor, would recognize Eddie from his past purchases of gold. While the mechanic is in the coin store, Eddie gets out of the MGB, and takes a look at the newer cars in the parking lot. Not seeing the classical steel bumpers from his era, Eddie wonders why most cars have no longer have bumpers. Eddie is also wondering what is taking the mechanic so long.

Back in the coin store, the mechanic finds out the price of gold is about $1,850.00 per ounce. Jimmy gives the mechanic a deal on the commission, netting $1,800.00 per ounce. Jimmy is able to redeem all five ounces for cash. The mechanic informs Jimmy he has some more that he wants to sell. Jimmy tells the mechanic to just give him a few days' notice, and he can have the cash available. Selling five ounces, the mechanic walks out of the store with $9,000.00 cash, in one-hundred dollar bills.

The mechanic returns to the car, and Eddie asks, "what's the matter? Cars have no bumpers anymore?" Giving Eddie some interesting news, the mechanic informs him, "cars are made out of plastic these days. They don't make them like they used to. The engines run good and they're reliable. But, if you get in an accident, the bodies fall apart." They both get in, and the mechanic hands Eddie the cash, and tells him to put it in the glove box. Looking at the stack of bills, Eddie is amazed. Eddie asks, "how much is that?" The mechanic replies, "$9,000.00, which is a couple Summers of lawn cutting. Let's go pick up the vitamins." The mechanic heads back in the direction of the service station, passing it on the way to the chiropractor.

On the way to the chiropractor, the mechanic breaks the news to Eddie that he cannot bring back $85,000.00 back with him at one time. The mechanic, however, has a plan. He tells Eddie to hide some gold and cash in the MGB. The MGB will remain in the same location, and not move until Angelo tells Eddie he can have the car. This makes the MGB the perfect place to hide anything. Angelo does not care about the MGB, which can rust away to nothing as far as he is concerned. When they get back to the service station, the mechanic's plan is to give Eddie a key to the MGB, and show him how to hide the cash.

The mechanic and Eddie arrive at the chiropractor's office. Dr. Bobin, the chiropractor, is inside, sorting through the mail while he is waiting. The mechanic instructs Eddie to get a few hundred dollars out of the glove box. Eddie asks the mechanic, "vitamins cost that much?" The mechanic replies, "everything cost a lot more now. On average, anything cost ten times what it does from when you came from."

Eddie walks in with the mechanic, and the doctor greets them both. Introducing Eddie as "George," a kid from high school, the mechanic tells the doctor he is interested in cars. The doctor asks the mechanic, "what did you need today?" The mechanic replies, "the vitamins and the methylfolate. And, do you have anything to build up muscles?" The doctor asks, "would that be for George, or you?" "For George," replies the mechanic. Explaining the basics, the doctor tells them, "the branched-chain amino acids are a must. A free-form amino supplement will also help, and definitely some vitamins. The vitamins you usually buy would be good. But remember, resistance training, such as lifting weights is most important when building muscle. Supplements alone will not do it."

Asking the doctor for a favor, the mechanic asks, "can you tell George about the genetic problem I got? He's interested in this kind of stuff." The doctor replies, "sure, if I have your permission." Giving his permission, the mechanic replies, "sure, no problem." The doctor tells the mechanic, "let me get your file. It will be just a minute." Watching the doctor print the test results from a computer, Eddie is amazed at the technology he is witnessing. Laser printers and personal computers do not exist during Eddie's era.

The doctor returns with the report, which is an eight-page color printout, showing genetic variations that can be intervened with by using nutritional supplements. Showing Eddie the test results, the doctor explains the basics of genetics. Beginning his dissertation, the doctor explains, "the test we performed was a DNA analysis. You are born with two copies of each gene. One you get from your mother and the other one from your father. This column represents the name of the gene, this other column labeled 'genotype and risk' shows the genetic variation. If the risk in coded in yellow, then it is called heterozygous. In other words, one of the two genes is what we call a 'variant'. When you see the risk coded in red, both copies of the gene are variants. Variants are sometimes good, sometimes bad. These other columns have suggestions for nutritional intervention."

After the doctor goes over the basics, he begins discussing the mechanic's genetic report, which, unknowing to the doctor, is also Eddie's, who the doctor thinks is George. The doctor continues, "first, we'll look at this section labeled 'Methylation.' This gene, labeled MTHFR, stands for methylenetetrahydrofolate reductase. We see it is in yellow, meaning there is one defective copy. That results in about a 30 to 50 percent reduction in the enzyme efficiency. This gene, by the way, is why the mechanic can't take the heat in the Summer. The defective enzyme is what we call thermolabile. That's a fancy chemistry word that means that the efficiency of the enzyme gets worse in the hot weather, in this case, a lot worse. The MTHFR defect causes an accumulation of homocysteine, which a significant cause of plaque build-up in arteries. That will eventually lead to a heart attack or stroke. It also causes an increased risk of gastric cancers, such as stomach cancer. The good news is that the risk can be totally averted by taking methylfolate, vitamin B12, and a good vitamin B-complex." Interrupting himself, the doctor says, "let me get another report. This one will be very interesting. I'll be right back."

While the doctor steps away, the mechanic asks Eddie if he understood what the doctor was talking about. Eddie says he understands a lot of it, and that he has to take the right vitamins. The mechanic tells Eddie that, if he takes the vitamins, he will be changing his future, and he will be a lot more healthy. Eddie asks the mechanic whether the vitamins will help his athletic performance. The mechanic tells Eddie they will ask the doctor when he is done.

The doctor returns to the room with another genetic report. This report is a little more in-depth. Continuing with his narrative, the doctor continues, "here's another report with some interesting good news. Look at this gene here, the ACTN3 gene, which stands for Actinin alpha 3. This variant means that the mechanic has the genetics to be an awesome sprinter, which he told me he was a long time ago. There are couple other gene variants related to sprinting and muscle composition, which are present in the most desirable variation, all beneficial for an athlete."

Pointing to another line on the report that referenced the MAO gene. The doctor continues, "the MAOA gene, the variant type labeled here is rs909525 G. The report shows that the MAOA gene variation is the 2R, or 2-repeat version. This particular combination is known as the 'warrior gene'. Obviously, this is a desirable characteristic on the sports field, or, as the name 'warrior' suggests, on the battlefield. The MAOA gene, by the way, breaks down the neurotransmitters serotonin, norepinephrine, epinephrine, and dopamine in the synapse. Those are all excitatory neurotransmitters."

The doctor then addresses another gene that would suggest higher physical energy. Pointing to several other lines on the report, he continues, "all of these COMT variants slow down the elimination of some of the excitatory neurotransmitters from the body. The flip-side of this, however, is that, without exercise and physical activity, there's a tendency to not sleep well."

The doctor finishes, telling them, "it's all here. All the genetic makings of a super athlete. It's just too bad that all this wasn't known about 40 years ago. Otherwise, the mechanic probably could have made the Olympics." Eddie is amazed at what he is hearing from the doctor. In Eddie's era, a visit to the doctor amounts to not much more than looking down his throat and listening to his heart to make sure it's still beating.

The mechanic asks the doctor, "will the vitamins increase athletic performance, say, like in anyone?" Referring to George, the doctor emphatically states, "yes, especially at his age." The mechanic also asks, "how about me?" The doctor replies, "if you had these supplements when you were his age, you'd be even a better track star than you were. Unfortunately, the vitamins and supplements weren't available back then. This is part of the reason the athletes today are a faster and stronger than decades ago." Little did the doctor know that, because of the portal, the nutritional supplements will now be available to Eddie, back in his time.

The doctor asks the mechanic, "OK, so what did you want to pick up today?" "Let me get the vitamins, the methylfolate," the mechanic replies, and then asks, "and, what were the other two you mentioned?" "The free-form amino acids, and the branched-chain amino acids," the doctor replies, and asks, "do you want those too?" The mechanic responds, "yeah. Let me get those too. Give me two of everything, but three of the methylfolate. Give me the bigger sizes if you have them." While the doctor goes to the back and gets the products, the mechanic whispers to Eddie, "with the gold we sold today, your vitamins are essentially free."

In a moment, the doctor returns with the products. Explaining the protocol for taking the products, the doctor instructs Eddie, "you should take three of the vitamin capsules each day, one at breakfast, lunch, and dinner. The branched-chain amino acids are for building muscle. Take the free-form amino acids with the branched-chain amino acids. Two or three capsules of each between meals are a good amount." Handing Eddie the instructions for taking the vitamins and supplements, the doctor tells him, "the instructions are all here on the paper for you."

The doctor then figures out the bill for today's purchases. Pulling out some cash, the mechanic counts it, and hands it to the doctor. The mechanic tells the doctor to keep the change, which is about thirty dollars. The doctor tries to decline, but the mechanic insists, telling him he appreciated him coming in over the weekend. Knowing they just changed Eddie's future health, the mechanic and Eddie thank the doctor again for coming in over the weekend.

On the way back to the service station, the mechanic tells Eddie that he is going to have to come back for more vitamins. He also tells Eddie that the company that makes the vitamins and supplements did not exist back in his time. The mechanic also instructs Eddie to take the methylfolate in the morning. The mechanic suggests that Eddie take off the label, or find a different bottle to store the vitamins. Otherwise, it would be a mystery to all where they came from. It would, however, be no mystery to Eddie.

When they get back to the service station, the mechanic and Eddie take the vitamins and the cash from selling the gold inside. They exchange the newer bills for older ones that Eddie can take back with him. Eddie also has to take the remainder of the gold back with him, but he will make more trips to sell it a little at a time. The mechanic goes into the back of the office, and gets a spare key for the MGB. The mechanic explains to Eddie that there are two keys, a smaller one for the door lock and trunk, and the ignition key. He gives Eddie only the key for the door lock and trunk. Giving Eddie the ignition key is pointless, because the car won't start anyway back in Eddie's time.

The mechanic gives Eddie a brief tutorial on how to remove the sill plate of the MGB. Removal of the sill plate is quite easy, which Eddie is able to do with no problem. The mechanic also tells Eddie that he can also hide anything under the spare tire in the trunk. And the mechanic reveals the best hiding place of all, which is inside the battery compartment. The battery compartment is behind the seats, and has a lot of empty space. Removal of the cover, however, is time consuming. The mechanic informs Eddie that the battery box has been modified, so when he gets back, it will look different from its appearance right now.

Eddie tells the mechanic, "I'll come back again sometime around August 2011." The mechanic tells Eddie, "vary the dates a little when you sell the gold. But, if you come back on tomorrow's date to sell gold, Jimmy will remember from today. It doesn't matter how much you get for the gold. You're still way in the black." Eddie immediately understands, and realizes for the first time that the mechanic's wisdom is actually his own. Eddie decides to come back every few weeks to sell the gold.

As Eddie prepares to go back to his time, the mechanic tells him that, if he continues to take the vitamins, he will be much healthier in the future. Eddie packs his tool bag and handlebar bag with the gold and cash. He then places the bag containing the vitamins in the handlebar bag. The bag contains nine large bottles of supplements, which barely fits in the handlebar bag. Next time, Eddie figures he should bring something that will be more convenient to carry the vitamins, such as a back pack.

Before Eddie leaves, the mechanic tells Eddie, "you know, you can come to the future sometime and check out the beach." The mechanic explains, "when you come here to the station, we can conduct business, like redeeming the gold, or just talk." The mechanic gives Eddie some parting advice, "you can go to the future and have some fun. Ride around and see what the world will be like then." Eddie tells the mechanic, "yeah, I was thinking about riding to the beach, and checking it out." Still frequently visiting the beach, the mechanic tells Eddie, "well, that's the one thing that hasn't changed much."

As Eddie rides off to the portal, the mechanic opens his laptop, and continues where he left off this morning. On the way to the portal, Eddie takes a look at Mark's house as he passes by. Eddie notices that Mark's house looks very well maintained, which made him wonder what his house looks like in 2011. He decides that will be an adventure for another day.

As Eddie approaches the portal, he realizes this trip took up a lot of time. Looking at his watch, it looks as if he will be late for dinner. Eddie figures he'll have to ride fast to get home on time. Arriving at the portal, Eddie walks in, and walks out again, back to his time. Looking at his watch one more time, he notices that the watch has the same time as when he entered the portal earlier today. It looks like time stood still while he was away. Although Eddie was gone for several hours, no time has appeared to have elapsed on his watch. He arrived back at his time the same time that he had left. He did not realize time did not actually pass during other trips through the portal. This could be because the trips were shorter or because of some apprehensiveness that may have accompanied the other trips.

Eddie arrives home, and puts his bicycle away. The first thing he does after walking inside is to check the clock on the wall. The clock has the same time as his watch, which is good news. Bringing the vitamins up to his room, Eddie opens the bottles. Eddie decides to leave the labels on the bottles for now, so he does not get them confused. He wastes no time in going forward taking the supplements. Starting with the branched-chain amino acids and the free-form amino acids, Eddie takes two of each to begin with. The vitamin will have to wait for dinner time, and the methylfolate until tomorrow, per the instructions he received from the mechanic.

Dinner time arrives, with the menu tonight being chicken and tortilla chips with freshly made salsa. A salad also accompanies the simple meal. Eddie's mother made the salsa herself, with fresh vegetables from the garden. The salad, likewise, is all fresh from the garden. After dinner, Eddie takes his vitamin. Remembering the doctor told him that lifting weights and the amino acids will build muscle, Eddie decides to lift weights later in the evening.

As the evening arrives, Eddie heads downstairs to the basement to work out. He starts with the bench press, doing a warm-up set of ten reps with 90 pounds. He raises the weight to 150 pounds and does as many reps as he can.

Dropping the weight by ten pounds, he does as many reps as he can with 140 pounds. He continues this pattern for eight sets in total. This is known as the stripping method, which he learned from one of the books he read. Using the same method, Eddie works his back, shoulders, triceps, biceps, and forearms.

Eddie ends his workout by working his abdominal muscles by doing crunches. In the book, he read that the abdominal muscles are a stabilization muscle, and are meant to be engaged all day. The only way to make gains in the abdominal muscles, and get the coveted six-pack, is by working them to failure. To work the abdominal muscles properly, each set of crunches must be done to failure. This means doing reps until you can't do any more, resting for a minute, and then doing another set until you can't do any more. And, as if that wasn't enough, wait another minute and do a third set. After the workout, Eddie gets a large glass of water and takes his amino acid supplements. This time he takes three capsules of each.

The next day, Eddie hits the weights again. Today, he will work his lower body, starting with squats. Eddie does not have a squat rack, so he has to lift the weight over his head and lower it onto his shoulders. Having no squat rack limits the amount weight he can squat during a workout. To solve that problem, between sets he draws up plans for a squat rack, which he will build himself. Eddie then works his calves, doing calf raises, and reverse calf raises. After his workout, Eddie takes the amino acid supplements, and packs two bananas for a bicycle ride. This time out, he goes for a long bicycle ride North of the turnpike where there the hills are. This is no leisurely bicycle ride. During this ride, Eddie pushes himself as hard as he can.

Eddie now has a plan. One of Eddie's goals is to be the fastest guy in high school long before he is a senior. He also wants to be much stronger than currently he is. Eddie now has more knowledge about how to accomplish that goal. He will get his workouts down to a science, take the supplements, and train harder and smarter.

Let the Workouts Begin

Now that Eddie has some knowledge and vitamins, he goes ahead wide open with working out. His workouts consist of lifting weights, bicycling, and running. Eddie does not like to run long distances, so the running part of his workout is primarily sprinting. With the cooler weather of Autumn arriving, the county pool has been closed, so there is no opportunity to swim. Over the next few weeks, during the first semester of high school, Eddie will refine his workouts, getting them down to a science.

On Monday and Thursday, Eddie works his upper body. On Tuesday and Saturday, he works his lower body. The lower body workout on Saturday allows for a very long and strenuous bicycle ride after lifting weights. Eddie takes Wednesday and Sunday off, and does not usually lift weights on those days. On Sunday, however, Eddie will occasionally go on a bicycle ride.

In addition to working out, Eddie is faithfully taking his nutritional supplements. The methylfolate, as the mechanic told him, is taken in the morning. With each meal, he takes one vitamin tablet. Between meals, he takes three each of the amino acid supplements. He also notices that, since taking the supplements, he is sleeping better. Eddie is also more relaxed in general, and feels less stressed at school.

For the first time, Eddie notices that he can see rapid physical improvements to his body in the mirror. Eddie also notices improvements in the amount of weight he can lift. Leaving from a standing start, he can also deliver a lot more torque to the rear wheel of his bicycle. Every week, Eddie finds himself increasing the weight for every exercise. Improvements are noticed all around from week to week. Since last Spring, Eddie has grown two inches, and gained 25 pounds. A significant amount of the weight gain was in the last few weeks, since Eddie began taking the supplements.

In the middle of the Autumn semester, in gym class, the dreaded timed one-mile run is announced by Mr. Frazier without any notice. There will be another timed mile run in the Spring. Everyone's time is expected to improve over the school year. The amount of improvement from Autumn to Spring determines the student's grade for that event. Students are not stupid. They intentionally perform poorly in the Autumn, and do their best in the Spring to get a better grade. Gym teachers are not stupid either, for they know exactly what the students are up to. This year, however, Mr. Frazier has a surprise for the sophomores.

The class gathers in the gym. Mr. Frazier makes the most unpopular announcement of the day, "today, we will be running the mile, and you will be on the clock." Mr. Frazier will have his favorite device in his hand, his stopwatch. He then makes an announcement that comes as a surprise to everyone, "sophomores, you are expected to beat your best time from last year!" Then he starts naming names, "Anthony Ambrosini, last year you ran a 6:45. John Falberg, an 8:45. Jeff Davis, you ran a 5:54, and I know you can do better than that. Charles Smith, you ran an 11:55, which is almost a walking pace." Calling each sophomore's name, Mr. Frazier goes on, delivering the time they are expected to beat. This means the sophomores will have to actually run fast, not jog as they were expecting.

Mr. Frazier continues, "and, for all of you freshmen, I have a surprise for you too." Declaring to the freshmen, Mr. Frazier announces, "I have your times here from last year, courtesy of Mr. Harris." Mr. Harris, the middle school track coach and gym teacher, started giving Mr. Frazier the student's performance records this year. Surprising the freshmen, Mr. Frazier announces, "Edward Bogenskaya, last year you ran a 5:22, which is not bad. Axel Braden, a 5:18, also not bad. Robert Bradshaw, a 7:52. Daniel Gaspari a 7:44. Arthur Jones, an 8:55. Mark Svoboda, a 5:20, not bad. It sounds like the freshmen have some decent times here. John Walsh, an 8:43." Mr. Frazier continues until everyone's name is called, with the exception of one or two transfer students. Mr. Frazier then proclaims, "if I do not see an improvement compared to last year's time, you'll be running a mile every week until you do improve!"

The sophomores quickly realize that some of the freshmen, for some reason, have some awesome times for the mile. A few of the sophomores comment that the deck was stacked against them in the football game earlier in the semester. What they do not know is that half of the core members of the middle school track team are in their gym class. This core group is also among the best athletes of all the freshmen in the school.

Mr. Frazier tells the class, "everybody head out to the track." On the way out to the track, rumbling can be heard echoing the chords of discontent of many of the students. The thought of running a mile to some is worse than taking a final exam in math. To others, like Eddie or Mark, the mile run is like adding one plus one.

Mr. Frazier hunts down the other two gym teachers, Mr. Chubin and Mr. Zunde, who will help him record the times of the students as they pass the finish line. Mr. Chubin searches through the office for his stopwatch and, after a minute or so, finds it. This is not the case with Mr. Frazier, whose stopwatch is always worn around his neck like a piece of jewelry. If Mr. Frazier would lose his stopwatch, it would be about as traumatic as cutting out an internal organ.

The students are all ready to run, well, at least as ready as they can be. Mr. Frazier announces, "Mr. Zunde will be handing you a ticket with a number after you cross the finish line. Mr. Chubin and myself will record the time associated with that number." He continues, "I'll know your time by your number." He instructs the class to get ready. Most of the sophomores are lined up in front, with Mark, Eddie, and Braden on the outside. The outside is not exactly the best starting position but, with a pack of more than 30 students, you take the best position that you can get.

Mr. Frazier informs the students, "a mile is four laps." With no further ado, he announces, "ready, set," pauses for a moment, and announces, "go!" The pack is off. It only takes fifty yards into the race for Mark, Eddie, and Braden to separate from the pack. They are accompanied by two sophomores, Anthony Ambrosini, who is a running back on the football team, and Jeff Davis. Ambrosini has a score to settle with Eddie and his tribe. Eddie's tribe destroyed Ambrosini at his own game, football, earlier this year. Ambrosini now fully intends to beat Eddie, Mark, and Braden at their own game.

At the quarter mile mark, Eddie, Mark and Braden, and the two sophomores, still lead the race. Jeff Davis is falling a little behind, but is still having a good run. One hundred fifty yards behind the front runners are the majority of students. A smaller group of students is even farther behind. The goal of the last group is just to finish the race.

During the second lap, Eddie, Mark, and Braden begin messing with Ambrosini's mind. Mark sprints ahead of the group, with Ambrosini trying to keep up. Mark then slows his pace, leaving Ambrosini in the lead. Ambrosini then slows, keeping pace with Mark. Just as Eddie, Mark, and Braden catch up to Ambrosini, Eddie sprints ahead of the group. Braden, who does not want to be left out of the psychological warfare, runs right on the heels of Ambrosini. At the end of the second lap, Eddie slows his pace, and Braden takes the lead for a while. Continuing the cat and mouse game, Mark and Eddie allow Ambrosini to pass them by. On this lap, Braden passes a student who is still on his first lap. Following Ambrosini closely, Mark and Eddie push Ambrosini to his limit.

The first two laps were Ambrosini's race. The third lap, however, is not. Stopping the fun and games, Mark, Eddie, and Braden begin running at a competitive speed. Eddie and his tribe pour on the power, with Ambrosini desperately trying to keep up. Halfway into the third lap, Ambrosini has run out of juice. Jeff Davis, previously in fifth place, passes Ambrosini. Mark, Eddie, and Braden, now competing against each other, pass a few of the students who are still on their second lap. The truth is Eddie, Mark, and Braden don't care who wins this race. To them, it is all fun and games.

At the beginning of lap four, the large pack of students begins to pass Ambrosini one by one. Ambrosini appears to have completely run out of energy, being beaten again by Eddie's tribe. Mark, Eddie and Braden are all still running together, with only a few steps between them. With 220 yards left to go, none of the three runners is yet to make a move.

Halfway though the last lap, Braden says to Eddie and Mark, "lets just tie." That sits well with Eddie and Mark. Any of the three runners could win this race. With 50 yards to the finish, Mark, Eddie, and Braden are still head to head. Mr. Frazier can be heard screaming, "run, run, faster!" As they approach the finish line, Mark, Eddie, and Braden are running in perfect unison, as if this is a synchronized running event. With ten yards to go, Mr. Frazier is looking for a winner. Mark, Eddie, and Braden all cross the finish line at nearly the same time.

Mr. Frazier, looking at his stopwatch, is not disappointed. A few yards farther down, on the track, Mr. Zunde hands Mark, Eddie, and Braden their ticket. Jeff Davis finishes in fourth place, with a respectable time. Following Davis, every few seconds a runner crosses the finish line. Mr. Chubin records their time, and Mr. Zunde hands them their ticket. Recording the times on paper,

Mr. Chubin yells out, "five minutes and twenty seconds," to Mark, Eddie, and Braden. That time was not any better than they ran last year, but they had a lot of fun running the race.

Walking off the track toward the football field, Mark mentions, "I could have ran a lot better time." Eddie and Braden agree that they could have run a better time as well. If they weren't messing with Ambrosini, any one of them could have run a better race. To them, this run did not mean too much. They are sprinters. They had more fun messing with Ambrosini. If that was today's goal, they have all succeeded.

Ambrosini, who conceded a while ago, is still nowhere to be seen. He finally crosses the finish line with a time of 8:44. Ambrosini was more concerned with beating the competition rather than competing against his previous time. Burning himself out too early, Ambrosini simply did not have the strength nor stamina to run a decent time. If he had paced himself, he probably could have run a respectable time.

While Eddie and his friends are talking, they are joined by Jeff Davis, who just ran the mile in 5:50. Jeff Davis tells Mark, Eddie, and Braden that he is on the track team and that they should try out. Joking around, Mark asks Davis, "do you think we'd make it?" Davis responds, "you might." Braden whispers to Eddie, "we just kicked his ass, and he says we 'might' make the team?" Davis tells Mark that the mile is his event. Davis could have run the mile faster than he did, but this is gym class, not a track meet. Eddie thinks to himself that he, Mark, and Braden just beat one of the milers on the track team, without even trying. This makes Eddie now wonder how fast he could have run the mile. Beating Davis also gives Mark, Eddie, and Braden more confidence that they will make the track team.

After the run, Mr. Frazier tells everyone that they will play a quick game of football. Mr. Frazier picks two students and random, and appoints them to be team captains. After the run, most of the students are physically worn out, so it will not be much of a game.

Gump and Ambrosini are on opposite teams, playing quarterback. When Mark, Eddie, Braden, Bobby B., and Gump are not on the same team, the energy level of the game is drastically reduced. That is exactly the case today. As Mr. Frazier watches the two lazy teams pretend to play football, he has decided to schedule another sophomore versus freshmen game. Mr. Frazier also contemplates a few sophomore versus freshmen basketball and baseball games for this class. As the teams hit the locker room, Eddie has plans for later that day. He will move forward with his plans to build his squat rack.

Eddie's plans for his squat rack were already done by mid week. Now, all Eddie had to do is to build it. Not knowing where to begin, he rides his bicycle to Angelo's Service Station after school. Perhaps Angelo could shed some light on the best way to build it, and where to get the materials. Arriving at Angelo's, Eddie finds Angelo taking his dinner break. It is almost the end of the day for Angelo, so he is mostly finished with his mechanics' work. The rest of the day will be pumping gas and waiting for customers to pick up their repaired automobiles.

Angelo, finishing a bite of food, greets Eddie, asking him, "hey Eddie, what's up?" Eddie sits across the desk from Angelo, and shows Angelo his plans. Eddie tells Angelo, "I'm building a squat rack. I was hoping you can tell me the best way to do it and where to get the metal." Angelo takes a close look at the plans, and tells Eddie, "this is easy. You need a few pieces of square tubing, in the three-inch range, that fit inside each other." Eddie asks, "where do you get tubing like that?" Angelo quickly answers, "DeLeo Brothers, down the street next to Vinnie's Body Shop."

Vinnie's Body Shop is across the street from Angelo, on the other corner. At the end of the short dead end street is DeLeo Brothers, a metal fabrication and supply shop. Angelo tells Eddie, "I can pick it up for you tomorrow." Eddie asks Angelo, "how much will it cost?" Having built many things with metal before, Angelo replies confidently, "not much. Not much at all." Eddie tells Angelo to go ahead and get the tubing. This is the step in the right direction Eddie was hoping for. Angelo says he'll pick it up in the morning, before he opens.

The next day, after school, Eddie rides his bicycle to Angelo's to see his tubing. This is again the end of the day for Angelo. Angelo has just finished eating dinner when Eddie arrives. As Eddie walks into the office, Angelo stands up and, pointing to the service area, tells him, "your tubing is over there, against the wall. Come, and I'll show you." Angelo and Eddie walk back to the far side of the shop, where all of the machining equipment is set up.

Three pieces of square tubing are leaning against the wall, one much longer than the others. Delivering some unexpected news, Angelo tells Eddie, "I started working on the rack. Let me show you what I did." Eddie is surprised, thinking he would have to figure out some way to get the tubing home, which comes in ten-foot lengths. That would be quite the task, since Eddie's only mode of transportation is his bicycle. Eddie takes a look at the base of the squat rack that Angelo has already made, and all he can say is, "wow." Angelo has also cut the uprights to the squat rack to length. He also drilled a hole in the side of the upright for a pin to adjust the height of the rack.

Using a band saw, and cutting wheel, Angelo shows Eddie how to cut the square tubing so it will fit together. Before making any cuts, he first sets up a fence to get a straight cut, and sets a stop-block at the desired depth. He then carefully cuts the metal slightly to the inside of the tubing wall, two-and-three-quarter inches deep. He then makes the same cut on the other side. Angelo then places the tube in a vice. Angelo removes the metal between the two cuts on each side of the tube using a pneumatic cutting wheel. Using a grinding wheel, Angelo cleans up the rough edges. The result is a U-shaped channel that will slide nicely onto the base. Angelo then shows Eddie how the pieces will fit together. Eddie is amazed that this took Angelo less than five minutes.

Angelo announces to Eddie, "OK, man, it's your turn." Angelo hands a pair of safety glasses to Eddie, telling him, "get to it." Eddie takes the tubing, and lines it up on the band saw. Angelo tells Eddie, "the most important thing is to keep the tube square against the fence." Eddie moves the tube effortlessly through the saw, compared with the hacksaw he thought he'd be using at home. Angelo tells Eddie, "when you back it out, be very careful to keep the tube square against the fence, and pull it back very carefully." Eddie then cuts the other side of the tube, which goes equally as well. Taking the tube over to the vice, Eddie clamps it in. Using the cutting wheel, Eddie begins to remove the metal between the cuts. Watching as Eddie works, Angelo quickly realizes that Eddie is quite competent working with tools. After finishing the cut, Eddie turns to the master mechanic and asks, "how does that look?" Inspecting Eddie's work, Angelo says, "it looks good. Now do the opposite side." Eddie flips the tube over in the vice and makes the second cut with the cutting wheel. Using the grinding wheel, Eddie cleans up the cuts. Angelo and Eddie take the tube over to the base to check the fit. The piece fits perfectly. Eddie, proud of his work, wants to continue with the project.

Getting the base of the squat rack, Angelo brings it over to the drill press. Angelo tells Eddie to bring the uprights. Making a few measurements, Angelo draws a line on the base on each side where the uprights should be. Fitting the upright into place, Angelo drills a small hole for the temporary screw that will hold it in place when he welds it. Angelo instructs Eddie to fit the other side. Eddie gets the hang of working with metal very quickly. He places the upright into position, and drills the hole. Angelo tells Eddie, "now, we weld it. Well, now I weld it." At this time, Angelo thinks it is best to weld the piece himself.

They take the upright over to the bench, and Angelo prepares to weld the uprights to the base. Angelo uses an arc welder for this project. Angelo explains to Eddie, "the first weld is the most important." He further explains, "with the first weld, you tack the work together, at exactly 90 degrees. Then you weld the rest." Angelo makes the tack weld. He shows Eddie, "this is why we cut the metal to two-and three-quarters inches," pointing to a one-quarter inch gap between the upright and the bottom of the three-inch base. Angelo points out to Eddie, "this is where one of the welds will go." Angelo instructs Eddie not to look at the welder when he is working. Welding the two pieces together, Angelo works very slowly and carefully. When he's finished, Angelo tells Eddie to come over and take a look. Eddie is impressed by Angelo's work. Angelo tells Eddie, "we'll let that cool, then I'll do the other side." Eddie is amazed how Angelo makes everything look so easy.

After a few minutes, Angelo turns the base over and welds the other side. After that side cools enough, Angelo and Eddie lift the squat rack off of the bench and place it on the floor. Angelo asks Eddie, "well, how does it look?" The mechanic in training answers, "awesome!" Angelo tells Eddie, "that's enough for today. Tomorrow, we cut the braces for the uprights and install them. And that steel over there," pointing to the unused ten-foot piece of tubing, "that will fit inside the upright, to adjust the height of the rack." "One more thing," Angelo informs Eddie, "I'll have to find a steel plate to hold the bar." Eddie then heads home, astounded by the amount of progress that occurred in the last hour. It was at that moment Eddie decided, for sure, that he wants to be a mechanic.

Eddie returns to Angelo's on the next day, hoping to continue working on his project. As Angelo is working on an engine, he sees Eddie riding up on his bicycle. Angelo points to the other side of the shop where there is a completed squat rack. Looking at the squat rack, Eddie says to Angelo, "wow, you finished it!". Angelo responds, "yeah. I had a little time and I thought I'd finish it." Angelo asks Eddie, "are you ready to test it?" Eddie, somewhat puzzled, does not see any barbells around to test it. Eddie asks, "how are we going to test it?" Angelo says, "wait here for a second. I'll show you." Using the lift, Angelo raises the car he has been working on.

Angelo tells Eddie, "help me bring the squat rack over here." Angelo and Eddie place the squat rack underneath the rear axle of the automobile that is on the lift. As Eddie watches in amazement, Angelo slowly lowers the automobile until it is almost touching the squat rack. Aligning the squat rack perfectly with the rear axle, Angelo lowers the car a bit more. The rear end of the automobile is now partially supported by Eddie's squat rack. As if that is not enough, Angelo lowers the car even more, as the tires of the car are raised off of the lift. The rear end of the automobile is now entirely supported by Eddie's squat rack. The master mechanic asks Eddie, "how does that look?" Eddie replies and asks, "wow! How much weight is that?" Angelo looks at the car on the rack, and says, "probably a little more than a thousand pounds." Satisfied with the strength of the squat rack, Angelo lifts the car, and they move the squat rack over to the side.

Eddie has trouble expressing his great appreciation for what Angelo did for him. Eddie asks, "OK, so how much do I owe you?" Angelo tells Eddie, "the steel was about thirty dollars." A little confused, Eddie responds, "no, for the whole thing." Angelo tells Eddie, "just the thirty dollars. I'm just happy that someone like yourself is interested in how to make something. Anyone could buy something like this in a store, but this is a fine work of art, and much stronger." Pointing to a customer's vehicle, Angelo tells Eddie, "help me put it in that truck, and we'll take it to your house."

As they load the squat rack into the pickup truck, Angelo asks Eddie where he lives. Eddie lives about one mile from the station, which is a short drive away. "Follow me," Eddie tells Angelo, "I'll ride my bicycle." Angelo, thinking he'll be driving five miles per hour, reluctantly agrees. Getting on his bicycle, Eddie rides down the road, and Angelo follows. After about a quarter of a mile, Angelo is impressed by how fast Eddie can ride his bicycle. Eddie, riding as fast as he can, is breaking the speed limit, which amuses Angelo. Angelo must also break the speed limit to keep up with Eddie.

They arrive at Eddie's house, and unload the squat rack. Eddie's parents, who are quite surprised, come out to say hello to Angelo. If an automobile needs to be repaired, and Eddie's father or uncle can't fix it, they take it to Angelo. Occasionally, Eddie's father Dominik helps out Angelo with certain projects. Angelo shows Dominik and Nina the squat rack, telling them their son had a great design. Eddie's father looks over the squat rack, and is quite impressed. Angelo tells Eddie to acid wash the squat rack and put a coat of primer on it as soon as possible. Eddie's father says he has some phosphoric acid, which will remove any surface rust. Eddie, his father, and Angelo take the squat rack into the garage, where Eddie will paint it before bringing it inside.

Nina hands Angelo a bag of fresh vegetables that were picked from the garden earlier today. The Autumn crop ripens in stages. Nina staggers the planting of the vegetables, so there is always something to harvest. Angelo is happy to take them, as he heads back to the shop to finish his day. Before Angelo is even out of the driveway, Eddie's father has found the container of phosphoric acid and a spray can of primer. Eddie shows his father the part he cut and fitted together. Inspecting his son's work, Eddie's father remarks that the workmanship looks very good. Eddie's father tells him he should wash the squat rack down tonight and get the primer on before he goes to bed. This will prevent any rust from occurring.

When the Saturday comes, Eddie works out in the basement, perhaps more than usual today. He has a project to keep him busy at home, so he won't be riding his bicycle today. The squat rack is in the garage, and has received the first coat of paint before Eddie's workout. After his upper body workout, Eddie will put on the second coat of paint. Tomorrow, if all goes well, Eddie will get to use the squat rack for his lower body workout.

Sunday arrives, and Eddie is looking forward to using his squat rack later in the day. Eddie is moving a little slow today because of his strenuous workout the previous day. Eddie's mother tells him to hurry up and get ready for church. His mother anxiously exclaims, "Eddie, hurry up and get ready! We want to get a good seat!" Eddie comes downstairs and eats breakfast, which his mother has already prepared and is waiting for him. Eddie's mother tells him again, "we didn't go to Sunday school today, so we need to get there a little earlier today to get a good seat." Eddie moves a little faster, but he is still half asleep.

Eddie, his brother, and his parents arrive at the church 20 minutes early, and enter the sanctuary. The sanctuary is empty when Eddie's family walks in. Most everyone either is in Sunday school or have not yet arrived. They walk to the front to get a good seat but, as usual, people have unofficially reserved seats by putting their Bible, a jacket, or some other item in the pew. When the people get out of Sunday school, they will go to the seat they reserved for themselves earlier in the morning. This happens every week, even though the pastor asks people not to reserve a seat with their personal items.

Eddie's parents walk to the back of the sanctuary and strike up a conversation with someone who just walked in. Eddie comes up with a plan so they can get a good seat. Since all the seats in the front have been reserved by inconsiderate people, Eddie decides to rearrange the reservations. Eddie says

Eddie - The Freshman Year

to his younger brother, "let's rearrange all this stuff." His brother asks, "what do you mean?" Eddie tells him, "we'll move all the stuff in the front seats to the back, and then the front seats will be open." Eddie and his brother pick up the jackets and books from the pews in the front and randomly distribute them throughout the sanctuary. Eddie whispers to his brother, "hurry up, we got to move faster." Picking up more books and jackets, Eddie and his brother move them to the back seats in the sanctuary. When they have finished their good deed for the day, fulfilling the pastor's wish, Eddie and his brother take a seat in the front, at the end of the pew. Eddie, for some reason, always likes to sit on the end. They want to have a good seat to watch the confusion when the masses pour in from Sunday school.

A few people who didn't attend Sunday school today begin to trickle in, and take a seat in the front. Eddie's parents, having no clue what Eddie and his brother were up to, walk to the front. Their father says, "oh good! You found us a seat up front." Eddie replies, "yeah, no one was sitting here," which was true. No one was actually sitting there. Within a few minutes, the front pews begin to fill as people arrive.

With five minutes before the service begins, the front doors leading into the sanctuary open. A mass of people, who are just getting out of Sunday school, enter the sanctuary, moving to the seat that they reserved using their books and jackets earlier that morning. It takes only a few seconds for a look of confusion to come across their faces. Walking around the pews, they desperately look for their reservation materials they left in the pews only an hour ago. The same questions echo through the sanctuary, "did you see a book here?" or "was there a jacket here when you came in?" Everyone got the answer they were not looking for, "nope. I hadn't seen it." A few people eventually find their items, but not anywhere near where they left them.

Eddie and his brother sit back and watch the confusion, trying not to laugh. Still clueless about what is happening around them, Eddie's parents talk with someone they have not seen in a while. The pastor comes in, along with the music director, and encourages everyone to take a seat. His request, however, is slow to be fulfilled. He notices people seemed confused, so he steps up to the microphone, and says, "please have a seat, and we'll get started." He continues, "some of you look a little confused today. Let us be reminded of 1 Corinthians 14:33, which states, 'for God is not the author of confusion.'" Today, however, Eddie and his brother were the authors of confusion.

When Eddie gets home after eating lunch out with his family, he wastes no time moving his squat rack into the basement. The paint won't be fully cured for a week, but Eddie will be careful not to scratch it. Taking a little time to rearrange his workout area, he positions the squat rack against the wall next to his bench. This requires moving a few things around, but he finally gets everything set up the way he wants it. Eddie's home gym is now complete, at least for a while.

Eddie starts his workout with a warm-up set of squats. After each set, he raises the weight. Since he never had a squat rack before, he does not know the maximum amount of weight he can squat. After a few sets, Eddie has run out of weight. The 250 pounds of weight that he has is not quite enough. While this presents a problem, it is a good problem to have. All those years of bicycle riding significantly developed Eddie's leg muscles. He begins dropping the weight after each set, and continues with as many sets as he can. Eddie, absolutely fatigued, moves on to calf raises, and then reverse calf raises, conveniently using his new squat rack to support the weight between sets. At the end of the workout, Eddie, who is barely able to make it up the stairs, is done for the day.

After his strenuous workout, Eddie decides to take a couple of extra amino acid capsules. A while later, he eats an entire cantaloupe, and takes an extra vitamin. After the cantaloupe, he is ready for a nap. It's no wonder that Eddie's mother sees her grocery bills going up, which is to be expected when there is a teenager in the house. Between yesterday's workout and the workout today, Eddie pushed himself to the limit. The body rebuilds itself during rest and sleep, for which the nap will allow. Needing a nap is also a sure sign Eddie has had some really good workouts.

Eddie continues to work out, pushing himself to the limit each time. He bought four additional 50 pound weight plates, bringing his total inventory up to 450 pounds. Eddie also bought a few fixed dumbbells to complement his equipment. As the weeks go by, he finds himself getting stronger and faster. Occasionally, Mark, Bobby B., or Braden will work out with Eddie at his house. Eddie and his tribe, as they are now known, make good training partners. They push each other beyond what they will normally do on their own.

Right after the Thanksgiving break, gym class brings another surprise. Since it is a rainy day, Mr. Frazier announces, "today, you will be lifting weights!" With Mr. Frazier, just the act of lifting weights is not enough. There has to be a competition. So, as expected, Mr. Frazier continues, "there will be a winner.

There will be a winner in the bench press, a winner in the squat, and a winner in the dead lift!" Mr. Frazier, explaining the reality of life to the students, adds, "the rest of you, who are not the winners, will unfortunately be the losers." As if that is not enough, Mr. Frazier adds, "your grade will be based on how well you perform. Just like in your other classes, some of you will fail. Your grade is based upon two things, which are your body weight and how much weight you can lift. Mr. Zunde has a chart on the wall, showing how much weight you'll need to lift to earn a certain grade. When we get into the weight room, be sure to take a look at it." The short dissertation by Mr. Frazier finally comes to an end, but has set the tone for the next hour of class.

Mr. Zunde, a thirty something year old well-built man who still has his German accent, is the Athletic Director for the school. Mr. Zunde, who looks like a gold medalist in Olympic weight lifting, made the grading chart. A casual look at the chart suggests that Mr. Zunde probably used his own abilities to define a grade of A. Mr. Zunde is also the school's strength training coach. He works primarily with the football team during the Autumn. In the Winter, he works with the track team's field athletes and the wrestlers in the weight room, helping to develop their strength. In the Spring, he is found primarily working with the track team's field athletes.

The class enters the weight room, followed by Mr. Frazier. Even though this is a weightlifting competition, Mr. Frazier still has his stopwatch around his neck. Mr. Zunde and Mr. Chubin are already in the weight room, waiting to record the weight each student can lift. Some of the students are familiar with the equipment. To other students, the weight room looks more like a sophisticated torture chamber.

Mr. Frazier breaks the class into three well thought-out groups. The three groups represent Mr. Frazier's assessment of the overall fitness of the students. He assigns group number one to the bench press station, group number two to the squat station, and group number three to the dead lift station. Eddie's group is all too familiar to him. Eddie, Mark, Braden, Bobby B., Gump, Anthony Ambrosini, and Jeff Davis are all in group one, among a few other athletic types. It is no secret to the class that someone in group number one will be wining each event.

After Mr. Frazier gives some minimal instruction, the competition begins. The energy in the weight room suddenly rises dramatically. In Eddie's group, the competition will be more like warfare. You can be sure that, with Eddie and Mark, psychological warfare will also play a role. With Ambrosini in the group, just as on the football field, some serious and heated competition is expected.

Once a student fails at the current weight, they must go across the room and watch the rest of the competition. A student is allowed to pass at a lower weight, and begin competing at a higher weight if he so chooses. If the student cannot lift the weight they go in at, unfortunately they will receive a grade of F for the event.

Mr. Frazier has the bar loaded with 100 pounds on the bench, which everyone should be able to lift. Ambrosini goes first, intending to show everyone how it's done. He is able to lift the weight with no problem. He is followed by Braden, who makes the lift look as if he is lifting a baby's rattle. Eddie is next. Eddie lifts the weight with no problem. He is followed by Mark, Gump, Bobby B., all who also have no problem lifting the weight. Everyone in the group is able to lift this amount of weight.

After a few rounds, the weight is up to 175 pounds. Eddie's tribe, and Ambrosini are the only ones left in the competition. Everyone else has gone out at a lower weight. Ambrosini lies on the bench and, with a good fight, is able to lift the weight. Mark, the master of psychological warfare, comments to Braden, "that looked kind of weak." Mark's comment was fully intended to perturb Ambrosini. Ambrosini returns the fire to Mark, "yeah, well you try it!" Mark laughs, knowing he can easily lift the weight. Going out of sequence, Mark gets on the bench and pretends to struggle with the weight on his chest. This prompts Ambrosini to hurl the insult, "talk about weak!" Mark then lifts the weight off his chest with ease and places the bar on the uprights. Braden and Gump are both able to make the lift. Eddie goes last, and is also able to make the lift.

Mark suggests, "let's stop this Mickey Mouse stuff and raise it to 200." No one objects, and 200 pounds is placed on the bar. Ambrosini lies on the bench, and attempts the lift. He lowers the bar to his chest and, giving it his best, fails to raise the bar an inch. The spotters lift the bar from his chest, and Ambrosini joins the group of losers standing off to the side. Mark, who stares at Ambrosini with a look that can kill, is next. Ambrosini is watching, fully expecting the bar to crush Mark's chest. Mark raises the bar, lowers it to his chest, pauses, and with perfect form raises the weight. Eddie, who has been working out like a madman, gets on the bench next. Much to the surprise of many, Eddie is also able to lift the weight with perfect form.

The weight is now up to 220 pounds. Mr. Frazier is quite amazed that the competition has even come this far. From against the wall, Ambrosini fires off his mouth again, saying, "they're all going to go out." Mark, looking across the room at Ambrosini, replies with his normal answer to such comments, "shut up, junior." Mark gets on the bench, and makes the lift. He is followed by Gump, Bobby B., Braden, and Eddie. After this round, Eddie, Mark, and Bobby B. all remain. Braden, who has the build of a bodybuilder rather than a power lifter, is unfortunately out.

The next round begins with a weight of 235 pounds on the bar. At this weight, Bobby B. surprisingly goes out. Bobby B. has bench pressed this much weight before, but misjudged the weight and failed to complete the lift. After this round, Eddie and Mark are the only two who remain in the competition. Mr. Frazier instructs Braden and Bobby B. to be the spotters for the next round.

The weight is raised to 250 pounds. Neither Mark nor Eddie has bench pressed this much weight before. Mark goes first, and fails to complete the lift. Eddie is next. Eddie's tribe is now chanting, "Ed-Dee, Ed-Dee, Ed-Dee!" Getting on the bench, Eddie lowers the bar to his chest. As his tribe continues to chant, Eddie raises the weight, albeit slowly at first. The tribe chants louder, somehow transferring all their energy to Eddie's muscles. Eddie then completes the lift. Getting off the bench, Eddie raises his right arm into the air, and screams, "yes!"

First place in the bench press goes to Eddie, second place to Mark, and third place to Bobby B. Being the winner, Eddie is the only one in the group who does not know his maximal lift. What surprised Eddie is that he can lift a lot more weight when people are watching. Mark had noticed the same thing. Ambrosini, against the wall, looks worried and bothered. Bothering Ambrosini most, however, is the chanting that began when Eddie was on the bench.

The groups all switch stations. Group number one now moves on to the squat station. Mr. Zunde informs the new group, "the winner of the last group was able to squat an astounding 125 pounds." Seeing that the new group is better physically fit, Mr. Zunde asks, "how much weight would you like to start with?" No one answers, so Mr. Zunde humourously suggests, "would you like to start with 500 pounds, or shall we add some more?" Eddie, knowing he can squat 240 pounds, responds, "I'm a bit tired today. How about 200 pounds?" Eddie also knows that Mark and Braden can also squat that amount.

Ambrosini comments to some of the others in the group, "those guys are real morons." Mark kindly informs Ambrosini, "hey, twinkle toes. The girl's gym is down the hall!" Before Ambrosini can respond, Mr. Zunde tells Mark and Ambrosini to settle their differences on the squat rack. Mr. Zunde decides to start the competition at 125 pounds, the weight at which the previous group left off. Mr. Zunde tells the group, "this will be a good warm-up weight. Do as many reps as you want."

Ambrosini, again, goes first. He is able to squat 125 pounds with no problem. Eddie goes second and takes a pass. Mark, following Eddie's lead, also takes a pass. Braden, Bobby B., and Gump all follow suit. By taking a pass, Eddie and his buddies have really ticked off Ambrosini. After the first round, the weight is raised to 150 pounds.

Ambrosini walks up to the bar. Lifting the bar off the rack, he displays some unsteadiness. He manages to complete the lift, but with considerable more effort than at 125 pounds. Eddie, again, takes a pass. Mark, Braden, Bobby B., and Gump also take a pass. At 175 pounds, Ambrosini is the only one able to lift the weight. Everyone else is out. Mr. Zunde raises the weight to 200 pounds.

Ambrosini, who is quite angry, steps up to the bar, and raises it off the rack. With considerable effort, he is somehow able to complete the lift. Now it is Eddie's turn. Eddie comments, "I wonder how heavy that is." Eddie knows exactly how heavy the bar is. He is only saying that for the benefit of annoying Ambrosini. Eddie decides to go in at this weight. Getting under the bar, Eddie lifts the bar off the rack. He takes a step back, drops down, and raises the bar effortlessly compared to Ambrosini's last attempt. Eddie tells his tribe, "it's kinda light. It's good for a warm-up." Mark, Braden, Bobby B., and Gump all give it a try, and all succeed. Sitting at his desk recording the student's accomplishments, Mr. Zunde is quite amused at Eddie and his friends.

After this round, five students remain. Mr. Zunde raises the weight to 225 pounds. Ambrosini, the second string running back, looks worried. Ambrosini is psyching himself up. Mark, on the other hand, is psyching Ambrosini down. Mark humorously says to Ambrosini, "it's not going to get any lighter by staring at it." Ambrosini then gets under the bar, and attempts his lift. As he goes down, it looks as if he will fail. Mustering every last ounce of energy he has, Ambrosini is able to complete the lift, although with lousy form. If Mark had not antagonized Ambrosini, Ambrosini would have probably failed. Eddie goes next. Eddie gets under the bar, and, without hesitation, lifts the bar, drops down into a full squat, and raises the bar in perfect form. Mark, Braden, Gump, and Bobby B. all are able to squat 225 pounds easily. No one is out after this round.

Mr. Zunde calls for 250 pounds but, after quick reconsideration, calls for 240 pounds. Ambrosini steps up to the bar, and raises it off the rack. Eddie, and his tribe, are all standing with their arms crossed, watching Ambrosini. They expect him to fail. Taking a step back, he goes down to the squat position. Not able to get up, Ambrosini allows the bar to crash onto the safety cage. Mr. Zunde calls for the spotters to place the weight back on the upper rung. The spotters even have trouble lifting this weight. Now it's Eddie's turn. Eddie steps up, and gets under the bar. Squatting this much many times before, Eddie is very confident. Lifting the bar, he goes down into the squat position, and raises the bar. The rest make their attempt, and all succeed.

Mr. Zunde now calls for 275 pounds. Eddie goes first at 275 pounds. Mr. Zunde calls for Bobby B. and Braden to spot. The safety cage would normally catch the weight should the lifter fail, but it doesn't hurt to have additional spotters. Walking up to the bar, Eddie looks it over, and gets under it. Eddie comes down into the squat position. After a brief hesitation, he lets out a primal scream, and raises the bar. The whole class looks over to see what happened, many of them wondering how much weight Eddie just lifted. Mark goes next, and repeats in Eddie's footsteps. Gump and Braden go out this round, leaving Eddie, Mark, and Bobby B.

Ambrosini stands off to the side, thinking to himself that he is going to have to step up his game. In this gym class, Ambrosini is at the top of the sophomore food chain. There are five freshmen that are making Ambrosini seem like he is in elementary school, and he does not like it. Eddie and his tribe have not only buried Ambrosini in the competition, but have splattered his ego with psychological warfare.

In the next round, the weight is raised to 300 pounds. Eddie, Mark, and Bobby B. have already received a grade of A for their lifts. This round, and any round following, is only to decide a winner. Eddie goes first. The other students are heard making comments that can be heard around the room, such as, "here he goes." With the whole class watching, Eddie steps up to the bar, and wastes no time raising the bar from the rack. After stepping backwards, he goes down into the squat position. Eddie lets out a primal scream that, this time, can be heard down the hall in the administrative offices. Eddie raises the weight, much to everyone's amazement. Mark goes next, and is unable to lift the weight. Eddie and Braden, spotting for Mark, help him raise the weight. Bobby B. is up next. Bobby B. gets under the weight, steps back and gets down into the squat position. He raises the weight, with a slight hesitation, but is able to complete the lift with no problem. Bobby B. looks strong in this event. It is now understood why he is known as the doctor of the shot-put.

For the next round, Mr. Zunde asks the final two competitors how much weight they want on the bar. Confident in his own abilities, Bobby B. suggests 325 pounds. Eddie goes along with it, but he has never squatted 325 pounds before. The bar is loaded, and Eddie goes first. After lifting the bar off the rack, he takes a step back, and lowers his body into the squat position. Giving it all he has, halfway up to the upright position, Eddie just does not have enough strength to complete the lift. Bobby B., the shot doc, is next. Getting under the weight, the shot doc lifts the bar off the rack, and steps back. Bobby B. lowers the bar, and gets into the full squatted position. Eddie, Mark, and Braden begin to cheer him on. The class joins in, chanting, "Bobby B., Bobby B., Bobby B!" This gives the shot doc just extra motivation he needs to succeed. As the shot doc slowly raises the weight, the cheers get louder. Halfway up, it's home free for the shot doc, as he is able to complete the lift. In the squat, first place goes to Bobby B., second place to Eddie, and third place to Mark.

The first group moves on to the dead lift station. This station is manned by Mr. Chubin. Mr. Chubin is finally happy to see some students who might be able to lift more than 150 pounds. Eddie asks Mark, "how much can you dead lift?" Mark replies, "somewhere around 350 pounds." Braden joins in and says, "I can do in the upper 300 range on a good day." Mark asks Bobby B., "how about you?" Bobby B. answers, "350, yeah. I can do 350 when I'm asleep." Ambrosini, eavesdropping on their conversation, tells Bobby B., "no, you can't." Mark replies to Ambrosini's unsolicited comment, "hey! If you can't run with the big dogs, junior, stay on the porch." Mr. Chubin comments to Eddie's tribe, "when your convention is over, we can begin." Mr. Chubin decides to start the competition at 135 pounds.

Ambrosini, still determined to win something today, goes first. Ambrosini steps up and grasps the bar, performs the dead lift, and lowers the bar. He makes the lift look easy. When Eddie's turn comes, he takes a pass. Mark, Braden, and Bobby B. also take a pass when their turn comes. In this group, everyone who made an attempt is able to lift the weight.

The competition goes on for a few rounds. At 250 pounds, Ambrosini is beginning to struggle. He completes the lift at this weight, but he looks as if he is at his limit. Eddie remarks to his group, "are you guys ready for a warm-up set?" They all nod yes. Eddie's comment really annoys Ambrosini, who is having trouble keeping his emotions under control. Eddie's comment, on the other hand, amuses Mr. Chubin, who tries to keep his laugh under his breath, but is hardly successful. Eddie steps up to the bar. Grasping the bar, Eddie performs the 250-pound lift easily. Mark, Braden, and Bobby B. are also able to lift the weight with absolutely no problem. After this round, Ambrosini, Eddie, Mark, Braden, Bobby B., Gump, and Davis remain.

Mr. Chubin, recognizing that Ambrosini is the weak link among the remaining students, asks him, "how much weight do you want for the next round?" Mr. Chubin already knows Ambrosini will go out next, so he gives him the option. Ambrosini, who doubts his own ability to lift that much, boasts, "I'll take 275 pounds." The bar is loaded with 275 pounds. Ambrosini grasps the bar, and begins the lift. The lift ends quickly, with Ambrosini unable to maintain his grip on the bar. Eddie asks Mr. Chubin, "can I pass at this weight?" Mr. Chubin asks the group, "does anyone else want to pass?" Eddie said this not because he wanted to pass, but to further annoy Ambrosini.

The tribe talks it over, and Eddie asks Mr. Chubin, "can we move it up to 300 pounds?" Mr. Chubin replies, "go for it." Everyone remaining has already received a grade of A for their efforts in the dead lift. The remainder of the competition is again only to determine a winner. The bar is loaded with 300 pounds. All of the remaining contenders are able to perform the 300-pound lift.

Mr. Chubin comments, "I was wondering when the men were going to show up. Last week, the girls were lifting more than some of the guys. Next week, maybe we'll have the girls play the sophomores in a game of football." Ambrosini, not surprisingly, is irritated by Mr. Chubin's comment. The rumor around school is Mr. Chubin is a little on the crazy side. With the athletic students, he pushes them beyond their athletic limits, developing their abilities even further. His inherent personality is quite intimidating to the students who have below par athletic ability. He often pushes the less athletic types beyond their emotional limits.

The next increment raises the weight to 325 pounds. The weight now on the bar is a significant amount of weight for a freshman to dead lift. Eddie decides that he will go first. Stepping up to the weight, Eddie grips the bar, checking his grip carefully. With one big explosion, Eddie lifts the bar, holds it for the required time, and lowers the bar. Mark goes second. Mark steps up and grasps the bar. Remembering his earlier exchange of words with Ambrosini, Mark gets an additional adrenaline rush. Mark gives it his best, and lifts the weight, but appears to be at his limit. Bobby B. is up next. Stepping up to the bar, the shot doc wastes no time, and performs the dead lift slowly, but with perfect form. At 325 pounds, no one goes out. Eddie, Mark, and Bobby B. all remain.

Mr. Chubin instructs the students, "since you are all looking a little weak today, load the bar with 350 pounds." He is not expecting anyone to succeed at this weight. Neither does Ambrosini. Without much delay, Eddie steps up to the weight. Gripping the bar, and using the same strategy as the prior attempt, Eddie gives it all that he has. Eddie is not able to fully complete the lift, and has to drop the bar. Mark is next, and steps up to the bar. Grasping the bar, and getting into the proper position, Mark pulls with all the strength he has. Mark, however, is also unable to lift the weight. Now, it's all up to the shot doc. Bobby B. has never lifted this much weight in a dead lift before, and he is soon to find out whether he can. Stepping up to the weight that defeated the previous two contenders, Bobby B. grasps the bar. Again, the class begins to chant, "Bobby B., Bobby B., Bobby B!" After checking his grip, he makes one or two check motions, making sure he is set. Borrowing Eddie's primal scream, Bobby B. picks up the bar, raising it slowly, which seems like an eternity to the shot doc. Bobby B. completes the lift, but not without making a monumental effort. Nearly the entire room cheers and clap their hands after Bobby B.'s performance. In the dead lift, first place goes to Bobby B., and second place is a tie between Eddie and Mark.

In the back of the room, standing near the door, are two guys who did not clap. One of them was Ambrosini. The other was a five foot, eight inch well-built guy, with a military haircut, who looks like he is the poster boy for the ROTC program. His name is Paul Mahoney. Paul Mahoney, unknowing to anyone, was watching the competition for the last half hour. Knowing that the weightlifting competition was on the schedule in gym class this rainy week, Ambrosini cut class to check out Eddie and his tribe. Mahoney quietly slips out the door, as Ambrosini mixes with the class again.

The next day, in health class, Mark asks Eddie, "how did you get stronger that fast?" Eddie tells Mark, "I've been working out a lot more, a whole lot more." Mark replies, "no, you must be doing something else too." Eddie confesses, "well, I've been taking a few supplements too. You know, vitamins and that kind of thing." Eddie wonders whether he should tell Mark about the portal, after all they have been friends since kindergarten. If Eddie did tell Mark, Eddie reasons that would think he is crazy. Mr. Zunde, who also teaches health, walks in, and class begins.

In health class this month, the topic is, yet again, illicit drugs, and why you should not take them. The topic of illicit drugs shows up in every health class syllabus. This is because, after the students hear how bad drugs are, none of them will ever take them. Today's topic is hallucinogenic drugs, and how they will damage your brain. Mr. Zunde, the instructor, is describing the types of hallucinogenic drugs, and what the effect is on someone who takes them. He goes over marijuana, LSD, and then comes to psilocybin.

While Mr. Zunde is discussing psilocybin, Mark whispers to Eddie, "how do you spell that?" Eddie replies, "spell what?" Mark whispers, "that psilo thing." Eddie looks at the notes of the girl sitting next to him and tells Mark, "p-s-i-l-o-c-y-b-i-n." Mark tells Eddie, "I'm never going to remember that for the test." Explaining word association to Mark, Eddie tells him, "psilocybin sounds like psycho Chubin, so remember it that way, psycho Chubin." Mark says to Eddie, "yeah, yeah! Psycho Chubin, like the crazy gym teacher. I got it!" Eddie tells Mark, "yeah, you got it. Mr. Chubin is psycho, like he took some crazy drug, so, you get psycho Chubin." Mark now has it down.

When the next health class arrives, so does the test. Mr. Zunde instructs the students to place their books on the floor, and hands out the test. Tests in health class are not too difficult, and everyone usually passes. As Mark is working on the test, he comes to a question that looks kind of simple. The question reads, "List three hallucinogenic drugs." Mark, remembering his word association for one of the drugs, is quite confident. He writes his answer, and moves on to the next question. At the end of the class, Mr. Zunde collects the tests, and the students move to the next class.

The next time health class meets, which is the last time for this semester, Mr. Zunde hands back the student's tests. Handing Eddie his test, Mr. Zunde tells him, "very good." Next to Eddie is Dawn, who receives the compliment, "excellent," from Mr. Zunde. Mr. Zunde then comes to Mark, and hands him his test. Mr. Zunde tells Mark, "reasonably good, Mark, but psilocybin is the name of the hallucinogenic drug. The name of the drug is not psycho Chubin. Mr. Chubin is one of your gym teachers." The class bursts out laughing, including Eddie, and surprisingly, Mr. Zunde himself. With Mr. Zunde and Mr.

Chubin both being gym teachers, it is a sure bet Mr. Chubin has already seen Mark's test paper.

With the Autumn semester coming to a close, Mark, Eddie, Braden, and Bobby B. have proven themselves on the athletic field. The athletic field this time, however, was gym class. In gym class, the skill level of the athletes is the broadest range that one could imagine. Next semester, the athletic field will be the track. Eddie and his tribe will be competing against the best of the best for a position on the track team. One thing is for certain, Paul Mahoney will not be willing to give up his spot as the team's star sprinter. And, Paul Mahoney is not going to go down as easily as Ambrosini.

Over the Christmas holiday Eddie will be doing everything he can to increase his performance on the track. Mark will be doing the same. It's a sure bet that Paul Mahoney, after catching a glimpse of the weightlifting competition, will be doing some last minute training as well. Tryouts for the track team will begin during the first week of the Winter semester. By the end of that week, the team will be selected. The athletes will have three days to secure their spot on the team. Anyone who does not make the team will have to wait for Spring, when they can try out again.

Right before Christmas holiday, Mark tells Eddie that he wants to get a bicycle. Mark's parents told him that he can have one for Christmas. Since Eddie knows a lot about bicycles, Mark asks Eddie to go to Vito's Bicycle Shop with him to help pick it out. Eddie agrees to help Mark make his selection. They plan to meet on a Saturday afternoon at Vito's. Eddie will ride his bicycle there, and Mark will be driven by his parents.

When Saturday comes, Eddie rides to Vito's to meet Mark. Eddie walks in and Vito, who was working in the back, comes to the front to greet him. Mark has not yet arrived. Vito asks Eddie, "are you here to trade your bicycle in already?" Eddie replies, "no. I'm keeping it for a long time. But, Mark wants a good bicycle, something like mine. He's on his way with his parents." Vito, knowing his inventory down to the last valve cap, shows Eddie the two track bicycles that he has. One bicycle, which similar to Eddie's, has dual rear sprockets, and is suitable for road use. The other one is designed purely for track use, with no brakes and a single rear sprocket, coming in at a weight of just 15 pounds.

Mark arrives with his parents, who look around at all the bicycles lined up on the floor and hanging from the ceiling. Vito, walking up to greet them, says hello to Mark and his parents. Taking a look at Eddie's bicycle, Mark's father asks Mark, "so, this is what you want?" Mark replies, "yeah. Something like it. It doesn't have to be exactly the same." Looking over Eddie's bicycle, Mark's father is quite impressed with the workmanship.

Meanwhile, Vito shows Mark a bicycle similar to Eddie's. Mark takes the bicycle over to Eddie's and compares them side by side, as Vito talks with Mark's parents. Eddie tells Mark, "you've ridden mine. Ask Vito if you can take it out for a ride to compare." Mark yells over to Vito, "hey Vito! Can I take it for a spin?" Vito walks over, and asks Mark, "have you ever ridden a track bike before?" Mark replies, "yeah. I rode Eddie's a few times." Vito then tells Mark, "sure, take it out and give it a try."

As Mark takes the bicycle outside, Eddie decides to take a short ride with Mark. Mark and Eddie ride up the side street up to a long, rarely traveled road. Testing the bicycle for speed, Mark gives it all that he has. Eddie, the more experienced bicyclist, easily keeps up with Mark. Mark, nevertheless, is able to get up some good speed. The two cyclists turn around, and ride back to Vito's. It did not take Mark a lot of deliberation to decide whether he wants the bicycle. He definitely wants it. Mark mentions to Eddie, "so this is how you get to the beach and can run so fast?" Eddie replies, "yeah. I really don't run a lot. Actually, I hate running distances."

When they return from their ride, Mark and Eddie walk into Vito's. Vito immediately asks, "so, how did you like it?" Mark, with no hesitation, replies, "a lot." Looking over at his father, Mark asks, "can I get it?" Mark's father walks over to Vito, and starts talking about the bicycle, primarily the price. Mark's father looks over the bicycle, realizing that this bicycle is no toy store brand of bicycle. It is a genuine racing machine built by craftsmen. His son, Mark, is also a racing machine in his own way. Mark's father tells Mark, "yes, we can certainly get this for you." Suddenly the happiest person in town, Mark will now have the opportunity to expand his athletic endeavors.

Eddie tells Mark he is going to ride home. Mark asks his father, "can I ride my bicycle home?" Mark's father replies, "no, it's not Christmas yet." Although Mark is disappointed, but he understands. He will have to wait for Christmas day. Eddie heads home, while Mark's parents buy the bicycle, and load it carefully into the back of the pickup truck.

Over the Christmas holiday, Eddie makes a few trips to the various coin stores he frequents to buy gold. Buying voluminous amounts of gold, Eddie knows which merchants he can trust, and those that he can't. Occasionally, he has walked into the department store that has the coin and stamp counter, and walked out because a certain clerk was on duty. He somehow knew not to trust this person. But, with the price inching up slowly, he accumulates as much gold as he is able to this month. Making a few trips to the future to sell the gold, Eddie gets a considerable return on his investment. He also brings back a supply of vitamins and supplements, which he sees is making a big difference in his athletic performance.

One night over the holiday, Eddie loads his handlebar bag with gold and a little bit of money, and makes a trip to Angelo's Service Station. Eddie is planning to hide some gold and money in the MGB, as the mechanic instructed him. The streets are somewhat quiet late at night and, since it is dark outside, it would be a good time to hide some of his profits.

Eddie arrives at Angelo's and parks his bicycle between two junk cars near the MGB. The street lights are on the other side of the road, so the station is relatively dark. Eddie squats down, and walks low over to the MGB. To the casual observer, it is obvious that Eddie is up to something. He tries the key, and is able to open the door. He removes the sill plate, as the mechanic instructed, which goes easier than expected. Before he walks back to his bicycle, he looks around to make sure the coast is clear. Back at his bicycle, he gets the gold and the money, and walks over again to the MGB. He places the gold and the money in the sill, and replaces the sill plate. Closing the door quietly, he locks it, then makes sure it is secure. Sneaking back to his bicycle, Eddie thinks to himself, "that was kind of easy." Eddie rides his bicycle around for a while, burning off his excess adrenaline he got from his undercover activities.

By buying gold in the current time, and selling it in the future, Eddie is amassing a huge fortune. Eddie, however, has no idea how much money he has saved. Even though Eddie has nothing against hard work, he figures that having some extra money will give him more time to do what he wants to do in the future. Eddie has also decided to cut lawns again next Spring, and not slack off. Cutting lawns is a workout, and will give him more money to invest for the future.

Indoor Track Tryouts

Now that Christmas break is over, it's back to school for everyone. As usual, no real work gets done in the classroom the first day back from break. The talk in Eddie's circle is all about track tryouts, which begin this afternoon after school. Last year, in middle school, Eddie, Mark, Axel Braden, Bobby B., Eric Johnson, and Gary Mitchell did not really have to try out for the team. They only showed up for tryouts to set the standard no one else can meet. This year, however, it will be a little different.

As the school day comes to a close, the day is just beginning for a certain group of students. Tryouts begin for all the Winter sports. Gump, who secured a position on the football team earlier this year, will hopefully be on the wrestling mat over the Winter. Indoor track brings a different set of events than does Spring track. Marginal track and field athletes will not likely make the Winter indoor track team. With fewer events, the competition is tougher. Bobby B. is happy that the shot-put event is held in Winter track, which is not part of the Winter season events in some regions. During the indoor track season, for Mark and Eddie, there is no 100-yard dash for which to try out. Instead, the sprints are less than 60 yards. In Eddie's school district, the sprint during the indoor track season is the 40-yard dash.

As many of the students head for their busses, this year's Winter athletic hopefuls all head for the locker room. Wrestlers, basketball players, and track athletes all pour into the locker room. Eddie, and his crew, meet in the hall after class, and walk in together. As the athletes are getting dressed for the tryouts, Mr. Zunde announces, "basketball tryouts are in the main gym. Wrestling tryouts are in the auxiliary gym. If you are trying out for track, please meet in the hallway outside the locker room." Mark asks Braden, "we're meeting in the hallway? Where are we going to run?" Braden replies, "I guess we'll find out." Johnson surmises, "maybe, we'll be practicing on the outdoor track."

The track team hopefuls meet outside the locker room, waiting for Mr. Frazier to arrive. Eddie, and his tribe, are off to the side. They are joined by a few members of the middle school track team from last year. The upperclassmen form several smaller groups. Looking around, it is no secret who the seniors are. The students look each over carefully, somehow thinking that there is a way to assess someone's speed by observing their stationary body.

Paul Mahoney, who is conversing with Anthony Ambrosini, is looking in the direction of Eddie. Ambrosini comments to Mahoney, "there are a lot more of them. Where are they all coming from?" Mahoney replies, "it looks like the guy in the red and the two guys next to him are juicing[2] it," referring to Eddie, Mark, and Braden. After checking out the competition a little further, Mahoney mentions, "they look a little big for freshmen." Mahoney is correct. They are somewhat well developed for freshmen. Their size is the result of genetics and having worked out for many years.

Mr. Frazier walks out from the athletic office, and announces, "this is the meeting place for indoor track. If you are trying out for another sport, you are in the wrong place. If you are trying out for track, please follow me." Any student in the wrong place is out of luck getting any assistance from Mr. Frazier today. Mr. Frazier walks down the hallway, pulling out his keys to open a door with no number, sign, or markings. The upperclassmen know exactly what is behind this door, but the freshmen, who have no clue, are about to find out.

Mr. Frazier unlocks the door, and the upperclassmen enter first. Behind the door is a very wide steel stairway, which goes to the basement of the school. Few students know there is a basement to the school, and even fewer have been there. The side of the stairway has an open railing, allowing a panoramic view of what is downstairs. Eddie, along with the other freshmen, walking down the steel staircase, look in awe at what they see in the basement. Underneath the classrooms is a full-sized 220-yard indoor track with a composite rubber surface. Off to the side, disconnected from the oval, is a long track for the sprinting events. In the center of the track is where the high jump and shot-put events are held. To either side of the track are bleachers for the spectators. At the corners of the arena are benches to hold up to four competing teams, each complete with an adjoining locker room.

---

[2] Juicing: A slang term for using anabolic steroids.

Eddie looks at Mark, and remarks, "wow, this is the big time!" Braden, looking at the setup, is at a loss for words, if one can imagine that. As Mr. Frazier instructs everyone to have a seat on the bleachers, Mr. Zunde walks down the staircase. Mr. Frazier begins, "I want my sprinters over here on this side, with me." Pointing across the room, Mr. Frazier continues, "I want the distance men and the field athletes across the track on the other set of bleachers. If you are middle distance, I want you with the distance men." Delivering some interesting news to the freshmen, Mr. Frazier announces, "and, if you run the 440, you are now a sprinter! In high school, the 440 is the 440-yard dash. It is no longer a leisurely jog around the track." Mr. Frazier then instructs the students to move to the correct side of the track.

Mr. Zunde helps Mr. Frazier out with the training, primarily working with the shot-put athletes. The athletic director, Mr. Zunde is the school's strength training coach. He works extensively with the football team in the weight room during the Autumn, and with the shot-put athletes during the track season. Today, and during the next few days of tryouts, Mr. Zunde will also be working with the distance runners. Once the team has been finalized, Mr. Zunde will then be working exclusively with the shot-put athletes in the weight room.

Gary Mitchell, having a respectable cross country season, walks across the track with the distance men. Mark, Eddie, Braden, and Johnson all sit together, along with a few dozen students who hope to be sprinters. Braden is not his hyper energetic self today, somewhat due to the uncertainty of the higher level of competition. Addressing the sprinters, Mr. Frazier explains the events for which they will be trying out. Mr. Frazier explains that he will be deciding who runs in which event, based upon their performance. Mr. Frazier tells the sprinters, "I want you to stretch, take a warm-up lap, two, three, whatever you need." He then announces, "the first event will be the 40-yard dash, and everyone will be running it for time." The students jog around the track, stretch, run in place, doing whatever they need to get warmed up.

Mr. Frazier instructs everyone to stand behind the starting line. He announces, "you will be running two at a time." This is because Mr. Frazier has only two hands and therefore can only work two stopwatches at once. Having a foot-operated buzzer at the other end of the track, Mr. Frazier is a one man Timekeeper. He tells the students, "pair up, preferably with someone of your own skill level." Mark pairs up with Eddie, and Braden pairs up with Johnson.

Up first is the ROTC poster boy himself, Paul Mahoney. Mahoney is paired up with Darryl Bell, who is a junior this year. Bell, although not as fast as

Mahoney, was one of the top sprinters last year. Mahoney and Bell step up to the starting blocks, adjusting them to their liking. Mr. Frazier announces, "on your marks," as he waits for the runners to get ready. He then announces, "set." Once the runners are in the "set" position, he waits two seconds and hits the starting buzzer. The runners leave the blocks with lightning speed. Mark and Eddie all of a sudden get serious. This looks like real competition. Halfway down the track, Mahoney has a step or two lead over Bell. About six seconds later, they both cross the finish line, Mahoney first, and Bell a few steps behind him. Setting the initial standard, Mr. Frazier announces, "Mahoney, 5.5 seconds. Bell, 5.7, seconds."

After hearing Mahoney's and Bell's times, Mark asks Eddie, "is that good?" Eddie thinks about it for a moment, as the second group of runners takes off. Eddie, unsure of his math, replies, "I don't think so. That seems like it would be a 14-second 100-yard dash. I thought a good time in the 40-yard dash was like in the upper four-second, not five-second, range." Mark replies, "I think you're right about that." Eddie comments, "last year, in middle school, I ran the 50-yard dash in 5.8 seconds in gym class one day. That guy just ran 40 yards in 5.7 seconds."

The upperclassmen, who were all at the head of the line, complete their heats. Now the freshmen are up, which catches Eddie and Mark's attention. As Eddie and Mark continue chatting, Johnson and Braden get behind the starting blocks. They have not been paying too much attention to the previous runners, but rather stretching to prepare for their own run. Mr. Frazier announces, "on your marks." The runners all get ready. He then announces, "set," and the runners get set in the blocks. Mr. Frazier hits the starting buzzer. Johnson and Braden are off, with Johnson taking a slight lead at the halfway mark. Crossing the finish line in what seems to be no time, Johnson edges out Braden by a split second. Mr. Frazier makes the announcement, "Johnson, 5.3 seconds. Braden, 5.4 seconds." Eddie tells Mark, "5.5 was the time to beat, and Johnson ran a 5.3." It does not take Mark and Eddie too much time to realize that they will also beat Mahoney's time. Johnson, although he is awesome at the 220, 440, and 880 yard events, presents no competition for Mark or Eddie in a short sprint.

Another two runners get set in the blocks as Mark and Eddie get psyched up, for they are up next. After the heat, the announcement comes from Mr. Frazier, "6.0, and 6.3 seconds." Mr. Frazier, unimpressed with those times, exclaims, "do I need to get a calendar out to measure these times?" That was all Mark and Eddie needed to hear to get their adrenaline going and raise their energy level. Mark whispers to Eddie, "his timing is really consistent," referring to the time that elapses between Mr. Frazier announcing, "set," and the buzzer going off. What that means to Eddie and Mark is they can anticipate the buzzer.

Mark and Eddie walk up to the blocks, with their adrenaline levels now through the roof. This is their moment, what they have been training for. At the end of the track, with Mr. Frazier, are a few of the other sprinters. One of them is Paul Mahoney. Mahoney has heard a lot about Mark and Eddie, but has never seen them in formal track competition. Standing with Mahoney is Darryl Bell, who both have reasonably good times thus far today. They are both standing with their arms crossed, waiting to see what the two freshmen can deliver.

Mr. Frazier announces, "on your marks," and waits for the runners to get ready. He then announces, "set." Once the runners are set, he hits the starting buzzer after the predicted two seconds. Mark and Eddie, who both anticipated the buzzer well, are off. Out of the blocks, they are head to head. Looking down the track in amazement is Mahoney, who cannot believe what he is seeing. At the halfway mark, there is no clear leader. When Mark is up against Eddie, neither want to lose. For a split second, it looks like Mark might have been ahead but, closer to the finish line, Eddie may have a quarter step advantage. Crossing the finish line first is Eddie, who edges out Mark by about a quarter step. Mark and Eddie are both immediately wondering if they ran a qualifying time to make the team.

Mr. Frazier, looking at his stopwatches, is checking one watch against the other. It seems as if eternity passes before the times are announced, especially to Mark and Eddie. Also waiting to hear the times is Mahoney, who does not have a good feeling right now. Mr. Frazier announces the long awaited result, "we have a tie! Eddie, 4.8 seconds, and Mark, 4.8 seconds! That was an awesome run!" He looks at his stopwatches again, just to make sure the time is really 4.8 seconds, and not 5.8 seconds. Seeing that both stopwatches agree, the times are confirmed to be 4.8 seconds.

Eddie's and Mark's times of 4.8 seconds is in the upper one percentile for their age group. Giving each other high-fives, they are both ecstatic that they have the best time of the day. Most track athletes run better in competition, rather than during time trials. Mahoney and Bell, even though they did not have the best time of the day, are not to be underestimated. Neither are Mark and Eddie to be underestimated. Being freshmen, Mark and Eddie are delivering the same blow to Mahoney as they delivered to Ambrosini and the sophomores in gym class.

Meanwhile, in the center of the track, the high jump and shot-put tryouts are in full swing. The field events in Winter track are somewhat limited, mostly because it is difficult to throw a discus, hammer, or javelin indoors. The field athletes generally keep track of their own performance. Bobby B., having a good day, has the second best performance of the afternoon. A senior, Matt Wood beat out Bobby B. by several feet. Bobby fits in well with the others in this event, who all let him retain his title as the doctor of the shot-put even though he is a freshman. After today, there is no doubt that Bobby B. will make the team.

The next race to be run is the 220-yard dash, which is one lap around the oval track. To give the sprinters the same amount of rest, Mr. Frazier instructs the contenders to run the 220-yard dash in the same order in which they ran in the 40-yard dash. The distance group, who just completed the last one-mile run, is now taking a short rest. The distance group will also be participating in the 220-yard dash along with the sprinters. Mark, Eddie, Braden, and Johnson catch up with Mitchell, who just ran a 5:23 in the mile, beating out Jeff Davis, the sophomore miler from Eddie's gym class.

Mitchell, who is upset with his time, is counseled by one of the upperclassmen, Louis Zaino, who is also a cross country team member. Zaino explains to Mitchell that his times are going to be slower on a 220-yard track. This is because, on a 220-yard track, the curves are sharper and are not banked. Zaino also explains to Mitchell that the pace of the race is determined by the front runner. If the pace is fast, everyone runs faster. If the pace is slow, everyone seems to run slower. This makes sense to Mitchell, who had a decent run for the day.

Mr. Frazier tells the sprinters to get ready for the 220-yard dash. Mr. Frazier and Mr. Zunde will be both keeping time, so four runners will be in each heat. The starting blocks are placed into position as the first group gets ready. Mr. Frazier announces that, within each group, the runner with the best time gets the inside lane, and the worst time, the outside lane. Paul Mahoney is in the first group, with Bell, who are in the inside and second lanes respectively. The slower runners get the outside lanes.

There is a long-standing argument whether the inside lanes or the outside lanes on an unbanked 220-yard track are the most desirable. The inside lanes have a bit of a sharper curve to them, potentially slowing the runner to a slight degree. The outside lanes have only a moderate curve, which may prove to be a slight advantage. If the curves are banked, there is no expected performance difference between the inside and outside lanes. On a 440-yard track, the difference in the sharpness of the curve in each lane is negligible. Interesting to note is that a runner with a greater mass will have an advantage running in the outside lanes. With a staggered start, the runners on the inside lanes start the race in a position physically behind the runners in the outside lanes. This gives the runners in the inside lanes a much better visual of what is transpiring during the race. Nevertheless, runners seem to always prefer the inside lanes.

Mr. Frazier announces, "on your marks," as he waits for the runners to get ready. He then announces, "set." Once the runners are set, he hits the starting buzzer, and the runners are off. With the staggered start, it is difficult to see who is ahead. Johnson is watching carefully because the 220-yard dash is his race. Halfway around the track, Mahoney is clearly ahead. His lead appears to be increasing, but it is still difficult to judge because the runners remain staggered until the final straightaway. As the runners come out of the final curve, it is becomes obvious that Mahoney is going to win, and Bell will be in second place. Mahoney crosses the finish line with a time of 33.3 seconds, followed by Bell with a time of 34.2 seconds. The other two runners, with times in the upper 30-second range, will probably not make the team.

Johnson's heat comes up. Johnson is paired up with Braden, Jeff Davis, and Jimmy O'Brien, whose father is a teacher in the high school. O'Brien possesses little or no athletic ability, and made the track team in middle school only because his father is a teacher. This is, however, high school. O'Brien will have to rely on his own skill if he is to make the team. Johnson, who has never run a staggered start race, is aware he will appear like he is winning because of the staggering. He does not want to be blind sided and lose a place on the team, especially since this is his best event.

Mr. Frazier again announces, "on your marks," as he waits for the runners to get ready. Announcing, "set," Mr. Frazier has his eyes on Johnson. Once the runners are set, he hits the starting buzzer. Johnson is out of the blocks as fast as he was for the 40-yard dash. Halfway around the track, Johnson is clearly ahead, but he is not aware of this. He senses the runners are catching up, and gets the false impression he is falling behind. This is the nature of a staggered track. As the runners get closer to the finish line, the runners in the outer lanes appear to be quickly catching up. Johnson, vying for his place on the team, pours on all the speed he has. Braden, thinking he is behind by a large margin, is trying to catch Johnson. Into the straightaway, Johnson is in the lead, with Braden following closely behind. Johnson crosses the finish line first, with Braden crossing a second or so behind. Jeff Davis, who ran a mile earlier, is still coming out of the turn when Braden crosses the finish line. O'Brien, turning in a dismal performance, is just entering the final curve when Jeff Davis crosses the finish line.

Mr. Frazier confers with Mr. Zunde to compile the runner's times. After recording the times on paper, Mr. Frazier announces, "Johnson, 31.5 seconds. Braden, 32.8 seconds. Davis, 42.3 seconds. And O'Brien, you ran a 58.4, which would have been a good time if you were running the 440-yard dash!" Mark has a good laugh after hearing O'Brien's time because Mark can run 440 yards faster then O'Brien can run 220 yards. It will be interesting to see if O'Brien makes the team this year.

After a few more heats, it's Eddie and Mark's turn. They are teamed up with two runners who are the upperclassmen that ran before Eddie and Mark in the 40-yard dash. Eddie gets the inside lane, and Mark is in lane number two. It is embarrassing for the upperclassmen to be in the outer lanes, but that is where their prior performance landed them. Most of the athletes are standing in the center of the track or sitting on the bleachers, relaxing as they watch the last race of the day. Mahoney, standing next to Mr. Frazier at the finish line, no longer needs an explanation as to why Ambrosini refers to this group of freshmen as Eddie's Tribe.

Mr. Frazier, wondering how Mark and Eddie will fare in the 220-yard dash, announces, "on your marks." He announces, "set," watching the group carefully. As he hits the starting buzzer, Mr. Frazier tries to see which of the runners are the fastest out of the blocks. Mark and Eddie leave the blocks, racing against the clock, each other, and Mahoney's time. Around the first curve, Eddie and Mark have to contend with curve in the track, which slows their times a bit. On the back straightaway, Eddie and Mark sprint as fast as they can before entering the second curve. Coming out of the curve, Eddie has a slight lead over Mark. Mark tries to catch up, but there is not enough distance left in the race to catch Eddie. Eddie crosses the finish line first, with Mark following closely behind. After Mark finishes, the remaining two runners break out of the final turn. Twelve seconds after Mark, the final runner crosses the finish line.

Mr. Frazier, speaking longer than usual with Mr. Zunde, writes the runner's times on paper. Then comes the announcement. Breaking the news, Mr. Frazier announces, "Bogenskaya, 28.3 seconds. Svoboda, 29.1 seconds. Smith, 39.7 seconds. And, McDaniel, 41.3 seconds." Mr. Frazier is exhilarated that Eddie, Mark, and the rest of the freshmen are delivering the level of performance he saw last Spring during the final track meet of the year at the middle school.

Closing out the afternoon, Mr. Frazier reminds everyone, "although we are competing against each other today, we are a team, and soon we will be competing against the real opponents." This does not raise Mahoney's spirits. Just like Ambrosini was taken down on the football field, Paul Mahoney is now being taken down on the track. The good news is all indications are that Mark, Eddie, and the rest of the tribe, have a place on the team.

Mr. Frazier instructs the candidates to all return tomorrow, at the same time and place. Tomorrow's events will be the 440-yard dash, the 880-yard run, and the relay events. Mr. Frazier informs the athletes that, after tomorrow's tryouts, the first cut will be made. He tells the students that the list of successful candidates will be posted on the window of the administration office the day after tomorrow by the time they arrive at school.

In the locker room, the discussion turns to the previous two hours. Mahoney is heard saying, "it's only tryouts. No one is running their best." Another senior informs Mahoney, "some of the new guys are looking quite good." Mahoney answers, "yeah, but they haven't run against me yet." Meanwhile, Mark, at the other end of the locker room, overhears Mahoney's conversation and tells Eddie, and Braden, "they're talking about us." Braden, back to his hyper energetic self, replies, "yeah, well let 'em talk! We kicked their ass and we're gonna do it again!" Eddie reminds Braden, "remember, we're all going to be on the same team." Braden responds, "yeah, I know! But, until then, every single one of them is my opponent!" Braden has a valid point. Today's goal is to make the team. Tomorrow's goal is to beat the competition.

The second day of tryouts arrives, and the talk around school is how Mahoney was beaten at his own race. Mahoney brushes off the comments, repeating, "it's just tryouts." Mahoney, however, is worried. The confidence of Mark, Eddie, Braden, Gary Mitchell, and Eric Johnson reach an all-time high. As freshmen, they find themselves able to compete at the high school level quite competently.

At the end of the next school day, the day is just beginning for the indoor track candidates. The students head to the locker room again for the second day of tryouts. Inside the locker room, there is an eery silence today when compared with yesterday. Today is the second session of tryouts for the big three, basketball, wrestling, and track. The coaches have a good idea of who will make their respective teams, but the students do not. Not making the team could be a devastating blow to some, yet, to others, it will be no big deal.

The track team candidates exit the locker room one by one and move into the hallway. Today, there is a lot less chatter than yesterday. Mahoney, who usually commands a lot of attention, gets none. Mark and Braden mess around, and get into a boxing match, just for fun. This sends the signal that they are not stressed in the least. It also creates the center of attention. Braden does not try to be the center of attention, but his energetic personality seems to focus it in his direction all too often. Mr. Frazier and Mr. Zunde walk down the hallway from the administrative office, and signal the team to follow them downstairs.

Once in the arena, Mr. Frazier instructs everyone to sit on the bleachers. He addresses the team candidates, "many of you gave an awesome performance yesterday, but some of you were not giving it your best. Today, I expect a lot better. Today, we will be running the 440-yard dash followed by the 880-yard run. Afterwards, we will be doing relay drills. During the drill, I will be looking how well you handoff and receive the baton. We will not be running relay races for time."

Recalling last semesters' gym class, Mr. Frazier makes the announcement, "Mahoney, Eddie, Mark, Braden, Johnson, Bell, Ambrosini, and O'Brien, all of you come and see me." He instructs the rest of the runners, "the rest of you form groups of four." The eight runners approach Mr. Frazier, wondering what's up. Mr. Frazier informs Mahoney, Eddie, Mark, and Braden that they will all be running in the same heat, and that they will be going first. Mr. Frazier informs Johnson, Bell, Ambrosini, and O'Brien that they will be running in the second heat together. Mr. Frazier threw O'Brien into Johnson's heat to show O'Brien what real competition is. He prearranges a couple of other groups in order to compare certain runners. Mr. Frazier then tells all the runners to get ready, "stretch, take a few warm-up laps, and do whatever you need to warm up. Your place on the team may depend on it."

After blowing his whistle, Mr. Frazier tells the runners to stand along with their group to the side of the track, near the starting line. He calls for the first group, assigning Braden to lane one. This is the inside lane, and is usually reserved for the fastest runner. Mahoney thinks this should be his lane but, Mr. Frazier, by assigning this lane to Braden, implies Mahoney should try harder. Eddie is assigned to lane number two. Mark is assigned to lane number three.

Mahoney, as a surprise to all, is assigned to lane number four, and is not the least bit happy.

Mr. Frazier then instructs the runners, "440 yards is one quarter mile, which is two laps around this track." He continues, for those who do not know, "after the first lap, you do not have to stay in your lane." There are markings on the track denoting a staggered start for both 220 and 440 yards. Mr. Frazier could have staggered the start in such a way that the runners would stay in their lane during the entire 440 yards, which is often done in indoor track, but today he chose not to. Mr. Frazier already knows that Eddie, Mark, and Braden can run a 54-second quarter mile. He is more interested in how the runners interact with each other and jockey for position on the track. This will also make the race more interesting.

The runners stand behind the starting blocks, and Mr. Frazier announces, "on your marks." Waiting for the runners to get ready, he then announces, "set." The runners get set, and are ready to go. The buzzer goes off, and the runners leave the blocks as if they are running for an Olympic gold medal. Mahoney, leaving the blocks, raises his legs high during his stride to show off, which does not afford him any extra speed. Mark and Eddie, in their usual competitive spirit, leave the blocks with enough speed to convince anyone they are running the 40-yard dash. Braden, in lane one, is not fooling around. The 440-yard dash is his race, and he refuses to let anyone show him up. This race is the reason Braden is here.

Halfway around the first lap, not even Mr. Frazier can discern the leader. Coming around the curve into the straightaway, it becomes apparent that Braden is in front. Eddie and Mark are head to head, with Mahoney in last place. The runners drop in behind Braden, with Eddie closely following, and Mark right behind Eddie. Far behind Mark is Mahoney. If Mahoney is going to win this race, he will have to do it in the back straightaway. Mahoney has nothing to lose by sprinting along the back straightaway, but surprisingly finds himself losing ground. Eddie keeps pace closely with Braden, which is a smart move on his part. If Mark is to pass Eddie and drop in, he must pass Braden too. At the end of the back straightaway, no one is able to change their position. As the runners clear the final curve, Braden, Eddie, and Mark fight it out. Eddie tries to pass Braden, but is unable. Mark, who is in third place, tries his best to catch Eddie. And Mahoney, who is now far behind, has burned out early and lost a lot of ground. Braden crosses the finish line first, quickly followed by Eddie, and then Mark. Mahoney, even though he ran a respectable time, arrives at the finish line last.

Mr. Frazier and Mr. Zunde speak with each other and record the runners times. Mr. Frazier gives some encouragement to the group, announcing, "this is the kind of running I like to see! I want to see everyone give this kind of effort!" Then, the announcement comes, "Braden, 54.2 seconds. Bogenskaya, 55.0 seconds. Svoboda, 55.7 seconds. And Mahoney, 59.8 seconds." Mr. Frazier reminds everyone that this race was a time trial, and he expects the athletes will perform better in competition.

As the next group gets ready, Mark and Braden move off to the side, and Eddie walks over to talk with Bobby B. for a moment. Johnson will be in this next heat, so they will be watching closely. As Eddie is talking with Bobby B., he overhears Mahoney talking with Matt Wood, the senior shot-putter. Wandering a little closer to hear what is being said, Eddie hears Mahoney telling Wood that he hates the 880-yard run. The 880-yard run is the next event, and will take place after everyone completes the 440-yard dash.

The buzzer goes off and Johnson's heat begins. While Johnson is running, Eddie gets an idea. Eddie tells Mark and Braden what he overheard between Mahoney and Matt Wood. Eddie, Mark, and Braden also don't like competing in the 880-yard run. It is not a sprint, and it is not distance race. Braden sees the 880-yard run as a race with which you get stuck. Eddie tells Mark and Braden, "look, we hate the 880, and so does Mahoney. We did really good in the sprints. We beat Mahoney and everyone else." Revealing his idea, Eddie whispers to his friends, "if we let Mahoney win the 880, we won't have to run it, and he'll probably get stuck with it." Braden likes the idea, since running both a 440-yard dash and an 880-yard run in one meet is not exactly his idea of fun. Mark, who detests the 880-yard run, has no problem letting Mahoney win. If Mark had to run 880 yards in competition, he'd probably quit the team.

Too busy talking about their plan, they missed the finish of Johnson's race. They walk over to Johnson, and Braden asks, "how did it go?" Johnson, still somewhat winded, replies, "sub-60, like 58 something. I won." Mark asks Johnson, "hey, do you like the 880?" Johnson replies, "hell no!" Mark lets Johnson in on their plan. Johnson points out, "if Mahoney wins, he may not act like a such jerk anymore." Eddie, Mark, and Braden are all in on the plan. Also in on the plan, Johnson tells the group, "that sounds like a good plan to me. I'll take it easy on my heat too."

Most of the 440-yard dash heats go well, but no one came close to the times of the first group and Johnson. Eddie, Mark, Braden, and Johnson are at the top of their game. The worst quarter mile time was delivered by O'Brien, who ran a time that would rival the best half mile times. Some people wonder why O'Brien, who is still expecting to make the team, is even at the tryouts.

Mark suspects the same groups that ran the 440-yard dash will have to run the 880 together, and he is right. Mr. Frazier makes the announcement to prepare for the 880-yard run, telling the groups they will run in the same order. Braden, all fired up after yesterday's tryouts, exclaims, "I'm hot, I'm hot! Ain't no one stopping me, no one!" He said this, however, not to get his own adrenaline levels up. He fully intended for his ranting to get Mahoney's adrenaline levels up so that Mahoney runs a better race.

Mr. Frazier instructs the runners, "880 yards is one half mile, which is four laps around the track. After the first lap, you do not have to stay in your lane." Eddie asks, "are we in the same lanes?" Mr. Frazier responds, "no. To be fair, we will reverse the lane assignments. If you were in lane one, you will be in lane four. If you were in lane two, you will be in lane three, etcetera." This sounds simple enough, but someone is bound to screw it up along the way. The runners take to their lanes. There are no starting blocks for the 880-yard run, a somewhat foreign way to start a race to the sprinters. Standing proud in lane one is Mahoney, who is not about to lose another race. Mahoney is unaware that he has a few runners who are going to help him win.

Mr. Zunde, wasting no time, tells the runners, "get set," and immediately hits the buzzer. Mahoney is the first one out of the blocks, and takes the lead. Mark and Eddie, who expected a delay after Mr. Zunde said, "get set," suffer a delayed start by a second or so. Braden, in the outside lane, starts out strong, pushing Mahoney. Not about to lose another race, Mahoney is not allowing Braden to catch him. For the first lap the runners keep pace with each other. At the end of the lap, the runners leave their lanes and drop to the inside lane of the track. Mahoney is in first place. Braden drops in behind Mahoney into second place. Eddie is in third place, and Mark is last place. Braden makes Mahoney work hard, following him closely. Eddie and Mark are several steps behind Braden. By the end of the second lap, Mahoney is still in the lead, with Braden right behind. Eddie and Mark maintain a good distance behind the leaders.

Just into the third lap, Braden perceives Mahoney is making a move, and speeding up. To Braden, this is the perfect time to slow his pace, causing Mahoney to appear even faster. Mark and Eddie see themselves catching up to Braden, and so they also slow their pace. Mahoney, clearly ahead, widens his lead by a good margin. At the end of the third lap, Mahoney thinks he has the race wrapped up. He has learned not to underestimate Eddie's tribe, so he sprints as fast as he can. Braden, seriously not wanting to run the half mile in competition, begins to slow his pace even more during the last lap. Eddie and Mark, who are again catching up to Braden, also drop their pace. On the back straightaway, Eddie slows his pace even more, prompting Mark to follow suit. While Eddie and Mark are still on the back straightaway, Mahoney crosses the finish line. Braden, who is just entering the final turn when Mahoney wins, momentarily slows to a fast jog in order to get a slower time. Braden crosses the finish line, eventually followed by Eddie, then Mark.

Mr. Frazier, looking at the times on his stopwatches, meets with Mr. Zunde. They record the times. The announcement comes as a surprise to many, but not to Eddie, Mark, and Braden. Mr. Frazier gives the good and bad news, "Mahoney, 2:30. Braden, 2:44. Bogenskaya, 2:49. Svoboda, 2:55." Looking at Mark, Mr. Frazier asks, "what happened?" Used to running on a 440-yard track, Mark replies, "the 220-yard track threw me off. I guess I'm not used to it." Eddie adds, "we never run the 880. I'm not too familiar with the strategy. And, I'm not used to the smaller track either." Mr. Frazier reassures them, "you'll get used to it. Don't worry." Meanwhile, Mahoney is celebrating and getting high-fives from his teammates. Braden, Eddie, and Mark head over to the bleachers to watch the rest of the heats. They are done for now, until the relay practice.

Mark mentions to Eddie, "I think that worked." Eddie remarks, "yeah, I'm not running no 880." Braden chimes in, "me neither." Thinking more in depth about the race, Braden adds, "but, I think I could have beaten that guy." Mark comments, "well, Mahoney ran a good race. Hopefully it'll be his." As they are talking, Mahoney walks by Eddie and his tribe. Braden stands up and gives Mahoney a high-five, and says, "good run, good run!" Eddie and Mark also give Mahoney a high-five. Mahoney, for the first time during tryouts, is in a good mood. Mahoney moves on, not realizing he potentially committed himself to running the 880-yard run, a race of which he does not want any part. Eddie, Mark, Braden, and Johnson were the real winners of this race.

Mr. Frazier calls the group together, having everyone sit on the bleachers. He addresses the group, "we're now going to run relay drills." Instructing the runners how this will be accomplished on the 220-yard track, he tells them, "there will be one group on this side of the track. There will be another group on the other side of the track." Mr. Frazier describes the drill, "you will line up, and take turns receiving the baton, run 110 yards, and hand it off, and get in the back of the line." Mr. Frazier then describes what he is expecting to see in the drill, telling them, "I'm not looking at your speed. I'm only interested at your handoff skills and how well you transfer the baton."

The drill begins with one of the seniors running the requisite 110 yards, and handing it off to the next runner. The handoff skill taught by Mr. Frazier is a nonvisual-nonverbal exchange, which is the same technique taught by Mr. Harris at the middle school. Receiving the baton, the next runner runs his 110 yards, and passes the baton along. This drill continues for about five minutes. Once the students get the hang of it, Mr. Frazier calls for another three groups of runners in lanes two, three and four.

There is no competition for speed in this drill. Mr. Frazier and Mr. Zunde are making notes regarding each students skill. Mr. Frazier and Mr. Zunde are watching how the baton is transferred from one runner to the next, and looking at the runner's feet. Any hesitation or break in the runner's cadence is evidence of a bad handoff. Most of the runners appear to be reasonably skilled at handing off the baton. After the drill, they will compare notes to see who has the potential to excel in a relay race. They will then take the time trial data, and form the relay teams. The drill continues for about 30 minutes.

Mr. Frazier blows his whistle, and tells everyone that the tryouts are done for the day. Mr. Frazier then tells the students, "remember, tomorrow will be the first cut. When you get to school tomorrow, the results will be posted on the window of the administration office. If you have locked in an event, that event will be posted next to your name, and you have made the team. If there is no event next to your name, you have not been cut, but I haven't decided anything yet." And then the bad news is delivered, "if your name is not on the list, you have been cut." Seeing an event next to your name means you have made the team already. Not having an event next to your name means you are still trying out. Mr. Frazier dismisses the team, and everyone heads to the locker room. Most students, however, already know whether they made the team or not.

The day of reckoning arrives, with good news for some, and bad news for others. As the busses pull in, anyone who has tried out for a team heads straight to the window of the administration office. Bobby B., who walks to school, has already found out that he's in. Bobby B. has been sitting in the lobby for a while, waiting for his friends to arrive. Mark and Braden's bus arrives, and they walk through the door, not even noticing Bobby B. Bobby B. just sits back and waits for their reactions. Mark and Braden walk up to the list, looking for their name. Almost simultaneously, they scream out, "yes!" They both have made the team. After further examination, Mark sees that he is locked into the 40-yard dash and the 440-yard dash. Braden is locked into the 220-yard dash and the 440-yard dash. These are the events that they each wanted, and they are both are ecstatic.

Bobby B. walks up to join Mark and Braden in their celebration. Eddie walks through the door, and heads straight toward the list. Braden and Mark did not even look to see who else may have made the team. They were too busy celebrating. Eddie nervously looks at the list and finds his name. Bursting out in a happy laugh, Eddie exchanges high-fives with his friends. Eddie earned a spot in the 40-yard dash and the 220-yard dash, which is exactly what he wanted.

After they calm down a bit, they look to see who else is on the list. They see that Johnson, who has not yet arrived, has also made the team. Johnson has earned a spot in the 220-yard dash, which is his specialty. Gary Mitchell is locked into the mile and the 880-yard run, which is no surprise to anyone. Looking for Mahoney's name, Eddie points to the line, taps on the glass, and everyone else looks. Only one event is listed, which is the 880-yard run. Eddie, Mark, and Braden look at each other, and burst out laughing. Their plan worked and it worked well.

Watching bad news walk through the door, the group moves toward the center of the school lobby as Mahoney makes a beeline to the list. Looking at the list, Mahoney exclaims, "son-of-a, crap," as he punches himself in the thigh and kicks the wall. Eddie, standing 20 feet away with his back to Mahoney, says to the group, "well, he has the rest of the day to calm down." Braden contends, "yeah, but he won't." Johnson and Mitchell then walk up to the group. Johnson asks, "did we make it?" Eddie replies, "we did. We don't want to spoil it for you guys though. Go and look!" Johnson and Mitchell run up to the list and, after a quick look, engage in their own celebration. They then walk over to the group, everyone getting the best news of the year. They celebrate and talk for a while, and then head off to class.

At the end of the day, the team meets again. Everyone has the routine down by now. They go to the locker room, get dressed, and go downstairs to the arena. Today, Mr. Frazier officially announces who will be competing each event. After he gives everyone the news, he informs the team, "we still have a couple of open slots, and I have not chosen any relay teams yet. You will all get to compete in two or three events each." Mr. Frazier then announces today's agenda, "today, we will be running a few specific races to help me make my decision, and I don't want anyone to slack off." Mr. Frazier then issues a warning, "for some of you, I have already assigned you to an event. I can remove you from that event just as quickly, so I expect competitive times today, and every day."

Mr. Frazier instructs the team to warm up. After the warm-ups, he calls Eddie, Mark, Johnson, Braden, Mahoney, and Darryl Bell to meet with him. Mr. Frazier informs the six runners, "I need three sprinters in the 40-yard dash. We're going to run a race. The best time will be joining Mark and Eddie." Mr. Frazier then instructs the runners to get ready. While the runners are preparing, Mr. Frazier tells the rest of the students to sit on the bleachers and watch the race. He knows performance improves when one is begin watched.

At the other end of the track, Mr. Frazier announces, "on your marks." The room falls silent. The word, "set," follows. All the runners are set and are as ready as ever. The buzzer sounds, and the runners all leave their blocks, accelerating as fast as they can. Out of the blocks, Eddie and Mark are clearly ahead at ten yards. Johnson, surprisingly, is in third place. Johnson does not want any part of the 880-yard run, so he is giving it his all out best. Mahoney and Braden are right behind Johnson, with Bell in a not so distant last place. Halfway though the five-second race, Eddie and Mark have a good lead, which is adequate to win. No one is likely to catch them. Johnson, thinking about the potential agony of running the 880, is somehow able to find more speed than he ever has. In third place, Johnson is widening his lead over Mahoney. Braden, passing Mahoney, is willing to let Johnson beat him, but not Mahoney. A few yards before the finish line, Johnson has locked in third place. Eddie and Mark cross the finish line first, which appears to be a tie. Johnson, several steps behind, takes third place. Braden takes fourth place, and Mahoney fifth place. Braden and Mahoney were separated by only a slight margin. Bell, who was supposed to be the number two man this year in the sprinting events, finishes in last place.

At the finish line, Mr. Frazier and Mr. Zunde were only interested in the times of the top three. Mr. Frazier and Mr. Zunde record the times, and prepare to make the announcement. Eddie and Mark do not know who won, as the race was very close. Johnson knows that he came in third place, and that's all he cares about. When the runners return to the finish line, Mr. Frazier announces to everyone, "first place was a tie at 4.7 seconds." Whether Eddie or Mark won the heat is immaterial right now. Mr. Frazier is more interested in the runner who took third place. He continues, "in third place is Johnson, who I'm very proud of, 5.1 seconds."

Mahoney, who finished behind Braden, is not at all happy. This was supposed to be his race, along with Bell. This was his second chance at locking in this event, and he has failed. Bell asks Mahoney, "what's up with these guys? Where did they come from?" Mahoney, who was hoping for a scholarship in track, replies, "I have no idea. It looks like I'm going to have a lot of work ahead of me." Disappointed with his own performance, Mahoney exclaims, "I'm not getting a scholarship with these times!" Bell, at a loss to understand where all this talent came from, is even questioning his own ability. Bell, a junior, and Mahoney, a senior, have both been beaten by four freshmen. They both know that is nothing to be proud of.

Meanwhile, Eddie and Mark congratulate Johnson. Winning this race assures Johnson that he will not have to compete in the 880-yard run. Eddie has locked in the 40-yard dash and the 220-yard dash. Mark will join Eddie in the 40-yard dash, and will also run the 440-yard dash with Braden. Braden and Johnson will be running the 220-yard dash together. With any luck, the four sprinters will land on a relay team together.

Eddie's tribe takes a seat on the bleachers, while Mr. Frazier arranges a few other competitions. Just as they finally have a chance to sit back and relax, trouble comes their way. Mahoney, who is not so happy at the moment, walks up to the tribe, just as they are all ready to watch the rest of the events. Mahoney, not even knowing how to open the conversation, sarcastically asks, "what's up with you guys?" Eddie and his tribe look at each other, not knowing how to even answer Mahoney's question. Eddie, who remembers the encounter with Ambrosini on the football field and how Ambrosini and Mahoney seem to talk a lot, answers, "we're the tribe, that's what's up." Braden adds, "yeah, the tribe, dude." Johnson, who just defeated Mahoney, adds his two cents, "and, the tribe always wins." Mark, not wanting to feel left out of the highly intellectual discussion, comments, "if you want to be in the tribe, you got to win. But, you can't win unless you're in the tribe."

Mark's circular logic left everyone pondering the great depth of his philosophy. Mahoney, somewhat frustrated, exclaims, "don't you guys take anything seriously?" Braden, hammering his fist on the bleachers, responds quickly and firmly, telling Mahoney, "yeah, we do! Winning!" Quite startled, Mahoney walks away after Braden gave him something to think about. Braden's words of wisdom, "winning," will echo through Mahoney's mind for weeks to come.

After a while, Bobby B. and Mitchell wander over to join the group. Their day is over, as the competition begins to wind down. Mitchell mentions to the group, "I'm glad I'm running the 880." Mark asks, "I saw you running. What was your time?" Mitchell replies, "I ran a 2:20. Two seconds faster than last time. I came in first place." Eddie asks, "what did Mahoney run when he ran it with us?" Braden replies, "ten seconds faster than me." Eddie asks Braden, "well, duh! What did you run?" Braden replies, "a 2:44, I think." Mitchell says, "I beat Mahoney by fifteen seconds today." Mitchell is as happy as he can be, knowing he is going to be a solid competitor in that event. Mitchell has no problem running 880 yards. A half mile is a cake walk for the five-star miler.

Mr. Frazier announces that the tryouts are done for today. He reminds everyone, "check the list tomorrow morning. It will be posted in the same place. Tomorrow's list will have the final team, and your events. However, not all the relay events will be decided by tomorrow." Mr. Frazier explains his strategy, telling the team, "some relay teams may also change from meet to meet, like we did last year." Mr. Frazier, who is well aware of the competition, will often change the relay team members to gain an advantage. The team heads to the locker room, with their fate already sealed after today's events. Many will be waiting anxiously for tomorrow's news.

The final team roster is posted in the window the next morning. Bobby B., arriving again before everyone else, looks over the list. The final roster is not too much different from the previous day's list. Mark and Braden arrive, curious to see if there are any changes. The only change to their entry is "4x440" written next to their names, which stands for the 4 by 440 relay. Looking to see who else is on the 4 by 440 relay team, they find Eddie's and Johnson's names, who both just happen to be walking up. The newly assembled relay team celebrates, with cheers and high-fives. They move away from the roster, as other students search for their names.

Mahoney enters the school, casually walking up to the list with a walk suggestive that he's on the top of the world. Looking at the roster, he finds his name and notices there are no changes next to his name. Looking for his buddy's name, Bell, he also notices no changes. With no additional events next to his name, Mahoney will be an alternate to some events, or will be on various relay teams. Somewhat confused, he starts looking through the final roster, name by name. Mahoney is perplexed that the prestigious 4 by 440 relay event was assigned to four freshmen. He decides he will question Mr. Frazier later today about that decision.

Later that day, practice arrives and the team meets in the normal place. The team is addressed by Mr. Frazier, who goes over today's agenda. Mr. Frazier informs the students, "today, we will be running relay events for time. If you have already been assigned to a relay event, you will be running first." Then the interesting news, "if you have not been assigned a relay event, you will be running relays for time for the rest of the day." As Mr. Frazier addresses the team, Mr. O'Brien, and his son, Jimmy, who is in uniform and ready to run, walk down the stairs and take a seat on the bleachers. Jimmy, a bit too inept to be embarrassed, has been cut from the team, but still shows up to practice. Closing his instruction, Mr. Frazier tells the 4 by 440 relay team to get ready.

As the team prepares to run for time, Mr. O'Brien approaches Mr. Frazier and asks, "coach, how come Jimmy didn't make your team?" Brushing off the question by stating hard and cold facts, Mr. Frazier tells Mr. O'Brien, "he's not fast enough." Mr. O'Brien, not accepting of Mr. Frazier's answer, begins to argue with Mr. Frazier, which is a big mistake. Mr. Frazier, who does not argue, finally asks Mr. O'Brien, "so, please tell me. What event do you want Jimmy to run?" Mr. O'Brien replies, "the 440-yard run is his favorite event. He really likes the distance races." The 440-yard dash is hardly a distance race, making Mr. O'Brien sound a bit like an inept imbecile himself.

Mr. Frazier blows his whistle, causing dead silence to fall over the track. Mr. Frazier announces, "Svoboda, Bogenskaya, Braden, Johnson, and Mahoney, get over here now!" The five runners jog over to Mr. Frazier, wondering what is going on. Calling the runners off to the side, Mr. Frazier tells them, "you'll be running the 440-yard dash with Jimmy O'Brien." Mr. Frazier then whispers to them, "kick his ass, and kick it good!" Mr. Frazier tells the five team members and Jimmy O'Brien to get behind the blocks, and prepare to run a 440-yard dash. Not that it will make any difference, Mr. Frazier lets Jimmy even choose his lane. Braden, looking over at Jimmy, asks him, "are you ready for your ass whooping, junior?" Braden remembers quite well from last year how Jimmy O'Brien was always dragging the team down.

Mr. Frazier reminds everyone, "440 yards is two laps. The way the blocks are set, you are to stay in your lane for the entire race. Do not leave your lane! O'Brien, do you got that?" O'Brien replies, "yeah." Mr. Frazier wants O'Brien running in his own lane during the entire race, so he does not cause a collision on the track. Wasting no time, Mr. Frazier announces, "on your marks," followed by, "set." Once everyone is set, Mr. Frazier hits the buzzer.

Braden is out of the blocks first, with a very obvious false start, but Mr. Frazier does not care. In the first few yards, Braden is in first place, with Eddie, Mark, Johnson, and Mahoney slightly behind. Jimmy, as he enters the first turn, sees the other runners already well into the back straightaway. Johnson and Braden appear to be leading. Because of the staggering, however, it is difficult to know who is actually ahead. Coming into the second curve, the placement becomes more evident. Jimmy, who is entering the back straightaway, watches the group come out of the second curve. At the end of the first lap, it is Braden, followed by Eddie, Mark, Johnson, and Mahoney, in that order. Only three or four seconds separate the five front runners. Meanwhile, O'Brien, who is still in the back straightaway, begins to tire, slowing to a fast jog. As O'Brien enters the second turn, the pack is well into the back straightaway on their second lap, ready to catch him. O'Brien, still on his first lap, is about to be embarrassingly passed by the pack. Braden, who is ahead, appears like he will be definitely winning this one.

To Braden, however, winning is not enough. He wants to win by a significant margin. Braden sees O'Brien flailing, and wants to cross the finish line before O'Brien completes his first lap. O'Brien, just coming out of the curve, is in Braden's sites. Braden, halfway through the final curve, gives it all he has. Coming out of the curve and into the final straightaway, Braden sprints toward the finish line, and just edges out O'Brien, who has just completed lap one of a two-lap race. Two seconds later Eddie crosses the finish line. He is followed by Mark, Johnson, and Mahoney, in that order. O'Brien is determined to complete the race, finishes his last lap alone.

Once O'Brien crosses the finish line, Mr. Frazier looks at his two stopwatches, and wastes no time making the announcement, "the winning time is 54.1 seconds! Jimmy O'Brien, your time is 2:25, which sucks!" Mr. Frazier exclaims, "O'Brien, you took more time to run a quarter mile than Mitchell takes to run a half mile! And Braden just ran 440 yards faster than you can run 220 yards!" Mr. Frazier, all fired up, looks at Mr. O'Brien, and yells at him, stating, "and, that is exactly why Jimmy got cut!" After blowing his whistle to get everyone's attention, Mr. Frazier tells the mile medley team to get ready to run for time. Changing the agenda, he gives Eddie, Mark, Braden, and Johnson a chance to rest after demonstrating to Jimmy O'Brien how to run.

Hoping that something will change, Mr. O'Brien and Jimmy hang around for a while. After a few minutes, they walk up the steel staircase, somewhat disappointed. Jimmy will have to wait until Spring if he wants to try out for track again. If he does, he will have to do a lot more than just show up to practice and expect to make the team. Between now and then, he will have to be training, not sitting around watching television or taking it easy. With Jimmy, this is not likely to be the case. But, either way, the standard for making the team has been set.

After a few relay races, Mr. Frazier calls Eddie, Mark, Braden, and Johnson to run the 4 by 440 relay. Paul Mahoney, idle at the moment, sees the group setting up. This was supposed to be one of Mahoney's events, as it was during the last two years. Mahoney, who wants to discuss with Mr. Frazier his 4 by 440 relay team selection, approaches the coach and asks, "is there any reason why I didn't make the 4 by 440?" Mr. Frazier responds, "no. Your times are good enough for any relay team." Mr. Frazier continues, "these four guys, for some reason, run better and faster when they are together." Mahoney, a veteran on the team, responds, "yeah, I've noticed that." Making Mahoney an offer, Mr. Frazier tells him, "if you can put together a team who can beat them, I'd be glad to rearrange things and let your team run that event." Mr. Frazier could not have handled that situation any better. Mahoney walks away thinking about who could beat Mr. Frazier's 4 by 440 relay team. Mr. Frazier then steps off to the side, and talks to Mr. Zunde for a few minutes as the 4 by 440 relay team warms up.

Turning his attention back to the 4 by 440 relay team, Mr. Frazier asks, "are you guys ready?" Braden replies, "yeah. But, what order do you want us to go in?" Mr. Frazier, remembering the relay team well from the final middle school track meet last year, tells them, "we'll start with the same order you ran last year." Mr. Frazier does not remember in which order the relay team previously ran. He is sure that Mr. Harris, the middle school track coach, had his reasons for the order. Last year, Braden was the lead man, followed by Johnson, then Eddie, and lastly the anchorman, Mark.

Braden, the lead man, is ready, as Eddie, Mark, and Johnson finish some last minute stretching. Mr. Frazier announces, "on your marks." Running up, and interrupting Mr. Frazier, Mahoney exclaims, "I got a team who'll beat them!" This is exactly what Mr. Frazier wants to hear, competition and a challenge. Mr. Frazier asks the 4 by 440 relay team, "are you guys OK with that?" Eddie and Mark, standing off to the side with their arms crossed, nod yes. Johnson replies, "sure." Braden, a bit more vocal, breaking into a dance and pointing the baton at Mahoney, cries out, "bring it on! Bring it on, junior! Ain't nobody stoppin' me now, just bring it on! Bring it on! It's ass kicking time, and I'm ready!" This is exactly what Mr. Frazier was talking about when he told

Mahoney, "these four guys, for some reason, run better and faster when they are together."

Mahoney waves to the runners he selected, which include Darryl Bell, Anthony Ambrosini, and Louis Zaino. Mr. Frazier looks Mahoney's team over, and tells them to get ready. Eddie also evaluates the team, and comments to Mark, "Ambrosini again? Really?" Johnson asks, "who's that other guy?" Mark replies, "Zaino. He's really good, but we're better. Don't worry." Eddie, Mark, and Johnson are now confident in their ability to beat Mahoney's team. Braden, on the other hand, was already confident. Zaino walks up to the starting line, and will be Mahoney's lead man. Eddie, catching Braden's eye, gives him a thumbs up.

Mr. Frazier makes the announcement, "on your marks." Braden, behind the blocks, spins on one foot, gracefully becomes airborne, and lands in front of the blocks. He then positions himself to get set on Mr. Frazier's command. Mr. Frazier, who can hardly contain his laugh, announces, "set." Both runners get set and are ready to go. Mr. Frazier hits the buzzer and the runners explode out of the blocks.

Braden, who is out of the blocks first, is clearly ahead after 50 yards. Halfway around the track, on the back straightaway, it is evident that Braden is extending his lead over Zaino. As Braden approaches the starting line, Eddie yells out to Braden, "faster, faster." On the last lap of his leg, Braden pours on all he has. Zaino, although a reasonably good runner, is no match for Braden today, who is more than fired up. On the back straightaway, Braden again widens his lead over Zaino. Coming around the final curve, Braden eyes Johnson, who is waiting for the baton. Next to Johnson is Ambrosini, who has already had the pleasure of competing against, and losing to, Johnson. The transition between Braden and Johnson goes perfectly, and Johnson takes off. Just as Johnson enters the curve, Ambrosini receives his baton.

Johnson, unfamiliar with Ambrosini's ability in the 440, does not want to be passed. On the back straightaway, Johnson sprints and, upon entering the curve, sees that Ambrosini has not gained any ground. Johnson runs both laps of his 440-yard leg as if he is running a 220-yard dash. On the second lap, it appears Johnson has gained significant ground over Ambrosini. As Johnson approaches the transition zone, Eddie is waiting, and ready to go. So is Bell, who is a better opponent than the previous two runners on Mahoney's team. Eddie leaves the transition zone running like a machine. Bell receives his baton as Eddie comes out of the first curve.

Back at the starting line, Mark mentions to Braden something about déjà vu. Braden asks Mark, "déjà what?" Mark replies, as he is watching Eddie gain ground over Bell, "McCrutchen, remember that guy from last year?" Braden, remembering that race, says, "oh, yeah. That guy." Before Mark can explain, Mr. Frazier walks up to Mark and Braden, and informs Braden, "you will be running the anchor leg." Mark, somewhat perplexed, replies, "what?" Mr. Frazier tells Mark, "I'll explain later," and tells Braden to get back on the track. Equally perplexed, Braden enters the track a second time.

Back on the track, Eddie and Bell fight it out, both trying to gain a better advantage for their respective anchorman. After the first lap, Eddie has gained a little ground over Bell. During his second lap, Eddie, who does not want to lose his position on the relay team, sprints the last 220 yards as if he is running the 40-yard dash. He does not care that he might burn himself out. For Bell, there is already too much ground to make up to win the leg or the race. Coming out of the final curve, Eddie, expecting to see Mark, sees Braden in the transition zone. With the switch, Eddie is wondering what's up. Eddie hands off to Braden, who is running his second 440-yard dash within four minutes. Mahoney receives his baton 23 seconds later.

Mr. Frazier takes Mark aside, telling him, "you still have your spot on the relay team, so don't worry." Mr. Frazier explains to Mark, "they've challenged your team, and this is how I defend my decision." Mark quickly figured out that, if Braden beats Mahoney, Mr. Frazier will not be questioned again. Mark also understands that, if Braden wins this leg, Mahoney will be totally embarrassed.

Braden maintains his significant lead for the first lap. If Braden wins, Mahoney knows he will have a truck load of egg on his face that will look as if it were placed there by a jet engine. Mahoney, with all he has, tries to catch Braden. Entering the second lap, Braden begins to drop his pace a little, but is still running at a highly competitive speed. On the back straightaway, Mahoney is closing in on Braden's lead. Mahoney wants this win but, even if he wins, he has lost. Braden, however, refuses to be beaten by Mahoney. Around the final curve, Braden finds a third wind and sprints toward the finish line. Mahoney, coming out of the curve, also sprints toward the finish line. Mahoney, however, does not have enough distance remaining to catch Braden. At the finish line, Braden crosses first, with Mahoney crossing fourteen seconds later.

Mr. Frazier, even more amazed at the 4 by 440 relay team's performance, didn't even look at the time on his stopwatch. The time did not matter, for it was not a valid time nor a valid race. What is valid is that the 4 by 440 relay team, with one fatigued and burned-out runner, still beat Mahoney's team. Braden was apparently correct, when he said a few days ago, that he could have beaten Mahoney in the half mile.

After catching his breath, Braden rejoins the rest of the 4 by 440 relay team. Braden gives a high-five to each of the other three team members, along with his very vocal celebration. Braden exclaims, "ain't no one beating the tribe, no one!" Focusing his attention toward Mahoney, Braden exclaims, "I kicked your puny little ass, not once, but twice! And I'm gonna kick it again and again, junior!" Mahoney has no business responding to Braden, for he has been beaten, and beaten badly.

After Braden's rant, Mr. Frazier looks over at Mahoney, and says absolutely nothing. Nothing had to be said. At times, silence conveys more than if words were used. This was one of those times. Today, Mahoney learned why Mr. Frazier is the coach. It is unlikely that Mahoney will be questioning Mr. Frazier anytime soon.

Braden's dramatically increased enthusiasm is almost contagious. After watching Braden run, anyone running next is blessed with a higher energy level. Mr. Frazier congratulates the relay team, and apologizes to Mark and the 4 by 440 relay team for not allowing Mark to run his leg for this time trial. Mr. Frazier then informs the 4 by 440 relay team that they do not need to prove themselves by running for time. Mr. Frazier already knows that no other combination of runners on the team can match their performance level.

After a few more races, and running laps for training, Mr. Frazier then instructs the team to sit on the bleachers, as he reviews the team's performance. Mr. Frazier goes over each event, telling the runners what is good and what areas may need improvement. As he is speaking, three very athletic looking girls walk down the metal staircase and sit with the team on the bleachers. Mr. Frazier then makes the announcement to the team which runners will be performing in each relay event during the upcoming meet.

When he is finished discussing the events, Mr. Frazier says, "Barbara, Kathy, and Paula, please come up here." The three girls walk up to Mr. Frazier and stand beside him. Mr. Frazier continues, "many of you know Kathy and Barbara from last year. This year, they are joined by Paula. They are my spies." Mr. Frazier, explaining further what the three girls do, tells the team, "they snoop around, flirting when necessary, to get any information they can for me. If they flirt around with you during the meet, play along! They're also part of the team. Their job is to distract the competition." Mr. Frazier then gives the team some final words of wisdom for the day, "and most important, do not let Kathy, Paula, or Barbara distract you when you are running!"

Mr. Frazier finishes by telling the team what the three girls really do, "Kathy, Barbara, and Paula are my team assistants. The majority of what they do is to gather information about the competition during the meets. They are our team statisticians. They will be working closely with you over the next several weeks. Barbara will be working with the distance group. Kathy and Paula will be working primarily with the sprinters. Pay very close attention to what they tell you. You might actually learn something."

With all of the preliminary work out of the way, Mr. Frazier and the team can now get down to serious training. The team members have been selected and the events have been decided. With the first meet only a week away, now it's time to train. Eddie and his tribe are not content with just training during track practice. They also do some extra training on their own. This what sets Eddie and his tribe apart from many other members of the team.

After Mr. Frazier has finished addressing the team, everyone heads to the locker room. On the way to the locker room Eddie joins up with Braden and Mark, who are discussing the 4 by 440 relay. Mark, joking with Braden, tells him, "hey, thanks for running my leg, and for giving me the day off." Eddie joins in the conservation, telling Braden, "if you want, you can run my leg next time." Braden, not missing out on the fun, says, "yeah, and I'll also run Johnson's leg if I'm up against those guys, and I'll still win!" Braden's confidence is well backed by his performance. Not too many can make that claim, and then deliver.

On the way to the locker room, Mahoney mentions to Bell that he is interested in Kathy, one of Mr. Frazier's team assistants. Mahoney says to Bell, "at the end of the Spring season last year, I wanted to ask Kathy out on a date, but it never happened. Over the Summer, well, I didn't know where she lived." Bell pointing out the obvious to Mahoney, replies, "well, how about this year?" Mahoney, as if he were struck by lightning, points out the obvious to himself and Bell, "that's a good point. I could ask her out this year!" Bell responds, "duh! But, will you?" Mahoney tells Bell, "I'm definitely going to ask her out this year." Whether Mahoney asks Kathy out on a date or not this year is yet to be seen. But, since Mahoney failed on the track, perhaps he can succeed elsewhere.

With the team selected, and most of the events filled, the rest of the semester will bring practice and meets. Now, the real competition begins. Out of the many students who tried out for the team, the best have been identified. The best will now compete against the best. The last few days will prove to be a cake walk compared to the competition that is ahead.

Eddie - The Freshman Year

Winter Semester

In addition to training with the track team, Eddie is also continuing his training at home. Since it is cooler out and the days are shorter, he does not have as many chances to ride his bicycle. On one particular Saturday, however, the temperature is in the high 60s, which is unusual for this time of year. He calls Mark, and asks if he wants to go on a ride to the beach. This is the perfect time for Mark to give his new bicycle a good test ride. Mark agrees, and Eddie gets ready to go. Packing a few pieces of fruit, water, and some amino acid supplements, Eddie rides to Mark's house.

When Eddie arrives, Mark is ready to go. Eddie points out to Mark that he is not ready to go. Eddie tells Mark to go inside, and get some food and water because he will need it once he gets to the beach. Mark goes back inside, and returns with some fruit and a few bottles of water. The cyclists head toward the parkway, and take the paved path to the beach. As they ride along the path, Eddie glimpses toward the portal, wondering if Mark would believe him if he told him about it. Eddie decides to save that discussion for another day.

Eddie and Mark are having a highly energetic ride. Surprising to Eddie, Mark is able to keep up reasonably well. Eddie and Mark alternate who is in the lead, giving each one a chance to set the pace. As they approach the beach entrance, Eddie takes the lead since he is more familiar with the area. When they come to the turnabout, which has an obelisk in the center of it, they make the circle and go down the road to the left. A half mile down the road is a large parking lot, which they enter. At the end of the parking lot, there is a concession area. The concession area is closed because it is Winter. Between the parking lot and the road, there is an Olympic sized swimming pool for those who prefer fresh water. But, just like the concession area, the pool is also closed for the Winter.

Eddie and Mark get off their bicycles, and walk onto the nearly abandoned beach. Staring out at the ocean, Eddie asks Mark, "so, what do you think Mahoney does on a Saturday?" Mark replies, "sit on his ass and worry about Braden." Eddie, recalling the 4 by 440 relay race during which Braden ran two legs, laughs, and says, "yeah, you're probably right about that one."

Looking over at the ocean, Eddie tells Mark, "if this were Summer, I'd be in the water right now." Mark replies, "what about your bike?" Pointing to the concession stand at the end of the parking lot, Eddie tells Mark, "there's a bike rack over there. It's even bolted down. I just bring a lock." Mark looks around at the ocean, the miles of beach, the pool, the concession stand, and compliments Eddie, "you got a really good set up here. It's no wonder you're always headed down to the beach." Eddie remarks, "yeah, the only thing missing today are the girls."

Eddie and Mark walk back up to the parking lot. Eddie asks Mark, pointing farther down the road, "do you want to ride to the last parking lot up there, turn around, and head home?" Mark, not knowing how far away the parking lot is, says, "sure." As they slowly ride down the road that parallels the beach, the sound of crashing waves relaxes the two riders. The last parking lot, which is a much smaller one with no amenities, turns out to be only two miles down the road.

Eddie and Mark stop in the parking lot and have their snack and drink some water. Eddie also takes his supplements, prompting Mark to ask, "what are those?" Eddie replies, "they're my supplements, the amino acids. It's for building muscle." Mark, although he is curious, does not ask Eddie any other questions just yet. They turn around, and head down the road back to the beach entrance. At the entrance, they hang a right, and the relaxing part of the ride is over.

The ride home is the second part of the workout. Eddie tells Mark that the trip is about eleven miles each way. This is not a long distance for either of them to ride, but the workout is in the speed at which they ride. Riding up the path, an unofficial competition begins. Eddie, in the lead, speeds up, with Mark trying to keep up. Mark keeps up reasonably well, but the seasoned cyclist Eddie is faster. Eddie slows his pace, and lets Mark take the lead. Now it's Mark's turn. Eddie drafts behind Mark, conserving his energy at the expense of Mark's.

At the end of the path, Eddie and Mark stop and chat for a while. Mark asks Eddie, "how do you keep up so easily?" Eddie tells Mark, "I draft off of you." Mark asks, "you what?" Eddie replies, "I follow you closely, and it breaks the wind resistance. You do all the work, and I use less energy." Mark mentions, "I wonder if that works in running too." Serious, but joking, Eddie replies, "yes, but don't tell Braden. He's always out in front." Thinking about this, Mark figures it out and suggests, "so, if we run close behind each other, and trade off the lead, we conserve energy." Eddie replies, "yeah, and you'll run a better time. That's why Mitchell is always running on someone's heels in the mile. And that's how he whooped Mahoney in the 880. So, Mitchell always lets the other runner set the pace, and burn out. Then he has a lot left at the end, and wins the race." Mark says to Eddie, "we have to tell everybody about this." Eddie replies, "I thought everyone knew about drafting." Apparently not everyone knows, so the tribe may have just stepped up a notch or two in skill level. Mark, who has always relied on brute strength and speed, now has added a skill to his repertoire.

Mark and Eddie continue the short ride toward Mark's house. As they approach Mark's house, Mark heads up his driveway, and Eddie rides home. It's a sure bet that Mark will be seen at the beach a lot more this next Spring and Summer. Riding a bicycle eleven miles to the beach is much easier and faster than running eleven miles. And, the beach has the added benefit of being able to go into the water to cool off.

Monday's track practice comes as usual after school, but with a surprise to the freshmen. Mr. Frazier announces that the meet next Saturday will be a 4-way meet, meaning four teams will be competing. The upperclassmen, who were on the team last year, are all too familiar with a 4-way meet. In a 4-way meet, the competition is always more challenging. Instead of one opposing team having one or two star runners in every event, there are three opposing teams, each with their own one or two star runners. It doesn't take long to figure out that there will be a lot more losers than winners. Mr. Frazier also mentions that everyone will be running two events, not three. The team will practice Monday through Thursday for the week before the meet. On Friday, the team will be allowed to rest, allowing for complete physical recovery before the big event. Fortunately, for the team, it is a home meet, so they will have the advantage of not having to wake up early and travel.

Everyone already knows who the opposing teams are because the meet schedule is published at the beginning of the season. Before practice one day, Eddie checks the schedule to remind himself who will be the opposition. On the list of schools that will be competing is Centerville. Eddie thinks to himself, "what was the deal with them last year?" Then it occurred to Eddie, thinking to himself, "oh, yeah. McCrutchen. That guy again." Eddie, headed to the locker room, intends to tell Mark.

In the locker room, Eddie finds Mark, who is talking with Braden. Announcing his entrance, Eddie says to Mark and Braden, "guess who's back on Saturday?" Mark and Braden look at each other, at a loss to figure out whom Eddie is talking about. Eddie just tells them, "McCrutchen. One of the teams is Centerville." Mark grins, and says, "yeah, we worked him over good last year." Braden throws a monkey wrench in the conversation, stating, "I wonder if he even made the team." Mark comments, "he'd better be on the team. I want to mess with his mind some more." Braden has no problem reminding everyone, "yeah, we kicked their ass big time last year, and we're gonna do it again."

After practice, Mr. Frazier calls a short team meeting and has the team sit on the bleachers. Mr. Frazier tells the team everything he could dig up regarding the opposition for the upcoming meet. As he is speaking, Kathy, Paula and Barbara, the team assistants, walk down the metal staircase and sit with the team on the bleachers. Mr. Frazier tells the team, "Kathy, Paula and Barbara will now talk to you. Pay close attention to what they have to say." Going through the events one by one, Kathy, Paula, and Barbara offer the names of some of the competitors, and what their best-known time is for each race. After going through the running events, they move on to the high jump and shot-put. When the girls are done, Mr. Frazier dismisses the team for the day.

As the team walks up the metal stairway to the hallway, Eddie turns to check out Kathy, Paula, and Barbara from a higher vantage point. With his eyes on the girls rather than where he is going, Eddie trips and stumbles into Mark, taking Mark, who is also checking out the scenery, down with him. Braden, following Eddie, trips over Eddie, causing a domino effect on the stairway. Mr. Frazier, not missing a beat, yells out to them, "you guys can run, but it looks like you need a little help walking!" Mr. Frazier was clueless what caused the commotion, but everyone on the stairway knew.

In the locker room, Braden mentions to Eddie and Mark, "well at least there's one for each of you." Eddie and Mark laugh off Braden's comment, but Braden couldn't be closer than the truth. Braden, not letting the moment pass, asks Eddie, "so who gets who?" Eddie replies, "I'll take Kathy." Mark, who is glad to hear that, replies, "OK, then, I'll go with Paula." Eddie then says to

Braden, "well, that leaves you with Barbara." Braden, not missing a beat, replies, "I ain't shopping. I still have Wendy." Johnson pipes up and says, "remember, the coach said their job is to flirt," which is apparently the only thing Johnson remembers about the girls. Everyone eventually heads home, with a couple of new things to now think about.

Saturday morning arrives, and so do the busses transporting the competition, and a few spectators. Saturday morning meets usually begin at 10:00 a.m., and are usually done by 1:00 p.m. As the teams arrive, some student volunteers direct them to the proper location. Meanwhile, Mr. Frazier and the team are going over some last minute details. The most important detail that Mr. Frazier is discussing is that he wants to win. He reminds the team that, since this is a 4-way meet, there will be medals for the winners of each event. Medals issued for first, second, and third place are supposed to induce the runners to perform better.

At the requisite starting time, all of the runners are on the track, ready to go. The first event is the 40-yard dash. Since there are four teams, and each team is allowed to have three contestants, twelve runners will be competing. There will be two preliminary heats. The fastest six times will compete in the 40-yard dash final. Past performance determines whether a runner is in the first or second heat. As the coaches are discussing procedural issues, which they seem to do every year, Eddie spots McCutchen warming up. He points McCutchen out to Mark, who hopes to run against him in some event today.

Mr. Frazier walks over to his sprinters, and tells Eddie and Mark that they are in the first heat, and tells Johnson that he is in the second heat. Mr. Frazier tells Mark, Eddie, and Johnson, "don't let me down." That is all that the three sprinters need to hear in order to run a better race. The Meet Announcer tells all of the runners of the 40-yard dash to make their way to the starting line. The lane assignments for the preliminary heats are based upon qualifying times. Eddie is assigned to lane two, and Mark to lane four. McCutchen is not found among the sprinters.

As the runners get ready, the Centerville coach, Mr. Ruff, is complaining to one of the Timekeepers that the sprint is a 40-yard dash, not a 50 or 55-yard dash. Mr. Ruff makes this complaint every year. In Winter track, the sprint can be a 40-yard, 50-yard, 55-yard, or 60-yard dash, depending on the track size. Not to mention, the 40-yard dash happens to be the divisional standard. Mr. Ruff's complaining gets him nowhere, as one of the Timekeepers explains to him that it is a regulation track.

The Starter, who is the official that starts the races, makes the announcement, "on your marks." Ready to run their first high school meet, Eddie and Mark are filled with adrenaline. They are both aware that this is now real competition. The Starter, with a long drawn out tone, announces, "set." Waiting for the buzzer, the runners are in the "set" position and are motionless. Time appears to stand still. The Starter hits the buzzer, and the runners are off.

All of the runners are quickly out of the blocks. A few steps out of the blocks, the runners are all approaching their top speed. At ten yards there is a clear leader, Eddie. He is followed closely by Mark. One step behind Mark are two runners that are head to head. At the halfway point, Eddie quickly realizes that this is no easy race. Although he is in first place, if he does not keep up his speed, or move faster, he could be easily overtaken. At 30 yards into the race, it appears that Eddie has the race wrapped up. Out of his peripheral vision, he sees a runner to his right gaining ground. The last thing a runner wants to do is to turn his head to see who it may be. Turning your head during a sprint will cause you to slow your pace and run erratically, and perhaps lose your lead. Eddie, focused on the finish line, crosses first, followed very closely by Mark. After Mark, two runners cross at nearly the same time. The runners in fifth and sixth place are not too far behind, but will probably not make the final heat.

Wasting no time, the Meet Director tells the runners in the second heat to get ready. Eddie is watching the officials to see how they work together. He is looking for a way to anticipate the buzzer. He notices there are two officials operating the buzzers, one at the far end of the track and one at the starting line. Eddie, near the finish line, watches the runners as they get ready. He sees Johnson in lane four. The Starter at the starting line announces, "on your marks," as Eddie watches intently. The Starter then announces, "set." Off to the side of the track, the Starter fixes his gaze at the runners. Once the runners are set, he nods his head. Eddie hears the buzzer go off, but the Starter at the starting line did move his foot to operate the buzzer. Eddie surmises that the nod of the head signals the other Starter to hit the buzzer while the one at the starting line looks for a false start. If there is a false start, the Starter at the starting line would hit his foot switch, sounding the buzzer a second time. Eddie decides he would watch this more closely the next chance he got.

Meanwhile, during Eddie's deep thought, Johnson just came in second place is his heat. Eddie, Mark, and Johnson exchange high-fives, and will be in the final heat. As the attention turns toward the 4 by 220 relay race, the group heads back to the team bench to watch that event.

After some discussion between the Timekeepers, the Meet Announcer declares the results, "competing in the 100-yard dash final, Edward Bogenskaya, 4.5 seconds. Mark Svoboda, 4.55 seconds. Lucius Clay, 4.6 seconds. Alan Williams, 4.8 seconds. John Brady, 4.6 seconds. Eric Johnson, 4.7 seconds." With his three sprinters in the final, Mr. Frazier could not be more pleased with the results. Mark asks Mr. Frazier, "how did I get a 4.55?" Mr. Frazier explains to Mark, "Eddie got a 4.5, third place got a 4.6, so they assign the guy between them, you, a 4.55." Mark is not accustomed to a race where less than a tenth of a second potentially determines the winner and loser.

During the 4 by 220 relay event, Kathy, one of Mr. Frazier's team assistants, comes up to Eddie, and says to him, "so, you're Eddie?" Eddie simply replies, "yeah. That's me." Kathy tells Eddie, "that was a really good race you ran." Eddie, not used to the attention, tells Kathy, "yeah, but it's not over yet." Looking at her clipboard, Kathy tells Eddie, "you have the best time today." Eddie sees on Kathy's clipboard that the winner of the other heat ran a 4.6. Quickly flipping the page, Kathy looks at her stopwatch, and writes something down as Mahoney passes the baton to the next runner.

Kathy mentions to Eddie, "Mahoney's having a bad day." Eddie tells Kathy, "I don't really talk to him much." Kathy giggles, and tells Eddie, "that's because he doesn't like you. You're running his events. You're faster than he is, and he doesn't like it." Eddie, without thinking about what he is about to say, tells Kathy, "using his logic, no one should like me because I'm the fastest one here." Eddie thinks to himself, "wow, did I just say that?" Attracted to Eddie's confidence, Kathy tells him, "I'll have my eyes on you the whole time during the final." Touching Eddie on his arm, Kathy warmly says to him, "good luck," as she goes about her team duties.

At the end of the relay, Kathy confers with Mr. Frazier, and records the team's time. Kathy, Paula, and Barbara, each with several stopwatches hanging from their necks, also record the other team's approximate split and composite times. With the efforts of his three team assistants, Mr. Frazier has all the statistics he needs going into future competitions. Unknown to the other coaches, Mr. Frazier is running a high-tech organization.

The next event is the mile. Each team is allowed three runners, making for a crowded field on the 220-yard track. Following the one mile run will be the 40-yard dash final. The position of the 40-yard dash final within the order of events varies from meet to meet, with the coaches coming to a consensual agreement. This is because the finalists are scheduled for other events, and no coach wants their runners in back-to-back races. More so than the coaches, the runners also do not want to be in back-to-back events.

While the mile is underway, Eddie walks toward the starting line for the 40-yard dash. While he walking, he catches Kathy glancing his way, smiling at him when he catches her eye. Mark, already at the starting line, asks Eddie, "are you ready?" Eddie replies to Mark, "more than ever." Eddie sees Johnson headed their way. With six runners in the final, four of them were from Eddie's heat, and two from Johnson's.

Once the mile is completed, all eyes are on the 40-yard dash. The two Starters operating the buzzers move into position. The lanes are assigned to the finalists by another official. Eddie is in lane four, Mark in lane two, and Johnson in lane six. The better qualifying times are usually assigned the inside lanes. There is also an unofficial rule to not place runners on the same team next to each other if possible. At the finish line, there are two officials with Polaroid cameras, to get a photo of the finish. This will give objective evidence in the event of a close race.

Eddie, looking down the track, sees Kathy, looking right at him. Eddie remembers what she said a while ago, which is that she would have her eyes on him whole time. Mark walks over to Eddie, and whispers to him, "the guy in lane three has the best time of the competitors. I'm going to mess with his head." The Starter asks the runners if they are ready. Everyone indicates that they are ready. The Starter then announces, "on your marks." The runners position themselves in the blocks. When they are almost in position, Mark says to the runner in lane three, "I thought you told him you were ready." A split second after Mark's comment, the Starter announces, "set." Somewhat distracted, the runner in lane three turns his head and looks at Mark. Mark whispers to the runner in lane three, "your shoelaces." Taking Mark's advice, the runner in lane three examines his shoelaces. Eddie, meanwhile, has his eyes fixed on the Starter on the other end of the track. With the runner in lane three physically set, but not mentally ready to run, the buzzer sounds.

Eddie, as he saw the Starter's foot move, was out of the blocks first. The runner in lane three, who was distracted by Mark, was clearly out of the blocks last. This is the runner that had a time close to Eddie's during the qualifying heats. His slowness out of the blocks, which came as a great surprise, is noticed by all who are watching. Leaving the blocks last on a 40-yard race is a sure sign you will lose, for there is not sufficient distance to make up any lost time.

Eddie - The Freshman Year

At ten yards, Eddie and Mark are nearly tied, with Eddie having a slight lead. A group of three runners, which includes Johnson, are a few steps behind. The guy in lane three, who was distracted by Mark, is in last place. Eddie, remembering he told Kathy that he is the fastest person in the arena, must now deliver on his claim. Eddie, somehow finding some extra energy, is beginning to take a slightly greater lead over Mark.

Halfway through the race, Eddie is clearly ahead. Mark, however, is still close behind. Johnson is still in the middle of the pack of three. The runner in lane three is catching up to the pack, but is too far behind to catch the leaders. At 30 yards, Eddie will be the clear winner. It appears Mark will take second place. Third place, however, cannot be called with ten yards remaining. Eddie, who is too focused on the race, does not see Kathy, just beyond the finish line, watching his every step.

At the finish line, Eddie, knowing he has ran his fastest race ever, crosses the finish line first. Mark crosses second, a mere one yard behind Eddie. When the next of group of runners approach the finish line, third place is too close to call. As the runners cross the line, several flashes go off to catch it on film. The last place runner, three yards behind the photo finish crowd, finally crosses the finish line more than one second after Eddie.

The officials meet, examining the photographic evidence to find out who has earned third place. Some of the coaches want to see the photos, which they will, but won't be able to until after third place is called. Meanwhile, the guy who ran in lane three, distracted before the race by Mark, has some words to exchange. The lane three guy alleges to Mark, "you screwed up the whole race, you idiot! It needs to be run over." Mark simply tells the guy, "hey, it ain't my fault you can't run. Maybe you should practice sometime." Mark's comment did not sit well with the lane three guy, who tells Mark, "yeah, well, I'll kick your ass." Mark laughs quite audibly, and responds, "yeah, right. I'd love to see that." The lane three guy walks away, knowing that Mark has beaten him three times. Once before the race, again during the race, and finally after the race. The officials and coaches were too busy waiting to see who got third place to notice the exchange between Mark and the loser of the race.

The officials have made their decision. The coaches are now allowed to examine the photos. After careful examination of the results, none of the coaches object. Separating third and fourth place is only a few inches, which is common in this type of race. The Head Timekeeper takes the pleasure of declaring the final times. He announces, "Edward Bogenskaya, 4.4 seconds. Mark Svoboda, 4.5 seconds. Lucius Clay, 4.6 seconds. Eric Johnson, 4.65 seconds. Alan Williams, 4.65 seconds. John Brady, 5.1 seconds." Paying close attention is Brady, who now knows the name of his new opponent, both on the track and off. Paying close attention to Eddie is Kathy, who congratulates Eddie for his awesome victory.

Next up for Eddie is the 4 by 440 relay. The 4 by 440 relay is always the last event to be run. This is because the best runners are usually assigned to this relay race. Scheduling the race last gives the runners the most time to recover from their other events. For now, the attention is turned to another relay, the mile medley, which is owned by veterans this year. In the mile medley, there are two legs of 220 yards, one leg of 440 yards, and one leg of 880 yards. Mahoney gets the pleasure of running the 880-yard leg of the race.

Eddie, however, pays absolutely no attention to the race. Taking a seat on the bench to rest for a while, he has his first chance to observe what is happening as a spectator. Eddie hears the coaches telling the runners to run faster. Being a runner himself, he can assure the coaches that the runners are running as fast as they can. He can equally assure the coaches that the runners don't hear them screaming because they are too focused on running the race. Eddie also sees no less that three dozen people with stopwatches. One of them is Kathy, who seems to be paying more attention to Eddie on the bench than the race. Eddie catches Kathy looking in his direction a couple of times, and each time she is smiling.

Eddie is joined by Mark, Braden, and Johnson, who have all completed their individual events for the day. Braden tells the group, "I won the 440! I took first, second, and third place!" Braden was joking, for he only took first place. Mark points out to Braden, "the only way you can do that, bro, is if you're the only one in the race." Braden thinks about that for a second, and fires back, "I am the only one in the race! No one can beat me!" They all have a laugh at Braden's comeback. Johnson mentions, "I got second place in the 220. Some of these guys are fast."

While they are having their conversation, Kathy walks up to the relay team. Showing them her what is on her clipboard, she tells them, "your race is after this one. This is what you'll be up against." Kathy also mentions, "the times next to their names are not exact. But, the times are their best as far as we know." As they look over the list, Mark points to a line and says, "McCrutchen again. So, that's where they put him." Eddie also sees another name who is familiar to Mark. Eddie points to the runner's name, and says, "yeah, and there's Brady, from the 40-yard dash." Kathy adds some valuable information, "the good news is Brady can only run a 60-second quarter mile, and that's on a good day."

Braden asks, "do we know what order they go in?" Kathy, who acquired the information earlier, replies, "this is their order." Braden, the lead man, will be up against McCutchen and Brady. Mark asks Kathy, "can we change our order?" Braden interjects, "why?" Mark replies, "it's not every day that I'll get to kick McCrutchen's and Brady's ass in one race." Kathy tells Mark, "you'd have to ask Mr. Frazier about that." Kathy tells the team, "good luck," placing her hand gently on Eddie's back as she walks away.

The relay team approaches Mr. Frazier to see if they can change the order. Mark asks, "Mr. Frazier, can we change our order in the race?" Mr. Frazier replies, "what do you mean?" Mark asks Mr. Frazier, "can I be the lead man, and Braden the anchor?" Mr. Frazier asks the expected question in the form of a statement, "tell me why." Mark explains, "McCrutchen and Brady are the lead men for the other teams. I want to kick both of their asses at once, in one race!" Mr. Frazier smiles and laughs, and replies, "sure, go ahead. But, you'd better kick their ass!" Mr. Frazier explains to Braden, "hold the baton, and give it to Mark right before the race begins." Mark curiously asks, "why?" Mr. Frazier tells Mark, "they can make last minute changes as well, so you don't want to give them the chance." Mr. Frazier's reaction to their request was priceless. He also raised the energy level of the relay team, who is now even more fired up.

The officials tell the runners of the 4 by 440 relay teams to prepare for the final event. The teams meet at the starting line, with Braden holding the baton. Also holding batons are McCutchen and the veteran Brady. As McCutchen, Brady, and some unknown guy from Madison High all enter the track, Braden tosses the baton to Mark, who also enters the track. Mark points to McCutchen's shoes, invoking a little déjà vu in his mind. McCutchen remembers Mark well from last year's meet. Mark also points to Brady with his baton, and stares right into his eyes. Mark knows from Kathy that Brady can only run 440 yards in the lower 60-second range. Mark's display of playfulness, confidence, and relaxed attitude can only distract the opponents.

The Starter tells the runners, "on your marks." The runners get into position. The next command seems like it is delayed. Sure enough, McCutchen is not positioned yet, and is checking his shoelaces. The Starter announces, "set."

With the runners ready to go, the buzzer sounds. Mark leaves the starting blocks with enough speed to convince everyone he has something to prove. Casually looking at the runners, it is clear that Mark is in the lead. In second place is Brady, who has a score to settle. McCutchen, in third place, has many scores to settle with Mark. After the first lap, at 220 yards, Mark is clearly ahead of the other three runners. For the remainder of the first leg, the relative position of the runners remains the same, but the gap between each runner widens. Brady is desperately trying to catch Mark during the last lap, but simply can't. Mark passes the baton to Johnson, and leaves the track, returning to the starting point to join the other runners.

After Brady and McCutchen leave the track, they also return to the starting point. Brady looks at Mark, and has no words to say this time. Braden, however, has words for everyone to hear. Braden, giving Mark a high-five, impulsively blurts out, "you kicked their ass, big time!" McCutchen gets up the nerve to say to the tribe, "the race ain't over yet." Braden, reassuring everyone around, says, "oh yeah, it is! It was over when it started!"

Back on the track, Johnson is maintaining a solid lead. After the first lap is completed, the runner on McCutchen's team passes the runner on Brady's team. This is not good news for Johnson, for he is next on the runner's list to be passed. On the back straightaway of the last lap, the runner is gaining on Johnson but, with about 100 yards to go, Johnson sprints to the transition zone. Johnson delivers the baton to Eddie, and is the first runner in his leg to complete the transition.

Eddie leaves the transition zone running with the same speed with which he won the 40-yard dash. Eddie widens his lead over the other runners, who seem to be bunching up halfway through the leg. Another positional change occurs between Riverdale and Centerville, but all attention is focused on Eddie. With the rest of weekend to recover, Eddie sprints the last 100 yards. With Braden in his sites, Eddie hands off the baton, quickly looking back to see where the other runners are. Eddie knew, when he saw the runner in second place just coming out of the curve, the race has already been wrapped up.

Just as Eddie joins his other team members, Brady asks Eddie, "where did you guys come from? We haven't seen you before." Brady, a senior, does not remember Eddie, Mark, Braden, or Johnson from any previous meets. Mark, deciding to be the spokesman, answers, telling Brady, "we're freshmen. This is our first meet. It was good practice." McCutchen, a little distance away, was eavesdropping on their conversation. McCutchen mumbles to a teammate, "four more years of this shit to come. Oh wonderful."

Braden, with a comfortable lead, is taking no chances. He remembered Mr. Frazier told him to "kick their ass." Well, Mr. Frazier told the whole team to kick their ass, but kicking ass is somehow Braden's specialty. On the back straightaway, it becomes apparent that Braden has more than a 100-yard lead, or greater than ten seconds. After the first lap, Mr. Frazier knows Braden has the race all wrapped up.

As Braden is on his last lap, Kathy tells Eddie, "all of you ran a sub-60! It looks like Braden will too." Eddie asks Kathy, "what was my time?" Kathy replies, "you can't tell exactly because of the handoff, but it was definitely in the 54-second range." The focus shifts toward the finish line as Braden comes around the final curve. Braden crosses the finish line while the runner who is in second place is still in the final curve. In second place is Riverdale, which is Brady's team. They are followed by Centerville, which is McCutchen's team. In last place, from Madison High, is a relay team that ran as if it was the first relay race they've ever ran together.

With the meet now over, the officials make the announcement regarding the final score. Mr. Frazier is ecstatic when he hears his team won, but he suspected that would be the case halfway through the meet. The Meet Announcer instructs the spectators to move to the sides of the bleachers, opening up the center area for the runners. The official then tells the teams to have a seat on the bleachers for the awards ceremony. In just a few minutes, the winners will receive their medals. With more than 125 athletes in the arena, it takes several minutes to get everyone where they should be.

Standing behind the podium, the Meet Announcer addresses the runners, saying, "when I call your name, I want you to walk up to your coach, and receive your medal. You will stand behind your coach after you receive your award." The group of athletes standing behind their coach is the coach's reward for the meet. To both the left and right of the podium stand two coaches, spread out in the center of the oval track. Kathy, Paula, and Barbara stand with Mr. Frazier and Mr. Zunde to the far left side of the oval.

The official begins the announcements. "In the 40-yard dash, first place goes to Edward Bogenskaya. Come up please." Eddie walks up to Mr. Frazier, as an official hands the medal to Mr. Frazier. He continues calling the names of the winners, "in second place, Mark Svoboda, and in third place, Lucius Clay."

The Meet Clerk distributes the medals to the appropriate coach. The Meet Announcer then tells the coaches, "you may now drape the medals." Mr. Frazier hands the first place medal to Kathy. Simultaneously, Kathy drapes Eddie and Mr. Frazier drapes Mark. Some people notice that Kathy does a little more than draping the medal around Eddie's neck. She places her hands gently on his shoulders, and is very slow to remove them. The runners then stand behind Mr. Frazier, Mr. Zunde and their three team assistants. Mark whispers to Eddie, "bro, she likes you."

As the awards continue, Mr. Frazier's group is getting to be, by far, the largest. By the time the medals are to be distributed for the 4 by 440 relay event, Eddie's entire tribe is behind Mr. Frazier. Bobby B. placed third in the shot-put. Mitchell placed second in the 880-yard run and placed second in the mile. Johnson placed second in the 220-yard dash. Braden placed first in the 440-yard dash, letting everyone in the arena know that he won the gold medal in that event. This is not bad for freshmen, who were competing against mostly juniors and seniors. As for the rest of the team, the majority of the Northside track athletes are now standing behind the Northside coaches.

The official then announces the result of the 4 by 440 relay, "in first place, for Northside, Axel Braden, Eric Johnson, Edward Bogenskaya, and Mark Svoboda," which was the order in which they were supposed to run. With everyone looking at the bleachers waiting for the winners to come forward, the relay team, each already decorated with a medal, steps out from behind Mr. Frazier. The official announces the second and third place winners of the event. Second place goes to Riverdale, and third place to Centerville. The official instructs the coaches to drape the medals. Mr. Frazier hands one medal to Barbara, one to Paula, one to Kathy, and keeps one for himself to drape. He then tells the girls, "pick one," referring to a runner to drape. It did not take much time for Kathy to end up standing behind Eddie again. Kathy got behind Eddie so fast, it's a wonder that she's not on the track team herself. Mr. Frazier and his assistants proudly drape the four runners.

With the meet now over, the winners shake the hands of their opponents. The center of the oval track serves as the winner's circle. Eddie and his tribe mingle with the crowd for a few minutes. Some of the runners who are on the bleachers come down to congratulate the winners. After a while, the crowd thins out, and the visiting teams head to their busses.

On the back row of the bleachers, watching the meet, was Mr. Moreno, the football coach. Mr. Moreno was more interested in looking for a potential running back, wide receiver, or free safety than in the outcome of the meet. During the 4 by 440 relay, Mr. Moreno was visualizing the runners running with a football rather than a baton. He had his own clipboard, and was silently taking names. Mr. Moreno quietly slips out of the arena, unnoticed by all.

Eddie and his tribe have their own celebration in the locker room. This was their first big meet, and each of them walked away with at least one medal. Braden, showing off his medals, exclaims, "I finally got some proof that I kicked ass!" Bobby B., who took third place in the shot-put, is very excited. Mark comments, "imagine what it'll be like when we're seniors." A comment is then heard around the corner in the locker room, "if you ever get to be seniors." Eddie looks around the corner, as Mark asks, "who said that?" Eddie looks around the corner again, pretending not to know the team member making the comment, replies, "I don't know who he is." Mark, looking around the corner, says, "I think that's Mahoney." Eddie, getting Mark's drift, questions Mark and everyone else, "oh, so that's Mahoney?" Eddie and Mark have been ignoring Mahoney, and pretending not to know who he is. Mahoney has not learned that messing with the tribe is something you just don't do.

The locker room eventually empties out, and everyone goes home to have lunch and a relaxing afternoon. Eddie and Mark, who rode their bicycles to the meet, ride home together. As Eddie and Mark ride down the parking lot to the road, Kathy comes out of the front of the school hoping to find Eddie and talk with him for a while. She has been hanging out in the hallway, waiting for Eddie to come out of the locker room. She sees Eddie off in a distance, riding away, and is deeply saddened because she really wanted to see him. What she didn't know is that Eddie's and Mark's bicycles were locked up in the locker room, and Eddie and Mark left out of the back door near the gym. Her next chance to see Eddie will be Monday, if she can even find him before practice. Kathy starts her walk home alone, thinking all about today's meet on the way.

As Monday arrives, word gets around school that the team did well in the track meet. The wrestling team also had a good meet this weekend, with Gump beating his opponent in under a minute. After school today, Mr. Frazier will go over the meet, and again congratulate the winners. But, in the meantime, it's back to academics. During every class change, Kathy searches the halls for Eddie to at least say "hi," but has no such luck today. Being a sophomore, Kathy's classes aren't usually in the same area of the school as Eddie's.

After school, it's back to track practice for the team. Once the team is in the arena, Mr. Frazier instructs them to have a seat on the bleachers. Eddie, and his tribe sit near the end, closest to the metal stairway. Mr. Frazier addressing the team begins, "we had an awesome meet this weekend! I want to bring your attention to a few items. The first is in the individual events. We took more gold and silver medals than any of the other teams! And, we took more medals overall than all the other teams combined! I am proud of every single one of you!"

As Mr. Frazier continues speaking, Kathy, Barbara, and Paula walk down the metal stairway. Barbara walks up to Mr. Frazier and hands him a piece of paper, as Kathy and Paula have a seat on the bleachers. Kathy takes a seat next to Eddie, with Paula joining her. Mr. Frazier continues, "Barbara has given me a list with your approximate split times in the relay races." Mr. Frazier gives the team some interesting news, "the first thing I want to address regarding the relays is that some of your handoffs need a little work. So, that's what many of you will be working on today." He then continues, "now for your times. In the mile medley, Bell, your 220 was about 32 seconds, not bad." Mr. Frazier continues announcing the split times, with everyone listening for their name.

While Mr. Frazier continues to announce the times, Kathy places her hand on Eddie's thigh, whispering to him, "don't worry. Your times were seriously awesome, and Mr. Frazier has some good news for you!" Bell, who is seated in the row behind Eddie, but a little farther down, catches a glimpse of Kathy placing her hand on Eddie's thigh. Bell whispers to Mahoney, "he's got your events, now he's going after the girl you like." Mahoney looks to his left, and turns about as red as a ripe tomato. Kathy, knowing what is on the paper that Barbara gave to Mr. Frazier, whispers to Eddie, "here's your time coming up now." Mahoney, catching a glimpse of the whisper, can only presume what Kathy whispered in Eddie's ear.

Mr. Frazier then announces, "and, in the 4 by 440 relay, everyone ran a sub-60 second time!" He then gives the approximate times, "Mark, you ran a 54. Johnson, you ran a 55. Eddie, a 53, a 53! And Braden, you ran a 54." Mr. Frazier tells the team, "Braden said this team was going to kick ass, and they delivered! I'm very proud of this relay team!"

Mr. Frazier finishes by making the announcement, "in eight weeks, there will be a State level competition in the coliseum." He gives some further details, telling the team, "in order to be invited to this meet, you must first qualify. In order to qualify, you must simply deliver a qualifying time." A qualifying time is defined by the sport organizers, which is usually somewhere in the upper three percentile, based upon the statistics for the last few years. Then Mr. Frazier gives some good news, "some of you have already qualified!" Kathy whispers again in Eddie's ear, "that's the good news I was telling you about. You're going to the State invitational meet."

Mr. Frazier then tells the team to stretch and take a warm-up lap before practice begins. During the warm-up lap, Mahoney runs up next to Eddie and gives him a warning, "stay away from Kathy. She's mine." Eddie replies to the buffoon, "shut up, loser. The only thing that's yours is last place." Eddie starts running faster, not wanting to listen to Mahoney's babbling. Mahoney chases him, trying to prove that he is not a loser, but is unable to catch Eddie.

After the warm-up lap, Mr. Frazier assigns everyone to a group, and gives them their workout drills for today. Kathy, Barbara, and Paula will be helping Mr. Frazier with today's practice. They will be recording times, and working with the runners, giving them some ideas to help improve their performance. With so many qualifiers and the State invitational meet coming up, Mr. Frazier wants the best team he can deliver. Mahoney, whose best performance this past weekend was third place in the mile medley relay, is assigned to a group that will be working on their handoffs. Eddie, Mark, Braden, and Johnson are assigned to a group that will be running sprints for time. Mitchell will be running nonstop for the next hour with the other distance men. Bobby B. will head up the metal staircase to the weight room, joining the others in the shot-put event.

Mr. Frazier assigns each one of the three girls to work with a particular group. Mr. Frazier, himself, will be working with the runners who need help with their handoffs, since he is an expert in this area. Mr. Frazier assigns Kathy to work with the sprinters. Barbara, being a distance runner herself, will be working with the distance runners. Paula, who is new to the team of assistants, will be trading off between helping both Kathy and Barbara.

Mr. Frazier instructs Kathy to work on getting the runners to improve their start out of the blocks. Two things are important when running a sprint. The first is getting out of the blocks as fast as possible. The second is getting to your top speed as fast as possible. These two factors are often the difference between first and second place. Today, Kathy will be reviewing with the sprinters how to accomplish that goal.

Kathy has the sprinters prepare as if they are going to run a sprint. She picks six of the runners, and tells them to pick a lane. Included in the six are Eddie, Mark, Johnson, and Braden. Kathy explains, "the drill is to only run ten yards after leaving the blocks. Me and Paula will be watching to see who is the fastest out of the blocks." Paula is equipped with a Polaroid camera, to document who is the fastest out of the blocks. Kathy also tells the runners, "Mr. Frazier says you should be at your top speed three or four steps out of the blocks."

The runners are in their lanes and ready to go. Kathy announces, "on your marks," followed by, "set." After sounding the buzzer, the runners are out of the blocks as fast as they are able. Simultaneously, Paula snaps a photograph just after the buzzer goes off. The runners run ten yards, as Kathy makes a note of who was ahead at five yards. After the photograph is ready, Kathy and Paula are ready for the next group. The next group steps up to the blocks, and performs the same drill. Gathering around Paula as she is holding the photograph, the runners can easily see who was out of the blocks fast and who was not.

Eddie's group gets another turn. But, before they perform the drill, Kathy will explain the proper foot placement in the blocks. Calling Eddie to step up to the blocks, Kathy will use him for an example. Kathy explains to the group, "the position of the front starting block should be one-and-a-half to two times the length of your shoe from the starting line." Telling Eddie to get in the "set" position, Kathy adjusts the front block to Eddie's optimal position. Kathy tells the runners, "when it's your turn, memorize the setting on the front starting block, and don't forget it."

She then tells the group that the position of the rear block depends on the height of the runner, which is generally two-and-one-half feet to three feet from the starting line. Kathy, holding onto Eddie's rear leg, adjusts the rear block to his optimal setting. Kathy tells the runners, "the front leg should be bent to 90 degrees at your knee, and the back leg should be at 120 degrees when you are in the 'set' position." She tells the runners, "when it's your turn, you will look at the setting of the rear block, and memorize that number too."

The last things Kathy checks for are that Eddie's hands are three inches in front of his shoulders and three inches outside of his shoulders, and that his waist is bent at 45 degrees. Kathy comes over to Eddie, and places his hands in the correct position, which may have been a fraction of an inch off. Eddie hands were actually in the correct position, but Kathy seems to be giving Eddie a lot of extra attention today.

Meanwhile, watching Eddie and Kathy carefully from the oval track is Mahoney, who is performing relay drills. Mahoney, who is about to receive the baton, has his eye fixed on Kathy positioning Eddie's hands rather than the runner behind him. Next to Mahoney is another runner, also about to receive a baton. Mahoney, still looking at Kathy with her hands on Eddie, catches the runner about to handoff to him in his peripheral vision. He then comes back to reality, and realizes he should have started running a second or two ago. As he starts running, the runner handing off has to drastically slow his pace, and trips over Mahoney during the delivery. They both go down on the track, taking down with them two other runners who were also in the middle of a handoff. With four runners down on the track, Mr. Frazier blows his whistle. Mr. Frazier, who saw exactly what happened, is not happy at the moment.

Back at the sprinting drills, everyone turns to see what happened. Mark, who usually has some interesting commentary, states the obvious, "well, that didn't go exactly as planned." Braden replies, "yeah, I'd say. There's Mahoney and Ambrosini thinking like they're playing a game of Kill the Man with the Baton." The runners lay on the track for a while, and are slow to get up.

Kathy instructs Eddie to get ready again, making sure he is properly positioned. She tells Eddie, "on your marks," which he already is. She then tells Eddie, "set." With Eddie perfectly positioned, Kathy sounds the buzzer, and Eddie leaves the blocks. After sprinting ten yards, he returns to the starting line. Kathy asks Eddie, "do you notice any difference?" Eddie replies, "yeah! Big time! I'm definitely out of the blocks faster and stronger." Kathy then tells the group, "it also looked like Eddie may have been up to his top speed faster." Kathy tells the group, "I want the first group to set the blocks using the information I just went over. Then, we'll run another drill." Eddie, Mark, Johnson, and Braden, who are in the first group, get ready for the drill. Kathy and Paula help each runner with their optimal block position.

Once everyone has their blocks set, Kathy tells them to memorize their block settings. When they are ready, Kathy announces, "on your marks." She then announces, "set." Once everyone thinks they are in the "set" position, Kathy checks all the runners, making sure they are actually in their optimal position. After sounding the buzzer, the runners are all out of the blocks. Paula snaps another photograph after the buzzer goes off. The runners run their requisite ten yards and return to the starting line. Kathy asks, "OK, now! How was that?" Everyone agrees that they were able to leave the blocks a little faster and stronger. Kathy tells the runners, "check your blocks and make sure you have your setting numbers memorized." She then goes through the procedure with the rest of the sprinters.

Kathy takes Paula aside, telling her, "it looks like Mark needs a little extra help with the blocks." Paula, who seems quite naive, tells Kathy, "actually, it looks like he's doing really good." Kathy, whispering to Paula, explains to her, "he's looking more at you than the blocks, or anything else. Don't you see it?" Paula responds, "I just thought he was paying attention to what we were telling them." Kathy, again explaining the facts to Paula, "yeah, he's paying attention, all right. To you! He knows how to run. That's obvious. He doesn't need much help in that area." Paula finally concedes, and tells Kathy, "OK, I'm going to watch him and see."

While the other sprinters are getting set up, Eddie thinks back to the meet this past weekend. No one really paid too much attention to the way their blocks were set up. Many of the runners, Eddie recalls, just used the blocks where they were already positioned. He also wonders how Kathy knows so much about the art of sprinting. Eddie, who previously relied on pure strength and speed, quickly realizes that sprinting is more complicated than he originally thought.

At the end of practice, Mr. Frazier has the team sit on the bleachers. As usual, he goes over the good and the bad. The good news today is that the sprinters have all improved their starts. Mr. Frazier, after examining the photographic evidence, announces, "it looks like Eddie, Mark and Braden are the fastest out of the blocks." Mr. Frazier also tells the team, "Mitchell, it looks like you're ready to run a marathon." Today, Mr. Frazier has an abundance of good news and compliments for the team.

The only bad news the runners heard is about the relay handoffs. Mr. Frazier announces, "some of you still need a little help on your handoffs." He then mentions, "and, Mahoney! Make sure you have collision insurance next time you get on the track!" Everyone laughs at Mr. Frazier's comment, except for Mahoney of course. Mr. Frazier, however, did not say this to be funny, but to make sure that a collision like that never happens again. Mr. Frazier dismisses the team, and they all head to the locker room.

As Eddie leaves the locker room, he walks toward the front door. Kathy is sitting on a bench in the school lobby waiting for him. Kathy, standing up and walking with him, says, "that was a really good workout." Eddie replies, "yeah, I learned a lot today. You're really good." Kathy softly asks Eddie, "are you headed home?" Eddie replies, "yeah. I'm walking." Hoping that was the case, Kathy replies, "I'll walk with you."

Today, Kathy finally gets her time alone with Eddie. As Eddie and Kathy walk out together, Kathy asks Eddie, "OK now, I have to ask. You're a freshman, and you're faster than all the seniors. How is that? What's up?" Eddie, who wasn't even sure he'd make the track team, answers, "I don't know. I ride my bicycle a lot, work out, and take some vitamins. I have some weights at home, a bench, and a squat rack that I sort of built myself." Kathy tells Eddie, "wow, you'll have to show it to me sometime." It is clear to anyone, just by looking at Kathy's body, that she also works out.

Kathy, who is getting really interested, then asks Eddie, "where do you ride to?" Eddie replies, "well, over the Summer, I ride to the beach a couple of times during the week." Kathy says, "wow, that's like a long ride." Eddie replies, "it's only eleven miles. It's really not too far." Also liking the beach, Kathy tells Eddie, "I really like the beach too, but I never thought about riding my bicycle there." Eddie asks, "do you ride a lot?" Kathy replies, "mostly to get to my friends' houses." Eddie and Kathy have a nice conversation on their way home.

Kathy's house, which is around the corner from Bobby B., is on the way to Eddie's house. When they arrive at Kathy's house, Kathy tells Eddie, "well, this is my stop." Before she goes inside, Eddie asks Kathy, "do I get to know the last name of the girl I just walked home?" Kathy replies, "oh, yeah. Well, um, to start with, my real name is not Kathy." Eddie asks the obvious, "wow! Then what is your name?" Kathy replies, "Katarina Karakova." Pausing for a moment, Eddie repeats to Kathy, "Katarina Karakova. Wow! That's the most beautiful name I've ever heard!" Giving Eddie a hug, Kathy leaves absolutely no mistake about her level of interest in him. She expresses to Eddie, "I've enjoyed our walk. See you tomorrow?" Eddie replies, "yeah. That would be really nice, Katarina Karakova." Kathy smiles, gives Eddie another hug, and walks up to her house. Eddie continues walking home, thinking that high school has just gotten a lot better.

The next day before school starts, Kathy, sitting on a bench in the school lobby, anxiously waits for Eddie to arrive. As she is waiting, Mahoney comes up to Kathy and strikes up a conversation. Mahoney's dialog goes about as smooth as 40-grit sandpaper on silk. Mahoney, who finally gets up the nerve to ask

Kathy out on a date, asks, "do you want to go and get some pizza with me after track practice today?" Kathy declines, telling Mahoney, "you shouldn't be eating pizza when you're in training!" Kathy then sees Eddie walk into the school building. She abruptly ends her conversation with Mahoney, telling him, "I'm sorry. I got to go." Mahoney, a bit puzzled by Kathy abruptly ending their conversation, watches as she runs across the lobby.

Kathy runs up to Eddie. She takes him by the arm, and locks elbows with him. As they walk through the lobby, Kathy tells Eddie, "good morning! I've missed you!" Kathy's warm good morning leaves absolutely no doubt as to her intentions. Kathy walks Eddie to class as Mahoney tries to pull the dagger out of his chest. Kathy, walking Eddie down the hall, does so in a way that is noticed by all. When they arrive at Eddie's class, Kathy walks in with him in a way that advertises to everyone that Eddie is now with her. Kathy tells Eddie, "see you after school." Eddie replies, "yeah, definitely."

Walking over to the window, Eddie takes his seat near Mark, Braden, and Bobby B. Mark asks Eddie, "so, what's up with Kathy?" Not wanting to become the center of attention, Eddie replies, "I think she likes me." Braden says, "yeah, so tell us something we don't know." Wendy brilliantly stays out of the conversation, seeing it as "guy talk." Mark comments, "yeah, she likes you all right. Everyone can see that. It's been obvious since the first time she met you."

Braden, who is very observant, tells Mark, "yeah, and I've noticed that Paula has been looking at you a lot more recently." Mark asks, "really? She has?" This is good news to Mark, who has had his eye on Paula for a while. Braden tells Mark, "yeah, she's got her hands all over you when she's helping you with the blocks." Miss Starr walks into the classroom, sparing Eddie from the game of 20 questions with his friends. Mark, however, wanted the conversation to continue, as he wanted to hear more. If he is lucky, Mark might hear more from his buddies during the next class.

The next class is science class, specifically Earth Science. The group walks into class, and takes their usual seat, near the window. Somehow, for Eddie, just staring out at an open field is sometimes more interesting than listening to some of the crap they teach in school. Mr. Lambert, the teacher, tells everyone to have a seat so he can begin. Today's discussion is about the weather, specifically lightning.

During the lecture, Mark whispers to Eddie, "so, honestly, do you think Paula likes me?" Eddie asks Mark, "honestly?" Mark replies, "yeah." Eddie drops the bombshell, "bro! It's obvious to everyone but you. She does, no doubt." Mark replies, asking, "you ain't shittin' me, are you?" Eddie replies, "no. She's looking at you all the time, and she has her hands all over you every chance she gets."

Mr. Lambert hears Eddie talking to Mark during class. With all of his craftiness, Mr. Lambert asks Eddie, "Eddie, I presume you are discussing my lecture with Mark. Did you have a question, or can I clear something up for you?" Eddie replies, "yes." Mr. Lambert replies, "OK, Eddie, what is it?" Clearing up any doubt that he was listening to Mr. Lambert, Eddie replies to him, "you said lightning strikes the highest thing in the area, right?" Mr. Lambert confirms, "yes, that is correct." Eddie then asks his question, "so, if lightning strikes the highest thing in the area, that means you should not smoke pot during a thunderstorm, right?"

The whole class bursts out in laughter, including Mr. Lambert, who desperately tries to hide his own amusement. Mark, with an inside joke, adds, "or take psycho Chubin." Eddie, Braden, Bobby B., and anyone else who remembers that incident from health class, begins to crack up even more. Mr. Lambert, realizing the best thing to do is just let the laughter run its course, has a problem containing his own laughter. After five minutes or so, the class is finally back to order, and Mr. Lambert continues his lecture. One thing was learned today. You can't outsmart Eddie on the track or in the classroom.

At the end of the day, it's back to track practice for the team. Practice is uneventful, other than Mahoney giving Eddie the occasional evil eye. Eddie has no knowledge of what transpired between Mahoney and Kathy before he got to school this morning. During practice, Mahoney asks Ambrosini, "how much did Eddie bench in gym class that day?" Ambrosini, who cannot remember, replies, "something like 250 pounds. The rumor is that he can do a lot more." Ambrosini tells Mahoney, "those four guys are animals." Mahoney was asking because he is attempting to compare Eddie's strength with his own. Mahoney quickly realizes he comes up short in that category too.

At the end of today's practice session, Kathy asks Eddie, "do you want to go get pizza after practice today?" Eddie says, "sure! Let me just call my mom and tell her not to wait for me for dinner." Kathy, happy as can be, says, "OK then! It's a date!" This, of course, is overheard by Mahoney, who is now pulling the second dagger out of his chest today. Mahoney, who tries to forget about it, keeps thinking about Kathy's earlier comment, "you shouldn't be eating pizza when you're in training."

Eddie and Kathy walk to the pizzeria, which is only a minor detour from their walk home. The team members in the front of the school see Eddie and Kathy as they walk away, holding hands. Since it is cold out, they are walking close together. No one really thinks too much about Kathy and Eddie walking together, except for Mahoney, who is red with envy.

Kathy and Eddie talk about track on the way to dinner. Eddie asks Kathy, "so how did you learn all about setting the blocks?" Kathy tells him, "oh, that's an easy one. My dad is an Exercise Science professor over at the University, which means he's basically a glorified gym teacher. My dad, Mr. Frazier, and Mr. Zunde are friends." Kathy again tells Eddie, "I'm still amazed how fast you are. Not only you, but your friends." Eddie says, "oh, you mean the tribe." Kathy, in wonderment, asks, "the tribe?" Eddie responds, "yeah. Me, Mark, Braden, and Bobby B." Eddie explains, "Anthony Ambrosini said to me in gym class one day during a football game, 'what kind of tribe are you running?' Since then, we've been known as 'the tribe.'" Kathy tells Eddie, "I like that, 'the tribe.'" In an afterthought, Eddie adds, "oh, yeah. Johnson and Mitchell are also in the tribe." Once they get to the pizzeria, shop talk is over, and the conversation shifts more toward other topics.

Following a two-hour dinner at the pizzeria, Kathy and Eddie begin to walk home. The sun set a while ago, so the temperature is quickly dropping. After walking down the main road, they turn right onto a dark road leading toward Kathy's house. Being cold and dark outside, the road is mostly deserted, with an occasional car driving by. As they get within view of Kathy's house, Kathy tells Eddie, "I really liked our day." Eddie replies, "yeah, me too." Kathy stops, turns toward Eddie, and asks, "what are we doing tomorrow?"

Before Eddie can even answer the question, Kathy's puts her arms are around his neck, and tells him, "I don't want to go. Make the night last longer!" Kathy touches her lips to Eddie, surprising him with a little more than a goodnight kiss. Eddie and Kathy embrace each other again, this time longer, as they hug each other tightly. As they finish their walk home, both know something changed just then. When they get to Kathy's house, Kathy sighs and says, "well, here's my stop again. We should have taken the long way." Eddie tells Kathy, "this has been my favorite day ever." Kathy and Eddie walk up to the door, and say good night to each other. As Kathy goes inside, Eddie walks to the sidewalk and makes his way home.

The next day at school, Kathy is sitting on the bench in the school lobby again waiting for Eddie to arrive. When Eddie walks in, Kathy runs up to meet him. Kathy takes Eddie's arm and walks him to class, getting there a little early this time. They talk in the hallway for a while. But, as the halls empty out, Kathy has to get to class or she'll be late. In front of the open classroom door, Kathy gives Eddie a quick kiss before she heads down the hall. Kathy, in essence, made it a point to let everyone around know that Eddie is now unavailable.

Eddie walks into the classroom, and takes his usual seat. Braden, the only one to make a comment, says to Eddie, "that looks like a little more than just liking you." Eddie, who has his mind elsewhere, just replies, "I guess so." Meanwhile, Mark is busy copying an assignment he failed to complete for the next class. Mark is hoping for the conversation to come back to Paula, but there is no such luck today. Bobby B., just staring out the window, is not even fully awake yet. Eddie, the only energetic one in the group, cannot wait until school is over so he can see Kathy again.

For the next few weeks, the team practices several times a week. The meets, which are primarily held on the weekends, all go well. Eddie and his tribe gain a lot of confidence over the season, especially in the 4 by 440 relay. With the State invitational meet in the near future, Mr. Frazier and his team assistants give some additional attention to the athletes who have been invited to the event. Eddie still does some extra training at home, and is taking the vitamins and amino acids that were recommended by the doctor.

Kathy has also been spending a lot of time with Eddie, but not just in the capacity of helping out with the team. One afternoon after school, Eddie invites Kathy over to see his workout area. Kathy has been wanting to see it, and today is her chance. It's not so much that she wants to see the workout area, but that she wants to be with Eddie. Eddie and Kathy walk home from school, and stop by Kathy's house. They walk inside, and drop her stuff off. Kathy tells Eddie, "I'll be right back," as she runs upstairs for a few minutes.

As Kathy comes downstairs, Eddie looks and sees that she changed into workout clothes. Eddie, stating the obvious, says to Kathy, "you changed." Kathy replies, "yeah! You didn't think I was just going to look at your equipment! We're using it!" Eddie, surprised that Kathy wanted to work out, is definitely excited. Kathy gets her jacket, and they head out the door.

When they get to Eddie's house, Eddie introduces Kathy to his mother. After a short conversation, Eddie's mom asks Kathy, "would you like to stay for dinner?" Without any hesitation, Kathy replies, "oh, I'd love to! Let me just call my mom and make sure it's OK." As Kathy is calling her mom, Eddie is thinking that he'll have more time to be with Kathy if she can stay. After Kathy hangs up the phone, she says to Eddie and his mom, "well, the answer is," and after a long pause she says, with excitement, "I can stay!" Eddie's mom smiles and says, "OK, I'll set another plate."

Eddie and Kathy head downstairs to work out. Kathy, looking at Eddie's bench and squat rack, says, "wow! Nice set up!" Eddie asks, "what do you want to work on first?" Kathy replies, "we're doing bench first. Do you think you can keep up with me?" Eddie smiles, and replies, "probably not, but I'll give it a try." This is something Eddie really likes about Kathy. She is very assertive, and has no problem expressing herself. Eddie loads the bar with 50 pounds, and Kathy does a warm-up set. Eddie is impressed that Kathy knows exactly what to do.

Eddie continues to raise the weight for Kathy, getting up to 100 pounds. Kathy, laying on the bench, tells Eddie, "OK, spot me." Kathy lowers the bar to her chest, and raises the bar without any help. All energetic, Kathy tells Eddie, "let's do 120, please, please, please!" They put ten more pounds on each side, and Kathy gets back on the bench. Laying on the bench, Kathy tells Eddie, "I've never done 120 before." Eddie, giving Kathy some confidence, tells her, "yeah, but you will today." Kathy lowers the weight to her chest, and starts to raise the bar. Eddie tells her, "come on, you can do it, you can do it!" As Kathy raises the bar, Eddie tells her, "push, push!" After Kathy returns the bar to the uprights all by herself, she gets off the bench. She gives Eddie a high-five as she exclaims, "new max! Awesome!"

Kathy tells Eddie, "OK, now it's your turn!" Eddie gets on the bench and does a warm-up set. While Eddie is doing his warm-up set, Kathy takes two dumbbells and starts doing overhead dumbbell presses. After Eddie finishes his warm-up set, he looks over at Kathy working with the dumbbells. Teasing Eddie, Kathy says, "you didn't think I was going to just sit around and watch, did you?" Eddie replies, "it almost looks like you've done this before." Kathy humorously replies, "yeah, maybe once or twice." It is clear to Eddie that Kathy is no novice at working out. Kathy and Eddie have more fun working out together than they could have imagined. After working out for about an hour, Kathy and Eddie head upstairs for dinner.

After dinner, it comes time for Eddie to walk Kathy home. Kathy tells Eddie's mom and dad, "thank you so much for having me over for dinner. It was really good!" Eddie's mom tells Kathy, "we've enjoyed having you. Come over anytime." Eddie is certainly glad to hear that. Eddie's mom says to Kathy, "it's cold out. Would you like me to drive you home?" Kathy replies, "no, thank you. It's only a half mile, and we like to walk." As they walk out the door, Eddie tells his mom, "I'll be back later."

On the way, Kathy tells Eddie, "we're taking the long way home today." Eddie replies, "which way is that?" Kathy tells Eddie, "when we get there, I'll show you." As they approach the elementary school, Kathy takes a detour into the schoolyard. There is another smaller entrance for kids who walk to school on the other side of the field, which is actually a shortcut to Kathy's house. Eddie tells Kathy, "this looks like it's a short cut." Kathy, leaving Eddie wondering, tells Eddie, "no, it's the long way. You'll see."

Walking through the field, Eddie tells Kathy, "I really had a great time today." Kathy replies, "me too. We'll have to work out together more often." As they are walking, they come up to a small row of bleachers next to the pee wee ball field. Kathy sits on the bleachers, and Eddie sits next to her, holding her hand. Kathy gets up and sits on Eddie's lap. Putting her arms around Eddie, Kathy looks Eddie in the eye, telling him, "this, Eddie, is the long way home." Kathy kisses Eddie, with an embrace so warm it could melt the light snow that is beginning to fall. Kathy and Eddie make out on the bleachers for quite a while, each wondering where the other has been their entire lives.

Eventually, they have to continue their way back to Kathy's house. As they stand up, and walk, neither Kathy nor Eddie can walk straight. Seemingly drunk with each other's passion, they stumble toward the school entrance on Kathy's street. Eddie tells Kathy, "I really like the long way home." Kathy, passionately tells Eddie, "when I say, 'let's take the long way home', well, this is the long way home."

As they approach Kathy's house, Kathy sighs because the evening is coming to an end. She says to Eddie, "well, here's my stop again." Eddie walks Kathy to the door. They kiss goodnight, and Kathy passionately whispers in his ear, "see you tomorrow." Kathy goes inside, as Eddie walks to the sidewalk. As Eddie walks away, Kathy watches through the window, sad that Eddie has to make the half mile walk home by himself. To Eddie, who can easily run a half mile in less than two minutes and thirty seconds, but the trip home seems like it takes forever without Kathy.

A few days later, Eddie's mother, Nina encounters Mark's mother, Mariana, at the local farmers market. They both shop in the same markets, and see each other quite frequently. Nina tells Mariana, "Eddie's got a girl now, so he's not home as much. She's good for him. They really like each other." Mariana replies, "Mark's got his eye on someone too, some girl helping out with the track team." Nina tells Mariana, "I guess they're at that age." Bearing some good news, Nina tells Mariana, "Eddie and his girl, Katarina, go out and eat after school a lot. He's even saving me a little on my grocery bill!" Nina and Mariana compare notes as usual about what is fresh or a good deal. They then continue shopping on their own, only to meet again on another day.

With the State invitational meet just around the corner, Eddie invites his parents, his friends, and everyone he knows. Eddie knows that, with people watching him, he will run a better race. Mark, Braden, and Johnson, Mitchell, and Bobby B. also invite their parents, who were all going to show up anyway. Mitchell also invites his girlfriend, Amber Amy, who is still in middle school. Forming their own cheerleading squad, the tribe will definitely gain a slight edge over the competition. Paula and Barbara also invite their parents to the meet. Kathy, however, has a surprise for Eddie about her parents attending the meet.

The day of the State invitational meet finally arrives, and the team meets at the school. They will take the bus together to the coliseum, which is about eight miles away. Mr. Frazier is proud to have a good number of competitors going to the meet this year. Most schools are lucky to have one or two runners who qualify for the State invitational meet. Eddie will be running the 40-yard dash and the 4 by 440 relay today. Mark and Braden will be running the 440-yard dash, and will be later joining Eddie and Johnson in the 4 by 440 relay. Johnson, taking first place in a 220-yard dash during a 4-way meet late in the season, qualified for that event. Mitchell, who qualified in the mile, will also be competing today. Darryl Bell, who also qualified in the 220-yard dash, will be joining Johnson in that event. A handful of other runners, who are mostly juniors and seniors, fill the rest of the bus. Conspicuously missing from the bus today is Paul Mahoney, who's best performance this season was third place in the 880-yard run.

Sitting on the bus next to Eddie, not surprisingly, is Kathy. Kathy, who was present at the State invitational meet last year, knows how tough the competition can be. Kathy tells Eddie, "this is going to be the hardest meet of the year. Mr. Frazier was so happy last year when the team took home one medal." Eddie optimistically replies, "hopefully, we can do better than that this year." Kathy, holding Eddie's hand during the entire trip, knows this will be a really hard meet for Eddie. Eddie has placed first in every event he ran this year, so she is hoping he doesn't get too upset if he doesn't take home a medal today. Eddie tells Kathy, "I invited my whole family. Maybe I'll run faster." Kathy tells Eddie, "my mom is going to be watching too." Eddie asks, "how about your dad?" Kathy smiles, and tells Eddie, "oh, that's a surprise! You'll see."

After a short trip, the bus arrives and the team disembarks. Mr. Frazier instructs the team, "OK everyone, follow me, and don't get lost." Mr. Frazier has been to the coliseum many times before, and knows his way around well. After Mr. Frazier checks in with the security guard, the team enters through a gate which leads to a long tunnel. At the end of the tunnel are the entrances to the locker rooms. The team gets settled in their assigned locker area. Once everyone is ready, the team heads out another tunnel to the arena. When Mark sees the track, he exclaims, "OK, now this is really the big time!" The team meets up with Kathy, Barbara, and Paula, who entered the arena through the women's locker room.

The first event up is the 40-yard dash. Mr. Frazier tells Eddie that his best time this year is in the top four of the field of 28 runners. This is encouraging, since no one really wants to come in last place. Coming in last place will make the event feel like a wasted effort. Once the 40-yard dash gets underway, the meet will move along quickly. Until then, most of the runners sit around nervously waiting for something to happen.

The announcement finally comes signifying the start of the meet. The Meet Announcer introduces the meet officials, including the Meet Director, whose name is Dr. Alexander Karakova. Kathy whispers to Eddie, "I told you I had a surprise for you." Eddie whispers back, "wow, I'll be running right in front of you and your dad." The Meet Announcer then introduces the teams that are present, and opens the meet with a prayer. After the announcements, the Meet Announcer tells the contestants in the 40-yard dash to meet at the starting position in ten minutes. Nearby is a bulletin board that has the heat and lane assignments for each runner, which each runner checks before the race.

Eddie, in the second heat, feels like he is under enormous pressure. Kathy tells Eddie, "remember your block settings. Good luck, sweetie. I'll see you at the finish." Kathy jogs over to the finish line so that she can be there when Eddie finishes. As the first heat gets ready to run, Eddie, and the rest of the second heat, lines up a few yards behind them. Once the runners appear to be ready, the Starter tells the runners, "on your marks." Eddie watches carefully to observe the procedure. The Starter then announces, "set." Eddie looks around, and sees nothing unusual, other than there are many more officials than usual. The buzzer sounds, and the runners are out of the blocks. In five seconds the race, which that Eddie paid little attention to, is over. As the second heat gets ready, Eddie notices another race, the mile, has already started.

The Meet Announcer tells the second heat to get ready to run. Eddie, assigned to lane four, adjusts the blocks with the settings given to him by Kathy. Eddie also notices that, even though this is a State invitational meet, some runners do not pay attention to the block settings. The Starter tells the runners, "on your marks." In a few seconds, the Starter announces, "set." Eddie is set, and is ready as ever for the buzzer to sound. The buzzer sounds, and Eddie is out of the blocks like a madman on a mission. At ten yards, Eddie is in the lead, and presumably at his top speed. He hears the runner to his right gaining on him. He knows the sound of a runner right behind him very well. Eddie, somehow, is able to move his legs even faster. With ten yards to go, Eddie adds to his lead. In another second, Eddie crosses the finish line first, winning his heat.

The runner in lane five, who was gaining on Eddie, came in second place. Third through fifth place, however, is up for discussion. While the officials must determine the third, fourth, and fifth place runners and their times, technically it does not matter. In this particular heat, anyone finishing after second place will not be in the final. Their times were simply not good enough. As the officials examine the photographs, Eddie walks over to Kathy and Mr. Frazier, standing in the coaches area.

Mr. Frazier congratulates Eddie, giving him a high-five. Eddie asks Mr. Frazier, "what was my time?" Mr. Frazier tells Eddie, "we both clocked you at 4.5! But, they won't publish the official times until all of the heats are over." Eddie asks, "why not?" Mr. Frazier explains, "in the preliminaries, to be fair, if you knew the time to beat, you'd have an advantage." Eddie understands, but is nevertheless ecstatic with his unofficial time. Mr. Frazier tells Kathy and Eddie, "I'm going over to Mitchell. He's running the mile."

Kathy, who has to act more reserved around Mr. Frazier, lets out her excitement, as Mr. Frazier jogs away. With Mr. Frazier gone, Kathy gives Eddie a high-five and exclaims, "you ran really, really good!" Eddie asks, "do you think it's good enough for the final?" Kathy whispers to Eddie, "so far it is." Just then, the Starter announces, "on your marks." Kathy tells Eddie, "OK, I got to get back to work." Kathy, clipboard in hand, is ready to time the next heat and record any times she can. Eddie goes back to the team bench area, waiting for his next event, which will hopefully be the 40-yard dash final.

When the preliminary 40-yard dash heats are completed, Kathy walks over to the team bench. She whispers in Eddie's ear, "you made the final. You're the number three seed." Kathy then walks over to Mr. Frazier, who is talking with Johnson. Johnson is about to run in the 220-yard dash, and will have a tough race. Kathy lets Mr. Frazier know what she found out, telling him, "Eddie's in. He's the number three seed." Mr. Frazier grins ear to ear, seen by Eddie all the way over at the team bench. Kathy goes over to the bulletin board, and writes down the runner's names and lane assignments in Johnson's heat. Getting her stopwatches ready, Kathy goes to work with Paula, recording as many of the runner's times as they can. This information will prove valuable to Mr. Frazier and the team in future meets.

Meanwhile, Barbara notices the times were posted for the 40-yard dash. She writes them down on her clipboard, and delivers them to Mr. Frazier. Mr. Frazier, looks over the list, and tells her to show the list to Eddie. Barbara walks over to the team bench, and hands Eddie the list. Eddie looks over his competition, and notices his time was a 4.6, not a 4.5. Two other runners were clocked at 4.5. The other runners were all in the upper 4-second range.

Eddie wonders why his times were slower than in the other meet. He mentions to Louis Zaino, a junior who is looking over the list with him, "I wonder why my time is not as good as the last meet. I thought I ran faster." Eddie's teammate tells him, "it's the Timekeepers. As long as the same Timekeepers are working the clocks, everything's consistent." Eddie asks Zaino, "so, my best, which is a 4.4, could have been a 4.6?" Zaino says, "exactly, but winning is the only thing that counts." Explaining further, Zaino tells Eddie, "you're at this meet because you won a lot of races, not only because of what your times were." Zaino has a point. Eddie decided he would be more focused on winning than on his times for today.

The last call for the 40-yard dash final is made. The Meet Announcer broadcasts, "will the 40-yard dash contestants please check the roster located on the bulletin board. If you are a finalist, please be at the starting location for that event in five minutes." None of the runners have to look at the roster. They've all already looked at it immediately after it was posted a while ago.

The finalists know who they are, and what lane they are in. But, nevertheless, the official announcement has to be made.

Eddie walks over to the starting area, and Kathy joins him on the way. Mr. Frazier is already positioned near the finish line, and is wise enough to let Kathy escort Eddie to the starting area. Mr. Frazier is no idiot. He sees what is going on between Eddie and Kathy. If her presence can make him run faster, Mr. Frazier will stay out of the way. Kathy tells Eddie, "remember your block settings." Eddie tells her, "don't worry about that. I got those down now." Kathy, informs Eddie, "I have to go over to the finish line. I'm still working." Before she leaves, Kathy whispers in Eddie's ear, "run this one for me." Kathy then walks to the finish line to join Mr. Frazier.

The Starter tells the runners, "this is the final for the 40-yard dash. Please take your lanes." The runners set their blocks, and stand behind them when they are ready. Eddie, the third seed, is in lane five. In lane four is none other than John Brady, the top seed, who Eddie beat in a 4-way meet earlier this year. This is the guy Mark threw off base during that meet just before the buzzer sounded, causing Brady to lose the race. Eddie, learning from Mark, thinks of a plan to distract Brady again.

The Starter announces, "on your marks." This is it, the final. In a few seconds, there will be a winner. The runners get themselves positioned in the blocks. The Starter then announces, "set." As everyone moves into the "set" position, Eddie whispers to Brady, "you again?" With everyone ready to go, Brady briefly turns his head, looking at Eddie. The buzzer sounds, and Eddie is out of the blocks as fast as he has ever been. Brady, being distracted, is out of the blocks last. Sharing the lead at ten yards, Eddie is head to head with the runner in lane three. At the midway point, the runner in lane three is leading. Eddie is trying his best to catch him. With 10 yards remaining, Eddie finds himself a few feet behind the leader, with not enough distance left in the race to catch him. The runner in lane three crosses the finish line first, with Eddie a split second behind. Eddie takes second place, being edged out by a senior who already has scholarship in track. Brady, distracted again, did not medal in the race.

Mr. Frazier congratulates Eddie on a fine run, giving him two high-fives and a fist bump. Mr. Frazier tells Eddie, "that's second place in the State meet! And you're a freshman!" Eddie is jubilant that he got second place. Learning from Zaino, Eddie is not concerned with his time. This time, his time didn't matter. What did matter is that he earned a medal for second place. Mr. Frazier congratulates Eddie again, and then has to go to monitor the mile medley relay, which is up next.

After Mr. Frazier walks away, Kathy, all excited, runs up to Eddie. Kathy gives Eddie a high-five and a hug, telling him, "second place! Awesome!" Eddie looks at Kathy, remembering that she said, "run this one for me." A tear comes from Eddie's eye, and Kathy immediately asks, "what's wrong, sweetie?" Eddie tells her, "I lost." Kathy tells Eddie, "no, no, you won! Trust me. You really won! You're a freshman. Most of these guys are seniors." Eddie, all emotional, confesses, "when you said, 'run this one for me,' I wanted to give you better than second place." Kathy gives Eddie a big hug, telling him, "you're first place in my book." Kathy tells Eddie, "you've given me more than I ever wanted, and it's found right here," placing her open hand over Eddie's heart. Eddie gives Kathy a big hug, and they start walking back to the bench.

After many events, the end of the meet approaches, and so does the final event of the afternoon, the 4 by 440 relay. The Meet Announcer makes the final announcement for the event, and instructs the runners to get ready. There will be eighteen teams competing in this event, which will require three heats. There is no runoff, so the best time will take first place. Eddie, and his relay team, will be in heat two. The first heat gets ready, but Eddie, Mark, Johnson and Braden pay no attention. They are too focused on their own upcoming performance, not on someone else's race.

After the first heat is over, the Meet Announcer tells the second heat to get ready. The team will run in their new order, which was instituted after the first 4-way meet of the season. Mark will be leading off, followed by Johnson, then Eddie, and finally the anchorman, Braden. Braden, who likes to "kick ass," makes a good anchorman. Braden was shifted to the anchorman position because his body is good at delivering what his mind conceives. Braden, however, is unusually quiet today. This is the State invitational meet. If Braden is caught bragging and cannot deliver, he will look a bit too much like Mahoney.

Mark, the lead man, walks up to the starting position with the team. Mr. Frazier, Kathy, and Paula are with the relay team as they prepare to run. Kathy tells Eddie, "just run your best. That's really all that you can do." Paula, who has the baton, hands it to Mark. Paula tells Mark, "you are one of the fastest in your leg, but Johnson's going to be up against trouble in his leg." Putting her arm around Mark's shoulder, Paula tells him, "you really have to run your best today." As Paula walks back to where Mr. Frazier is standing, Eddie winks to Mark, and says, "see?" Mark now understands that Paula might just like him after all. And, it certainly took Mark long enough to figure it out.

The long awaited announcement comes from the Starter to get ready for the second heat. Once the runners are all on the track, Kathy, who is very familiar with the rules, points out to Mr. Frazier that the runner in lane four is wearing a wristwatch. Wearing a watch during a race is grounds for immediate disqualification. This is part of Kathy's job, to do anything to give the team an edge. Mr. Frazier takes note, and confides with Kathy, "thank you. If the officials don't catch it, I'll point it out to them after the race starts." Mr. Frazier, reconsidering, tells Kathy, "on second thought, I'll let you point it out to the Lane Judge. Just wait until I tell you. But, don't tell anyone on the team yet." Wisely, Mr. Frazier does not want to bring the infraction to the attention of the officials until the race starts. This is a quick and easy way to eliminate one team from the competition.

The Starter announces, "on your marks." The runners position themselves in the blocks, including the runner in lane four wearing the wristwatch. The Starter tells the runners, "get set." Four seconds later, which is longer than usual, the buzzer sounds, and the runners are off. Mr. Frazier, pointing to an official, tells Kathy, "OK, point it out to that Lane Judge. But, remember, don't tell anyone on the team yet." Kathy jogs over to the Lane Judge and says to him, "Mr. Frazier, our coach, wanted to let you know that the guy in lane four is wearing a watch." The Lane Judge tells Kathy, "ut oh. That's not good. I'll take a look when he comes around the curve." As the runners come around the curve, it looks like Mark is having an awesome run. The Lane Judge says to Kathy, "there it is. I see it. Thanks." The Lane Judge walks over and mentions it to the Timekeeper assigned to that lane, just so there is more than one person who sees the infraction.

When Kathy returns to the relay team and Mr. Frazier, Eddie asks, "what's up?" Kathy tells him, "Mr. Frazier wanted me to tell him something." Eddie, who is up next, didn't think much of it. As they watch the handoff from Mark to Johnson, Eddie tells Kathy, "it looks like I'm up next." Kathy gives Eddie a hug, as they both get back to work. Eddie looks over the field, and sees that Johnson is in second place, although the race is close. As Johnson, on his first lap passes by Eddie, Eddie waits a bit, and then enters the transition zone to receive the baton.

As Johnson enters the transition zone, Eddie takes the baton from him as fast as he can. Somewhat observant, Eddie recognizes that he is in second place after receiving the baton, but could not see which team is ahead. Since this is a relay, no one wants to disappoint the other team members, so they go all out. Eddie sprints the first 110 yards to gain some ground. Realizing he hadn't gained much ground, he must also sprint the second 110 yards as well. After the first lap, Eddie says to himself, "what the hell. I'll just sprint for the whole race." Eddie, still in second place, is giving it all he has, and then some. It is better to go all out than to find out later that, with a little more effort, the race could have been won. For Eddie, the good news ahead is that Braden, the chief ass kicker, is in the transition zone. After handing off to Braden, Eddie walks off his 440-yard sprint, watching Braden as he runs his leg.

Braden, back to his hyper excitable self, is running to win. The expression on his face as he is running says victory. As Braden enters his second lap, Kathy tells Eddie, who is still recovering, "you ran better than 54 seconds on your leg. I just wanted to tell you the good news." Eddie tells Kathy, "I feel like I just ran a 44." Kathy and Eddie watch Braden, as he is finishing the last lap. The 54 second time, which is approximate, has not yet sunk into Eddie's mind. Fixed on the finish line, Eddie, Kathy, and the rest of the team watch as Braden gives it his best. At the finish line, Braden crosses second, with the runner whose team was assigned to lane four crossing the finish line first.

Mr. Frazier and Kathy are exuberant that the team did so well. Mr. Frazier tells the team, "congratulations. You guys are awesome. You won your heat!" The relay team, however, is perplexed. They saw Braden take second place. Mr. Frazier informs the team, "the lead man in lane four was wearing a wristwatch, so they're disqualified." Brady's school, Riverdale, is still unaware they've been disqualified. They will find out later but, as of now, they think they are in the lead. Kathy tells Eddie, "Mr. Frazier said not to tell anyone." Mr. Frazier, overhearing Kathy, says to everyone, "I said that because, if you guys knew they were disqualified, you may not have run as fast!" Mr. Frazier then exclaims, "oh! And, by the way, that was your best time of the year!" Since their event is over, the team heads to the bench, to sit and rest.

With heat three underway, Mr. Frazier tells the team some good news. Mr. Frazier whispers to the team, "don't get too excited but, according to my stopwatch, you guys are unofficially in first place." Mr. Frazier has his stopwatch timing the current heat, as Kathy, Barbara, and Paula record some 440-yard split times of the current runners. The winner of the event, however, will not be known until the last heat is over. This is because, in the relay race, the best time wins. There is no runoff or final, so everyone must run their best during their heat.

With the last race over, and the meet over, the entire team finally relaxes together on the bench. The work is all done. The team is anxiously waiting to hear who won the 4 by 440 relay. Afterwards will be the awards ceremony. As the last heat is over, Kathy, Barbara, and Paula return to the bench. The three girls share with Mr. Frazier their final statistics but, right now, Mr. Frazier is only interested in one statistic, who won the 4 by 440 relay.

After considerable time, the Meet Announcer comes to the microphone to deliver the results of the 4 by 440 relay. The delay in the announcement is due to the disqualification, which had to be brought to the attention of the Meet Clerk. The Meet Announcer finally announces, "in the 4 by 440 relay event, in first place, Northside High." The Meet Announcer continues to announce the results, but Eddie and the rest of the relay team are cheering so loud they miss hearing the rest of the results.

Jumping up and down and celebrating, the 4 by 440 relay team is exchanging high-fives with the rest of the team. Kathy and Eddie give each other a big hug. Kathy yells out to Eddie and everyone else on the relay team, "you guys won State! You guys did it!" Braden, back to his usual self, is running around ranting, "we did it! We kicked ass! And, there's gonna be a lot more ass kicking in the Spring!" Even Johnson, who is a little on the reserved side, is giving high-five to everyone he can find. Mark, however, is no longer cheering along with the team. Mark has moved a little farther away from the main celebration, and having his own celebration. Paula is giving Mark a hug, a hug that lasts a little bit longer than a victory hug.

The Meet Announcer tells the crowd, "the awards ceremony will begin in fifteen minutes." The Meet Announcer instructs the teams, "coaches, please have your teams return to your benches." Mr. Frazier is totally ecstatic at the team's performance today. Mr. Frazier has not delivered this well of a performance at the State invitational meet during his entire career. It is quite rare for any coach to have one student go to the State invitational meet. This year, Mr. Frazier had quite a few.

Meanwhile, still discussing the outcome of the 4 by 440 relay with Alexander Karakova, the Meet Director, is Riverdale's coach, Mr. Lyons. Mr. Lyons tells the Meet Director, "wearing a watch shouldn't disqualify my team. It was completely unintentional." Dr. Karakova simply asks the coach, "then, you want me to take the rule book, tear out a page, and throw it away?" Dr. Karakova continues, "the rules explicitly state that a runner may not wear a watch while he or she is running." The coach continues to argue, "but, it was a 440! It's not like he was timing himself!" Dr. Karakova finally explains to the coach in no uncertain terms, "look, this is why we have Lane Judges. They caught it, and I have absolutely no grounds to overturn their decision." The Riverdale coach walks away, severely disappointed. The relay team that was disqualified will be even more disappointed once they hear the news.

Beginning the awards ceremony, the Meet Announcer addresses the crowd, "this has been a most excellent competition. We have had quite a few close races this year. The talent present here in the arena is among the best we have ever seen. Every single one of our athletes has given it their best this year." After a few more announcements, the Meet Announcer then moves on to the core of the ceremony. The Meet Announcer tells the runners, "when you hear your name, please come up to the stage and stand on the appropriate tier for your place in the event." He continues giving instruction, identifying where the runners in first, second, and third place should stand. This is not hard to figure out, but he has to make the announcement anyway.

The Meet Announcer begins with the 40-yard dash. Opening the delivery of the awards, he announces, "in first place, from Henderson High, Damien Harrington." As the first place winner approaches the stage, he continues, "in second place, from Northside High, Edward Bogenskaya." Eddie, sitting next to Kathy, stands up to go and receive his medal. Kathy, stands up with Eddie, and gives him a hug in front of everyone in the arena, telling him, "I'm so proud of you! You did so good!" Kathy sits on the bench, as Eddie walks up to the stage, not paying attention to who took third place.

Standing on the second place tier, Eddie waits to receive his medal. The officials drape the medals around the three winners' necks as the crowd applauds. Cheers can be heard from the benches of the winning teams. Eddie is actually able to hear Kathy cheering from the stage where he is standing. Kathy wishes she could drape the medal around Eddie's neck, but is very happy just seeing him on the winner's stage. The medalists return to their benches, and the Meet Announcer then moves on to the winners of the next event.

When Eddie returns to the bench, Mr. Frazier stops him and takes a look at the medal. Mr. Frazier congratulates Eddie again, telling him again how proud he is of Eddie and the rest of the team. When Eddie takes his seat, he lets Kathy hold his medal. Kathy has never held a State invitational meet medal before. Last year, Mahoney and Bell won third place in a relay event. The other two runners in that race were seniors, and have since graduated.

The mile medley team placed third in their event. The medalists are Darryl Bell, Louis Zaino, Mark, and Mitchell. Mark occasionally runs this event when assigned to do so. It just so happened that when Mark substituted for Ambrosini, and Mitchell substituted for Mahoney, the relay team took first place and ran a qualifying time. Unfortunate for Mahoney, he has not beat Mitchell all year in an 880-yard run, either in the 880-yard event itself or in an 880-yard relay leg. The best Mahoney could hope for is to hear about the race during school Monday. Consisting of two juniors and two freshman, the mile medley relay team will be back next year.

The ceremony moves along quickly, with the medals being distributed in the same order the events were run. The Meet Announcer gets to the final event. He announces, "in the final event of the day, the 4 by 440 relay, first place goes to Northside High. Running for Northside High in the 4 by 440 relay event, are Axel Braden, Eric Johnson, Edward Bogenskaya, and Mark Svoboda." He instructs the winners, "please come up to the stage." Eddie and the group stand on the first place tier, and await the second and third place winners to come up. Mr. Frazier, back at the team bench, cannot contain his excitement, primarily because his first place relay team consists of all freshmen. Mr. Frazier will have them for another three years. Kathy and Paula, sitting on the bench together, have tears of happiness rolling down their cheeks.

Once all the teams are on their tier, the officials award the final medals of the meet. The officials drape the medals around the winners' necks. Eddie, and the rest of the team, experience one of the highest points of their life. Winning is what they all have worked for by training for years. First place is the result of lifting weights and working out day after day. Standing on the stage is the result of running down the paved path along the parkway in the heat, cold, and rain. A gold medal is the result of bicycling and swimming to work out, not just for fun. Today is payday for the work of the last several years. The winners receive their medals, and the crowd claps and cheers. Everyone joins in to celebrate their victory.

The relay event winners return to their teams, and the celebration continues. Mr. Frazier congratulates the relay team, giving each member a high-five, handshake, and fist bump. Eddie, now with two medals draped around his neck, removes the first place medal he won in the relay event and drapes it around Kathy's neck. Eddie tells Kathy, "this one's for you." Kathy, at loss for words, does the only thing she can, which is give Eddie a hug and a kiss.

Eddie did not like coming in second place in the 100-yard dash. Keeping the second place medal for himself, it will serve as a constant reminder to work harder and train harder. He gave his first place medal to Kathy, who put her heart and soul into helping the team train. Eddie clearly understands Mr. Frazier's point of second place being the first loser. He has vowed never to stand on the second place tier again.

With the ceremony over, the parents and spectators are now able to mingle with the teams. Some of the parents come down from the stands to meet with their sons. Eddie's parents find Eddie, and meet his coach, Mr. Frazier, for the first time. Kathy's father, Alexander, the Meet Director, comes over and talks with Kathy. Alexander then takes the opportunity to talk with Mr. Frazier, Mr. Zunde, and Eddie's parents. Some of the other parents, who finally get to meet each other, join in on the conversation. Sure enough, Nina and Mariana are talking with each other, proud of Eddie's and Mark's accomplishments.

While the adults are having adult conversation, Eddie and Kathy mingle with the tribe, celebrating their win. The team members all seem to agree that Eddie's medal in the 4 by 440 relay looks better on Kathy than it would on Eddie. The team also deeply expresses to Kathy, Barbara, and Paula how much they appreciate them working with the team this year. Kathy, who is just as happy as the 4 by 440 relay team, can see how the decorated athletes are so appreciative and nice to her. This year, Eddie and his friends have made Kathy and the other girls feel like they are part of the team, not just the team assistants.

The team heads to the locker room and back to the bus. Mark's parents offer to drive him home, but he declines. Mark tells them he wants to take the bus with the rest of the team, which is understandable after their big victory. Eddie also takes the bus with Kathy, just so they can be together. Today, on the bus ride home, something is a little different. Paula is sitting next to Mark, leaving a little less doubt as to their interest in each other.

When the bus arrives back at the school, Mr. Frazier again congratulates the team. Mr. Frazier also tells the medalists, "if you've medaled in the State meet, you have a place on the outdoor track team. But, you'll need to come to tryouts anyway. I hope to see every one of you at tryouts in a week." This is the end of the indoor track season for this year. The Spring season, right around the corner, is sure to put forth a very competitive team.

Before everyone goes home, Mr. Frazier asks the medalists to come inside so that he can get a couple of photographs. The team enters the main gym, and sits on the bleachers for the photograph. While Mr. Frazier hunts down someone to take the photograph, Paula takes it upon herself to pose the medalists for the picture. Paula volunteered herself for this task because she has an ulterior motive. Paula has Eddie sit on the left side, with Kathy on his lap. She has Mark sit to the right, leaving a space between them for Mr. Frazier and Mr. Zunde to sit. Braden and Johnson sit on the row behind them, with Barbara between them. Bell, Zaino, and Mitchell, who placed in the mile medley relay, sit on the row behind Barbara, Braden, and Johnson. Paula tells everyone, "make sure you are wearing your medals."

When Mr. Frazier returns with the recruited photographer, Paula tells him he is to sit next to Mr. Zunde. Paula, at the last minute before the photographs are taken, takes her seat on Mark's lap, which is quite the surprise to Mark. The photographer starts taking pictures, documenting not who won medals this year, but also who is now with whom.

On Monday, following the weekend of the State invitational meet, word gets around school that the track team took home nine medals in three events. Winning nine medals in a State invitational meet is virtually unheard of, suggesting that perhaps something about this team is special. All of the medalists are wearing their medals during school today. Anyone walking around the halls has no doubt who the medalists are. With the team needing some well needed rest, they get a one week break from training. Tryouts for the Spring team begin next week, which usually brings a bigger field of students attempting to make the team.

Monday morning starts with English class, which is quite a departure from the events of the weekend. As Eddie, Braden and Mark sit in their usual place near the window, it's back to academic reality. Miss Starr walks in, who is quite aware of the events that occurred over the weekend. She asks Eddie, Mark, and Braden to come to the front of the classroom. Braden says, under his breath, "uh oh. What did we do now?" Braden knew that they were not being called to the front of the classroom for reasons of academic excellence. Miss Starr tells Eddie, Mark, and Braden, all wearing their medals, to stand and face the classroom.

Miss Starr, announcing to the rest of her class, informs them of the good news, "Eddie, Mark, and Axel have taken first place in the State track meet this weekend in a relay race. Eddie also won second place in the 40-yard dash.

Mark also got third place in another relay race. Everyone please give them a round of applause." The class cheers, applauds, and whistles, which can be heard all the way down the hall. The three medalists return to their seats with a feeling that this week is starting off great.

By midweek, the athletes have found a special place to keep their medals at home. Kathy, however, is still wearing Eddie's gold medal around her neck that he won in the 4 by 440 relay, which is noticed by everyone in school. Mahoney is very upset, to say the least, that he was not invited to the State invitational meet. For some strange reason, Mahoney thinks the medal around Kathy's neck should be his. After all, this is his senior year, and he should have been the star of the team. He is constantly reminded of his failure to qualify for the meet by the medal around Kathy's neck. Seeing Kathy wear Eddie's medal before school, in the hall during class change, and after school motivates Mahoney to train harder. The Spring track season is his last chance to prove himself, and get the scholarship that he has wanted since he's been running track.

After school, on Wednesday, Mahoney runs into Kathy in the school lobby. Mahoney, stating the obvious, tells Kathy, "so, you're still wearing Eddie's medal." Mahoney's opening line simply cannot go anywhere constructive. Kathy, as cordial as she can be, replies, "yeah, the team did really good! It was an awesome race!" Mahoney points out to Kathy, "yeah, well I heard somebody ratted out the first place team. Something about wearing a watch, so they got disqualified." Kathy, now between a rock and a hard place, just tells Mahoney, "I wonder who would do that." Mahoney callously answers, "some jerk, probably." Kathy replies to Mahoney, "well, Karma's a bitch." Mahoney understood Kathy's statement to involve the Karma of the person ratting out the other team. What Mahoney did not understand is that Kathy was referring to Mahoney, who just called Kathy a jerk.

Kathy sees Eddie walking down the hall to the lobby, which could not have come soon enough. She abruptly tells Mahoney, "I'm sorry. I got to go." Mahoney is ticked off that Kathy again ran off to see Eddie. Mahoney, still interested in going out with Kathy, has no idea of what is going on between her and Eddie. Mahoney decides to do a little investigation into Eddie, and find out more about him.

Kathy runs up to Eddie, and asks, "what are we going to do today?" With no track practice, and lots of free time after school, they have more time to spend with each other. Eddie replies to her, "how about we see a movie, get some pizza, and take the long way home." Kathy is all in. Eddie's plan is perfect for the afternoon. Once tryouts begin next week, there will be less time for social activities. For today, homework and tests can wait.

Kathy and Eddie walk to Kathy's house and drop their stuff off. On the way to the movie theater, Kathy asks Eddie, "have you figured out what you want to do when you graduate?" Eddie answers her, "I sure have. I want to be a mechanic." Eddie is used to people being disappointed in him choosing to be a mechanic. Kathy, however, tells him, "that's wonderful! I think you'd make an awesome mechanic!" Eddie asks Kathy the same question, "how about you? Do you know what you want to do?" Kathy's answer is a bit less surprising, "I want to be a gym teacher. Like what I'm doing now with the track team." Kathy also tells Eddie, "I like gym class. I like track. That's what I really want to do." Eddie tells Kathy, "that's awesome! If that's what you really want to do, go for it!" Eddie then points out, "actually, you're already doing it!" Kathy replies, "wow! Yeah, I am!"

When they get to the movie theater, they check out what is playing. Since they are not in training this week, it looks like the movie choice will be a chick flick. This week is for relaxing. They decided to save the energetic movies for before a workout or while in training. Eddie buys the tickets, and they walk in. The theater is mostly empty, so they find a good seat in the back. During the movie, Kathy lays her head on Eddie's shoulder as they hold hands. Kathy likes romantic movies. Eddie never really paid much attention to them but, now that he's with Kathy, he finds he actually likes them. Or, perhaps it is watching the movie with Kathy that he likes.

After the movie, they head to the pizzeria. Eddie asks Kathy, "so what did you think of the movie?" Kathy tells him, "it was pretty good. It was a little bit of a departure from the usual script." Eddie asks, "the usual script? What's that?" Kathy replies, "yeah, the usual script. Boy gets girl, boy loses girl, boy gets girl back." She explains to him, "that's the usual script for romantic movies, but sometimes it's girl gets boy, girl loses boy, girl gets boy back." Eddie tells Kathy, "wow, you got it all down." Kathy tells Eddie, "well, there is the other script too." Eddie asks, "OK, which one is that?" Explaining the other script, Kathy tells him, "boy gets girl, they fall in love, girl dies, and boy goes on living without her." They both have a laugh at Kathy's understanding of chick flicks, but her assessment is not far from the truth.

Pizza time comes, and they walk into the pizzeria. Inside, Joe, the man behind the counter, greets them as they walk in. Joe yells out to them, "hey, it's Kathy and Eddie! You always look so happy together!" Working in the pizzeria for years, Joe remembers everyone from the time they were four years old and had their first slice of pizza. Joe knows everyone who frequents the shop, even Vito from down the street. Joe asks them, "what can I get for you today?" They decide to split a calzone, and get a slice of pizza each.

As they are eating, Joe yells out to Kathy and Eddie from behind the counter, "if I charged by the smile, I could retire when you guys come in!" Joe knows when the young kids are happy, and he sees it in Eddie and Kathy. Joe's comment makes everyone around them smile too. Everyone inside seems to be having a good time, but there is someone who just drove up looking in the window that is not. Mahoney, who was going to go into the pizzeria, is sitting outside in his car watching Kathy and Eddie through the window. As Kathy and Eddie get up to leave, Mahoney drives off. Mahoney, who is still clueless about the depth of Kathy and Eddie's relationship, still thinks he has a chance with her.

After dinner, they walk back in the direction of Kathy's house. Eddie asks Kathy, "are we taking the long way home?" Kathy responds immediately, "you betcha." They take the detour into the schoolyard, and make their way to the bleachers. Kathy sits on Eddie's lap, telling him, "this is life, hon." Before he can even respond to what she said, Kathy kisses Eddie, as the two seem to leave the real world, and enter their own world of passion. It seems their time alone together never comes soon enough. The time they have together is always not enough, and the time to go always comes too fast.

But, it is getting late, and tomorrow's a school day. Leaving the schoolyard, Kathy stops and turns to Eddie with a tear rolling down her cheek. With a quivering voice, she tells him, "no, I can't do this. I can't let you go right now. Please, don't go." Kathy and Eddie hug each other tightly, not knowing what more to say to each other. They hug each other and kiss for a while longer. They remind each other that they will see each other tomorrow. As they walk to Kathy's house, they keep reminding each other, "there's always tomorrow."

As they get to Kathy's house, Kathy again turns to Eddie, and holds him tightly. She whispers in his ear words from her innermost being, "I don't know if I can go inside. I can't leave your side right now. I can't do it." Tears roll down Kathy's cheeks again. Eddie tells her, "let's go sit on the grass." They sit on the neighbor's lawn, and hold each other. Hyperventilating, Kathy tells Eddie, "OK, you know my secret now." Eddie asks, "secret? What secret?" Kathy unveils to him, "yeah, well, I break down like this sometimes." She explains to

Eddie, "sometimes I get really, really emotional, maybe more than I should." Exposing her innermost feelings, she tells Eddie, "but, this is real. I'm sorry. I just get like this." Eddie, holding her tightly, tells her, "it's going to be OK, I promise." Kathy whispers to him, "sometimes when I break down, it ain't pretty." Kathy begins to calm down, she whispers to Eddie, "OK, let's try this again." They get up and walk to the house, and on the way, Kathy calms down.

As they make it to the door, Kathy says, "OK, I can do this." Eddie whispers to her, "when you go to sleep tonight, think of me and I'll be there with you." Eddie also tells Kathy, "when I go to sleep, I'll think of you, and then we'll still be together." Kathy and Eddie kiss goodnight. Before Eddie turns away to go home, he whispers in Kathy's ear one more time, "remember, think of me."

Eddie walks to the road, and begins the long walk home alone that he has taken many times. On the way, he thinks of Kathy, and how he treasures her in his heart. As he gets close to his house, he realizes all of his school books are still at Kathy's house. Eddie figures out a plan. He will wake up early, and walk to school. He'll be waiting for Kathy when she leaves for school the next morning. As Eddie walks inside, a car drives down the road. This is not just any car. This is Mahoney's car. Mahoney, who lives clear across town, is somehow found driving by Eddie's house very late at night. What Mahoney has been up to during the last few hours is anybody's guess.

The next morning comes and it's back to school again. After getting ready, Eddie walks to school today. He has to get to Kathy's house before she leaves so that he doesn't miss her. Eddie sits on the sidewalk in front of Kathy's house, propped up against a street lamp post waiting for Kathy to walk out the door. Kathy walks out of her house, and seeing Eddie sitting on the sidewalk, yells out, "Eddie!" Kathy drops her school books and his, which she was carrying to school for him. They run to each other, and give each other a big hug and a good morning kiss.

Eddie tells Kathy, "good morning, sweetie!" Kathy replies, "oh, yeah! That it is!" After another long good morning kiss, they walk back and pick up their books, and walk to school together. On the way, Eddie expresses to Kathy, "you know, if you're going to give me this kind of good morning, I'll walk to school every day." All excited, Kathy replies, "that sounds like a plan to me!" Eddie asks Kathy, "did you think of me when you were falling asleep?" Kathy replies, "oh, Eddie, I had the best night's sleep ever!" Kathy then whispers to him, "I actually felt like you were holding me."

On the way to school, Kathy tells Eddie from deep within her heart, "I'm sorry I broke down last night. Really, I am." Eddie replies to her, "no, please don't be sorry. If that is you, just be you." Kathy warmly replies to him, "you are so sweet. Everyone expects you to act a certain way, and sometimes you just can't." Reassuring Kathy, Eddie tells her, "just be who you are. Anything else would be a fake." Eddie then tells her, "I want to know the real you."

Eddie continues, "can you imagine telling Braden to speak using proper English? That's just not him." Kathy, finishing Eddie's thoughts, translates Braden's pre-race energetic rants into proper English, "my fellow team members, I do perceive that we are going to beat the opposing team by a significant margin, unmatched in either speed or stamina. And, as an added bonus, I shall figuratively place my foot into a very personal posterior part of their anatomy using great force. And then, I shall inform the opposition of our superior performance level and compare it with their inferior performance level using an abundance of very descriptive metaphors." Eddie laughs, and says with an energetic voice, "we're going to," and Kathy, knowing where this is going, joins in, and they both say, "kick ass." They have a good laugh together, and have a wonderful start to their day.

Before Spring track tryouts, Mahoney is trying to find out all he can about Eddie and his friends. After following Eddie and Kathy around, Mahoney continues his investigation by talking with anyone who might know something about Eddie's training protocols. He also attempts to find out more about Eddie's family, prying information out of anyone he can. Mahoney, who was literally left in the dust during the indoor track season, cannot let this happen again during the Spring. It is apparent to all that Eddie and his friends have some sort of secret, or train in a way that enhances their running. While Mahoney does not find out much about their training, he does come across what he considers interesting information about Eddie. Mahoney, who is still obsessed with Kathy, intends to find out more.

Eddie - The Freshman Year

Spring Tryouts

When Monday arrives, so do tryouts for the Spring sports teams. Mr. Frazier has assured the medalists from the indoor track team that they already have a place on the Spring team. That, however, will not afford them the luxury to be lazy. The Spring track season usually brings out many more students vying for a place on the team. Mr. Frazier has to weed through the pack quickly in order to trim the field down to the most competitive athletes.

At the end of the day, the locker room again becomes the most popular place on campus. Students are trying out for baseball, lacrosse, swimming, golf, and, of course, track and field. There is some unfounded belief that track and field is some sort of unskilled sport that anyone can do. Some of the students think that anybody can run, so many of them try out for the team. They will be in for quite a shock once they hit the track and find out what it really takes.

Mr. Zunde enters the locker room, and makes the announcement for those students who have missed the sign on the door telling the athletes where to report for each sport. Mr. Zunde announces, "if you are trying out for lacrosse, you will meet out on the lacrosse field. If you are trying out for baseball, you will meet in the main gym for a short meeting. If you are a swimmer, meet at the pool. If you are trying out for track and field, you will meet in the auxiliary gym for a short meeting. And finally, if you are trying out for golf, you are in the wrong place. You should have taken the bus that would have brought you to the golf course. Better luck next time." Mr. Zunde does not bother with students who cannot get to the proper location for their tryouts. He does not put up with bullshit from students using lines such as, "I didn't know," or, "no one told me." He just tells them, "welcome to the real world."

While the athletes are getting dressed, Kathy, Paula, and Barbara load up the Cushman[3] and bring the equipment out to the track. They set up the starting blocks and set up the high jump and pole vault equipment. Finally, they place both the sixteen and twelve pound shot-puts near the shot-put pad and the discus near the discus pad. They drive the Cushman back to the school making the second trip, bringing out the hammer, the javelin, the poles for the pole vault, and a few other items. They then head back to the school to join the meeting. After practice, they'll load the Cushman again, and return the equipment to the storage room.

As the track and field team hopefuls gather in the auxiliary gym, it appears that certain cliques appear to form. Eddie and his tribe are no different. They hang out together, joined by a few of the freshmen from last year's team. This time, however, it does appear that you can judge a person's speed from the appearance of their stationary body. Many of the students appear out of shape, and obviously will not make the team. Well, it is obvious to the well-conditioned athletes anyway. Braden, looking over the field of athletes, says to the tribe, "it looks like we got a lot of fat ass to kick today!" Eddie starts laughing, recalling what he and Kathy said last week about Braden using proper English.

Mr. Frazier walks into the gym, and tells everyone to get seated on the bleachers. As he is waiting for everyone to take a seat, he looks over the sign-up sheet. Kathy, Barbara, and Paula walk through the door, ready to go to work. With more than a hundred students trying out, you can bet there will be a lot of work to do. The large turnout this Spring is due to many students hearing of the success of the indoor track team at the State invitational meet.

Mr. Frazier opens by telling the students, "this is Spring track. We do not have a lot of time to get the team ready for the first meet." He then informs the students, "tryouts are today, and for the next two days." Mr. Frazier then gives the not so good news, "when you come to school tomorrow, check the roster posted on the window to the administration office. If your name is not on the list, you have been cut. Do not bother showing up tomorrow." As Mr. Zunde walks into the gym, Mr. Frazier, getting right down to business, tells the students, "if you are trying out for a field event, Mr. Zunde will take you out to the track right now. Please follow him."

---

[3] Cushman: (a corporation) A utility vehicle, larger than a golf cart, used to transport small items.

Mr. Frazier then tells the runners, "there are only two races that are run in Spring track. The two races are the 100-yard dash and the 440-yard dash." Some of the athletes can be heard making comments, such as, "he's crazy," or, "what is he talking about?" Mr. Frazier continues, "the 220-yard dash is nothing more than a very long 100-yard dash. If you can run one, you can run the other. The 880-yard run, the mile, and any distance race is nothing more than a 440-yard dash. The last 440 yards are where the race is won or lost. There is only one difference between any of the distance races. That difference is how much of a warm-up you must perform before running the last 440 yards." Mr. Frazier tells them, "the next time you see a track meet on TV, you will see exactly what I'm talking about." Eddie looks at Mark, and mentions, "you know, that really makes a lot of sense."

Mr. Frazier introduces his three team assistants to the team, "these three women are my assistants. They will be working with you today." He then issues a warning, "I want you to treat them with the same respect as you would treat me. If you don't, you will be cut from the team." Wasting no time, Mr. Frazier tells the students, "if you are a distance runner, including middle distance, you will be working with Barbara today. Please follow her out to the track right now." Before she leaves with the group, Mr. Frazier whispers to Barbara, "six minutes and fifteen seconds, and run a steady pace."

As part of the gym empties out and follows Barbara, Mark says to Eddie, "wow, he's getting right down to business today." Eddie replies, "yeah, I guess he's got to get rid of some of these guys." Braden adds, "yeah, and the faster the better." Braden is now very confident in his abilities, and freely displays it. Mr. Frazier continues, "if you are a sprinter, please follow Kathy and Paula out to the track right now." Mr. Frazier then leaves the gym with the sprinters, leaving a few people sitting on the bleachers who apparently have no idea for which event they showed up. They eventually get a clue, and follow the rest of the students to the track.

Once the distance group is warmed up, Barbara, who has a distinct British accent, tells the group, "we are now going to run a mile for time." She informs the candidates, "just for fun, today I will be running with you." She then instructs the runners, "if you finish the mile before me, I want you to please move to the inside of the track and wait. If you finish after me, I want you to please move to the outside of the track." Then she gives them some words of advice, telling them, "you must run the best race you can right now, today." She gets the runners positioned at the starting line, and tells them, "when I blow my whistle, we will start." Barbara then announces, "get ready," and two seconds later she blows her whistle. The field leaves the starting line along with Barbara. The seasoned runners know what they are doing, and pace themselves appropriately. Some of the novice runners begin sprinting as if they are running a 100-yard dash, and think they can keep that pace for the entire mile.

Halfway through the mile, some of the runners are beginning to fall significantly behind. Mitchell and Davis are leading the pack at the halfway mark, with Davis slightly ahead. It's no secret that Mitchell will pass Davis during the last lap. Barbara, running with a stopwatch, plans to run exactly a 6:15 mile, running each 440-yard lap in about 94 seconds. Barbara, who is a junior, can run this time easily. With one lap to go, Mitchell makes his move and passes Davis. Mitchell crosses the finish line first, with Davis right behind. A few other runners cross the finish line after Davis. Barbara then crosses the finish line, exactly 6:15 after the race began. About twelve runners, who finished before Barbara, are waiting inside the track. Barbara then waves the other runners off the track to stand on the outside as they cross the finish line. When the last runner crosses, about 30 runners have accumulated on the outside of the track.

Mr. Frazier walks up to the 30 runners finishing after Barbara, and informs them, "Barbara ran a 6:15 mile, and you could not beat her?" Mr. Frazier informs this group, "if you can't run a sub-six minute mile, unfortunately you are not competitive enough for the team." Delivering the bad news, Mr. Frazier tells them, "unfortunately, I have to cut everyone in this group, so please head on back to the locker room. But, keep practicing and train hard, and try out again next year." This is Mr. Frazier's quick and easy way to eliminate noncompetitive runners who will not make the team. Barbara then records the names of the runners who ran the mile in less than 6:15, most of whom were on the track team over the Winter.

Kathy and Paula, working with the sprinters, arrange their own competition. Kathy calls out, "Eddie, Mark, Braden, and Johnson, please come up here and meet with Paula." While Kathy is addressing the other runners, Paula tells the group of four runners, "warm up. You have to show these guys how to run. We're going to have some fun today." The four medalists from the indoor season get ready for their debut performance in the 100-yard dash.

Announcing to the field of 40 or so runners, Kathy announces, "these four guys are going to run the 100-yard dash. This year, they will set the standard that you will be compared to. After they run, the rest of you will get your chance to show us what you can do!" One upperclassman is heard saying, "they're freshmen. They'll be easy to beat." Another upperclassman comments, "I guess they're starting the bar out pretty low this year." They will be in for a surprise.

Kathy, who is very observant, notices Eddie, Mark, Johnson and Braden all carefully setting their blocks. Paula will be the Starter. Kathy and Mr. Frazier will be the Timekeepers. Kathy, moving to the finish line, tells the rest of the field, "follow me to the finish line." Kathy and Mr. Frazier want all of the runners to see the finish of the upcoming race. Kathy arrives at the finish line where Mr. Frazier is waiting for her. They both have two stopwatches, and will record the time of each runner. Mr. Frazier instructs Kathy, "I'll take first and third place, you take second and fourth place." Kathy replies, "second and fourth. Got it."

As the group of sprinters is moving to the finish line, Paula bumps her hip to Mark's and whispers to him, "hey, do you want to go out with Eddie and Kathy and get pizza after practice?" Mark quickly replies, "yeah. That would be awesome." Paula's casual comment to Mark gets his energy level up, as the two have not been out together before. Eddie hears the comment, and sees Mark getting all fired up. Eddie, however, is not about to let Mark beat him, and gets fired up himself.

Paula, announcing to the runners, says, "on your marks." The runners get ready in their blocks, which appears easy to those watching from a distance. Paula announces, "set." When the runners are set, Paula fires the gun and the runners are out of the blocks. Eddie and Mark take a quick lead, with Braden and Johnson not far behind. The field of 50 or so onlookers watch the runners intently, many not believing what they are seeing. Halfway through the race, Eddie is ahead, with Mark slightly behind. Johnson and Braden are tied at the halfway mark. As the runners approach the finish line, Eddie crosses the finish line first, Mark second, Johnson third and Braden fourth.

Mr. Frazier and Kathy look at their stopwatches, and compare the times. Kathy says to Mr. Frazier, "wow, is this for real or what?" Mr. Frazier tells her, "yeah, these are right. They fit the finishing distances between the runners, and they seem to correlate." Knowing Kathy's passion of wanting to be a gym teacher, Mr. Frazier tells her, "I'll let you tell them their times." Kathy replies, "really?" Mr. Frazier responds, "yeah! Go ahead, and have some fun." Kathy then makes the announcement to the field, "Eddie, who came in first place, ran a 9.7. Mark, who came is second place, ran a 9.8. Johnson, in third place, ran a 10.1. And Braden, in fourth place, ran a 10.2." Eddie,

Mark, Johnson, and Braden give each other high-fives. While Kathy breaks the news to the runners, Mr. Frazier reflects upon the times that were just delivered. He looks again at his stopwatch, in total amazement at what he just saw. Normally, he would be exclaiming the time to the runners. Today, however, he is at a loss for words, for it was freshmen that ran those times.

Mark leaves the group quickly, to share his time with Paula. Kathy, meanwhile, looks over at Eddie, with the biggest smile on her face that one could imagine. Eddie walks over to Kathy, who gives him a high-five, and exclaims, "awesome, winner!" Eddie asks her, "do you think I'll make the team?" Kathy, with her quick sense of humor, replies, "I don't know. These other guys haven't run yet." Eddie, with his unusual sense of humor asks Kathy, "how about those slow guys that were behind me? Do they stand a chance?" Kathy replies, "it looks like they could use a little work." Kathy and Eddie often surprise each other with their sense of humor, and they never miss a beat.

Mr. Frazier instructs the runners, "form groups of four, and you will all be running the 100-yard dash for time." Some students can be heard commenting about the times of the first group. Mahoney, who will be running shortly, is having difficulty believing the times delivered by Eddie and his tribe. Last year, Mahoney's best time was a 10.4, which he could run consistently, but never able to beat. As the runners are forming their groups, Mahoney mentions to Bell, "I wonder if those times were real." Bell, responding authoritatively, tells Mahoney, "you know that Mr. Frazier doesn't make up times." Mahoney agrees, replying, "yeah, you're right." Mahoney, now thinking to himself, whispers under his breath, "not this shit all over again."

The students run in groups of four, as Mr. Frazier and Kathy record theirs times. As Mahoney's heat comes up, one upperclassman is heard saying, "here it comes. He's going to beat those four guys." Another upperclassman responds to him, "yeah, no one beat Mahoney last year." As Paula instructs the runners to get ready, all eyes are on this race. In this heat is Mahoney, Darryl Bell, Louis Zaino, and a wrestler, Mack Clark. Clark was not on the indoor track team because it conflicts with the wrestling season.

Once the runners are ready, Paula tells them, "on your marks." She then announces, "set." The gun goes off, and the runners are out of the blocks. After ten yards, all the runners are at their top speed. Mahoney is clearly the leader, with Bell slightly behind. Halfway through the race, Bell has not lost any ground to Mahoney, which is surprising. Zaino and Clark are somewhat falling behind, but the 100-yard dash is not their primary race. At the finish, it is Mahoney taking first place, with Bell right behind taking second place. They are followed by Zaino, and then Clark, who were not too far behind.

Mr. Frazier did not appear too happy after this heat. He and Kathy record the runner's times, which were not as good as expected. Mr. Frazier makes the announcement, "Mahoney, 10.7 seconds. Bell, 10.8 seconds. Zaino, 11.0 seconds. And Clark, 11.1 seconds." Mr. Frazier then comments, "all four of you ran better times last year!" Making another comment that pierces the heart the runners in that heat, Mr. Frazier informs them, "and there's a guy in middle school named Jimmy Hoffer that can beat three of those times!" Hoffer, who will join the team next year, ran a 100-yard dash in less than 11.0 seconds when he was in the seventh grade.

After Mr. Frazier examines the times, he tells the field of sprinters to prepare to run a 440-yard dash. Braden, who lost his heat in the 100-yard dash, is exclaiming, "now, it's my turn to kick ass! This is my race, and ain't no one gonna beat me!" He then questions the crowd, "who want's their ass kicked first? Come on, who's first?" Braden, even though he came in fourth place in his 100-yard dash heat, still had the fourth best time of the day, which was not a bad time at all.

Mr. Frazier smiles, and tells Braden, "you will be kicking the ass of your 4 by 440 relay team, and I'm throwing in O'Brien." Jimmy O'Brien, who did not make the indoor track team, decided to try out for Spring track. Thinking about it a little further, Mr. Frazier adds, "and, Mahoney! You're running in this heat too!" Mr. Frazier tells Braden and the rest to get ready to run. Mr. Frazier knows that Eddie, Mark, Braden, and Johnson always run better together. Throwing in O'Brien is just adding more fuel to Braden's fire. Throwing in Mahoney adds even more fuel to Mark's and Eddie's fire. Mr. Frazier is not stupid, and he knows this.

Jimmy O'Brien's father, who is a Social Studies teacher, is present today at the tryouts. Mr. O'Brien wanted to make sure Jimmy didn't get a raw deal, so he decided to come and watch the tryouts. Jimmy O'Brien will get his fair chance today. But, oddly, Mr. O'Brien has a tendency to be harder in the classroom on the athletes than the other students. Mr. Frazier completely ignores Mr. O'Brien, primarily because any conversation with him will go nowhere.

As the runners prepare to run, Mr. Frazier tells the field, "on your marks." He waits about fifteen seconds for Jimmy to get himself ready. Making sure that Kathy and Paula have not fallen asleep as they are waiting for O'Brien, Mr.

Frazier makes sure they are ready to start their stopwatches. The girls signal to Mr. Frazier that they are ready. Mr. Frazier finally announces, "set." The gun sounds, and the runners are off. The first 100 yards are run by the tribe as if that was the total distance in the race. Mark, Braden, and Eddie are in the lead, in that order. Johnson, fifth place, is on the heels of Mahoney, but will not be there for long. As for Jimmy O'Brien, well, at least he got out of the starting blocks.

At the halfway mark, Braden takes the lead, with Mark right behind him. Mark remembers what Eddie told him about drafting during their ride to the beach earlier this year. Also at the halfway mark, Johnson makes a move and passes Mahoney. Johnson, whose strength is at the end of the race, is catching up to the leaders. Three quarters the way around the track, Braden is ahead, with Eddie and Mark tied for second place following Braden very closely. Johnson is now right behind them, narrowing the gap. Braden glances to his left, and sees O'Brien has barely made it past the 110-yard point. Eddie takes a slight lead over Mark as they approach the finish line. This is Braden's race, and he is not about to let anyone else beat him. Braden sprints to the finish, with Eddie right on his heels. Braden crosses the finish line first, followed by Eddie. Mark finishes in third place, right behind Eddie. Johnson finishes two or three steps behind Mark. Mahoney finally crosses the finish line eight seconds later.

While everyone is paying close attention to the finish, Mark points out Braden to Eddie, and exclaims, "look! What's he doing?" Braden never stopped running at the end of the race. Braden is taking a second lap around the 440-yard track and has not slowed his pace. Eddie, still recovering exclaims to Mark, "he's trying to catch O'Brien again!" Mr. Frazier finally sees what is happening, and starts laughing uncontrollably out loud. Mr. Frazier exclaims, "there goes Braden! He's going to kick ass twice in one race!"

Mr. Frazier looks across the track at Paula and Barbara and yells out to them, "does anybody have him on the clock?" Barbara, who is timing O'Brien, screams back, "I got it!" Mr. Frazier yell back to Barbara, "forget O'Brien! Catch Braden's time!" Everyone turns to watch Braden as he is gaining on O'Brien. Braden is halfway around the track when O'Brien is three-quarters the way to the finish line. The last half of the race is usually O'Brien's weakest. He tends to flail and jog, which he is doing as expected. In the last 100 yards, Braden is gaining on O'Brien at an enormous rate. With 50 yards left to go, O'Brien is slowing down to a fast jog, and Braden is speeding up, passing O'Brien. Braden slows his pace just a bit, since his mission is accomplished.

Braden crosses the finish line a second time. Crossing the finish line a few seconds later is O'Brien, naively thinking he almost beat Braden.

While Braden is walking down the track to recover, Mr. Frazier, Kathy, and Barbara record the quarter mile times. Mr. Frazier, who clocked Braden's quarter mile, asks Barbara, "what did you clock his half mile at?" Barbara replies, "two sixteen." Mr. Frazier exclaims, "a 2:16 half mile, that was a 2:16 half mile! That's the new standard!" Braden, finally cooled down, returns to the finish line.

After Braden's run, many of the students standing around have lost any sense of confidence they have in their own abilities. Mahoney is amongst them. Braden not only beat Mahoney in the 440-yard dash, but just shattered Mahoney's best half mile time as well. When Braden is told his times, he exclaims, "I said I was gonna kick ass, and I did!" Braden, all fired up, points to O'Brien, and exclaims, "twice! I kicked your ass twice in one race! Put some ice on your ass, junior." Eddie, Mark, and Johnson all have a good laugh listening to Braden. To them, watching Braden rant and rave is free entertainment.

Mr. Frazier then tells the remaining sprinters to form groups of six. As they get ready to run, Eddie and his tribe walk off to the side of the track, and sit on the bench. Their work is done for today. Wendy, who was watching with a few others from the bleachers, comes down to meet Braden. Joining the group, Wendy tells Braden, "you looked pretty good out there today." Braden tells Wendy, "yeah, I won the 440 and the half mile, all in one race!" Mark, humorously says, "we let him win every once in a while." Eddie, joining in the humor, adds, "today was Braden's day to win anyway." Even Johnson, who is a little on the quiet side, says, "we didn't want to make him look too bad today." Braden, taking all this in, laughs along with them, has the final words, "yeah, right! I'm just getting warmed up!"

Bobby B. and Mitchell come over to join the group and the conversation. Bobby B., the shot doc, has some good news, telling the group, "I'm in. I made it!" Johnson asks Bobby B., "in what, the shot-put or the high jump?" Bobby B. replies, "neither. I made the 100-yard dash. I'm taking over!" Johnson replies, "yeah, I heard you run the 100-yard dash in the ten range. Ten minutes, that is." Bobby B., returning the humor, tells Johnson, "yeah, well the rumor is that you can throw the shot-put around 60 or 70. That would be 60 or 70 inches, with the wind behind you." After a hard day's work, they all have a good laugh together.

Mitchell tells Braden, "I saw your 440 and half mile. That looked really awesome!" Braden says, "yeah, I even kicked Mahoney's ass too!" Mitchell, the honor roll student, points out, "you do realize you just signed up for the half mile, don't you?" Braden responds, "dang! Dang! I hate that race. Dang! What did I have to go and do that for?" After Mitchell's statement, it became obvious to everyone that Braden, in fact, may now be running the half mile. The group hangs out until tryouts are over, then everyone heads to the locker room.

Eddie, Kathy, Mark, and Paula meet after practice and walk to the pizzeria. Kathy takes Eddie's hand, which quickly prompts Paula to take Mark's hand. On the way, they talk about the tryout session. Kathy tells everyone, "Mr. Frazier cut half the students today." Paula adds, "yeah, and that was interesting how he cut the distance guys." Paula was not a team assistant last year, so everything is new to her. Mark mentions, "what was cool is that Barbara ran the mile in exactly the time Mr. Frazier told her to." Kathy informs Mark, "Mr. Frazier tells her how fast to run the mile, and she does, right down to the second. Last year he told her how fast to run each lap, and she hit it spot on."

As they sit for a moment and decide what they want to eat, Kathy tells everyone, "only me and Paula get to eat. You guys are in training. You don't get to order pizza." Eddie starts laughing, and responds, "OK, you order it then, and I'll just eat it." Mark and Paula join in laughing. Joe, seeing the laughter from behind the counter, yells out to them, "I tell you, if I charged by the smile, I could retire when you guys come in."

Eddie and Mark go up to the counter and place their order, and return to the table with the drinks. Eddie tells Kathy and Paula, "we ordered two pizzas, one for each of you." Paula, not quite familiar with the guy's sense of humor yet, replies, "we can't eat a whole pizza!" Mark chimes in and says, "well, I guess we'll have to help then." Eddie tells Mark, "but, we're in training. They said we can't have pizza." It's quite amazing how the four friends can have such a good time joking about something so simple.

After dinner, the group heads in the direction of the school. Halfway back to the school, Kathy tells the group, "well, here's my exit." Mark, who lives back in the other direction, thinks to himself that he doesn't even know where Paula lives. Kathy tells Paula and Mark, "we've really enjoyed going out with you guys." Paula replies, "yeah, it's really been fun. We have to do this more often." Paula is clearly hinting to Mark that she wants to go out with him more.

The girls give each other a hug, as the guys give each other a fist bump. Eddie and Kathy head to Kathy's house, as Mark and Paula turn around and walk in the direction of Paula's house. Kathy looks back at Paula and Mark, and says to Eddie, "look! I think they really like each other!" Eddie, looking back at Mark and Paula, replies, "maybe we can all ride to the beach together someday." Kathy tells him, "yeah, that would be nice. Summer is right around the corner."

As they are almost to Kathy's house, they pass the side entrance to the elementary school, and Kathy takes a detour. Kathy starts running into the schoolyard and tells Eddie, "catch me!" Eddie starts chasing Kathy, as she starts running in circles. It takes the track star a little longer to catch Kathy than he thought. Eddie can run in a straight line faster than anyone at school but, Kathy, running in circles, is really giving him a good run for his money. After a minute, he finally catches up to her. Kathy turns to Eddie, and jumps up onto him, locking her legs around his hips and arms around his neck. Looking Eddie in his eyes, Kathy says to him, "Edward Bogenskaya, I love you!" Eddie, holding Kathy and seeing the joy in her eyes, tells her, "Katarina Karakova, I love you." They kiss each other passionately, both knowing, at that moment, something again changed. Eddie slowly squats to the ground, with Kathy still on his lap. They kiss passionately, wanting their time together to go on forever.

Since tomorrow is a school day, the night comes to an early end. As they walk back to Kathy's house, she reassures Eddie, "don't worry, no emotional breakdown today." Eddie tells Kathy, "well, you seem extra happy today." Kathy replies, "well, Edward Bogenskaya, that's because I am!" Kathy then asks Eddie, "hey, after tryouts tomorrow, do you want to see my gym?" Eddie asks, "you have a gym?" Kathy answers, "I sure do!" She then prepares Eddie, telling him, "it's nothing like yours. It's totally different." Kathy then whispers to him, "you have to promise me one thing though." Eddie whispers back, "what's that?" She tells him, "you can't laugh. You got to promise me that you won't laugh." Eddie says to Kathy, "OK, I promise. But, now you really got me wondering." Kathy replies, "good! I hope you wonder all night, dream about it, and wonder all day tomorrow!" Eddie tells Kathy, "OK, now you're torturing me." The time comes when they have to say good night to each other again. They give each other a goodnight embrace, and Kathy goes inside. Eddie walks home, wondering on the way what kind of gym Kathy could possibly have. His mind, however, quickly wanders back to Kathy's words, "Edward Bogenskaya, I love you!"

The next day, Eddie is again sitting against the street lamp post waiting for Kathy. She is unusually late today, and Eddie begins to wonder where she is. Thinking that maybe he missed her, he stands up walks up to the door. On his way up the walk, Kathy walks out of her house, and is all ready for school. They run to each other, and give each other a morning hug. Eddie tells Kathy, "I though I missed you." Kathy, still half asleep, replies to him, "I couldn't sleep, and I woke up late." Kathy tells Eddie, "I kept hearing you say, 'Katarina Karakova, I love you,' and I think I was up half the night." Eddie looks at Kathy again, and says to her again, "Katarina Karakova, I love you." Kathy melts into his arms, telling him, "oh, Eddie, I love you." The good morning hug turns into a very affectionate good morning kiss.

At school, they both walk in late. They stop by the office to get a late pass, following school protocol. On the sign-in sheet for late students, there is a column heading "Reason for Tardiness." Eddie writes in, "tired from track practice." Kathy, seeing what Eddie wrote, uses a different excuse, "took the long way home." The school secretary, Mrs. Marlowe, looks at the sign-in sheet, and looks at Kathy and Eddie. Mrs. Marlowe says to Kathy, "the long way home? Really?" She explains to Mrs. Marlowe, "yeah. I got sidetracked and got home real late." Mrs. Marlowe just sighs, and hands them their passes. When they get into the hall, Eddie tells Kathy, "that was a good one." Kathy replies, "well, it looks like it worked." As they walk out of the office, Eddie asks Kathy, "should I check to see if I got cut from the team?" Kathy, affectionately bumping her hip to Eddie's, tells him, "nah, you made it." Kathy then goes to her class, and Eddie to his.

Eddie walks into English class late. As he is walking to his seat, Miss Starr tells him, "Eddie, I'm glad you could join us today." Handing Miss Starr his late pass, Eddie responds, "track tryouts were yesterday," letting her fill in the blanks. About 20 minutes later, Mark walks into the classroom, also quite late. Miss Starr says to Mark, "let me guess. Track tryouts?" Mark, looking at his friends, responds, "yeah! That's it. Track tryouts." Miss Starr tells the class, "these guys can run 100 yards in 9.7 seconds, but do you think they can they get to class on time?"

As the whole class starts laughing, Eddie asks Braden, "how did she know that?" Hearing everything that goes on in her classroom, Miss Starr catches Eddie's question to Mark. Miss Starr answers Eddie before Braden could, "I know because Axel told the whole class." She then adds, "at least three times!" Miss Starr also informs Mark and Eddie, "I also overheard Axel describe in vivid detail how he placed his foot in certain posterior anatomical locations of his opponents yesterday. Don't worry. I got the play by play." The students are now hysterical, which just about does it for class today. After a few minutes, the bell rings, and it's off to the next class.

The end of the day brings the second session of tryouts. The students meet on the track, continuing where they left off yesterday. Announcing to the remaining field of athletes, Mr. Frazier says, "there are two more days of tryouts, including today." Mr. Frazier tells the field athletes to follow Mr. Zunde over to the filed event area. Surveying the field of the remaining track athletes as he is talking, Mr. Frazier yells out, "O'Brien, you were cut! Head to the locker room now!" Mr. Frazier then tells the distance athletes, "if you are running distance, you will be working with Barbara again today." He then instructs the sprinters, "and the sprinters will be working with me, Kathy, and Paula." Mr. Frazier already has a good idea who will make the team, and who will run each event. After today, the team members will be carved in stone. Tomorrow's practice will be for fine tuning the events.

Mr. Frazier instructs the sprinters to take a seat on the bench. Today, Mr. Frazier will attempt to further identify the better sprinters, and begin to assign events. Several of the sprinters will be running the 100-yard dash again for time, Mahoney included. Calling the sprinters by name, Mr. Frazier places four in each group. He tells them to be ready to run when their group is called. He then calls the first group. The first group steps up to the blocks, and gets ready to run. Mahoney is in the first group, wanting to be the one to set today's standard. Following the 100-yard dash time trials, Mr. Frazier will move to the 220-yard dash.

Eddie, Mark, Braden, and Johnson, however, were not assigned to any group. Their times were already good enough to make the 100-yard dash. They all sit back for a while on the bleachers and watch the action. Eddie tells Mark, "from what I can see, Paula really likes you." Mark replies, "wow! Yeah! I'd say so." Eddie jokes with Mark, "so, she kept you up past your bedtime, didn't she." Mark admits, "yeah, a little bit. Well, two hours." Eddie laughs, and gives Mark some advice, "just make it up in science class, and take a nap." Braden chimes in, giving his own advice, "just take your nap after lunch." Eddie questions Braden, "so, that's where you've been at lunch?" Braden replies, "yeah. Now that the weather's nice, me and Wendy go to the back of the school, and sit and relax." Mark answers Braden, "yeah, right. I can see that. You sitting and relaxing."

Wendy walks up to the bleachers where the guys are sitting and relaxing. Wendy, as she takes a seat next to Braden, asks, "why aren't you guys running?" Braden replies to Wendy, "Mr. Frazier is trying to make us fall asleep, just to make the next race fair." Wendy pokes Braden in his side, and asks, "no, why? Really!" Johnson, answering Wendy, tells her, "we're already in for this event. We'll be running in a few minutes." Mark, correcting Johnson, tells Wendy, "don't believe him. We all got cut." Wendy says to the group, "geesh, since you turned my question into a multiple choice question, I think I'll go with Johnson's answer." Wendy is easy to tease, easily falling for the guys joking around.

Mr. Frazier blows his whistle, announcing the beginning of the 220-yard dash time trials. Braden tells Wendy, "it looks like we have to go and check in." Wendy replies, "I'll be sitting here watching, and doing your homework for you." Eddie replies to Wendy and the guys, "well that certainly explains a lot." Mark, also commenting, adds, "now we know where Braden gets all the time to sit and relax and do all those other things he won't tell us about." All Wendy could say is, "you guys!" The guys head to the track, and Wendy starts working on her and Braden's homework, which Mark will undoubtably be copying tomorrow morning.

When they get down to the track, Mr. Frazier makes the announcement, "next up is the 220-yard dash." Mr. Frazier instructs the groups, "you will be running with the same group that you ran the 100-yard dash with." Eddie, Mark, Braden, and Johnson take a little time to warm up, since they have been sitting for a while. The group stretches, and runs a few short ten-yard sprints.

While they are warming up, Mr. Frazier calls for the first group that ran today to get ready. Mahoney, getting ready to run, starts babbling, imitating Braden, "I'm hot. Ain't no one kicking my ass today." Eddie quickly points this out to Braden, telling him, "look, you have some competition!" Mark says to Braden, "hey, he thinks he's you!" Mahoney continues his non energetic rant, telling everyone, "I'm doing the ass kicking today."

Braden has had enough. Braden jogs up to the starting line where Mahoney is getting ready. Repeatedly pointing to his chest, Braden yells to Mahoney, "I'm the chief ass kicker here. You ain't kicking nobody's ass but your own!" Mahoney, again trying to imitate Braden, yells back, "no, I'm kicking." Mahoney is sharply interrupted by Braden, who shouts back, "oh no, you ain't! Not with that Mahoney baloney jive you ain't! You ain't kicking no one's ass! Your fat, flimsy little ass is gonna have my footprint on it for a month!"

Mahoney, in a fit of rage, screams back to Braden, "who the hell do you think you are?" Braden, standing tall, responds, "I'm the one and only ass kicker around here! You got that, junior? Your job is to get your ass kicked, and my job is to kick it!"

While Mahoney and Braden are having their exchange, Mr. Frazier jogs to the starting line to find out what is going on. During part of Braden's rant, Mr. Frazier had to turn around for a moment to conceal his laughter. When he arrives, Mr. Frazier instructs Braden and Mahoney, "OK, now, everybody calm down." Pointing to Ambrosini, who is all ready to run, Mr. Frazier tells him, "sit out this heat. You'll run in the next one." Pointing to Braden, Mr. Frazier instructs him, "take his place." Mr. Frazier instructs the runners to prepare to run. Mr. Frazier then jogs to the finish line.

While Mr. Frazier returns to the finish line, the ranting continues, albeit in a much subdued tone. Braden is energetic as is possible. Mahoney, on the other hand, has a look of fear on his face. Braden, ignoring Mahoney, says, "gonna kick his puny little ass to the moon." Mr. Frazier gives the signal to Paula, who announces, "on your marks." Braden makes his own announcement to Mahoney, saying, "here we go! My foot is gonna kick your puny little ass!" Paula announces, "set." The gun goes off, and the ass kicking of the day is underway.

Not surprisingly, Braden is out of the blocks first. Braden already has a two-step lead before Mahoney is even out of the blocks. Braden is running down the track like a jet engine. By 50 yards, it is a one-man race. Mahoney, giving it all he has, can't catch Braden. The gap between Braden and Mahoney, not surprisingly, is getting wider. At the halfway mark, there is absolutely no hope of Mahoney catching Braden. At the finish line, Mr. Frazier clicks his stopwatch as Braden crosses the line. Kathy catches the time of Mahoney on her stopwatch, and the runner in fourth place. After catching Braden's time, Mr. Frazier was looking so intently at his stopwatch, that he failed to catch the time of the third place runner.

Mr. Frazier examines his stopwatch, and is very impressed by Braden's performance. He checks with Kathy, who is recording the times. Mr. Frazier waits for Braden and Mahoney to recover before he announces the times. Braden returns to the finish line, staring at Mahoney. Neither of them says anything. Nothing had to be said. The times Mr. Frazier has recorded on the stopwatches says it all. Mr. Frazier announces the times, "Braden, 24.7, and Mahoney, 30.7." Those times settle the dispute. Braden is the chief ass kicker, and Mahoney got his ass kicked. Mr. Frazier calls Barbara over, and telling her to work the 220-yard dash with Kathy. Mr. Frazier then goes on a short walk by himself, telling Barbara, "I'll be back in a few minutes."

As Mr. Frazier walks away, he thinks to himself, "how did I get so lucky to get all this talent in one year." He felt like he had to take a short break from the tryouts. Runners like Eddie, Mark, Braden, Johnson, and Mitchell come along once every five years. This year, he has five runners, and one shot-put star who will hopefully be with him for four years. Mr. Frazier also has been blessed with three team assistants, any of whom could easily coach the team in his absence. Mr. Frazier, feeling blessed, drops to his knees, and looks to the sky, and exclaims, "thank you, Jesus!" He looks back at the track, watching the action from a distance.

Kathy, Paula, and Barbara continue managing the heats where Mr. Frazier left off. As Mr. Frazier walks back to the school, no one knows why. Someone is heard saying, "he's probably going back to get another stopwatch. He's been staring at his like it's broken or something." Kathy blows her whistle, telling the second group to get ready, which is Eddie, Mark, and Johnson. She tells Ambrosini, who Mr. Frazier removed from the previous heat, to run in this one. He will take Braden's place, running against the tribe. Ambrosini is not happy with this decision, but that's the way the dice roll.

The tribe gets fired up, ready to crush Ambrosini's ego again. While they are getting ready, Paula mentions to Mark, "that was like a free comedy show watching Braden and Mahoney get at each other." Mark replies to her, "yeah, I wonder who Mahoney's going to try to act like next." Paula comically suggests, "maybe Jimmy O'Brien." Mark starts laughing, delaying the heat for a minute or so. Paula starts laughing too, causing another slight delay.

Finally, the runners are ready to run, and Paula tells them, "on your marks," followed by, "set." She fires the gun, and the four runners are out of the blocks. Halfway through the race, Eddie is clearly leading. Mark is usually right up there with him, but not today. The comical exchange at the starting line threw Mark off a bit. Mark and Johnson are tied at the halfway point, with Ambrosini far behind. At the finish line, Eddie is the clear winner. Johnson and Mark finish in second and third place, respectively. Ambrosini finishes in last place, but delivers a better time than usual because of whom he was up against.

Mr. Frazier returns from his walk, just in time to hear the results of the race. After Kathy and Barbara record and announce the times, Kathy tells Eddie, "you ran a 24.9! That was great!" Eddie asks Kathy, "what did Braden run?" Kathy replies, "a 24.7, but he was more fired up than ever." Eddie tells Kathy, "wow! I wish I was in that race. I would have done better." Kathy reassures Eddie, "it doesn't matter. You're in." Eddie replies, "yeah, well I guess I wanted to kick Mahoney's ass too." Kathy laughs, and tells Eddie, "now you're sounding just like Braden!"

Kathy then whispers to Eddie, "do you want to know a secret?" Eddie says, "you love me?" Blushing at Eddie's unexpected comment, Kathy replies, "that ain't a secret anymore!" Eddie tells Kathy, "OK, tell me." Telling Eddie the secret, Kathy whispers to him, "Mr. Frazier is going to let you, Mark, Braden, and Johnson choose your events, but he has you all down for the 4 by 440 relay. He mentioned that to me while you guys were sitting on the bench earlier." Eddie replies, "cool! I'll take the 100, and whatever else he has me in will be fine." Eddie, thinking for a moment, adds, "that would be good news to Braden. After yesterday's 440 that he turned into an 880, he thought he'd get stuck with running the half mile." Barbara tells Kathy, "Paula's ready." Kathy then tells Eddie, "OK, it's back to work for me."

When tryouts are over, Mr. Frazier reminds everyone to check the final roster, which will be posted tomorrow. Mr. Frazier then calls a few hand-selected runners aside, also asking his team assistants to stay for a minute. Eddie, Mark, Braden, Johnson, and Mitchell were among the group asked to stay. Mr. Frazier asks them, "is there any particular race you want to run?" Eddie, without hesitation, says, "the 100-yard dash." Mr. Frazier instructs Barbara, "write these down for me please." Mark asks, "can I have the 220 or the 440?" Mr. Frazier replies, "you got it." Mitchell says, "I'll take the half mile and mile, if that's OK." Mr. Frazier tells Mitchell, "no problem. They're yours." As Mr. Frazier questions the group, Braden claims the 440-yard dash and the 220-yard dash, and Johnson claims the 220-yard dash and 100-yard dash. Mr. Frazier asked few other runners what events they would like to run. Once the list has been compiled, Mr. Frazier tells them, "thank you for delivering a good performance. You guys are my core team this year." Mr. Frazier, almost forgetting, says, "oh, and the 4 by 440 relay, unless someone strongly objects, will be the same team as we had in indoor track." No one objects, and everyone heads to the locker room.

On the trip to the locker room, Eddie asks Kathy, "so, do I get to see your gym today?" Kathy replies, "oh, yeah! That's right!" All excited, she tells Eddie, "we're going to have fun!" Kathy's comment attracted a lot of attention from Mr. Frazier and the group of guys walking with them. Eddie does not know what to expect, but is looking forward to the workout. When they get back to the locker room, Kathy tells Eddie, "meet me by the front door."

Eddie comes out of the locker room, and walks to the school lobby. Exiting the school, he finds Kathy waiting for him. Kathy asks, "are you ready?" Eddie replies, "as ready as ever. I can't wait!" Kathy tells him, "you know, you're not going to be able to keep up with me." Eddie, showing a bit of confidence, says, "yeah, I will." Kathy reassures him, "oh no, you won't. Ain't no way." Eddie then asks, "OK, then, what is this gym?" Kathy replies, "oh, you'll see." Eddie tells his sweetheart, "you're already making this workout fun."

When they arrive at Kathy's house, they go inside. Kathy tells Eddie, "OK, wait here, I'll be right back." Kathy runs downstairs to the den, and opens the door to the backyard. After Kathy moves her equipment into the backyard, she runs back upstairs to get Eddie. She takes Eddie downstairs, and telling him, "close your eyes and don't peek." She takes his hand, bringing him out into the backyard. Kathy tells Eddie, "stand here, and remember, no peeking." Eddie is now wondering what this gym could possibly be. He's been waiting all day to see Kathy's gym, and the time has finally come.

Taking her special workout hoop, which is heavy and silent, Kathy begins hooping. She tells him, "OK, open your eyes, and remember, don't laugh!" When he opens his eyes, he sees Kathy hooping, in a way he's never seen before. As the hoop is spinning around her body, she raises it up to her chest, then up to her neck, and back down again to her waist. Then, with the hoop rotating around her waist, she places one arm behind her back. As she makes a half turn on her feet, the hoop is now overhead, rotating around her wrist. She lowers her hand to her waist, and the hoop seems to have magically moved back to her waist again. She then does the same move with the other hand. Eddie had no idea that what Kathy is doing with the hoop was even possible. Kathy says to Eddie, "this is my gym! There's one laying against the bush for you, over there." Eddie says to her, "wow, you are awesome at that!" Eddie gets the hoop, but right now he is more interested in watching Kathy as she is hooping. Kathy tells him, "go ahead, and give it a try!"

Eddie takes the hoop, and places it around his waist. He is able to get the hoop going around his waist, but right now his mind is stuck on watching Kathy. Kathy then does the ultimate, raising the hoop over her head, getting the hoop airborne. She moves quickly back under the hoop, catching it with her body. The hoop seems to have magically appeared rotating around her waist again. In the blink of an eye, Kathy reverses the direction the hoop is spinning, and does the move again. While concentering on watching Kathy, the hoop around Eddie's waist drops to the ground.

Kathy tells Eddie, "OK, throw me that hoop." Eddie asks, "how?" Kathy explains, "throw it over my head so I can catch it and make it spin." Eddie takes the hoop, and tosses it just over Kathy's head. Kathy takes a step back, and catches the hoop with her body, while she still has the other hoop going. Within a few seconds, both hoops are rotating around her waist. With one arm placed behind her back, she raises one hoop over her head, while the other hoop is rotating around her waist. She tells Eddie, "OK, now here's the hard part." She then reaches behind her back with the other arm, and raises the other hoop over her head. Eddie is totally amazed at what he is seeing. Kathy tells Eddie, "now, this is the really hard part." Kathy lowers one of her arms, with both hoops rotating overhead around her other arm. She lowers her other arm, and both hoops magically appear around her waist again.

Kathy stops hooping, and asks Eddie, "so, what do you think?" Eddie, at a loss for words, tells her, "that was awesome! It was so beautiful!" Eddie continues, "that is really artistic, like dance." Kathy tells him, "well, it kinda is like dance." Tossing Eddie a hoop, Kathy tells him, "lets hoop together." They start hooping, but this time Kathy keeps the hoop around her waist. Eddie's hoop falls off a few times, but he quickly gets the hang of it.

Kathy tells Eddie, "I'm training for the Olympics in Hula Hoop." Somewhat puzzled and surprised, Eddie asks her, "they have Hula Hoop in the Olympics?" Kathy replies, "ha, ha, I got you! But no, unfortunately they don't!" Eddie laughs, as his hoop falls to the ground. Eddie picks up his hoop again and starts hooping again. While he is hooping, he is moving backwards slowly. Kathy tells him, "you better not back up any more. You might fall into the pool." Eddie says, "yeah, I saw that. I thought the pool was your gym, not the hoop." Kathy tells him, "yeah, in the Summer it is. Sometimes I swim laps."

After a while, Kathy asks, "so, how do you like my gym?" Eddie replies, "I like it! And you're really good at this!" Kathy tells him, "I try." Eddie says to her, "no, that's not just try. That's first place, gold medal, Hula Hooping!" Letting her hoop drop to the ground, Kathy walks over to Eddie and puts her arms around his neck. She tells him, "I just wanted to show you what I'm good at." Eddie reassures Kathy, "you're good at a lot of things." Kathy replies, "yeah, but you're really good at what you do. I just wanted you to see that I'm good at something too." Eddie hugs Kathy, telling her, "I'm really happy you showed me. You're not just good at it. You're awesome!"

After they are finished hooping, they sit on the grass and relax for a moment. Kathy then asks Eddie, "you're staying for dinner, right?" Eddie asks, "hmm, do I have a choice?" Kathy replies, "nope. I'll call your mom and tell her I have taken you captive, and you won't be home until later." Kathy jumps up and runs inside to call Eddie's mom. Eddie follows her, wanting to hear this conversation.

Kathy goes upstairs to the kitchen and calls Eddie's mom. When she answers, Kathy says to her, "hi, this is Kathy." Eddie's mom asks Kathy how she is. Kathy replies to her, "I'm good, but I've taken Eddie captive. Can he please stay at my house for dinner or maybe go out for pizza?" Eddie, listening to this conversation, is laughing in the background. Eddie's mom agrees, so Eddie can stay for dinner. Kathy tells her, "he's kind of hungry. I made him Hula Hoop, and it wore him out." Eddie can hear his mother laughing at the other end of the phone. After another minute of conversation, Kathy then whispers, "OK, bye," and she hears Eddie's mother hang up the phone.

Eddie, unaware that his mother is no longer on the phone, hears Kathy say, "and, after dinner, we're going skinny dipping." This quickly gets Eddie's attention, prompting him to whisper to Kathy, "no, don't tell her that." Kathy hands Eddie the phone, whispering to him, "she said it's still too cold outside to go skinny dipping. Here, you convince her that it's not." Eddie says, "hi," into the phone, quicky realizing that there is no one on the other end. Kathy exclaims, "ha, ha! I got you again! That's twice in one day!"

Eddie starts tickling Kathy, both quickly ending up on the floor. Rolling around on the floor, Kathy is clearly ahead in the tickling contest, probably because Eddie is allowing her to win. The contest abruptly comes to an end when Kathy embraces Eddie. Letting Eddie come up for air, Kathy tells him, "I won!" Eddie tells her, "I want a rematch!" Kathy whispers to Eddie, "that's what I like about you, you're light and airy." Eddie asks, "I am?" Kathy tells him, "yeah. Your energy is light and free. Nothing heavy can fly." Kathy whispers in his ear, "that's one of the reasons I love you." Eddie tells Kathy, "you're really like that too." Kathy replies, "yeah, and I'm going to stay that way." Dancing around the room, Kathy tells Eddie, "and I feel even lighter when I'm with you, everything is like waves and stars." Eddie, seeing a side of Kathy he's not seen before, expresses to her what he said to her a while ago, "Katarina

Karakova, I love you!" They embrace again, with Kathy listening for any hint of anyone coming home.

After Kathy and Eddie come back to this universe, Kathy asks, "so, do you want to eat here, or go out?" Eddie replies, "it doesn't matter. I'm starving. That Hula Hoop workout really wore me out." Kathy, making the executive decision, tells him, "OK, then. We're going out because dinner is not for another hour or two, and my mom's not home yet." Eddie asks her, "OK, then, where are you taking me?" Kathy tells him, "it's a surprise, and it's not pizza." They head out the door, and head in the direction of the pizzeria. The main street in the town has a lot of small restaurants, coffee shops, and delicatessens. Eddie will have to wait to see what Kathy has in mind.

On the way, Kathy asks Eddie, "so, what's your secret?" Eddie replies, "what do you mean?" Kathy tells him, "well, you know two of mine. I break down, and I Hula Hoop." Eddie tells Kathy, "you wouldn't believe me even if I told you." Kathy tells Eddie, "try me." Eddie tells her, "you'll think I'm crazy." Kathy tells Eddie, "I promise, I won't think you're crazy." Eddie, telling Kathy his secret, says to her, "I can go into the future." Kathy responds, "no! Really? Are you serious?" Eddie tells her, "I know it sounds crazy, but it's possible." Kathy tells Eddie, "OK, show me." Eddie tells Kathy about the portal, and where it is. Actually believing Eddie, Kathy wants to see it right after dinner. Kathy is not willing to let this wait until the weekend.

Kathy takes Eddie to a Greek sandwich shop that is on the way to the pizzeria. They both order a Gyro and a side salad. Over dinner, Eddie tells Kathy all about the portal, and how he found it. He explains that the portal is the way that he gets his vitamins and brings them back. Kathy, surprisingly to Eddie, does not think he is crazy.

Also during dinner, Eddie asks Kathy, "what did you mean when you said, 'nothing heavy can fly'?" Kathy explains herself, "heavy energy, like Mahoney. He's always mad and angry." Eddie says, "yeah, I've noticed that. Everyone stays away from him." Kathy further explains, "he's not a free spirit like you. That's why his times on the track are getting slower, and yours are getting faster." Eddie asks Kathy, "was he faster last year?" Kathy replies, "oh, yeah! No one knows what happened to him, but I do." Kathy continues, "look at Braden this afternoon. He's just being himself, and whooped Mahoney." Eddie quickly responds to that, "yeah, I still wish I was in that race."

Kathy asks Eddie, "do you want to know another secret?" Eddie responds, "sure, good things come in threes." Kathy thinks carefully how to word her answer, and tells Eddie, "this may not make too much sense, but I see things other people don't." She then gives Eddie an example, "like when I first saw you, I somehow knew you were different." The check arrives, and Kathy leaves the money on the table. Kathy abruptly tells Eddie, "OK, more about my superpower later. And don't let me forget. Take me to the future!" Eddie and Kathy get up and walk out of the restaurant so fast that the person sitting next to them thought they had an emergency. After dinner, they walk back as fast as they can to get Kathy's bicycle. From there, Kathy rides to Eddie's house as Eddie runs beside her. When they get to Eddie's house, he gets his bicycle, and they ride off to the portal.

Eddie and Kathy ride down the road, and make a left at Angelo's Service Station. Eddie glances over at his future MGB, making sure it is safe, which it is. They ride past Mark's house, and take the paved path along the parkway. Eddie is quite surprised at how well Kathy can keep up with him. Eddie yells out to Kathy, "we're almost there." Eddie slows his pace, and right before the portal, he gets off his bicycle. Pointing to the three boulders, he tells Kathy, "there it is, right up there."

Eddie and Kathy walk up to the portal, and Eddie tells her, "here it is, right here." Kathy asks, "how does it work?" Eddie tells explains to her, "you raise your right hand, and say when you want it to be, and you immediately get there." Eddie then asks, "when do you want to go to, 10, 20, 30 years from now?" Kathy replies, "lets try 25." Eddie asks, "how about in the Summer?" Kathy tells him, "well, maybe late Spring. I'm not dressed for Summer." Eddie tells Kathy, "OK, hold my hand," as he holds Kathy's hand with his left hand. Eddie raises his right hand, saying, "May, 25 years from now, in the afternoon." In a moment, Kathy asks, "are we there?" Looking around Eddie responds, "yeah. It got a little cooler, and the clouds are all gone." Kathy looks around, seeing the difference, asks, "OK, where are we going to go?" Eddie replies, "the beach, the school, maybe the park." Kathy exclaims, "beach!"

Eddie explains to Kathy, "if we stay here for four hours, when we get back, it will be the same time as when we left." Kathy asks, "how do we get back?" Eddie tells her, "we just walk back into the portal, and we're back to the time we came from." Kathy, who is not the least bit stressed or apprehensive, asks, "how far is the beach?" Eddie responds, "eleven miles. Well, eleven miles from my house." Kathy responds to him, "cake! Let's go." All excited, Kathy and Eddie head in the direction of the beach, making good time.

When they arrive, the beach is definitely open for business. Eddie and Kathy ride to the parking lot that has the concession stand and the pool. They ride to the bicycle rack, and Eddie locks their bicycles. Finally, they have time together. Kathy, jumps up onto Eddie's hips, and gives him a hug. Kathy tells him, "we made it!" While they are walking toward the water, Kathy then asks, "OK now what?" Eddie suggests, "let's take a walk along the shore."

On the way to the water, Kathy stops abruptly, and sits on the sand. Eddie sits with her, waits a bit, then asks, "are you OK?" Kathy replies, "no! Listen to that song." A couple sitting right near where Kathy sat is playing the song The Power of Love, by Céline Dion. Kathy, with a tear rolling down her cheek, tells Eddie, "that song! It's so beautiful." They listen to the song together, holding each other as they watch the waves crash onto the beach.

When the song is over, Kathy tells Eddie, "I've got to have that song. It's so beautiful!" Eddie tells her, "we'll find a way to get it for you." Before they continue walking to the water, Kathy asks the couple, "do you know what that song was that just played?" The girl responds, "that was by Céline Dion. The name of the song is The Power of Love." Kathy responds graciously, "thank you, thank you so much." She then asks Eddie, "help me remember that, 'Céline Dion, The Power of Love,' OK?"

Overhearing Kathy and Eddie's conversation, the girl asks Kathy, "do you want me to play it again for you?" Kathy asks, "can you?" The girl answers, "sure." The girl pushes a few buttons on her iPhone, and the song plays again through her wireless speakers. The girl's technology is totally foreign to Kathy and Eddie. This time they slow dance to the song, as the girl who played the song tells her boyfriend, "they are so sweet. Look at them." After the song is over, Kathy thanks the girl again for playing the song again. They walk to the water, keep repeating to each other, "Céline Dion, The Power of Love."

When they get to the water, Eddie asks Kathy, "so tell me about this superpower." Kathy replies, "oh, yeah. That's another one of my secrets." Eddie responds, "the more I find out about you, the more I love you, Katarina Karakova." Stopping on the beach, Kathy gives Eddie a hug and a kiss, telling him, "wow, our first kiss on the beach!" Getting back to Eddie's question, Kathy tells him, "somehow, and I don't know how, when someone doesn't tell me the truth, I know." Kathy continues, "that, my dear, is how I know you are truly someone special."

Bring up the flip side of her superpower, Kathy tells Eddie, "and that is how I know Mahoney is full of shit, excuse my French." Eddie, curious about what Kathy is telling him, replies, "tell me more. Keep going." Kathy goes on, "if someone is truthful, their energy is light and airy. If they are living a lie, their energy is heavy. That's what I meant when I said 'nothing heavy can fly' while we eating tonight." Whispering to Eddie, Kathy tells him, "when you said you can go into the future, I believed you." Planting both feet into the sand, and placing her hands on her waist, Kathy tells Eddie, "so then, detecting bullshit! That's my superpower!" A moment later, Kathy gives Eddie a hug, and whispers to him, "but really, my superpower is I can read people really well."

Kathy and Eddie take a walk farther down the beach, with Kathy secretly hoping she hears that song again. Kathy asks him, "do you remember the name of the song?" Eddie replies, "Céline Dion, The Power of Love." Kathy tells him again, "I really got to have that song!" Eddie reassures Kathy, "we'll get it somehow."

On their walk, Eddie mentions, "this place still really looks about the same." Kathy replies, "yeah, ocean and sand. Beaches haven't changed much over the last few thousand years." After Kathy's answer, Eddie tells her, "OK, I'm going to tickle you again." Kathy then runs in circles in the sand, with Eddie chasing her. Abruptly turning around, she runs to Eddie and jumps onto his hips, holding him around his neck. Kathy kisses Eddie, distracting him from any tickling he had planned. Kathy then whispers to him, "the power of love."

The afternoon on the beach comes to an end as the sun begins to set. Kathy asks Eddie, "can we please, please, please stay for the sunset?" Eddie replies, "sure. I'd like that." They find a place on the beach with a good view. Kathy asks, "so, when we get back, it will be the same time we left?" Eddie replies, "yeah. It's weird. But, that's what happens." Looking at her arms, Kathy asks, "does my suntan come back with me too?" Eddie, somewhat puzzled, answers, "you know, I don't know." While Kathy sits on Eddie's lap, they have a wonderful conversation as they wait for the sun to set.

With the beach nearly deserted, the sun begins to set. Kathy whispers to Eddie, "I haven't seen the sun set like this for years." Eddie confesses, "me either." Kathy whispers again in his ear, "this is the best sunset ever, because

I'm here with you." While the sun is setting, Eddie and Kathy hold each other, never expecting a day of track tryouts to end like this.

Once the sun has set, they both know that have to make the trip back. They get up and walk back to the bicycle rack where they locked their bicycles earlier. Eddie asks Kathy, "so are you up to riding eleven miles?" Kathy thinks for a moment, and replies, "no, carry me." Eddie picks up Kathy, and carries her back to their bicycles. On the way, Eddie, with a sense of humor much like Kathy's, asks her, "I ran all day, and now I have to carry you?" Thinking for a moment, Kathy tells Eddie, "if I remember correctly, you ran, let's think about this, a grand total of what, 220 yards?" Laughing so hard, Eddie has to put Kathy back on her feet. Eddie replies, "yeah, I guess so, 220 yards." Returning to the bicycle rack, they unlock their bicycles, and make the eleven-mile trip home.

Because it is dark out, Eddie has a little trouble finding the exact location of the portal. Kathy tells him, "oh good! We're stuck here forever together!" Eventually they find the portal, Kathy asks, "OK, now how do we get back again?" Eddie tells her, "we just walk back though it." They walk through the portal again, holding hands. While they are walking through, it immediately becomes daytime again. Kathy gives Eddie a high-five, screaming out, "awesome! We had a vacation together!" Kathy, looking at her watch, tells Eddie, "and look at that, it's the same time when we left!" Eddie thinks for a moment, and says to Kathy, "wow, that means we can leave for days and come back, and no one will ever notice." Kathy and Eddie then begin the short trip back to Kathy's house.

When they arrive at Kathy's house, Kathy sighs, telling Eddie, "well, I guess it's back to reality, homework and that sort of thing." Eddie replies, "yeah, and tomorrow we have another day of tryouts." Kathy reminds him, "tomorrow it's just relay drills and, by now, Mr. Frazier has the team picked." Eddie replies, "that should be easy, if it's like anything like Winter track." Kathy reassures him, "yeah, it'll be cake." Kathy and Eddie sit on the lawn and talk for a while longer.

When it comes time for Eddie to head home, Kathy tells him, "I don't want you to go." Eddie holds Kathy tightly, and whispers to her, "we can go to the beach again on Saturday." Thinking for a moment, Kathy replies, "yeah, or the pool but, next time, I'm bringing my swimsuit." Kathy then remembers, "oh, yeah. And we got to get that song." Eddie replies, "yeah, Céline Dion, The

Power of Love." Eddie and Kathy kiss goodnight, knowing that, after today, nothing will ever be the same again.

The next morning, Eddie is waiting for Kathy so they can walk to school together. Walking out of her house, Kathy sees Eddie waiting by the sidewalk. Kathy tells Eddie, "I'm really tired this morning, carry me." Eddie replies, telling Kathy, "well, we did have a 30-hour day yesterday." In an ah ha moment, Kathy tells Eddie, "yeah, you're right!" Kathy concludes, "well, we should have just slept on the beach and came back in the morning." When they arrive at school, Kathy tells Eddie, "see you at practice, maybe before." They kiss each other in the school lobby, and head to their classes. Anyone not knowing that Kathy and Eddie are together no longer has any doubt.

At the end of the day, the last session of tryouts begins. The team members have already been determined, and today the relay teams will be decided. With the team meeting at the track, Mr. Frazier discusses today's agenda. He begins by telling the group, "today, we are going to be running relay drills. While you will not be on the clock, your handoff will be done at full speed. Kathy and I will be right here in the middle, at the transition zone. We will be watching your handoff, and recording how well you do." Pointing to one end of the 220-yard straight track used for sprinting, Mr. Frazier tells the group, "Barbara will be at that end." Pointing to the other end of the straight track, Mr. Frazier tells them, "and Paula will be at that end. Barbara and Paula will tell you what to do." Mr. Frazier then makes an announcement to the team as to which runners will be at each end, and which six runners will initially remain in the transition zone.

Today, Mr. Frazier brings several hand-held two-way radios to the practice session. Since the venue is larger than the indoor arena, he often uses the radios during the Spring track season to communicate with his assistants. Giving one to Paula and another to Barbara, he will use the radios to communicate matching up certain runners on the handoff. Mr. Frazier and Kathy will be seated close to the transition zone, where they can watch the handoff. Kathy is happy that she gets to sit today because she is a little tired from yesterday's beach expedition.

The drill begins, and continues for a while. Mr. Frazier watches the actual handoff of the baton, and Kathy has been watching for any break in cadence involving either runner. Eddie, Mark, Braden, and Johnson have been working together for years, and they have their handoffs down to a science. Some of the other runners have also been working with each other for years, and their handoff is also great.

Mr. Frazier decides to see how well some of the faster runners handoff to the 4 by 440 relay medalists. As Bell delivers the baton to another runner, using the radio, Mr. Frazier tells Paula to put Eddie in lane three. Bell is instructed to get in lane three to receive the baton from Eddie. As Eddie enters the transition zone, he is running much faster than Bell expected. Bell quickly realizes this, and leaves slightly early. This allows for a smooth transition.

Just arriving in the transition zone, and handing off, is Mahoney. Mr. Frazier, on the radio, asks, "where's Braden?" Using the radio, Paula replies, "here with me." Mr. Frazier takes a quick survey of the field, and tells Paula, "put him in lane six next." Mr. Frazier tells Mahoney to get in lane six. Braden, receives the baton, and is at full speed long before the transition zone. Mahoney sees Braden coming, and takes off. Mahoney, not nearly close to full speed, is unable to take hold of the baton from Braden. Braden passes Mahoney, still holding the baton. Now outside of the transition zone, Braden leaves the track, and walks back to where Mr. Frazier is seated.

Mahoney advises Braden, "you really messed that up!" Mahoney's comment is not well received by Braden, who exclaims, "me? What do you mean, me?" Braden points his finger at Mahoney, telling him, "you're slower than an ice cube melting at the North pole!" Mahoney screams back, "you're just going to." Before Mahoney could finish his sentence, Braden interrupts and finishes for him, "yeah, I'm just gonna shove the baton up your flimsy ass next time if you don't take it." Braden, all fired up, continues with his rant, "and if you ain't moving fast enough, I'm gonna kick you in your fat ass to get you moving if I have to."

Meanwhile, Mr. Frazier, listening to the exchange between Braden and Mahoney, cannot contain his laughter. Kathy is also laughing uncontrollably, remembering what she told Eddie about Mahoney's anger yesterday. Mr. Frazier instructs Mahoney to get back in lane six. He instructs Braden to go to the end of the track and tells them both, "we'll keep doing it until we get it right." Mahoney, by attempting to make Braden appear incompetent in front of Mr. Frazier, made himself look bad instead.

The next transition between Braden and Mahoney goes a little better, but not the seamless transition that is needed for competition. Mr. Frazier mentions to Kathy, "I'm beginning to think that Mahoney and Braden are incompatible on the track." Kathy is thinking to herself that Mahoney is not compatible with anyone. Kathy, holding her tongue, replies, "yeah, I can see that. Last year, Mahoney was a lot faster. And, you know, Braden is kind of funny when he gets fired up like that." Mr. Frazier replies, "yeah, I know. And, after he rants like that, he runs better, so I'm not stopping it." Kathy points out to Mr. Frazier, "everyone else seems to run faster too." Mr. Frazier replies, "yeah, I think you're right about that."

A few minutes later, Kathy tells Mr. Frazier, "that stuff Mark and Eddie pull at the starting line is really funny too." Mr. Frazier asks, "oh? What do they do?" Kathy tells him, "well, for one, during the State meet, when the Starter said 'on your marks.' Eddie told Brady, the number one seed, 'you again,' which distracted him and caused him to lose the race." Kathy tells Mr. Frazier, "Mark pulls that kind of stuff all the time." Mr. Frazier asks, "what does Mark do?" Kathy explains to Mr. Frazier, "well, to start with, both of them scope out the highest seed in the race. When the Starter says, 'on your marks, Mark says to the highest seed next to him, 'I though you said you were ready.' The runner then questions everything, like the block settings, his position, and even if his shoelaces are tied. That throws the runner off." Mr. Frazier laughs, telling Kathy, "I didn't know that about them." Kathy informs Mr. Frazier, "yeah, those guys are really funny at the starting blocks. Even the Starters are entertained."

Tryouts finally come to an end, and everyone heads to the locker room. On the way back, Kathy asks Eddie, "did you hear Braden?" Eddie replies, "yeah. That was kind of funny. Especially that comment that Mahoney is slower than an ice cube melting at the North pole." Kathy tells Eddie, "yeah, even Mr. Frazier found it amusing." Eddie tells Kathy, "yeah, I see what you meant about Mahoney. He can't even run anymore." Kathy mentions, "something is sucking the life out of him big time." Eddie proposes that, "maybe it's Braden." Thinking about that for a moment, Kathy replies, "Braden couldn't suck the life out of Mahoney unless he lets Braden do it. It's Mahoney. It's got to be. He's his own problem." Eddie replies, "and he can have it." Kathy, with words of wisdom, says, "yeah, you don't want any part of that energy. All it can do is drag you down." When they come up to the school, Kathy tells Eddie, "catch you in a few."

Kathy and Eddie meet at the school entrance and walk home together. On the way, Eddie tells Kathy, "I ran more than 220 yards today. Carry me." Kathy stops, and tells Eddie, "I love you so much! You are so much fun!" As they start walking again, Kathy tells Eddie, "you're the one in training. You should be carrying me." Eddie stops, and tells Kathy, "hold my book." Eddie gets behind Kathy, putting his head between her legs. He grabs her hips, and raises her onto his shoulders. All bubbly, Kathy tells Eddie, "I didn't really mean that you actually had to carry me!" Eddie replies, "yeah, but it sounds like to me that you're liking it." Kathy exclaims, "yeah, I really am!" As Eddie walks down the street with Kathy on his shoulders, he tells her, "watch out for tree branches."

When they get to Kathy's house, Eddie lets her down, telling her, "now I can skip my workout tonight." Kathy jokingly asks him, "are you telling me I'm heavy?" Eddie replies, "no, I'm just weak. Remember? I get worn out after running 220 yards." They both have a good laugh, and sit on the grass and talk for a while. Since no school work has gotten done in the last few days, Eddie and Kathy have a bit of catching up to do. They give each other a goodnight kiss, and Eddie starts the long walk home.

The next day, the final roster is posted on the window of the administration area. As Eddie and Kathy walk in, they see Johnson, Braden and Bobby B. looking over the list. Braden tells Eddie, "it looks like we have our 4 by 440 relay team again. That's going to tick Mahoney off." Eddie, seeing that he is in the 100-yard dash, asks, "who else got the 100?" Kathy replies, "you, Mark, and Johnson." Kathy also adds, "Mr. Frazier hasn't made all the decisions yet." As they are talking, Mark walks up, and asks, "any news?" Braden answers, telling Mark, "no. It looks like Mr. Frazier gave us all exactly what we wanted, just like he said he would."

Looking at the roster, Braden casually mentions, "Mahoney got the half mile again." Mark, Eddie, Braden, and Johnson start laughing hysterically. Bobby B. asks, "what's so funny?" Kathy says, "yeah! Fill us in." Mark replies to both, "we'd better do this outside." Eddie, agreeing with Mark, says, "yeah, outside would be better." They all walk outside to the front of the school, and sit on the grass. On the way outside, Kathy tells Bobby B., "this is going to be good. I can feel it."

Kathy asks, "so, exactly what is it that you guys did?" Eddie starts the story by telling Bobby B. and Kathy, "during indoor track tryouts, I overheard Mahoney talking to Matt Wood. Mahoney was telling Matt that he hates running the half mile." Mark adds, "Eddie told us what he overheard, and none of us like running the half mile either." Eddie then tells Bobby B. and Kathy, "we figured that, if we let Mahoney win the half mile, he'll get stuck with it. After Johnson finished his race, we told him about it, and he was in on it too." Mark, explaining what Braden did, says, "and right before the race, Braden started his usual 'nobody's gonna beat me, I'm hot' rants, just to fire up Mahoney. And so, we all let Mahoney win the race."

Bobby B. starts laughing, with Kathy joining in. Kathy, now laughing uncontrollably, exclaims, "tell me you guys didn't!" Braden says, "oh, yeah! We did! And, Mahoney was so proud of winning that race and beating us. He was giving everyone high-fives." Braden is quick to point out, "I'm not running the half mile. I'll let junior run it." Mark adds, "and it worked! Mahoney won, and got stuck with the half mile." Kathy says to the group, "you guys just made my day!"

After a good laugh, they all go to class, starting the day in an awesome mood. On the way to class, Kathy tells Eddie, "at practice yesterday, I was telling Mr. Frazier what you guys do at the starting blocks, like how you distract the opponents." Kathy then adds, "he though that was too funny." Eddie says, "I hope Mr. Frazier doesn't find out about one we pulled on Mahoney." Kathy replies, "my lips are sealed. That is seriously funny! I can't believe you guys did that! I'm going to be laughing about that all day." As they walk through the hall and get to Kathy's classroom, Kathy says, "here's my stop, I guess I'll see you at practice." Eddie and Kathy kiss, having an awesome start to the school day.

The Spring Season

With the team members selected, and only a few days to practice before the first meet, the team has a lot of work to do. Before the first practice session, Mr. Frazier calls a short meeting in the gym. While the team is getting ready, there is a lot of chatter in the locker room about who is running in which event. Most of the runners have only been assigned one event, with some assigned to two events. Discussing the issue amongst themselves, they come to every conclusion except for the right one. Mr. Frazier has simply not decided yet.

The team takes a seat on the bleachers. Mr. Frazier walks in with Mr. Zunde, Barbara, Kathy, and Paula. Mr. Frazier then addresses the team. He begins by telling the team, "many of you have delivered a stellar performance during tryouts." He continues, "if you have excelled in an event, I have assigned you to that event." Many of the runners cheer. Mr. Frazier continues, telling the team, "Bobby B. has delivered a performance better than any freshman that I can remember in the shot-put." Mr. Frazier then announces, "the 4 by 440 relay that took first place during the Winter season will be running that event again during the Spring." Mahoney is heard saying, "second place," under his breath when Mr. Frazier made that comment. Mr. Frazier continues to deliver a considerable amount of good news.

Moving on to news that is not so good, Mr. Frazier tells the team, "I also have some bad news, which is that some of you have not delivered a stellar performance." Mr. Frazier then explains, "for some of you, your relay handoff gives me the impression you had three or four beers before tryouts yesterday." Someone seated in the back makes the comment, "yeah, like Mahoney." The whole team starts laughing hysterically. Mahoney, in self defense, blames his poor handoff skill on Braden again, saying, "that was Braden's fault."

Mahoney's comment fires up Braden, who abruptly stands up, taking control of Mr. Frazier's meeting. Braden, pointing to Mahoney, yells out, "that was your fault because you didn't get your fat ass moving fast enough! That's because you sit on your ass all day long! You sit on your ass in your car! You sit on your ass in class! And you even sleep sitting on your ass! And now, you even run sitting on your ass!" Mr. Frazier allows Braden to continue, seeing what else he may have to say. Braden continues, "I get up in the morning, lift weights, run for a half hour, get a shower, and then I walk to school." Braden now has Mr. Frazier's complete attention and interest. Going further, Braden shouts out, "then I come to practice, walk home, and lift more weights when I get home." Braden then makes the comment, "I don't work my damn ass off so you can sit on yours!" Braden finishes his dissertation, by telling Mahoney, "and if you can't grab that baton, next time I am gonna shove the baton right up your fat ass!" Half the crowd cheers, and the other half laughs. Braden then takes his seat. Mr. Frazier continues Braden's dissertation, telling the runners, "and, with that kind of working out and enthusiasm is how the 4 by 440 relay team won State!"

After Braden's pep talk, Mr. Frazier instructs Mr. Zunde, Barbara, Kathy, and Paula to take the team to the track. He then tells Braden, Eddie, Mark, and Johnson to remain behind. On the way out, Mahoney mentions to Bell, "good. Now they're really in trouble." Meanwhile, back on the bleachers, Johnson tells Braden, "uh oh, now you did it." Braden tells Johnson, "I wasn't even done! Mahoney couldn't even make the middle school track team. What's he even doing here?" Mark tells the group, "don't worry. The problem's Mahoney's anyway." Eddie is not worried. He knows the inside scoop from Kathy, which is that Mr. Frazier is not happy with Mahoney's performance.

Once the team is out of the gym, Mr. Frazier walks over to the bleachers where the gold medalists are seated. Braden, who is somewhat nervous, does not know what to expect from Mr. Frazier. Quite familiar with disciplinary action, Braden is aware that this is how it usually begins. Mr. Frazier opens by thanking Braden, "I would like to thank you for your energetic presentation to the team today." Mr. Frazier then confides, "you said things that I want to say but, for obvious reasons, I cannot." He continues, telling Braden, "perhaps you got something through to some of them." Mr. Frazier asks Braden, "is that really your workout routine?" Braden replies, "yes, sir. But, sometimes I do more, like on the weekends."

Knowing that Mark must also work out outside of track practice, Mr. Frazier asks him, "during your workouts, what do you do?" Mark replies, "in the morning, I take a run down along the parkway before school. If I have enough time, I'll lift weights before my shower. Then I lift weights again, every day before dinner." Mr. Frazier asks, "how about on the weekends?" Mark replies, "sometimes, my father puts me to work." Now quite curious, Mr. Frazier asks, "what does he do?" Mark explains, "he's a jobber. I carry 2 by 4s, help him build stuff, that kind of thing." Mr. Frazier asks, "what else?" Mark tells him, "I lift weights at least twice over the weekends. But, I usually take Friday evening off." Mr. Frazier cannot believe what he is hearing.

Coming to Johnson, who is the quiet one in the group, Mr. Frazier asks, "Johnson, how about you?" Johnson tells Mr. Frazier, "I lift after school, and then I get a run in before dinner." Mr. Frazier asks, "anything else?" Johnson tells him, "on the weekends, I ride my bicycle a lot. In the Summer, I ride my bicycle to my grandparent's house, cut their lawn, and ride home." Mr. Frazier asks, "how far is that?" Johnson replies, "ten miles, one way." Mr. Frazier asks, "how big is the lawn that you have to cut?" Johnson replies, "almost an acre. My grandfather can't do it anymore." Coming to the wrong conclusion, Mr. Frazier asks, "so, you use a riding mower?" Johnson, correcting Mr. Frazier, replies, "no, I use a push mower."

Coming to Eddie, Mr. Frazier asks, "Eddie, how about you?" Eddie replies, "I lift four or five days a week, and ride my bicycle a lot." Mr. Frazier inquires, "define 'a lot.'" Eddie replies, "usually about 50 to 75 miles a week. More over the Summer." Mr. Frazier asks, "what else do you do?" Eddie replies, "I carry Kathy home on my shoulders after school." The group, including Mr. Frazier, laughs over Eddie's commentary. Mr. Frazier asks Eddie, "when do you run?" Eddie tells Mr. Frazier, "I don't like running, so I usually don't. Well, except for on the beach, where I run there a lot in the sand." Mr. Frazier, in amazement, says, "you're the fastest guy in this school, and you don't like to run?" Eddie replies, "I ride my bicycle, swim laps, lift weights, cut eight lawns over the Summer, clean a few pools, so there's not much time to run."

Mr. Frazier tells the group, "well, this certainly explains a lot." Mr. Frazier tells the four runners, "it sounds like the team workouts are nothing for you guys." Mark replies, "well, it's fun." Eddie replies to Mark, "that's only because Paula's there." Mark replies back to Eddie, "until Kathy came along, I was faster than you." Braden, who is now a little chilled out, also replies, telling Mr. Frazier, "yeah, well the team workouts are where I get to kick ass." Mr. Frazier laughs, and replies, "and you're doing a great job of it! Just keep doing it!" Mr. Frazier then tells the group, "OK, let's get out there and start working." The four runners and their coach walk out to the track and join the rest of the team.

Out at the track, the first thing Mr. Frazier is working on is finding an alternate in the 100-yard dash. Mr. Frazier arranges a sprint between Eddie, Mark, Braden, Johnson, Bell and Mahoney. He tells the runners to get ready, and instructs Paula to be the Starter. He instructs Kathy to time the second place runner and Bell. Mr. Frazier will time the first place runner and Mahoney. Assigning the lanes, Mr. Frazier puts Johnson in lane one, Bell in lane two, Braden in lane three, Mark in lane four, Mahoney in lane five, and Eddie in lane six. The placement of the runners is by no means an accident. Mahoney is positioned between the two fastest sprinters in the school. The runners set the blocks, and are ready to race.

Mahoney, thinking that Mr. Frazier reprimanded Braden earlier in the gym, comments to Braden, "that'll teach you to shut up." Braden immediately gets irritated at Mahoney. Mark walks over to Braden, and calms him down. Mark whispers to Braden, "I'll get him, watch." In a few seconds, Paula commands the runners, "on your marks." Mark, immediately after Paula says, "set," tells Mahoney, "one of your laces isn't tied." Mahoney looks back to check his laces, and the gun is fired. Everyone is quickly out of the blocks, except Mahoney. The casual observer would think Mahoney's feet were glued to the blocks.

At the halfway point, Eddie leads, with Mark slightly behind. Johnson and Braden are tied, with Bell a few yards behind. Mahoney, who finally made it out of the blocks, is on his way to delivering a good middle school time. At the finish line, Eddie crosses first, followed by Mark. Johnson edges out Braden, taking third place. Bell, taking fifth place, finished not too far behind Braden today. Mahoney, delivering his most embarrassing performance of the year, finishes dead last.

Mr. Frazier and Kathy compare the times. Kathy tells Mr. Frazier, "I clocked Bell at a 10.8, and Mark at 10 flat." Mr. Frazier tells Kathy, "I got Eddie at a 9.7, but Mahoney ran a 12.9." Kathy writes down the runner's times. As she is writing, Mr. Frazier mentions, "I wonder what happened. That's a horrible time." Kathy thinks back about when she told Eddie that Mahoney is getting slower. Giving Mahoney the benefit of the doubt, Kathy replies, "it looks like Mahoney's times are getting worse. Maybe he's sick or something."

While Kathy and Mr. Frazier are talking, Mahoney starts yelling at Mark, attracting a bit of attention. Mahoney scolds Mark, telling him, "you messed up the race!" Mark tells Mahoney, "you got a problem, junior. Eat it." Mark, not wanting to listen to Mahoney's rant, walks away, and goes to talk with

Paula at the starting line. Mark does not choose to listen to such nonsense. It can lead to nothing constructive. Being ignored by Mark and getting no further attention, Mahoney kicks the ground and punches the air.

Not getting any response from Mark, Mahoney tells Mr. Frazier, "Mark cheated." Mr. Frazier asks, "oh, yeah? How exactly did Mark cheat?" Mahoney explains, "right before the gun went off, he told me my laces were untied." Breaking out in laughter, Mr. Frazier says to the senior, "and you fell for that?" Mahoney replies, "it's against the rules." Mr. Frazier counters Mahoney's argument, telling him, "it's against the rules to interfere with a runner once the race has begun. There is no rule against what Mark did, because it was before the race began. And, technically, what Mark did does not constitute interference anyway." Mr. Frazier then informs Mahoney, "by the way, you ran a 12.9. Get back to the blocks. I'll give you another chance." Kathy, who is listening to this conversation, remembers what she told Mr. Frazier yesterday, that Mark and Eddie distract the runner right before the gun goes off. Today, Mr. Frazier got to see first hand how well it works.

After the discussion between Mr. Frazier and Mahoney, Eddie asks Kathy, "what was my time?" Kathy tells him, "9.7." Eddie says, "that's what I ran last time." Kathy tells Eddie, "yeah, you've had no improvement in the last three days. I guess you'll have to carry me home every day until you get that time down." Eddie replies, "then I'll never get any faster because I like carrying you home." Kathy replies, "well, so far you only ran 100 yards today, so you're definitely going to need another workout." Kathy smiles and winks at Eddie, as she goes back to work. Mr. Frazier tells Kathy that he is arranging another sprint trial, and instructs her to round up certain runners.

Practice continues for another hour, with Mr. Frazier and his team assistants recording every bit of data they can. After this past Winter's indoor track season, Mr. Frazier has his eye on the State invitational meet again. This time, however, there will be no fooling around. He will do whatever he can to bring back as many medals as possible. What this means is the better runners will get the events in which they excel. As far as the relay events go, Mr. Frazier will strive to form relay teams that are virtually unbeatable.

With practice finished, the team begins to head to the locker room. Kathy, teasing Eddie, asks, "how many yards did you get in today?" Eddie replies, "not enough." Getting behind Kathy, Eddie raises her onto his shoulders. Kathy whispers to Eddie, "oh my! Eddie! I can't believe you're doing this!" Eddie replies, "I'm going to do this until I run a 9.6." Paula, walking beside

Mark and Eddie, bumps Mark's hip with hers, and asks Mark, "hey, how come I have to walk?" Without missing a beat, Mark lifts Paula onto his shoulders, and carries her back to the school. The two girls, high in the air and next to each other, give each other a high-five. Eddie tells Mark, "I hope she doesn't live far from the school." Mark replies, "she does. I guess I'm in big trouble." Once back to the locker room, they let the girls off of their shoulders, and plan to meet out front in a few minutes.

Kathy and Paula meet out front, waiting for Mark and Eddie. While the guys were getting dressed, Kathy calculated how much time Mark and Eddie actually ran today. Paula asks Kathy, "did you figure it out?" Kathy replies, "yeah. Eddie only ran for two minutes and twenty-five seconds, and Mark ran for a grand total of three minutes and fifty-four seconds." Paula replies, "so Mark worked out for less than four minutes today?" Kathy answers, "yeah. They are definitely carrying us home." Paula says to Kathy, "this is getting to be kind of fun."

The guys exit the front door, and meet up with Kathy and Paula. Kathy asks Paula, "are you going to tell them, or should I?" Paula replies, "I'll do the honors." Knowing the girls are up to something, Mark mentions, "uh oh, what's up?" Paula tells Mark, "you only worked out for three minutes and fifty-four seconds today, and Eddie only two minutes and twenty-five seconds." Kathy comments, "you can't really call that a workout, can you?" Eddie mentions to everyone, "I know exactly where this is going." Eddie gets behind Kathy, and lifts her onto his shoulders, and asks Mark, "what are you waiting for?" Mark then lifts Paula onto his shoulders. Eddie announces, "Kathy's house, in a half mile. Greek food, in three quarters of a mile. Pizza, in about a mile." The girls then yell out in unison, "pizza." Eddie says, "I knew that was coming." As they walk away, one of the baseball players says to another, "maybe we should have gone out for track. It looks like they're having a lot more fun."

Once they cross the main road, Kathy tells Eddie, "if you want, you can put me down." Eddie tells her, "you don't want me to put you down. You're having too much fun." As they walk down the sidewalk, many of the drivers honk their horns, and many whistle at the girls. Kathy and Paula wave back at the cars, having more fun than they could have imagined. No one would ever think that two guys carrying two girls on their shoulders down a busy road would attract so much attention.

Once they get to the pizzeria, someone opens the door for Eddie and Mark. Eddie tells the girls, "don't forget to duck," as they walk through the door. Once inside, everyone turns and looks at Kathy and Paula sitting on Eddie's and Mark's shoulders. Eddie and Mark let the girls off their shoulders. Joe, working behind the counter, yells out, "hey, it's so good to see you guys today!" Joe then asks, "how far did you guys carry your girls?" Kathy replies, "all the way from school!" Joe replies, "wow, you guys must be hungry. I tell you what, if you order two pizzas, one of them is on me!" Paula tells Joe, "Joe, that is so sweet of you." Joe replies, "well, you guys brought me some happiness today."

The group takes a seat, and decides what's for dinner. While Eddie and Mark go up to the counter and place the order, Paula whispers to Kathy, "I think I'm falling in love with Mark." Kathy whispers, "then tell him. Anyone can see the same in his eyes." Paula replies, "really?" Kathy tells her, "he just carried you a mile on his shoulders, so think about that for a moment! Stop second guessing yourself."

The guys return with the drinks and have a seat. The conversation abruptly shifts to the upcoming weekend. Paula asks, "what are you guys doing this weekend?" Eddie, looking at Kathy, replies, "maybe, if the weather is good, we were thinking about a ride to the beach. The water is still a little too cold, but it's kind of nice there." Paula asks, "do you guys want some company?" Kathy reluctantly agrees, telling Paula, "sure, that would be great." Kathy really wanted to go through the portal again, and get the song she loves, The Power of Love. She figures that could wait until another day. Dinner arrives, and the guys and gals dig in.

After dinner, everyone walks back in the direction of the school. Kathy mentions, "since you guys just ate, we'll walk ourselves." Paula says, "yeah, you shouldn't work out right after you eat." Mark suddenly starts laughing. Paula asks, "what is so funny?" Mark says, "maybe, I'll tell Mahoney the secret to running a good half mile is to eat a whole pizza right before the race." Eddie, Kathy, and Paula also start laughing. Kathy, laughing hysterically, exclaims, "he might just believe that!" Once they get down the road to the corner, the couples say goodbye for the evening. Eddie and Kathy walk to Kathy's house. Mark and Paula take a right, headed to Paula's house.

On the way, Kathy asks Eddie, "does anyone else know about the portal?" Eddie replies, "no." Kathy asks Eddie, "should we tell Mark and Paula?" Eddie explains, "once I was thinking about telling Mark, but I thought he'd think I'm crazy." Eddie also mentions, "I trust the guy, but he'd really think I'm crazy." Kathy asks, "how long have you known him?" Eddie replies, "since kindergarten." Kathy exclaims, "wow! I've known Paula since kindergarten too! But, I can definitely see how people might think we're crazy."

Eddie tells Kathy, "use your superpowers!" Kathy replies, "my superpowers?" Eddie says, "yeah. Remember you told me when we were at the beach you can read people really well." Kathy replies, "yeah, that's right! I can do that!" Eddie replies, "so, see if you can figure out if they'll believe it." Eddie suggests, "if you think they'll believe it, we can tell them about it." Flexing her biceps, Kathy replies, "yeah, I'll use my superpowers."

Once they arrive at Kathy's house, Kathy appears somewhat disappointed. Eddie asks, "is everything OK?" Kathy tells him, "yeah. Tomorrow's Friday, and I have two tests." Eddie replies, "uh oh. I have one, and I totally forgot about it." Kathy says, "yeah, I've been a real slacker this week." Eddie replies, "yeah, me too. I only ran for how long today?" Kathy replies, "exactly two minutes and twenty-five seconds, but you more than made it up on the way to the pizzeria." Kathy explains to Eddie, "I'd ask you to study with me, but nothing will get done." Eddie asks, "how do you know?" Kathy answers him, "trust me, I know." Kathy and Eddie give a long goodnight embrace, which makes it even harder for Eddie to leave. But, all good things come to a temporary end, and they will see each other in the morning.

The next morning arrives, and Eddie and Kathy walk to school together. Their conversation ultimately comes back to where they left off the night before. Kathy tells, "OK, so I'm going to see if Paula is going to believe us about the portal." Eddie asks, "how would you know?" Kathy explains to Eddie the best she can, "I don't know how I'll know, but I know that I'll know, if that makes any sense." Eddie replies, "actually, it does." Eddie then asks, "how about Mark?" Kathy replies, "Mark is easy to read. He'll go along if Paula goes." Kathy, who is very observant, relates to Eddie, "Mark is very confident. The only thing he wasn't confident about was believing that Paula liked him, but he's over that now." Eddie replies, "yeah, you're right about that." When they arrive at school, Kathy tells Eddie, "OK, I'm going to find out. I will definitely let you know."

Later that day, Kathy and Eddie meet at the front of the school. There is no track practice today, so they get a break. This, however, will not stop many of the team members from training over the weekend. With the first meet coming up shortly, everyone must be ready. Kathy mentions to Eddie, "since there's no practice, I'll give you the day off. You don't have to carry me." Eddie replies, "and I was so looking forward to carrying you!" Kathy, breaking the news to Eddie, tells him, "by the way, Paula will believe us about the portal." Eddie responds, "awesome!" Kathy then asks, "aren't you going to ask how I know?" Eddie, remembering yesterday's conversation, tells her, "I know that you know. It's your superpower." Kathy replies, "good, because I don't know how I know. I just know."

Just as Eddie and Kathy begin to walk home, Paula comes up, and asks, "are you guys still going to the beach?" Kathy replies, "yeah! Are you guys coming?" Paula replies, "sure! We'd love to." Kathy replies to Paula, "we have a big surprise for you." Spilling the beans all at once, Kathy tells Paula, "we're going to the beach of the future." Paula responds, "oh, really?" Thinking for a second, Paula tells Kathy, "this is going to be fun. I can feel it." Eddie reminds Paula, "bring a swimsuit and a towel. We're going in the water." Paula, knowing the water is going to be really cold, gives Eddie a weird look.

Feeling that Kathy has something interesting planned, Paula replies, "you guys are definitely up to something." Kathy, not sharing any more information, just replies, "yeah, we are." Paula, who has known Kathy for years, knows beyond a shadow of a doubt that Kathy has something big planned. Paula also knows that she is not getting any more information out of Kathy until tomorrow, so she doesn't bother asking. Kathy tells Paula, "when you see Mark, tell him." Paula replies, "OK, he's meeting me in a few." Eddie and Kathy start their walk home, all excited about tomorrow.

The next day, the two couples meet at Mark's house, since he lives the closest to the parkway. When Eddie and Kathy ride up, Paula is already there waiting. Kathy's opening line is, "are you guys ready for the trip of a lifetime?" Paula comments to Mark, "see, I told you they are up to something!" Kathy reassures Mark and Paula, "uh huh, we're definitely up to something." Mark comments, "well, whatever it is, I'm game." Eddie comments, "OK then, are we all ready?" Paula replies, "beach time! Let's go!" They all get on their bicycles, and head out to the beach.

Eddie, Kathy, Mark and Paula ride down the road to the parkway. Eddie points to the path so Paula knows where he is going. Once on the path, Eddie lets Kathy take the lead because he has a tendency to ride faster than most people can. A mile down the road, Eddie calls out to Kathy, "on the right."

Kathy pulls off the path, and walks her bicycle up to the portal. Eddie and the rest follow Kathy's lead.

Once they are at the portal, Eddie asks Kathy, "are you going to tell them or me?" Kathy replies, "please, please, please, let me!" Kathy, who often takes control of the situation, begins by saying, "OK, ladies and gentlemen, we are about to take a trip into the future." Paula whispers to Mark, "see, she's for real and she's definitely up to something." Kathy continues, announcing to everyone, "I am your cruise director, Katarina Karakova. Once we get to our destination, nothing will appear the same as it does today. Does anyone have any questions before we enter the time machine?" Mark asks Paula, "do you have my ticket?" Paula laughs, and replies, "I thought you had them!" Kathy asks Eddie, "I wonder if it works for me. Can I try?" Eddie replies, "sure. Do you remember how?" Kathy tells Eddie, "there are just some things that you'll never forget. This is one of them."

Kathy tells the group, "please follow me to the time portal." Once among the boulders, Kathy tells everyone to hold hands. Kathy asks everyone, "OK, are we all ready?" Paula, knowing Kathy is for real, holds Mark's hand tightly. Kathy, raising her right arm, announces, "June, 25 years from now, in the morning, please." Kathy then whispers to Eddie, "did it work?" Eddie replies to her, "it sure looks like it. The sky is clearer, it's warmer, and look at the cars," as he points to the parkway. Kathy then announces, "OK, everybody, we're here! Let's go to the beach!" Mark and Paula look around. Paula, after seeing Eddie point to the parkway, also looks at the cars. Paula exclaims, "wow, check it out!" Mark, previously not knowing what to expect, exclaims, "cool, the trees are all different too!" Mark knows this path better than anyone, for he runs along it nearly every day.

Kathy then continues, "I will be your tour guide for today. Please follow me." Eddie tells Kathy, "if I had to take a wild guess, I'd think you're really enjoying this." Kathy replies, "I sure am!" As she walks back to the path, Kathy tells everyone, "OK everybody, please follow me." Once they get to the path, they all start riding to the beach. The guys let the girls lead the way because today's trip is not a race. On the way, Mark can see things are very different. Paula, however, has not been on the path before. But, she is very aware that something has dramatically changed.

Once they approach the beach, Kathy lets Eddie take the lead. Eddie rides around the turnabout, and takes a left turn. A half mile down the road, they enter the parking lot, which is getting full since it is a nice day. Eddie rides to the bicycle rack near the concession stand, and they lock their bicycles. Kathy announces, "OK, everyone, we're here." They each get their duffel bags, and head to the water.

Once on the beach, Paula mentions, "wow, like everyone is dressed all differently." Kathy replies, "yeah, and listen to the music. It's stuff we've never heard before." Mark, who is usually on the confident side, exclaims, "wow, I can't believe this is happening!" Paula, holding his hand, reassures him, "it is, trust me. It is." Eddie tells Kathy, "good, I'm not crazy." Kathy reassures Eddie, "I never thought you were." Mark mentions, "well, the beach looks about the same." Eddie replies, "yeah, ocean and sand. Beaches haven't changed too much over the last few thousand years." Kathy bumps Eddie's hip with hers, and exclaims, "hey, that's my line!" Eddie starts laughing, with Kathy joining in. Mark finds an open place in the sand, and says to the group, "how about here." Everyone lays out their towels, and lay in the sun for a while.

Paula mentions, "wow, the music is so different." Kathy tells Paula, "yeah, I heard this song that just got to have." Eddie says, "yeah, The Power of Love, by Céline Dion." After a while, Mark asks everyone, "does anyone want to catch some waves?" Eddie replies, "sure," and they all get up and go into the water. When they walk into the ocean, Eddie tells Kathy, "the water seems the same too. It's still wet, as usual." Kathy, replies to Eddie's comment, "I love you so much. You're so much fun!" They all have a fun time riding the waves. Eddie notices that there are not a lot of people riding the waves, but most people stay in water up to their knees. After a while, they come out of the water, and dry off. Everyone is hungry after the ride this morning, so lunchtime comes a little early.

They head over to the concession stand, and everyone is surprised at the prices on the menu. Paula mentions, "well, we know the inflation rate over the next 25 years." Eddie tells everyone, "don't worry, it's my treat." Eddie and Mark order lunch, and the girls find a picnic table. While they are waiting for the guys, Kathy tells Paula, "what's awesome is that when we get back, it will be the same time that we left." Paula replies, "no, you can't be serious!" Kathy responds, "yeah, we'll have the whole day ahead of us." Paula asks, "how long have you known about the portal?" Kathy tells Paula, "Eddie showed me earlier this week. He didn't show me before because he thought that I'd think he's crazy." Paula replies, "yeah, I can see that." The guys return with the food, and they all have lunch.

After lunch, Mark asks, "do you guys care if me and Paula take a walk up the beach?" Eddie replies, "no, go ahead. We'll just meet back here later." Paula says, "we won't be too long, maybe an hour or so." Kathy thinks to herself, "yeah, right. That's going to be more than a walk." Mark and Paula take a walk down the beach, and Eddie and Kathy lay out on their towels for a few minutes. Eddie and Kathy then decide to go on their own walk.

Kathy and Eddie walk past the concession area, in the opposite direction of Mark and Paula. A little farther down, Kathy finds a group of sand dunes. She says to Eddie, "look, sand dunes. Let's check them out." They walk in and around the dunes for a few minutes. After looking around, Kathy tells Eddie, "here it is, the perfect spot." She sits in the sand with Eddie, telling him, "no one can see us here." Before Eddie can reply, Kathy embraces her sweetie. They spend the next hour among the dunes, having the private oasis all to themselves. All they hear are waves crashing, and a few seagulls in the background.

More than an hour goes by. Eddie and Kathy have no idea how long they've been in the dunes. They get up and walk in the direction of the shore. Making their way through the sand, they are walking like they are a bit drunk. Kathy tells Eddie, "look at what you did to me! I can't even walk straight." Eddie asks, "should I just carry you?" Kathy replies, "only if you don't drop me." Kathy whispers to Eddie, "do you have any idea what you do to me?" Eddie replies, "yeah. You do it to me too." Eddie, putting his arm around Kathy, tells her, "here, we'll just hold each other up." They walk along the shore, making their way back to their towels.

When they find their towels, they also find Mark and Paula laying out in the sun. Eddie mentions to them, "I hope you weren't waiting for us." Mark replies, "no, we just got back." Kathy tells Mark and Paula, "we got lost." What Kathy meant is that she and Eddie got lost in each other. By the way she said that, Eddie knew exactly what she meant. Mark and Paula pretty much figured it out too, because they got lost in the same way. All the sand in Kathy's and Paula's hair gives it away.

After another hour or so of laying out and riding waves, the time comes to make the trip back. Paula asks, "by the way, how do we get back home?" Eddie replies, "we just walk through the portal again." Paula says, "wow, that's easy." They gather up their stuff, and walk to their bicycles. As Eddie unlocks the bicycles, Paula tells everyone, "wow, this was really fun!" Mark replies, "yeah, the beach is Eddie's Summer hangout." Paula tells Mark, "and, it's going to be ours too." Not realizing she likes the beach so much, Paula has just planned Mark's Summer well in advance. Kathy doesn't really care where her Summer hangout is, as long as it is with Eddie. They all get on their bicycles, and begin the ride home.

When they come up to the portal, they get off their bicycles and walk up to the boulders. Kathy, being the tour guide for the day, tells everyone, "this ends our trip to the future today. I hope that you had a good time, and travel with us again sometime in the future." They all walk through the portal, arriving in the morning at the same time they left. Mark says, "wow, I still can't believe this." Eddie suggests, "maybe we can go to the future someday and watch a track meet at the school." Kathy adds her own suggestion, "I guess you can go to the future, and watch yourself run!" Kathy's remark makes everyone seriously think about what being able to go to the future means. They all then get on their bicycles again and ride to Mark's house.

Once they arrive at Mark's house, they sit on the lawn and talk for a while. Eddie says, "well, we still have the whole day ahead of us." Kathy points out, "yeah, and look! I got an awesome tan!" Paula still has not fully grasped what they have just experienced. Mark, sitting against a tree, asks, "I wonder if we can go back in time too." Eddie already knows the answer, which was given to him by the mechanic. Eddie replies, "yeah, we can." Mark then suggests, "we can go back to a track meet, and mess with McCrutchen twice as much." Eddie says to Mark, "then there will be two of you in the same place." Paula points out, "that will surely cause a mess." Kathy adds her two cents, "I think I prefer the beach." Then she remembers, and tells Eddie, "oh, and we've got to get that song!"

Mark then asks, "when is the first meet anyway?" Paula replies, "this coming Wednesday." Eddie asks, "against who?" Kathy replies, "I think it's Riverdale." Eddie then asks, "Riverdale? Why does that ring a bell?" Kathy answers, "Brady. He ran the 40-yard dash at State. He's mad at you guys." Eddie replies, "I guess I have a lot of work to do." Knowing Brady has fallen for the simplest tricks in the book, Mark tells everyone, "I'll think of a way to work him over good. He won't win."

After a while, Kathy asks Eddie, "can we go and get that song, please, please, please?" Eddie replies, sure! How about now? Kathy, all excited, tells Mark and Paula, "we're going back, I mean forward, to get that song. Do you guys want to come?" Paula replies, "I think we'll hang out here a while." Mark and Paula seem content sitting under the tree, and don't look like they are moving anytime soon. Kathy tells them, "OK, we'll be back in a while." Eddie and Kathy then ride off to the portal to seek out Kathy's treasure.

Once they get to the portal, Kathy asks Eddie, "where are we going to find it?" Eddie suggests, "we can try the record shop near the mall." The record shop is only a short distance from the portal, an easy ride for Eddie and Kathy. They walk with their bicycles among the boulders, and Kathy raises her right arm, saying, "May, 25 years from now, in the afternoon." They then find themselves where they were earlier this week, and they ride off to the record shop. The record shop Kathy and Eddie will be visiting is an international record store, stocking many releases intended for foreign markets that are not commonly seen in the United States.

When they get to the record shop, they walk in and nothing appears the same. The shop is packed with CDs, which is something totally unfamiliar to Eddie and Kathy. They manage to find a section that still has vinyl, which is more familiar to them. As they look through the albums, Kathy repeats to herself, "Céline Dion, The Power of Love." The clerk walks over and asks, "do you need any help?" Kathy replies, "I'm looking for Céline Dion, The Power of Love." The clerk then asks, "did you want the CD, or the vinyl album? Oh, and we might have the single in the back in 7-inch." Kathy looks at Eddie, as if the clerk is speaking a foreign language. Kathy asks, "do you have the 45?" The clerk replies, "OK, so you want the 7-inch. Let me check." While the clerk goes to look, Kathy puts her head against Eddie's shoulder, and telling him, "I really hope they have it."

The clerk returns, telling Kathy, "we have a 12-inch promotional disc, but not the 7-inch." Never hearing of a promotional disc, Kathy asks, "what's that?" The clerk replies, "it's the same size as an album, but it's a single. And, it has much better sound quality. They're made for radio stations, and DJs." Suddenly happy that they have her song, Kathy tells the clerk, "we'll take it."

The clerk goes to the back and retrieves the record. When the clerk returns, they go to the checkout counter. The record cost $19.95 before tax, which is actually a deal, since the store got it free. It would normally cost more than that, if you could even buy one. The clerk tells them, "that will be $21.35." Kathy has a look of surprise when she hears the price. Eddie takes out some money, and hands it to the clerk. The clerk hands Kathy the bag, and Eddie the change, and Kathy has bagged her treasure.

When they get outside, Kathy tells Eddie, "I didn't mean for you to spend that much." Eddie tells Kathy, "but, now you have your song, and we're going back to listen to it." Neither Kathy nor Eddie has ever heard of a 12-inch promotional single. What they also didn't know is Kathy's $21.35 single will be worth hundreds of dollars someday. Kathy, so happy that she got her song, cries in Eddie's arms, with tears of happiness. Eddie tells her, "lets go and listen to it." They get back on their bicycles, and head back to the portal.

At the portal, they walk through, and are back in their time. Kathy tells Eddie, "OK, we're riding to my house to listen to my song. I hope you can keep up with me." Kathy rides to her house, and is so focused on getting there that she did not realize she rode right past Mark and Paula sitting on Mark's front lawn. When they get to Kathy's house, Eddie mentions to her, "you are really fast on your bicycle." Kathy replies, "well, I really want to hear my song." Eddie replies, "so, I really don't have to carry you." Before Kathy could reply, Eddie tells her, "ha, I got you!" Kathy, caught off guard, says, "yeah, that you did!"

They go inside, and Kathy heads right for the stereo. She puts the record on, and they both sit back and listen. Kathy, sitting next to Eddie on the sofa, is listening to her song with her eyes closed. Tears of happiness and joy flow down her cheeks as she is listening. Eddie lets her listen, being careful not to disturb her when she has her eyes closed. When the song is over, Kathy plays her song again. This time she stands, taking Eddie by the hand, and they slow dance together. While they are dancing, Eddie whispers to Kathy, "this really is a very beautiful song." Kathy whispers back, "yeah, thank you so, so much for getting it for me." When the song is over, Kathy sighs, and tells Eddie, "you really made my day."

Kathy and Eddie spend the rest of the day together. Later that day, Mark and Paula come over to Kathy's house to hear the song she loves so much. The four of them listen together, and everyone now knows why Kathy wanted that song so badly. The problem is that, in Kathy's time, Céline Dion did not record the song yet, so Kathy cannot play it for anyone else. In fact, in Kathy's time, Céline Dion is not even in kindergarten yet. Kathy's treasured recording of The Power of Love will be her secret, shared by only a few.

Eddie and Mark talk about the upcoming meet, while Kathy and Paula immerse themselves listening to The Power of Love again. While discussing the upcoming meet, Eddie mentions to Mark, "Brady is the number one seed in the region." Mark replies, "we'll figure out something." Eddie asks Kathy, "do you know Brady's best time in the 100?" Kathy replies, "I don't know his best time, but his average is in the mid 9s." Eddie tells Mark, "that might be doable."

Thinking about the upcoming meet, Eddie mentions to Mark, "I got to get some training in." Mark replies, "yeah, me too." Kathy, overhearing their conversation, mentions, "if you guys want, you can go train, and we'll sit here and listen to The Power of Love some more." Eddie asks, "you don't mind?" Kathy replies, "no, go ahead." Eddie asks Mark, "do you want to go on a long bike ride?" Mark replies, "yeah. I'll give it a try," as if the 22 miles they rode earlier today were not enough. Eddie and Mark kiss their sweethearts goodbye for the time being and head off to train.

The day of the first meet finally arrives. Not one, but three busloads of students from Riverdale empty out into the parking lot. One bus carried the team, and the other two busses carried spectators. With Brady being the region's number one seed, he has attracted a lot of attention. A few college scouts are also attending the meet. They will have their eyes on only one person, Brady. This will put a lot of pressure on Brady to run a superb race. From Brady's vantage point, tens of thousands of dollars of scholarship money are at stake. From Eddie and Mark's perspective, it's still all fun and games.

Before the meet, Mr. Frazier has the team meet in the auxiliary gym. Making the team aware of what will be going on behind the scenes ahead of time, he announces, "during today's meet, there will be a lot of spectators for Riverdale. A few college scouts will be also observing today's meet. They will all be looking at Brady." Raising his voice, Mr. Frazier announces, "Mahoney, if you still want a scholarship, today's your chance!"

Mr. Frazier then continues, "Brady is their sprinter. He is the number one seed in the region, and number two in the State." Now being well aware of Mark's and Eddie's pre-race activities, Mr. Frazier adds, "anything anyone can do to distract him, go ahead and do it. I want the scouts looking at us, not them! And, Braden! Brady runs the anchor leg in the 4 by 440 relay. You know what to do!" Braden, not missing a beat, exclaims, "we're kicking their ass! I don't care what kind of reputation Brady has! It's going down the toilet, along with his ass!" Mr. Frazier then continues, "that is exactly the attitude I want everyone to have!" Mr. Frazier goes over a few other important details with the team before they head out to the track.

As they get ready to walk out to the track, Mark asks Mr. Frazier, "do we know the lane assignments yet in the 100-yard dash?" Mr. Frazier tells Mark, "yes, they've already been assigned." Mark asks, "what lane is Brady in, three or four?" The top seed usually gets one of the inside lanes, either lane three or lane four. Mr. Frazier replies, "it's probably lane three, since he is the number one seed, but we can check with the Timekeepers." Mark asks, "can you please check for me?" Not daring to ask Mark what he is up to, Mr. Frazier replies, "sure, no problem."

On the way to the track, Kathy tells Eddie some good news. Kathy explains to Eddie, "Brady's best times were all on composite tracks, where he ran with pin spikes." Kathy further explains, "this is a gravel track, so the times are usually a bit slower." Eddie mentions, "that's all I've ever ran on before indoor track this year." Kathy tells him, "your times will be slightly faster on a composite track."

Once they get to the track, Mr. Frazier checks with the Head Timekeeper regarding the lane assignments for the 100-yard dash. Mr. Frazier reports back to Mark, telling him, "Brady is in lane three, Eddie is in lane four, and you are in lane two." Mark, confirming what Mr. Frazier told him, asks, "are you 100 percent sure that Brady's in lane three?" Mr. Frazier replies, "I saw it on the lineup sheet myself." Mr. Frazier is still hesitant to ask Mark why he needs this information. Mark tells Mr. Frazier, "I'm going to go and warm up."

Mark catches up with Eddie, telling him, "Brady's in lane three, you're in four, and I'm in two." Eddie tells Mark, "we're up first. They changed the order of the events." Mark tells Eddie, "come with me. We're going to run some warm-ups." Eddie tells Mark, "but the meet starts in a half hour." Revealing his plan, Mark tells Eddie, "we're going to work lane three over really good, and loosen up the gravel." Eddie smiles, knowing exactly what Mark is up to. On the way to the starting line, they recruit Johnson to help. If the gravel on the track is loose, the track will not be as fast compared to compact gravel. Mark intends to loosen up the gravel in lane three, which is Brady's lane.

When they get to the starting line, Mark digs his spikes into lane three, and twists his foot, loosening the gravel. Eddie and Johnson begin to do the same. They run a few warm-ups in that lane to further loosen the gravel, but primarily to give the appearance they are doing something reasonably legitimate. After fifteen minutes of warm-ups, Mark tells Eddie, "let's try it out." Mark suggests Eddie get in lane three, and Johnson in lane one. Mark tells them, "just run 10 yards." Eddie and Johnson get ready. Mark gives the command, "ready, set," waits two seconds, and says, "go." Eddie and Johnson are both out of the blocks fast but, at 10 yards, Johnson is ahead of Eddie, something that has never happened before. Eddie, impressed with Mark's engineering skills, tells Mark and Johnson, "let's just pace up and down lane three, drag our spikes, and loosen it up even more until the race."

The Head Timekeeper, who is also serving as the Meet Announcer, notifies everyone that the meet will begin in five minutes. He tells the coaches that the 100-yard dash will be the first race. Kathy runs up to Eddie, asking him, "are you ready?" Eddie replies, "I'm ready, and I'm going to win." Kathy reminds Eddie, "remember, don't let your guard down. Brady is the number one seed." Eddie replies, "not anymore. I'm the number one seed." Kathy perceives Eddie is quite confident, and she clearly knows that Eddie, Mark, and Johnson are up to something.

The Timekeeper tells the runners to get ready. Brady, who recognizes Mark from the indoor track season, says to him, "you're not messing up this race." Mark replies, "I don't have to. You already messed it up yourself." That is not what a runner wants to hear 30 seconds before the gun goes off, especially when there are several college scouts watching. Brady's emotions are now on shaky ground, just like the lane he is about to run in. Mark, Eddie, and Johnson, however, are very confident.

Meanwhile, about 20 yards from the finish line, standing back from the track, are the college scouts. Each scout has their position from where they prefer to watch the race. One scout will even be filming the race. The bleachers have a significant crowd, considering this is a regular season track meet. Riverdale's two bus loads of spectators are all waiting for the meet to begin. Today, the 100-yard dash is the main event.

Once the runners appear ready, The Starter announces, "on your marks." The runners position themselves in the blocks. A few seconds later, the Starter announces, "set." Brady, in lane three, is physically set, but not mentally. The gun goes off, and the runners are out of the blocks. After ten yards, Eddie is in the lead. Mark is slightly behind Eddie, with Johnson and Brady tied. Halfway through the race, at 50 yards, Eddie is clearly in the lead, with Mark in second place. Johnson progresses to third place, and Brady is now in fourth place. Brady has now lost all confidence in himself. Brady begins to pick up some speed at about 75 yards, probably because the gravel is more compact. Eddie, knowing he is going to win, begins to pick up even more speed than Brady. At the finish line, Eddie is the clear winner. Mark takes second place. Johnson slightly edges out Brady and takes third place. Brady, taking fourth place, lost the race, any scholarship he had hoped for, not to mention his confidence.

Eddie, learning from Zaino over the indoor track season, does not care what his time is. Eddie, and the other two winners, cool down and return to the finish line. On the way Mark passes Brady, telling him, "I told you that you messed it up." Brady returns the serve, telling Mark, "shut up." Mark, taking the upper hand in the psychological warfare, ignores Brady's comment. Mr. Frazier, who is more excited than a kid at Christmas time, congratulates the three runners. Kathy, Paula, and Barbara also congratulate Eddie, Mark, and Johnson with high-fives. Kathy and Mr. Frazier make their way to the Head Timekeeper to find out the runners' times.

The scouts also approach the Head Timekeeper, attempting to discover the runners' times. The other Timekeepers attempt to keep the scouts away. Once the times are compiled, the Head Timekeeper makes the long awaited announcement, "Edward Bogenskaya, 9.6 seconds. Mark Svoboda, 9.8 seconds. Eric Johnson, 9.9 seconds. John Brady, 10.0 seconds. Alan Green, 10.8 seconds. And Vincent Clark, 11.0 seconds." After the announcement, the scouts surround Mr. Frazier. The scouts are desperately trying to get any information they can about Eddie, Mark, and Johnson. Mr. Frazier makes the announcement, "our three winners today are all freshmen. Please come back in three years." The Riverdale coach, hearing that Eddie, Mark, and Johnson are all freshmen, is beginning to look a little frightened.

Kathy comes up to Eddie again, telling him, "you did it! You beat your best time and the number one seed!" Eddie replies, "yeah! A 9.6! So, now I don't have to carry you anymore?" Kathy replies, "yeah. But, you know you will." Eddie exclaims, "yeah, I know, because you like it!" Recalling that this is a track meet and not just practice, Eddie then tells Kathy, "oh, and I'll have to carry you back to the school after the meet, since I'm only running 540 yards today."

Mark and Paula then walk up and join Eddie and Kathy. Kathy then asks, "OK, what were you guys up to?" Eddie replies, "when?" Kathy tells him, "before the race. You, Mark and Johnson, you guys were definitely up to something." Eddie replies, "we were warning up, and loosening up the gravel in lane three, Brady's lane." Kathy replies, "you didn't!" Mark confesses, "we all ran our warm-ups in lane three, and loosened it up more by twisting our spikes into the ground." Kathy starts laughing, and asks, "OK, whose idea was this?" Mark replies, "it was mine. I'll take the blame." Paula starts laughing along with Mark, attracting a bit of attention.

All of the hysterical laughter prompts Mr. Frazier to walk over and investigate what could possibly be so funny. Mr. Frazier walks over, and asks, "let me in on it. What's going on?" They explain to Mr. Frazier how they loosened up the gravel, and Mr. Frazier begins to laugh hysterically. Mr. Frazier then comments to Mark, "so, that's why you wanted to know what lane Brady will be in." Mark replies, "exactly." Still laughing hysterically, Mr. Frazier informs them, "well, I'm not aware of any rule regarding everyone warming up in the same lane!" Mr. Frazier then moves on to the 4 by 880 relay, which is already in progress.

The meet runs smoothly and progresses rather well. Eddie, Mark, Braden, and Johnson are getting ready to run the 4 by 440 relay. Meeting with the 4 by 440 relay team before the event, Mr. Frazier tells them, "any one of you can beat Brady in a 440. There are two runners we haven't seen before today. So, don't let your guard down." Mr. Frazier mentions, "one of them beat Mahoney in the half mile." Braden comments, "that ain't saying too much." Mark asks, "did he beat Mitchell?" Mr. Frazier replies, "no. Mitchell ran a very smart race." Mr. Frazier tells them to get ready, as they make their way to the starting line.

The scouts will be watching the 4 by 440 relay as well. Brady has one last chance at impressing the scouts. Although he is a good sprinter, Brady is not very competitive at running 440 yards. One of the Riverdale 4 by 440 relay team members was also on the indoor track season. The other two are presumably faster than the runners they replaced. Brady's relay teammates are intending to help him look good in the 4 by 440 relay. Eddie and his teammates, on the other hand, are intending to make Brady look as bad as possible.

The teams are all ready to run, with the runners congregating around the transition zone. Braden starts exclaiming, "whose ass am I kicking today? Which one?" Mark points over to the Riverdale relay team, telling Braden, "the one with his laces untied." Three of the four Riverdale runners, including Brady, look down and check their laces, which is not exactly a sign of confidence. Mark gets the baton from Paula, who tells him right in front of the opposition, "you're going to beat him, don't worry." This causes some worry in the opposing runner.

The Starter tells the runners, "on your marks." Mark takes his time to get to the blocks, staring down the opposing runner. Mark then points his baton at the opposing runner, who is now even more worried than he was after Paula's comment. Mark gets positioned, and the Starter announces, "set." The gun goes off, and the runners are out of the blocks. Mark takes the lead, yet another event to erode the opposition's confidence. Mark continues to enhance his lead over his entire leg. Meanwhile, at the transition zone, Braden also erodes Riverdale's confidence, yelling, "Mark's kicking their ass big time!"

Approaching the transition zone, Mark hands off to Johnson. Johnson has a comfortable lead, but he is up against one of Riverdale's unknowns. Braden continues, "and Johnson is kicking ass too!" Johnson maintains the lead throughout his leg, with no discernable change in distance between the two runners. Johnson hands off the baton to Eddie. As Eddie receives the baton, he hears Kathy scream, "go Eddie!" Kathy's voice motivates Eddie even more. During Eddie's leg, Braden gets even more fired up. Braden exclaims, "these guys aren't leaving me any ass to kick!" Braden continues, "why don't they put me up against someone who can run!" Brady, as he is looking over at Braden, prompts Braden to exclaim, "if I walk around the track, we'll still win!" Braden gets onto the track, ready to receive the baton from Eddie.

Braden takes the baton, and is long gone before Brady receives his baton. Braden is running at his sub-60 quarter mile pace, faster than he needs in order to win. Mark mentions to Eddie and Johnson, "it looks like we got this one wrapped up." Eddie agrees, telling Mark, "Braden's doing what he said he's going to do." Eddie, Mark, and Johnson all shout in unison, "kick ass!"

With Mr. Frazier distracted, one of the scouts approaches Eddie. The scout pulls Eddie aside, and asks, "are you Eddie Bogenskaya?" Eddie replies, "yeah. That's me." The scout then asks Eddie, "would you be interested in a free college education?" Not giving the scout much attention, Eddie frankly replies, "no." The scout asks, "may I ask why not?" Eddie replies, "because I'm going to be a mechanic." Eddie walks away from the scout, and focuses his attention back on the race, ignoring the scout. Overhearing the brief discussion with the scout is Mahoney, who thinks to himself, "oh, so he wants to be, a mechanic. That's it?" Mahoney shakes his head and laughs. After all, Mahoney wants to follow in his father's footsteps and be an attorney. It is not the fact that Eddie wants to be a mechanic that irritates Mahoney, but that Eddie is the star sprinter of the team.

Back on the track, Braden is approaching the finish line, with Brady too far behind to matter. With 50 yards left, Braden sprints to the finish line even though he could have run backwards from that point and still beat Brady. Braden crosses the finish line first, and the team celebrates not only winning the race, but the meet as well. The relay team members exchange high-fives with each other, congratulate each other, and walk away from the finish line just as Brady crosses.

At the end of the meet, the coaches and runners shake hands. Mark and Brady's path cross again, but this time Brady is a bit more cordial. Brady tells Mark, "congratulations, I don't know where you guys came from, but congratulations." Mark replies, "hey, thanks." Things begin to wind down rapidly. The spectators head to their busses, somewhat disappointed in their team's loss. Riverdale's team also heads to their bus, more disappointed than the spectators.

Eddie meets up with Kathy, who lands on Eddie's shoulders in no time. Paula didn't take too long to end up on Mark's shoulders either. They walk to the locker room together with the rest of the team, celebrating the season's first victory. Kathy asks Eddie, "what did that scout want?" Eddie replies, "oh, he said he wanted to give me a free college education." Kathy asks, "what did you tell him?" Eddie explains, "I just told him no, and that I wanted to be a mechanic." Kathy replies, "good for you!"

On the way to the locker room, Paula suggests, "hey, let's all go out and celebrate!" Kathy replies, "I'll go if Eddie carries me!" Eddie replies, "hey, I ran a 9.6!" Kathy replies to Eddie, "yeah, well, you only ran 540 yards today, and that's hardly a workout." Without any hesitation, Eddie agrees, telling Kathy, "OK, I'll carry you." Kathy then tells Eddie, "that's OK, I was only teasing you." Mark suggests, "hey, why don't we see if Braden, Johnson, Mitchell, and Bobby B. want to go too?" The girls agree, and suggest they also ask Barbara. Eddie mentions, "Wendy is probably around somewhere too." Mark then says, "we'll see who wants to go, and then we'll meet out front." Paula replies, "I'll try to hunt down Wendy." Eddie replies to Paula, "hey, when you find Wendy, you'll also find Braden."

After they get dressed, everyone meets out in front of the school. Mark asks, "OK, where are we going?" Paula and Kathy both reply, "pizza!" No one objects, so they all head down the road to the pizzeria. Eddie puts Kathy on his shoulders. Kathy exclaims, "oh my! Eddie!" Eddie tells her, "well, you wanted to be carried." Mark then puts Paula on his shoulders, followed by

Braden putting Wendy on his shoulders. Barbara, feeling somewhat left out, says to Kathy, Paula, and Wendy, "you guys have it made." Johnson makes the offer to Barbara, "hey, I'll carry you if you want." Barbara replies, "sure," as Johnson is already lifting her onto his shoulders. Johnson remarks, "so this is how you guys work out." Eddie replies, "yeah. It sure beats pumping iron." As they are walking down the road, Mahoney drives by in his car with Ambrosini. Mahoney, full of bitterness, looks over at the group knowing exactly where they are going.

They approach the pizzeria, and Mitchell opens the door for everyone. Kathy reminds everyone, "OK, don't forget to duck!" The group walking in brings a big smile to Joe's face. Joe yells out, "this looks like a celebration! Did you guys win?" Kathy and Paula yell out in unison, "oh, yeah!" Since the group is large, Joe tells them to have a seat where there are a few empty tables, and someone will take their order. Joe exclaims from behind the counter, "I tell you, if I charged by the smile, I could retire when all you guys come in!" Everyone has a seat, with the group spread over several tables. On the other side of the pizzeria are Mahoney and Ambrosini. Eddie and his group have not even noticed them.

After the group arrives, the energy level in the pizzeria rises tremendously. Once they are all settled in, Joe calls out to them, "what did you guys win?" Mark replies for the group, "everything!" Everyone decides what they are going to have. Most people decide to split a pizza with someone. Bobby B., the shot doc, decides to order a whole pizza for himself today. Kathy notices that Johnson and Barbara are seated at a table for two, located right next to her table. Kathy, who is very observant, knows long before everyone else that this was not by accident.

Arianna, the waitress, comes over, and sits with the team as she takes their order. The group orders a several pizzas, drinks, and a few large salads that they will split. High-fives continue at the tables as the team recounts their victories. Joe, himself, even comes over to the tables and personally congratulates everyone. Mahoney, seated across the floor with his buddy, wonders to himself why Eddie and his tribe get first class service and so much attention.

After the one hour long dinner and celebration, everyone heads outside and says their goodbyes. The group then heads out in different directions. Kathy is quick to notice that Johnson and Barbara walk away together. Eddie, Kathy, Mark and Paula head in the direction of the school. On the way, Kathy mentions, "did anyone catch Barbara and Johnson?" Eddie remarks, "no, what's up?" Mark replies, "Barbara is what's up. Up on Johnson's shoulders." The group has a good laugh, then Paula comments, "I saw that. They certainly were into each other over dinner." It's funny how the girls notice this kind of thing, but it flies right over the guys' heads at 10,000 feet.

For the next few weeks, the team practices together, and wins every one of their meets. By now, news has gotten around the region that Northside High is not to be taken lightly. The goal of the opposing teams is to walk away from the meet at least winning in some event. Mr. Frazier senses that this season is only the beginning of success. Mr. Frazier, who recently visited the middle school during a track meet with Kathy, got a first hand look at next year's upcoming talent. Hoffer, who will join the team next year, has delivered some promising times. Mr. Frazier has also identified a few other athletes who will make good additions to the team.

The end of the school year also brings the final meet of the year. This meet is against the team's rival, which is Centerville. Shortly after the final meet will be the State invitational meet, which Mr. Frazier and several of his star athletes will be attending. Eddie will be running the 100-yard dash in the State invitational meet. There is no doubt that Mark and Eddie will be up against McCutchen again in some event. Mark, Braden, Johnson, Mitchell, and Bobby B. will all be there as well.

The day of the Centerville meet arrives, which is after school on the home track. Eddie walks into English class, and is almost late. Mark, Braden, and Bobby B. are already seated. Braden asks Eddie, "another late night with Kathy?" Eddie replies, "yeah. School has really been getting in the way of life." Mark asks Eddie, "do you got enough energy for the meet this afternoon?" Eddie replies, "I have all day to rest. And hey, look who's talking!" Mark has been spending a lot of late nights with Paula, and Braden has been spending a lot of time with Wendy. None of them dare to continue this conversation.

Miss Starr walks in, telling the class, "everyone, please place your books on the floor, and we'll get started with the test." Braden whispers to Eddie, "we have a test?" Eddie replies, "yeah. Wendy didn't tell you?" Braden replies, "no, she didn't." Braden adds, "dang, I don't even have a pencil. And, it's not even Friday! It's Wednesday! Nobody gives a test on Wednesday." Eddie tosses Braden a pencil, which immediately catches Miss Starr's attention.

Miss Starr tells Eddie, "Eddie, please don't throw a pencil to someone. You can put somebody's eye out." Stressed because he was unaware of the test, Braden whispers under his breath, "that's a bunch of bullshit." Catching Braden's comment, Miss Starr asks Braden, "Axel Braden, would you please elaborate further on your comment?" Braden bluntly replies, "yeah. Throwing a pencil doesn't put somebody's eye out." Braden throws back a question to everyone, "how many people do you see who are walking around with their eye put out?" Answering his own question, Braden replies, "none. Nobody. Not a single one." Braden then comments, "we've been hearing this since kindergarten, and I ain't seen one person yet who has their eye put out from a pencil." The whole class laughs, including Miss Starr. Miss Starr should have seen something like this coming from Braden, but she rides with the tide and goes with the flow.

After the test, the pressure is off. Eddie and the rest can relax before today's meet. The word around school is that, during today's meet, there will be a rematch between Eddie, Mark, and McCutchen. Eddie and Mark both beat McCutchen badly last year in middle school. McCutchen, wanting to vindicate himself, has been training harder. He will not settle for anything less than first place today. Not losing a race all Spring, Eddie is not about to begin losing today either.

After school, Mr. Frazier calls a short meeting in the auxiliary gym, with Kathy, Paula, and Barbara joining him. Mr. Frazier starts by announcing who will be running each event. The team assistants then follow, giving insight regarding the competition. Mahoney, who will be running the half mile, and a subsequent half mile leg in a relay, is not happy at all. He still has his eyes on a scholarship, but has come up empty handed thus far. At the end of the meeting, Mr. Frazier asks, "does anyone have any questions?" Mahoney replies, "is there any chance that I can run the 100-yard dash today?" Mr. Frazier knows that this is Mahoney's last meet. Mahoney cannot deliver a competitive time, so Mr. Frazier simply replies, "no." The team then heads out to the track, with Mahoney infuriated.

Eddie, Mark, and Johnson will be up in the 100-yard dash right after the hurdles. On the way out to the track, Eddie asks Mark, "do you have any idea what are you're going to do to mess with McCutchen?" Mark replies, "I don't know. I hadn't figured it out yet." Johnson suggests, "maybe, he'll just lose without any help." Mark replies, "yeah, he will, but that will take the fun out of it." Johnson suggests, "maybe we can work his lane over like we did to Brady that time." Mark tells Eddie and Johnson, "I got it, when the Starter says 'set,' I'll whisper 'go.'" While Mark's plan sounds simple, it is enough to throw the runner off. Eddie replies, "you might not be next to him." Johnson replies, "we'll figure that out at the starting line."

The 100-yard hurdles event is up first. Eddie, Mark, and Johnson hang out around the starting line, waiting for their event. Prior to the race, Mark asks the Starter, "can you tell me what lane I'm in?" The Starter replies, "what's your name?" Mark replies, "Mark Svoboda, in the 100-yard dash." While the Starter looks down the list, Mark looks with him, and sees that McCutchen is in lane two. Mark sees that Johnson is in lane one, Eddie in lane four. The Starter tells Mark, "it looks like you're in lane three. Good luck." Mark returns to his group, telling their lane assignments, "yo, Johnson, you're in lane one. I'm in lane three, and Eddie is in four." Then Mark gives everyone the good news, telling them, "McCrutchen is in lane two, surrounded by us." Eddie replies, "awesome!" Mark tells the group, "I haven't decided what I'm going to say yet. But, whatever I say, just ignore me."

As the 100-yard hurdles event is underway, Eddie observes that the Starter holds the gun in the air. Eddie shares this information with Mark and Johnson. Eddie and his group know the Starter should have the gun behind his back where no one can see it. When they see the Starter's finger begin to move, they have a slight edge getting out of the blocks. Once the hurdlers are near the finish line, the 100-yard dash warriors approach the blocks.

Eddie, Mark, and Johnson set the blocks to their liking. While he is setting up his blocks, Mark mentions to McCutchen, "by the way, these are nonstandard blocks. Your settings might be off." McCutchen looks at Mark, not knowing whether to believe him or not. Eddie, overhearing Mark, winks at Johnson, telling him, "don't forget to add three to your setting numbers." Johnson, figuring out Mark's plan, pretends to adjust his blocks. This gives more credence to Mark's comment. McCutchen checks his blocks, and makes some unnecessary adjustments.

The Starter tells the runners, "on your marks." McCutchen gets himself ready, quickly realizing he should have left the blocks alone. The Starter announces, "set." Eddie, Mark, and Johnson have their eyes on the Starters finger, watching for it to move. Turning toward McCutchen, Mark whispers, "go." McCutchen turns his head for a second to look at Mark. Just as the gun goes off, Mark, Eddie and Johnson are out of the blocks, with McCutchen fooled not once, but twice this time.

At 25 yards, with six men in the field, it appears to be yet another three-man race. At 50 yards, one of the Centerville runners is closing in on Johnson, prompting Johnson to run faster. Eddie and Mark now hear too many footsteps behind them for comfort, so they give it all they have. At the finish line, Eddie crosses first, with Mark right behind him. Johnson takes third place, and the Centerville runner following closely behind takes fourth place. McCutchen finishes in last place, which is quite a surprise to his teammates.

At the finish line, after sweeping the event, the team has a brief celebration. Kathy smiles, and tells Eddie, "you ran a 9.7. It looks like you're back to carrying me again." Eddie replies, "oh good! It looks like I'll be carrying you then until next year's season." Kathy reminds Eddie, "but, there's the State meet." Eddie replies, "State doesn't count. It's not a regular season meet." Kathy, all excited, tells Eddie, "awesome! A whole Summer of carrying me around!"

Eddie has learned from Louis Zaino that, in some races, you only run as fast as you need to win. Louis explained to Eddie that if you try to set a record every race, you're more prone to injury. Eddie could have run faster, but to risk injury before the State invitational meet would not be wise. Zaino, a seasoned runner, will be going to the State invitational meet with the mile medley relay team this year. This is the same mile medley team that medaled in the State invitational meet during the indoor track season.

Eddie, Mark, and Johnson have a while before the final event, the 4 by 440 relay. Eddie goes over to talk with Bobby B., who is currently in second place in the shot-put event. Bobby B. was only about two feet shy of the senior, Matt Wood, in his first attempt. Eddie asks Bobby B., "how's it going?" Bobby replies, "well, we are going to win. They have nothing, so now it's between me and Matt." Eddie replies, "oh, really?" Bobby B. explains, "yeah. At the beginning of the season, I was four to five feet down, now I'm only a foot behind Matt on average." Eddie tells Bobby B., "wow, that's really impressive." Giving Bobby B. a high-five, Eddie tells him, "I'll be right back."

Eddie remembers from gym class how Bobby B. was able to squat more weight when he was being cheered on. Eddie thinks that might just work with the shot-put too. Eddie rounds up a few idle runners, including Mark, Johnson, and Braden. Mitchell is about to run the mile, which will take a few minutes, so everyone has a little time to spare. Eddie tells them, "lets go cheer for Bobby B. during his next attempt." They all head to the center of the track where the field events are held.

Eddie asks Bobby B., "when are you up?" Bobby B. replies, "I'm next. It's my second attempt." The runners gather around the circle, as close as the Field Judge will allow. When Bobby B. picks up the shot, they all start cheering, "Bobby B., Bobby B., Bobby B!" The cheering gets louder as the shot doc gets into position. Being watched and hearing his name over and over gives the shot doc a little extra energy. Bobby B. hurls the shot-put with all the energy he can find, letting out a primal scream that turns the heads of both teams and some of the officials. Two Field Judges measure the distance, with one of them recording it on paper. The Field Judge tells Bobby B., "congratulations! You're in first place. Your throw was five feet, eight inches better than your first attempt." The runners all give Bobby B. high-fives for what would later be known as the first place throw of the afternoon.

Eddie, and the rest of the runners, head back to the track just in time to watch Mitchell win the mile. Also watching the mile is Mahoney, who looks over at Eddie and his tribe with disgust. Mahoney will be glad to get this season over with. His senior year has been one dismal failure after another. Mahoney forgets that this is a team. Mahoney is not a team player. He is in it for himself. Mahoney had only one goal this year, which was to get a track scholarship, which he failed to do. He blames Eddie and his tribe for his failure. It has never crossed Mahoney's mind that his own performance might be the real reason he did not get a track scholarship.

The time comes for the last event of the afternoon, the 4 by 440 relay. The runners gather near the starting line. McCutchen looks over at his chief adversary, Mark. Last year, in middle school, McCutchen was the anchorman in this event. This year, in Spring track, McCutchen is the lead-off man. This means McCutchen will be up against Mark once again. McCutchen has been thrown off base many times in the past by Mark. Mark's presence is now all it takes for McCutchen to get distracted. The Starter tells the runners to get ready to run.

Paula hands the baton to Mark, and gives him a good luck kiss, which is noticed by everyone around. McCutchen, just seeing Mark and Paula embrace each other, is again distracted. The Starter tells the runners, "on you marks," as McCutchen looks at Mark, wondering what he has up his sleeve for this race. Mark ignoring McCutchen, gets ready. The Starter announces, "set," followed by the gun going off. Mark takes off so fast, seemingly leaving McCutchen at the starting line. Mark proceeds to give McCutchen his last running lesson of the regular season.

Johnson, who is talking with Barbara, is up next. Barbara sees Paula's good luck kiss gave Mark an edge, so Barbara gives Johnson a good luck kiss too. This is a surprise to everyone, but not to Kathy. Kathy knew that Johnson and Barbara were an item a while ago. Johnson gets on the track, and takes the baton from Mark. Next up is Eddie. Kathy will not allow Eddie to get on the track without his good luck kiss. Kathy gives Eddie a good luck kiss, which prompts the Centerville coach, Mr. Ruff, to complain to the Head Timekeeper. The Head Timekeeper reluctantly tells Mr. Frazier, "please have your team cool it a little." Mr. Frazier reminds the Head Timekeeper, "no rule has been broken." Mr. Frazier reacts by telling Braden, "get fired up! This is it!" Eddie receives the baton from Johnson, and is off to run his lap.

Braden, following Mr. Frazier's instruction, gets all fired up. While Eddie is running his leg, Braden is shouting, "where's my good luck kiss? What do you mean that I have to run this leg without a kiss? I got to kick ass all by myself, with no kiss? If I don't get my kiss, my foot is going to kiss someone's ass!" Wendy, in the bleachers, can hear Braden clearly, and blows Braden a kiss. Braden then shouts, "there, I got my kiss anyway!" Braden exclaims, "now, I'm ready to kick someone's ass!" The Head Timekeeper would have preferred that Wendy kiss Braden versus listening to his rant.

Braden gets on the track, waiting for Eddie to deliver the baton. Eddie arrives in the transition zone, and Braden is gone with the baton. A lot of people from Centerville are glad to see Braden leave. Braden is nearly halfway around the track when the Centerville runner receives his baton. Even after seeing the runner so far behind, Braden maintains his pace. With 50 yards remaining in his leg, Braden turns around on the track and begins to run backwards. Mr. Frazier is totally amused watching Braden's new running style. Braden crosses the finish line, still running backwards. Even with Braden running backwards, the Centerville anchorman had no chance of catching Braden. It is no wonder Northside and Centerville are rival schools.

The team walks away, not only with its final win of the season, but also an undefeated season. The walk to the locker room again brings Kathy on Eddie's shoulders, Paula on Mark's shoulders, and Barbara on Johnson's shoulders. Mr. Frazier could not be happier after today's meet. On the way to the locker room, the tribe plans for another victory celebration. They will probably end up celebrating in the ususal place, at the pizzeria, and agree to meet in the front of the school before they head out together.

Kathy, Paula, and Barbara all wait in the front of the school for the guys to shower and dress. They discuss what a great season the team had, and that next year's team will be even better. They have already decided where the celebration will be, which is no secret to anyone. In a few minutes, Wendy comes out to join them. Kathy tells Wendy that she should have come down from the bleachers and given Braden a kiss during the 4 by 440 relay. They all have a good laugh over that one. During the discussion, Paula, out of the blue, says, "shit, there's trouble right around the corner." Kathy asks, "how do you mean?" Paula replies, "I don't know, I just feel it." Barbara suggests, "maybe, it's just the stress of the day." The conversation then moves back to tonight's celebration.

Mahoney, who is through with track and the team, is the first one out of the locker room. He left without even taking a shower. Mahoney passes by the girls as he walks to his car. Barbara, putting her hand up to Mahoney for a high-five, says to Mahoney, "awesome season!" Mahoney, however, does not return Barbara's high-five. Instead, using both of his hands and all of his strength, he shoves Kathy over with enough force to knock Bobby B. over, landing her across the bushes and into the dirt. Paula yells out to Mahoney, "what's the matter with you!" Mahoney yells back, "I'm sick of this shit and all of you!" Wendy yells to Mahoney, "you're such an asshole!" Mahoney yells back to Kathy, "that guy's father is a jobber and he wants to be a mechanic! I'm going to law school!" Mahoney screams even louder at Kathy, "what the hell are you going out with that guy for?" Barbara tells the asshole, "just get the hell out of here, you piece of shit!" Barbara and Paula help Kathy, who is laying in the bushes and in the dirt, to sit up. Kathy, sitting on the ground in the dirt, is in tears. A crowd gathers around, wondering what happened. Paula, Barbara and Wendy are too involved helping Kathy to bother with the crowd.

Eddie comes out of the school, and sees all of the commotion. Eddie runs over, seeing Kathy sitting on the ground crying. Sitting beside Kathy and holding her, Eddie asks, "oh no, sweetie! What happened?" Kathy, still crying, tries to answer, but is unable. Barbara tells Eddie what happened, explaining, "I tried to give Mahoney a high-five, telling him, 'awesome season,' then he shoved Kathy over the bushes and onto the ground." Paula adds, "yeah, that jerk hit her pretty hard." Eddie, holding Kathy, reassures her, telling her, "you're going to be OK. Don't worry, sweetie." Kathy, still in tears and unable to talk, just cries and holds Eddie.

After about ten minutes, Kathy calms down a little, and stands up with Eddie's help. Still holding on to Eddie, Kathy tries to say something to him, but can't yet get words out. Eddie notices Kathy's clothing is torn from landing in the bushes. Eddie tells Mark and Paula, "I'm taking Kathy home. You guys go out without us." The group, however, waits around to make sure Kathy is going to be OK. In a few more minutes, Kathy tells everyone as she is crying, "I'm sorry, really, I am. You guys just go out without me. I'll be OK." Eddie and Kathy start the long walk home, with their friends walking along with them.

When they approach the corner to turn to go to Kathy's house, the group goes with Kathy and Eddie. Kathy tries to convince them to go to the pizzeria and celebrate, but they all choose to walk with Kathy and Eddie over to her house. Mark tells Kathy, "we can just celebrate another time." When they arrive at Kathy's house, Paula suggests, "we can order pizza and all eat it on your back patio. That is, if you're up to it." Kathy, much better than she was a while ago, replies, "yeah, let's do that. I'm not letting that moron ruin everyone's evening."

Kathy's father comes outside, wondering why the crowd has gathered. Eddie takes him aside, telling him what happened. Kathy's father immediately takes Kathy aside to find out more. Kathy assures him that she is going to be OK, and that she was just an emotional wreck for a while. Kathy's father assures Kathy and Eddie that this incident will not go unnoticed. When someone with a Ph.D., such as Kathy's father, uses the term, "will not go unnoticed," you can be quite sure that a hammer is about to come down.

The group takes a seat around the pool in the back yard, and orders pizza. While they wait, Kathy sits on Eddie's lap with her head on his shoulder for a few minutes. Kathy then tells everyone, "hey, everyone! Get bubbly!" Braden is the first to get bubbly, as Kathy put it. Braden exclaims, "I sense a major league ass kicking on the horizon!" Kathy replies, "yeah, and I'm going to do it myself!" After hearing Kathy's comment, everyone starts to get bubbly. Paula asks, "how are you going to do that?" Kathy stands up, showing everyone her clothing torn by the bushes, and replies, "to start with, this is what I'm wearing to school tomorrow." Paula whispers to Mark, "if she does that, Mahoney will be lucky to get out of that school alive." Mark replies to Paula, "it wouldn't hurt my feelings any." The conversation returns to the meet, and later to what everyone will be doing this weekend.

The pizza arrives, and the group asks Kathy's parents to join them. They gladly join the group, finally meeting some of the team members they've only heard about until now. Kathy's father says the mealtime prayer, and offers thanks to the Lord for bringing Kathy home safely, and for her many friends. Over dinner, the group fills Kathy's parents in on the meet. Kathy's father is quite amazed at the times the students are delivering on the track.

An Exercise Science professor at the local State University, Kathy's father jokingly asks, "so, who are my future Exercise Science students?" Barbara, raising her hand as if she were in a classroom, yells out, "me, for one!" Paula also yelling out, says, "me too!" Johnson also raises his hand, and says, "I'm seriously thinking about it." Kathy, much to her father's surprise, raises her hand, telling him for the first time, "surprise! Me too!" Kathy adds, "I was 100 percent sure after this year's track season." Kathy's father tells an inside joke, saying, "well, next year we'll be offering a Ph.D. in Hula Hoop." Kathy, smiling again, replies, "uh oh, my secret is getting out." Thinking he was joking around, Professor Karakova was surprised to learn that so many in the group are actually interested in Exercise Science and physical education.

Barbara asks Kathy, "what's this secret?" Kathy replies, "I Hula Hoop, but we call it hooping," thinking that was the end of the conversation. Barbara then tells Kathy, "please show us! I want to see!" Kathy looks at Eddie, who informs her, "you know you can't get out of this one." Kathy replies, "OK, but, nobody gets to laugh." Kathy goes inside and gets her hoop, secretly hoping that she is not too sore from being shoved to the ground by Mahoney.

Kathy returns with her hoop, and goes out onto the lawn. She starts her routine with the hoop spinning around her waist, which she lowers to her knees. She then raises the hoop back up to her waist, and reverses the direction of the hoop so fast that no one saw how she did it. Kathy then places one arm behind her back. She raises her arm overhead, and the hoop magically follows, spinning around her wrist. Lowering her arm, she has the hoop spinning around her waist again. In the next move, she places the other arm behind her back, raising the hoop overhead. Kathy then does a vertical split, as she transfers the hoop from her arm to the leg that is over her head. Much to everyone's surprise, has the hoop rotating around her vertical leg. She transfers the rotating hoop back to her arm, comes out of the vertical split, and returns the hoop to her waist. Kathy stops, telling everyone, "that's what I do!"

Everyone applauds, whistles, and cheers for Kathy. No one had the slightest clue that Kathy had such talent with a Hula Hoop. Even her dad is impressed by her performance. What started out to be a horrific evening, instigated by a hater, has turned out to be a wonderful evening, full of love. Kathy had no idea that her life long buddies and her newly found friends this year would stand by her so strongly. Kathy will definitely sleep better tonight knowing that her friends care for her so much.

As the evening comes to a close, every one of Kathy's friends give her a big hug before they head out. Braden mentions, "if that guy even looks at you, we'll kick his ass." Mark adds, "if he gives you any problems, just let us know. We'll take care of him." Eddie stays with Kathy for a while, assuring her that everything is going to be OK. They talk for a while longer, and then it comes time for Eddie to go. Eddie tells her, "I'll be here early to walk you to school, and to your class." Kathy replies, "yeah, that would be really nice." They kiss goodnight, and Eddie walks to the sidewalk.

As Eddie approaches the sidewalk, Kathy yells out to him, "no, wait!" Eddie returns, asking Kathy, "is everything OK?" Kathy tells Eddie, "yeah. But, I want to kick Mahoney's ass." Eddie replies, telling Kathy, "now you're beginning to sound a little like Braden." Kathy laughs, and says, "no, not that way." As they sit on the front lawn, Kathy asks Eddie, "we can we go back in time with the portal, right?" Eddie replies, "yeah." Kathy explains her plan, "if we get up early tomorrow, and meet here, then we can go to the portal after school tomorrow, and meet ourselves right here." Eddie replies, "I suppose so." Kathy replies, "good, we're doing that."

Eddie, asks, "OK, Katarina, what are you up to?" Kathy replies, "we are going to meet ourselves here, and go to Mahoney's house before school. There will be two of me and two of you, and we will scare the crap out of him. That's how I'm going to kick his ass. And bring your bicycle." Eddie asks, "do you want Mark and Paula to help?" Kathy replies, "I don't think so. This is my battle." Eddie tells Kathy, "OK, I'll be here an hour ahead of time." They give each other a goodnight kiss again, and Eddie begins the long walk home.

The next morning, Eddie is waiting for Kathy an hour ahead of the usual time. Kathy comes out of her house to meet Eddie. Eddie asks, "how are you doing?" Kathy replies, telling Eddie, "I'm doing better than I expected." Eddie asks Kathy, "now what?" Kathy replies, "we just sit here for an hour." Kathy tells Eddie, "after school today, we are going to the portal, and our future selves will be riding up right here on our bicycles." They then put Eddie's bicycle in the garage. Kathy tells Eddie, "OK, now we just wait." Eddie asks Kathy, "do you think this will work?" Kathy replies, "I was up for three hours thinking about this. It will work." After an hour, they walk to school, with Kathy reminding Eddie, "remember, this day will not be the same after I get done with it."

When Eddie and Kathy arrive at school, Kathy is wearing her torn clothing from yesterday. Her torn clothing attracts a lot of attention from both students and teachers. Rumors fly around in the morning and, by afternoon, everyone knows what happened yesterday after the meet. Whenever Kathy is asked about her torn clothes, she tells them, "it's a new style by a designer named Paul Mahoney."

Eddie, seeing Mahoney in the hall during class change, tells him, "I will kick your ass. I don't know when I'm going to do it. Maybe today, maybe next week, maybe over the Summer. But, I will kick your ass as sure as the sun rose this morning." Eddie's open ended threat leaves Mahoney with a high level of uncertainty, causing him to walk around in constant fear.

The end of the day arrives, and Kathy is ready to put her plan into action. Kathy and Eddie walk to Kathy's house, where Eddie's bicycle is. She also tells him, "he takes his car to school, and I hear he leaves a little early so he can drive past bus stops and show off his car." Eddie asks, "where does he live?" Kathy replies, "over on Rugby Road, off of Polo Drive." Eddie replies, "oh, over in the rich neighborhood. It figures." Kathy and Eddie arrive at Kathy's house. They leave their books, get their bicycles, and ride to the portal.

Eddie asks Kathy, "so, when we come back to this morning, will I still have my bicycle here?" Kathy tells him, "yes, it has to be here, because it was here this morning." Eddie asks, "and we'll be waiting there for ourselves?" Kathy replies, "yeah." Eddie is impressed that Kathy is so sure of herself. When they arrive at the portal, Kathy raises her right hand, and says, "today, 6:00 a.m." Kathy and Eddie are immediately transported back in time to this morning before school started. Eddie asks, "why so early?" Kathy replies, "I don't want to rush. I want to get this right."

Kathy and Eddie ride past Kathy's house, and then to the other side of the town where Mahoney lives. It only takes them a few minutes to get there. They pass Mahoney's house, and Kathy mentions, "there's his car." Mahoney's car, a current model year blue Corvette, is parked in the driveway. Eddie tells Kathy, "Mahoney was in school today. I saw him." Kathy replies, "good. All is going according to plan then." Kathy tells Eddie, "OK, now we go back to my house." They ride back to Kathy's house.

When they get to Kathy's house, they go to the side yard, and sit and wait. After a while, Kathy, who is all excited, points to the driveway, "here you come!" Kathy waves to Eddie, who arrived early this morning, as he rides up. She motions for him to come to the side of the house. Kathy mentions, "wow, now I have two of you." Eddie, who just came through the portal with Kathy, tells her, "wow, it worked just like you said." Kathy tells the two Eddies, "OK, now we just have to wait for me." In a few minutes, Kathy walks out of the house, looking for Eddie. Kathy whispers to her counterpart from behind a bush, "over here." Kathy and Eddie, with their early morning counterparts, get on their bicycles and ride to Mahoney's house. They, however, take slightly different routes for obvious reasons.

Once they arrive at Mahoney's house, they hide their bicycles behind some bushes. Kathy, who just came through the portal, tells her counterpart, "no changes, just like I, you, or is it we? Ha ha. Just as planned." Kathy tells Eddie and his counterpart, "squat down behind Mahoney's car where he won't see you." She instructs them, "if he gets physical, then come and rescue us." As planned, Kathy and her counterpart walk a little way down the sidewalk, waiting for Mahoney to leave for school.

Fifteen minutes go by, and Mahoney comes out of the front door. Kathy sees him coming down the walk, signaling to her counterpart that he is leaving. They both walk toward each other as planned, arriving in front of Mahoney's house at the same time. Kathy, wearing her torn clothing, yells out, "I am Katarina Karakova." Kathy's counterpart is wearing the same torn clothing, but is standing ten feet away. Her counterpart also yells out, "I am Katarina Karakova." Mahoney looks, and stares, and appears as if he is ready to panic. Kathy and her counterpart yell out in unison, "we are Katarina Karakova." With their arms motionless at their sides, Kathy, and her counterpart, walk very slowly toward Mahoney. Mahoney freezes, then goes into a full-blown panic. Kathy and her counterpart again yell out, "we are Katarina Karakova!" Mahoney panics, drops his books and his car keys on the ground, and runs back into his house screaming, "this can't be happening! I must have killed her! Nooooo!"

Kathy gives her counterpart a high-five. Eddie and his counterpart have been watching from behind the car as Kathy and Kathy's counterpart both scared the crap out of Mahoney. Once Mahoney is inside, Kathy instructs Eddie and his counterpart, "OK, back on the bikes! We're out of here." They all leave the scene, and stop around the corner. Kathy tells everyone, "that went right according to plan." Kathy then gives her counterpart a hug, telling her, "I might be the first person in the world to hug myself!" They all then ride back to Kathy's house.

Once at Kathy's house, Kathy tells her counterpart and Eddie's counterpart from this morning, "well, we're headed back to the portal, but you guys have to go to school." Kathy's counterpart asks, "what happens if we go to the portal, and you guys go to school?" Kathy answers, saying, "you know, I'm going to have to think about that one." Eddie and Kathy head to the portal, as their counterparts walk to school, knowing that Mahoney will now be absent today.

Once they return through the portal and get back from the past, Kathy remarks to Eddie, "oh, good. We're still here." Eddie asks, "how in the world were you able to figure all this out?" Kathy tells Eddie, "I missed a lot of sleep thinking about it last night." Eddie remarks, "yeah, that was pure genius." Kathy replies, "when that asshole knocked me over, I felt like he broke every bone in my chest. I thought I was going to die. He shouldn't be allowed to get away with that." Eddie replies, "he'll probably at least get suspended." Kathy replies, "no, he won't. His father's an attorney. He'll get the little twirp out of it." Kathy and Eddie ride back to Kathy's house, both wondering how they may have changed the future.

When they get back to Kathy's house, Eddie tells Kathy, "good news! I don't see any sign of us here." Kathy laughs, telling Eddie, "yeah, if we did, we'd probably feel like Mahoney did when he saw both of me." Kathy and Eddie go inside for a while and relax. Kathy puts on The Power of Love, as they both sit back and listen. Kathy closes her eyes, and begins to fall asleep. She tells Eddie, "I can't believe I'm so tired." Eddie reminds Kathy, "well, you've been through a lot in the last two days." Kathy replies, "yeah, I'll be a lot better in the morning, and tomorrow's Friday." Kathy then mentions to Eddie, "do you know what I'm going to say the next time I see Mahoney?" Eddie replies, "no, tell me." Kathy tells him, "I'm going to say to him, 'we are Katarina Karakova.'" Eddie and Kathy start laughing, and Eddie knows that Kathy is back to normal again. Eddie stays with Kathy for a while, and then he has to head home. Even though it's early, they give each other a goodnight kiss. Both of them desperately need sleep, so it will be an early night for both of them.

The next day at school, shortly after the morning announcements, another announcement comes over the loudspeaker. The expected words, "will Paul Mahoney please report to the principal's office." Kathy thinks to herself, "well, I know what that's all about." Another five minutes go by, and the same announcement comes over the PA system. Kathy then thinks to herself, "I guess he didn't make it to school today." If that is the case, it suits Kathy just fine.

She'd prefer not to see him around school anyway. All during the day, gossip flies about the incident after the track meet. Many students speculate what could have happened to Mahoney. A rumor is being spread that he was carted off to jail.

By the end of the day, one fact has emerged to dispel all of the rumors and speculation. Mahoney has been admitted to the hospital. Not just any hospital, mind you, Mahoney has been admitted to a psychiatric hospital. During the hospital admission, he is reported to have been repeatedly screaming, "there's two of her now! She's coming to get me!" The nervous breakdown after the final track meet, followed by seeing two of Kathy, was too much for him to handle. Mahoney's anger and bitterness have been brewing all year. After holding it in for the entire year, he finally snapped. It's a good thing for Mahoney that he is in the hospital. Dr. Karakova will be pressing assault charges. If Mahoney were not in the hospital, he would likely be headed to jail right now.

With the regular track season now over, Eddie and Kathy walk home together after school. Eddie asks Kathy, "did you hear about Mahoney?" Kathy replies, "yeah. And I don't care that he's in the hospital. Everyone is a whole lot safer now, especially me." Kathy also informs Eddie, "my dad is going to press charges against that jerk." Eddie reassures Kathy, "he's gone after this year anyway." Kathy sighs, and replies, "you're right. After this year, he's gone for good." Eddie asks, "so, is there anything you want to do? We have all this time." Kathy tells Eddie, "when I get home, I want to listen to my song, then we can go ride somewhere. I want to ride to somewhere that's quiet." Eddie replies, "yeah, I can see that."

Kathy listens to her song, and then they head to Eddie's house. Kathy tells Eddie, "I'll ride my bicycle, and you can run next to me." Eddie suggests, "I could just carry you and your bicycle." They both laugh, and decide that they would walk Kathy's bicycle to his house. Eddie needs a few days of rest from running anyway. Next week it will be back to training again in preparation for the State invitational track meet. When they get to Eddie's house, Eddie suggests a park that is not too far away. In fact, only few people know that the park is even there.

When they arrive at the park, it is completely deserted. They have the whole park to themselves, which suits Kathy just fine. They ride over to the swings, and they swing for a while. Eyeing a park bench in the shade, Kathy suggests they go over to that area of the park and sit for a while. They sit on the park bench for about a minute, then Kathy lands on Eddie's lap. Kathy and Eddie affectionately embrace each other, holding each other tightly. Kathy gets a little wild, and kisses Eddie like she never has before. They get off the bench, and lay on the grass continuing to embrace each other. As time goes by, it stands still for Kathy and Eddie, who are again in a world of their own.

After a while, Kathy lays with her head on Eddie's chest, as they fall deeper in love with each other. Kathy whispers to Eddie, "I think I might have a wild side." Eddie replies, "I suspected that. The Hula Hoop gave it away." Kathy replies, "my Hula Hoop? Really?" Eddie whispers, "no one can Hula Hoop like you do and not be a little on the wild side." Kathy sighs, and says, "yeah, maybe you're right."

They lay on the grass for a while, but the time to go home arrives too soon. Kathy tells Eddie, "my parents are going out for dinner tonight. I guess we need to get going." Eddie replies, "yeah, it's Friday, so my family is going out too." Kathy comes up with a wonderful idea, and tells Eddie, "hey maybe our families can all go out together!" Eddie exclaims, "yeah, that would be awesome!" They get on their bicycles and ride to Eddie's house to see if they can make the arrangements.

When they get to Eddie's house, Eddie and Kathy ask his parents if they want to go out to dinner with Kathy's family. Eddie's father tells Kathy, "sure, we'd love to go out to dinner with your parents." Eddie's and Kathy's parents have briefly met once before at the State invitational meet but, since Kathy's father had to fulfil his officiating duties, they did not get much of a chance to talk. Since Kathy and her bicycle are at Eddie's house, she decides she'll ride with Eddie's family to the restaurant.

Everyone decides on Italian food, since Eddie and Kathy have taken a liking to pizza recently. When they meet at the restaurant, Eddie and Kathy reintroduce their parents to each other. The parents order typical Italian dishes, whereas Eddie and Kathy split a pizza. Eddie's mother tells him, "Eddie, you shouldn't eat so much pizza. You're going to get fat." Eddie replies, "since I've been going out for pizza with Kathy, my times have gotten better, and I can lift more weight." Eddie's father mentions, "you can lift more weight and run faster because of Kathy, not the pizza." Everyone laughs, starting out the evening out with everyone displaying a good sense of humor.

After dinner, Eddie's and Kathy's parents agree that they must do this more often. Eddie and Kathy were certainly glad to hear of those plans. They love the time they have together, so more time is a good thing. On the way out, Kathy, mentioning to her parents, says, "my bicycle is still at Eddie's house. Can I ride back with him?" Eddie's younger brother mentions, "you just left it there so you have to come back to get it." Young kids do that sort of thing, so they figure the older kids do it as well. Eddie tells Kathy, "looks like he just busted you." Kathy replies, "yup, guilty as charged." Kathy gets to ride home with Eddie and his family. Eddie's brother sees that Kathy's well-thought out plan to purposely leave her bicycle at their house worked. Everyone has another good laugh, as they head out to their cars.

The next week goes rather well for everyone, except for Mahoney, who has not been to school all week. The State invitational meet is coming up in a week, so those who are invited practice after school. Most of the practice sessions involve the relay team members perfecting their handoff skills. Mr. Frazier gives the team Thursday and Friday off, so that they will be fully recovered for the meet on Saturday. Mr. Frazier did instruct the team, however, to not eat pizza on Friday night. Somehow the word got around that some team members frequent a certain pizzeria after practice. Pizza seems now seems to be the official food of the track team.

The morning of the Spring track State invitational meet arrives, and the bus leaves early, at 6:30 a.m. The track meet will take the entire day. For Eddie, the 100-yard dash is one of the first events of the meet, and the 4 by 440 relay is the last event. There will be a lot of time between the two events, hopefully giving Eddie and Kathy, Mark and Paula, and Johnson and Barbara some time to be together. It's a sure bet, however, that they won't be going out for pizza at lunch.

The bus arrives at the State University, which happens to be the school where Kathy's father is a professor. Dr. Karakova is today's Meet Director. He will be finding some time during the meet to watch Eddie run, per strict instructions from Kathy. As they are exiting the bus, Kathy tells Eddie, "now you get to see my dad's track. It's pretty awesome." Eddie asks, "what's awesome about it?" Kathy replies, "well, for one, there's a sand track, so it's like running on the beach." Eddie replies, "I'm not falling for that one!" Kathy replies, "no, really! Your 100-yard dash time will be about 25 seconds on the sand track." Eddie tells her, "you're up to something, I can tell." She replies, "no, I'm not, really! There really is a sand track."

When they get to the track, the entire team is impressed. The outdoor venue appears suitable to host an Olympic type event. Mr. Frazier takes the team to their designated area. Kathy asks Mr. Frazier, "can I go show Eddie something? It will only take ten minutes." Mr. Frazier replies, "show him what?" Kathy replies, "the new sand track. It's on the other side of the bleachers." Mr. Frazier replies, "sure. I'm coming too. I want to see it," then tells the rest of the team to unpack their equipment.

Mr. Frazier and Eddie follow Kathy to an area adjacent to the main track, partially behind the far end of the bleachers. When they come up to the 220-yard sand track, Kathy says, "see! A sand track!" Eddie knew Kathy had something up her sleeve. Kathy adds, "they put it in last year." Eddie asks, "what's it for?" Mr. Frazier answers, telling Eddie, "when you run on sand, especially barefoot, you force certain muscles to work harder, giving better leg development." Eddie mentions, "I run on the beach a lot over the Summer." Mr. Frazier replies, "yeah, I remember you mentioned that once." Mr. Frazier now has the idea that he should look into obtaining a sand track for the high school. As they head back to the team, Kathy bump Eddie's hip with hers, telling him, "see! There really is a sand track."

While the team settles in, the first half hour is filled with registration and paperwork for the coaches. Mr. Frazier and Barbara take care of the administrative work. The 100-yard dash is scheduled to begin early, so Eddie is stretching and doing some light warmups. Braden is looking up at the bleachers, trying to find Wendy. Johnson is not fully awake yet, but he doesn't need to be since his events aren't until later. Mark is sitting back, with his legs crossed and his hands behind his head. Mark is no doubt thinking of new ways to distract runners before the race. You can tell by the look in Mark's eyes that he has thought of a really good one.

After the hurdles are out of the way, the Meet Announcer tells the runners in the 100-yard dash to proceed to the starting line. Once they are all present, the Starter tells the runners, "you must run your best race. Only the top six times go to the final." Eddie is in the second heat, Mark in the first. Over at the finish line, Eddie sees Dr. Karakova, the Meet Director, where Kathy told Eddie he would be. The runners in the first heat are instructed to get ready. Mark looks at the field, recognizing most of the runners as someone he's beaten before. One of them is John Brady, who Mark worked over during indoor track, and then again in the Spring track season.

The Starter announces, "on your marks." Mark looks over at Brady, and says nothing. This is enough to shake up Brady, who seems to fall for every trick in the book. The Starter then announces, "set." The gun is fired, and six of the fastest high school runners in the State are off. At 50 yards, it is a two-man race between Mark and Brady. Brady, who is slightly ahead, is not about to be beaten by Mark. Brady is forcing Mark to run his best. At 75 yards into the race, Mark and Brady maintain their position, both running at about the same speed. At the finish line, Brady crosses first. Mark, who is very close behind, comes in second place. Finishing far behind Mark, it appears none of the other runners in this heat will make the final. Brady is now aware that Mark is a formidable competitor. If Brady makes the final, you can be sure he will run a faster race.

Eddie is up next. He knows Kathy and her father are at the finish line, so he wants to run a good time. The presence of Kathy's father at the finish line somehow causes Eddie to think back to the day Mahoney hit Kathy. This gives Eddie an additional adrenaline surge. The Starter tells them to get ready. The Starter announces, "on your marks," followed in a few seconds by, "set." As the gun is fired, Eddie is out of the blocks, already two steps ahead of the rest of the field by 10 yards. At 50 yards, it is a one man race, Eddie versus the clock. Eddie crosses the finish line first, with no one remotely close. Kathy's father mentions to Kathy, "that was a very impressive run." Kathy's dad goes over to the Timekeeper to find out Eddie's time. Kathy asks her father, "what did he run?" He whispers to Kathy, "unofficially a 9.6. He'll be in the final, but don't tell anyone until the official announcement. So will Mark, by the way."

After Eddie and Kathy talk for a while, Kathy has to go back to work, and Eddie returns to the team area. He sees Mark talking with Paula. Paula and Mark are pointing various areas of the track, and seem to be discussing something interesting. Paula then breaks into a few sexy poses, with Mark nodding his head yes or no. This spurs Eddie's interests, so he walks over and asks, "OK, what are you guys up to?" Paula replies, "nothing at all. But, we definitely need your help." Eddie remarks, "OK, this is going to be good, whatever it is."

Mark elaborates on his plan, and begins by telling Eddie, "Damien Harrington, the guy who took the gold in the 40 during indoor track is here, and Brady just edged me out." Eddie replies, "and?" Mark explains his plan, telling Eddie, "during the final, Paula is going to stand at the midway point of the track, looking really sexy. I'm going to tell Brady that Paula has had her eyes on him during the whole meet, and that she must like him. Then I'll point her out before the final and mention to him if he doesn't believe me, look at her while he's running." Eddie replies, "he'll lose a few steps and fall behind." Eddie then asks, "so, what do you need me to do?" Mark tells Eddie, "I need you to tell Harrington that Paula has her eyes on him." Eddie replies, "you got it, bro." Mark points out to Eddie, "we're all going to be standing around for at least five or ten minutes before the final, so that would be a good time to do it." Eddie agrees, and the plan is set.

After the 100-yard dash preliminary heats are completed, the Meet Clerk compiles and examines the times. The times and lane assignments for the final are posted shortly afterwards. As he is talking with the mile medley relay team, Mr. Frazier instructs Kathy to go and find out who is in the final. Kathy procures the requested information, and brings it to Mr. Frazier, who looks at the paper showing the finalists and lane assignments. Mr. Frazier is exuberant because Eddie and Mark are both in the final. Mr. Frazier tells Kathy to round up Mark, Eddie, Paula and Barbara for a brief team meeting.

Giving both Eddie and Mark a high-five, Mr. Frazier tells them, "congratulations, you're both in the final!" Mr. Frazier then gives them the scoop, "Eddie, you're the number two seed and you will be in lane four. Mark, you're number four seed and you will be in lane number two." Mark asks, "who else is in?" Mr. Frazier replies, "the number one seed is Harrington, who is in lane three. And there's Brady, who is in lane five."

Mr. Frazier then tells Barbara, "Barbara, I want you at the finish line with me." He continues, telling Kathy, "I want you in mid field, getting a photo of the runners." Mr. Frazier, coming to Paula, tells her, "and Paula, I want you at the start, and get a photo of the runners out of the blocks." Mark then asks, "can Paula and Kathy switch positions?" Mr. Frazier asks, "why?" Mark replies, "I have a plan." Mr. Frazier replies, "a plan?" Mark tells Mr. Frazier, "yeah. But, we need to have Paula at mid track." Mr. Frazier laughs, and replies, "I don't know what you guys are up to, but, OK, Paula will be at mid track. Fill me in about this plan after the meet." Mr. Frazier knows they are up to something big. He also knows that whatever plans they have conjured up are to gain an advantage, so he allows the change. Paula whispers to Mark, "this is going to work a lot better than you think."

The Meet Announcer makes the call for the 100-yard dash final. Paula quickly gets into position near mid track. The finalists congregate around the starting line. Mark whispers to Eddie that Paula is almost in position, and will be about 20 yards away until race time approaches. She will then move into her mid track position after Brady and Harrington get a good look at her sexy body language. Mark asks Eddie, "are you ready to go into action?" Eddie replies, "yeah. Let's go for it." Pointing out Harrington to Eddie, Mark tells him, "there's your target." Mark then mentions, "and here comes mine," as Brady walks up.

Changing his tone from the meet earlier in the season, Mark approaches Brady, telling him, "good luck." Brady, returns the favor, wishing Mark good luck too. Mark, pointing out Paula to Brady, asks, "hey, is that your girlfriend over there?" Paula watches Brady, waiting for them to make eye contact. When Brady catches Paula's eye, a sexy smile comes across her face as she waves. Brady, who now seems to be Mark's best buddy for pointing this out, asks Mark, "no. Who is she?" Mark, seeing Brady's reaction, points out to him, "I don't know. She was watching you during the preliminaries." Showing some interest, Brady replies, "really?" Mark then explains, "I thought she was looking at me, but then I realized it was you." Mark explains to Brady, "she was standing a little farther down during our first race." Setting Brady up for the fall, Mark tells him, "take a look. She'll have her eyes glued to you during the race." Brady, who is now distracted, looks down the track at Paula a few times as he is getting ready.

Meanwhile, Eddie approaches Harrington, telling him, "hey, congratulations on winning the 40 at the State meet this Winter." Harrington replies, "oh, thanks." Eddie, pointing to Paula, asks Harrington, "is that your prize too?" Harrington, somewhat confused, asks, "what prize?" Eddie replies, "the girl. I thought she was with you. She's been looking you over big time. I thought she was your girlfriend." Harrington looks at Paula, who smiles immediately when they make eye contact. After seeing Paula smiling at Harrington, Eddie mentions to him, "see?" Eddie then reveals, "someone said she was watching you during the preliminaries. They thought you two were together." Harrington mentions, "I wonder who she is." Eddie suggests, "glance over at her during the race, I bet she'll be staring right at you." Harrington, who keeps glancing down the track at Paula, is now hopelessly distracted.

The Starter tells the finalists to get ready. Harrington and Brady both look down the track at Paula. Paula, swinging her hips as she walks backwards to mid track, looks in their direction and waves. This clears up any doubt in Brady's and Harrington's mind about what they just learned. The Starter tells the finalists, "on your marks." Brady, who is taking a while to get ready, keeps looking down the track at Paula. Harrington's hormones have kicked in instead of his adrenaline, causing him to become more relaxed, and not physically ready for the race. The Starter announces, "set." The gun goes off and the runners are out of the blocks. At ten yards into the race, it's a close race that anyone can still win.

Harrington quickly develops a short lead, with Eddie right behind him. Mark appears to be tied with Brady, but it's too close to call who is ahead. At 40 yards into the race, Brady turns his head to the right to look at Paula. While he turns and looks, his stride veers slightly to the right, and he must quickly correct his bearing and cadence. This is enough to cause him to briefly drop down to fifth place, eventually regaining his position in fourth place. Mark, now in third place, has his hope set on a medal.

Harrington, on the other hand, waits until just before mid track to glance at Paula. Harrington turns his head abruptly to the right for a second to see if Paula is looking him over. When Harrington turns his head, he briefly steps out of his lane. He quickly regains his stride, never getting a good look at Paula. After Harrington's mishap, Eddie is now in first place.

Any sprinter knows, or should know, that you should not turn your head while you are running. Turning your head while sprinting will have a tendency to cause you to run in the direction your head is turned, potentially causing you to leave your lane. In addition, intentionally turning your head to one direction will disrupt your stride and cadence. Distance runners do not have this problem. Generally, in distance races, tenths of a second do not matter.

At the finish line, Eddie crosses first, taking the gold medal. Harrington follows right behind him, taking second place. Mark finishes right behind Harrington. Brady takes fourth place, completely unaware that Mark has thrown him under the bus once again. The other two runners also have a good finish, following Brady by only a tenth of a second or two.

After the race, one of the Lane Judges is seen walking down the track. The Lane Judge makes the Head Timekeeper aware that the runner in lane three stepped out of his lane. The Head Timekeeper asks the Timekeeper assigned to lane three if he saw it. Confirming the findings of the Lane Judge, the Timekeeper assigned to lane three added that he thought the runner almost tripped for a moment. Stepping out of your lane results in an immediate disqualification. With two officials seeing the infraction, Harrington has no leg to stand on.

Meanwhile, Mark, unaware of Harrington's disqualification, is happy that he got third place. Eddie and Mark exchange high-fives while the runners stand around waiting for the announcement. Eddie remarks, "the plan worked." Mark replies, "yeah, it took me a while this morning to come up with that one." If Mark was unable to distract one of the runners, Mark would have probably taken fourth place. Fourth place is no better than a participation trophy, worth absolutely nothing. But, why distract only one runner if you can distract two.

Due to the disqualification the announcement is delayed for a short time. With the times finally verified, the Meet Announcer declares the winners. The long awaited announcement arrives, as the Meet Announcer declares, "in first place, running for Northside High, Edward Bogenskaya. In second place, also running for Northside High, Mark Svoboda. In third place, running for Riverdale, John Brady." The announcer tells the winners, "congratulations to all of you, and we will see you at the awards ceremony this evening."

After the announcement, Mark, who is all excited, asks Barbara, "what happened? How did I get second place?" Barbara tells Mark, "the guy in lane three stepped out of his lane and was disqualified." Mark grins, and replies, "wow, awesome." Mr. Frazier, Mark, Eddie, and the three girls then head back to the team area, celebrating the victory on their way. Kathy is again on Eddie's shoulders, and Paula on Mark's. Both Brady and Harrington see Paula on Mark's shoulders. They both think, correctly for that matter, that Mark and Eddie had pulled something over on them. Brady and Harrington, who are both seniors, will not return next year.

When they return to the bench, Mr. Frazier asks Paula, "OK, what was all that about switching positions?" Paula replies, "well, it was Mark's idea." Mr. Frazier questions Mark, "what exactly were you guys up to?" Mark replies, "Eddie was in on it too. It wouldn't have worked without him." Mr. Frazier then asks, "will somebody please tell me what you guys were doing out there?" Mark then explains to Mr. Frazier in detail his plan, and how they conspired together. Mr. Frazier starts laughing, and asks Mark, "how did you come up with this?" Mark replies, "I needed a new way to mess with their heads, so I put it together before the meet started." Paula reminds Mr. Frazier, "well, you always said it's our job to flirt with the opponents if necessary." Mr. Frazier replies, "yeah, I did say that, didn't I? Guilty as charged!" Mr. Frazier tells Mark and Eddie, "you guys never cease to amaze me."

Kathy, who is crying with tears of joy, tells Eddie, "you did it! You got first place!" Eddie replies, "yeah, and just think, at the beginning of the year I was wondering if I would even make the team." While they are talking, Kathy's father walks up to personally congratulate Eddie. He tells Eddie, "that was a very fine run." Eddie replies, "thank you, thank you." Dr. Karakova informs Eddie, "by the way, you're a freshman, and you're running college times." Eddie asks, "what did I run?" The Meet Director tells Eddie, "a 9.5, but it's a rubber track so the times are usually a little faster." Eddie looks at Kathy, telling her, "see what happens to my times when I carry you all around town?" Kathy replies, "how do you know it wasn't all that pizza?" They all have a good laugh, but then the Meet Director has to excuse himself to resume his officiating duties.

Eddie, Mark, and the rest of the team sit back and relax for a while. Getting a break, Kathy, Paula and Barbara join them. The next race will be the mile medley relay, which will be right before lunch. Braden asks Kathy, "whatever happened to Mahoney?" Kathy, quick to answer, tells Braden, "he's still in the hospital, and I heard he's not getting out anytime soon." Kathy then reveals, "my father was going to press charges, but then he decided not to since Mahoney is in the loony bin. The attorney basically told us that Mahoney's jail time is being served in the hospital." Braden comments, "yeah, if that son of a bitch goes to a real jail, they will rip him a new hole where he never had one before." Barbara asks, "what?" Braden explains, "if you go to jail for assaulting a girl, you're in for a real ass whooping that's never gonna end until you get out." Kathy remarks, "yeah, well it's a good thing for him that he's in the loony bin." Braden also mentions, "if he goes to jail, they'll do some other shit to him too, but I ain't saying what that is." Eddie looks at Kathy, telling her, "well, the hospital sounds like a lot better alternative to jail." Kathy whispers back to Eddie, "I'm glad we helped Mahoney out then."

After a while, the call is heard for the mile medley relay. Zaino, Bell, Johnson, and Mitchell all get up and go to their race. Mr. Frazier tells Kathy to stay behind and find some lunch for the team. After Mr. Frazier is gone, Eddie tells Kathy, "you heard him! You're in charge of lunch. Break out the pizza!" Kathy sighs, and replies, "that's tomorrow." Kathy then tells everyone, "there's a cafeteria on campus. They're supposed to have some good food, and pizza. It's better than fast food." Everyone agrees to give it a try after the mile medley is over.

The mile medley team returns from their event, taking second place. This is a good accomplishment, considering the strong field of runners this year. The mile medley team almost ended up in fourth place, but Mitchell, who ran the 880-yard leg, ran a smart race, and pulled off the win right at the end. Johnson will have to run again later in the 4 by 440 relay. The team then heads to the cafeteria for lunch, where they will hang out as a group until later this afternoon. Mr. Frazier does not want the 4 by 440 relay team out in the heat all afternoon before the race.

About a half hour before the 4 by 440 relay, the relay team heads back out to the track. With the team now back in the team area, Mr. Frazier goes to check which heat the team will run in. Eddie remarks, "I'm glad we were in the air conditioning. It's getting hot out here now." Mark mentions to Eddie, "I wonder if we'll be up against Brady or Harrington." Eddie replies, "they'll be ticked off." Mark, changing the topic, asks, "someday this Summer, can you tell me how you got so fast so quick?" Eddie tells Mark, "sure. No problem. It's really easy."

Mr. Frazier returns with the good news. The news is the team will be up against Henderson, Riverdale, and Centerville in the same heat. Mr. Frazier also informs them that they are in the first heat. Braden asks, "Centerville, what was the deal with them?" Eddie answers for Mr. Frazier, "McCrutchen, McClutching, or whatever his name is." Mr. Frazier tells the team, "it looks like the first heat will take all the medals from what I can see." The higher seeded teams have been clustered together, ensuring they run their best race. Mr. Frazier then tells the team, "you have beaten all these guys in the past, but don't let your guard down. They have a score to settle." Mark replies, "yeah, more than one score." Mr. Frazier knows exactly what Mark is referring to, since the gold medal that Harrington had his eyes set on will be draped around Eddie's neck shortly. Mr. Frazier tells Mark, "see if you can think of something else to distract them since you have a few minutes."

The Meet Announcer issues the call for the 4 by 440 relay teams to meet at the starting line. The team heads over, and Mr. Frazier notices Mark is noticeably limping. Mr. Frazier suddenly gets concerned, and asks Mark, "is there something wrong with your leg?" Mark replies, "no, I'm just faking it so they think I'm injured." Mr. Frazier quickly sees Mark's plan. If they think Mark is injured, they may not think that his team will be much competition, and therefore not run their best. Mr. Frazier then decides to change the lineup, telling Mark, "OK, I want you to be the anchor." Having an injured runner as the anchorman may also give somewhat of an advantage, leaving the uncertainty alive as long as possible. Mark continues to limp to the starting line, as Mr. Frazier informs the other team members of the plan. Mr. Frazier tells Mark, "limp around, and make sure everybody sees you." Mr. Frazier also instructs Braden that he will be the lead man, and to be quiet at the beginning of the race. Braden, being quiet, will certainly be a feat.

At the starting line, Harrington sees Mark limping. Harrington will be Henderson's anchorman. Brady, the anchorman for Riverdale, looks over at Mark, watching him limp. Both Harrington and Brady now feel like they will be on vacation during this race. Mark remains quiet, having nothing to say to any of his opponents. Many of the runners are now all too familiar with Mark's psychological warfare, and they are glad to see him keeping to himself. Barbara hands Braden the baton, and Braden enters the track.

The Starter makes sure the runners are all in position and ready to run. Once he is satisfied, the Starter gives the command, "on your marks," shortly after announcing, "set." The gun fires, and the first heat of the last event is underway. Braden takes an early lead, but not a whole lot of people notice. Most of the attention has been drawn to Mark is sitting on the ground as Paula works on his leg. Brady, a short distance away, can be heard laughing, telling a teammate, "this race will be cake."

After Paula works on his leg, Mark gets up and walks around. Braden has already handed the baton off to Johnson, but many people have missed noticing that Braden was clearly in first place during the transition. Mr. Frazier is watching all of this as it transpires, wondering how Mark comes up with these ideas. Johnson, in the meantime, is making good time and maintaining the lead. No one is concerned about Johnson's lead because they figure Mark will quickly lose any lead Northside has managed to gain.

Eddie is on the track waiting for Johnson. Another runner, who is also on the track waiting for a handoff, tells Eddie, "it's not going to matter this time, dude. You guys are out of it." Eddie replies, "yeah, well, you still got to try." Johnson, who has maintained first place, hands off to Eddie. After Eddie receives his baton, Henderson, Riverdale, and Centerville all handoff in rapid succession. With Mark apparently injured, these three teams think they will be vying for first, second and third place during the final leg. Paula asks Mark, loud enough for the other competitors and coaches to hear, "do you think you can do this?" Mark replies, "I think I can finish." Mark gets on the track, waiting for Eddie. Eddie has widened the lead, but the opponents do not seem to care.

Eddie hands off the baton to Mark, who takes off like a jet plane. Harrington, waiting in the transition zone, watches Mark as he runs away with a perfect stride, wondering what in the world just happened. Mark was injured. Harrington, who is so focused on Mark's remarkable recovery, leaves the transition zone late, bungling the handoff. This ultimately causes Harrington to lose more time than he can make up, and dropping to third place.

Brady watches Harrington's bad handoff instead of focusing on his own. Brady's handoff is so poorly done, that the baton is transferred with both runners nearly stationary. McCutchen, from the arch rival Centerville, watches the commotion as it develops. McCutchen leaves too late, causing a bad handoff that resulted in him dropping the baton, losing at least ten precious seconds. Fortunately, for McCutchen, the baton does not leave his lane, otherwise his team would be disqualified. Meanwhile, Mark is clearly in the lead, leaving a train wreck behind him. Mr. Frazier cannot believe what he is seeing. Kathy, Paula, and Barbara are all laughing so hard at what just happened in the transition zone.

Mark sprints around the curve, headed toward the finish line without any competition in sight. Totally unaware of the carnage he left behind, Mark wonders where the other runners are. Mark crosses the finish line, with no one remotely behind him. He steps off the track, and exchanges high-fives with his other team members. Mr. Frazier and Paula fill Mark in on what transpired after he began his leg. Mark is quite surprised that his plan worked a lot better than expected. This was supposed to be the heat that produced the medalists. Instead, the handoff zone turned into a three-ring circus.

The team returns to their area as the other heats continue. On the way, the team celebrates, but they will have to wait a while to see where they placed. Kathy is again on Eddie's shoulders. Paula is on Mark's shoulders, giving credence to the fact there was never really anything wrong with Mark's leg. The other teams also return to their area, watching painfully as Mark carries Paula. Harrington's and Brady's teams, who were expected to medal in this event, will likely go home empty handed. If they had only focused on their own task and not pay attention to Mark and Eddie's distractions, they may have placed better in the 100-yard dash and the 4 by 440 relay.

After the final heat, the coaches surround the Meet Clerk. The times are checked, rechecked, and verified by several officials. The announcement comes, with the Meet Announcer declaring to the coaches, "first place goes to Northside." Mr. Frazier yells out, "yes!". He does not even wait to see who was in second and third place but, instead, he runs back to the team to deliver the good news. After Mr. Frazier leaves, one of the coaches remarks to another, "Frazier's team is going to be a problem in the next few years. Those guys are all freshmen." The other coach replies, "wow, so we're going to see three more years of this." Or worse, because the team is likely to be better in the upcoming years.

Mr. Frazier returns to the team and delivers the good news, "you guys took first place!" Celebration breaks out, with cheering that could be heard on the other side of the track. High-fives follow, followed by a celebration kiss between the couples. Mr. Frazier tells the team, "the medals ceremony is in 30 minutes. If you guys want to get a quick bite to eat, now is the time." Kathy and Paula look at each other and yell, "pizza!" The whole team, including Mr. Frazier, wastes no time and head to the cafeteria. They all decide to get pizza, including Mr. Frazier.

After dinner, the team rushes to the closing ceremony, which is held on the track. They get there with no time to spare. The Meet Announcer opens the ceremony, introducing the meet officials. He congratulates all the coaches and teams for their stellar performances. He then instructs the medalists to come down from the bleachers and meet at the shot-put pad. Once there, they will be lined up by another official in the order they will receive their award.

Following the awards for the hurdles, the program moves on to the 100-yard dash. The Meet Announcer states, "first place in the 100-yard dash, running for Northside, goes to Edward Bogenskaya." As Eddie walks up and stands on the first place tier, the crowd cheers. The Meet Announcer continues, "in second place, also running for Northside, Mark Svoboda." Throughout the stadium, cheering continues, especially from the Northside bench where a few distinct female voices can he heard. The Meet Announcer announces, "in third place, running for Riverdale, John Brady." Once the medalists are on their tiers, the meet officials drape the medals around the winners' necks. The cheering continues as some photos are taken. The ceremony then moves on to the next event. Mark and Eddie return to the shot-put area, waiting for their next award.

Johnson, Mitchell, Zaino, and Bell placed in the mile medley relay event, and are called to take their place on the second place tier. Zaino and Bell are secretly happy that Johnson and Mitchell were reassigned to the mile medley team. If Mahoney retained his assignment to the mile medley relay team, he would have insisted that Ambrosini be on the team as well, and Zaino and Bell would not have received their medal today. Zaino and Bell are juniors, and will return next year. Being beaten by a team with all seniors, the mile medley team has their eyes on a gold medal next year.

The last award to be distributed is for the 4 by 440 relay. The Meet Announcer, begins by introducing the winner, "in first place, in the 4 by 440 relay, running for Northside, Mark Svoboda, Eric Johnson, Edward Bogenskaya, and Axel Braden." The team comes up and takes their place on the first place tier. The Meet Announcer announces the teams taking second and third place, which go to Northport and Washington respectively. This is a great surprise to everyone, except for those who were present at the great handoff debacle during the first heat. The teams receive their awards and, after the photos, return to their team bench. Kathy runs up to Eddie and greets him with a big hug and a kiss.

After the filed athletes receive their awards, the ceremony is over. The parents, family members, and friends come down from the bleachers, and join the team. Eddie's parents congratulate him, and the other team members. College scouts make an attempt to talk to Eddie about furthering his education. With his team and team's family members all celebrating together, they are not able to get to him. Eddie drapes his 4 by 440 relay medal around Kathy's neck, which she will wear every day until school is over. The team heads to the bus, as this year's Spring track season comes to a close.

As Eddie and Kathy walk into school Monday, almost everyone notices Eddie's medal draped around Kathy's neck. Mark and Paula arrive at school, also with medals around their necks. As the lobby fills with students, they meet up with Braden, Johnson, and Mitchell. Bobby B. joins them, offering his congratulations. After the seniors graduate and are gone, next year Bobby B. will have a good shot at the State invitational meet. Throughout the day, they all receive congratulations from teachers and students for their achievements.

The group has a good time celebrating again in the lobby. Braden, wearing his medal from the indoor track State invitational meet in addition to his newly earned Spring season medal, tells everyone, "I had my Winter track medal engraved on the back." Eddie says to Braden, "uh oh. I can only imagine." Mark mentions, "I can't wait to see this." Braden shows everyone the back of his gold medal in the 4 by 440 relay that he earned during the indoor season, which is now engraved to read, "Axel Braden, Chief Ass Kicker." Eddie, who sees it first, starts cracking up. Mark, also after seeing the medal, starts laughing. Braden shows everyone, and in no time it seems like a party breaks out.

The last week of school is the week for final exams, so there will be tests followed by more tests. With one more week to go, Summer vacation is on the horizon. The students are counting down the days. Unknowing to the students, the teachers are also counting down the days. Truth be told, the teachers began counting down the days long before the students did. But, this will be a long week for everyone. But, once it's over, a few weeks of freedom begins.

The final bell of the school year finally rings, and Summer begins. Eddie and Kathy meet at the front of the school. They are joined by Braden, and shortly afterwards, Johnson. Since it's a beautiful day, everyone is walking home. Within a few minutes, the whole gang is together, and they head out. Paula mentions, "hey since we're all together, does anyone want to get pizza?" Kathy replies, "sure, why not! It's the end of the school year and we don't have to wake up early tomorrow." It's not that Kathy needed a reason to get pizza. Any reason will do when it comes to pizza with this group.

On the way out of the schoolyard, Mark notices Chuckie sitting under a tree with a few others. Mark mentions, "hey, do you want to invite Chuckie?" Everyone knew this was a joke, and they all break out in laughter. Braden sarcastically exclaims, "hey, look at that! Chuckie is smoking something!" Kathy quickly mentions, "yeah, pot." Hearing this, Eddie yells out, "hey Chuckie, don't you know doping[4] will get you disqualified?" Chuckie yells back, "shut up you bunch of jock heads." Mark tells Eddie, "look at that. He called you a 'jock head.'" Braden mentions, "he said, 'jock heads.' That's plural." Braden apparently learned something in Miss Starr's English class this year.

Eddie jokingly cries out, "oh, I'm so hurt. I don't know if I can take it any more!" Kathy reassures Eddie, "I think you'll get through this one. I know it's hard, but you'll make it." Kathy, on Eddie's shoulders, spreads her arms and yells out to Chuckie, "hey Chuckie, look at me! I'm an aeroplane!" Mark warns everyone, "you guys better be careful. It looks like Chuckie is the captain of the doping team. He looks tough!" They all then head down the road for the last pizza together of this school year.

---

[4] Doping: A slang term for increasing the number of red blood cells to boost athletic performance.

Summer Break

Now that Summer is finally here, Eddie can get back to serious training. Kathy is now training with Eddie. They often ride to the beach together. Once there, they go for a run in the sand. After all, who needs a sand track if you have a whole beach. Mark and Paula often join them. Paula, who is training with Mark, has discovered the beach is her home away from home. Occasionally they will all go to the beach of the future, just to check it out.

Eddie still takes regular trips to the future to sell the gold that he buys. He is amassing a great fortune, and has money to spend in the present time. Eddie buys the gold while he is out riding his bicycle, stopping in wherever he can to pick up some. Eddie has known for a while that he can go into the portal, and sell the gold in the future. He realized that he can then return to the present time, and immediately go back into the portal, choosing a different date to sell even more. This gives him a good workout. Eddie has also accumulated a lot of gold, which he can sell whenever he wants. While taking trips to the future, he also picks up the vitamins and supplements that he needs.

This Summer, Eddie is cutting lawns and maintaining a few pools. He has enough work to keep him busy three days a week, leaving the other four for himself and time with Kathy. Mark is helping his father a lot more this Summer, working a few days a week. More money means Mark can go out on more dates with Paula. Kathy, who is now sixteen, has a job teaching a morning class at a Summer day camp for kids three days a week. Not to anyone's surprise, one of the things Kathy is doing this Summer is teaching the kids to Hula Hoop. Paula also landed a job teaching at the same camp, also three days a week. Paula, however, is assisting on field trips, where she takes kids on nature walks.

During the first weekend after school is out, Eddie and Kathy decide to check out the beach. They decide to invite Mark and Paula to join them. It does not take much to convince Mark and Paula to go to the beach, or to get pizza.

They all decide to leave early, and agree to meet at 8:00 a.m. At 8:00 a.m. on a Saturday, most of the other teens are still in bed. The foursome, however, is up and ready to go. By the time the other kids their age wake up, the group will have already put in a full day's workout. They all agree to meet at Mark's house, since he is the closest to the path.

Eddie rides to Kathy's house so that she doesn't have to ride alone. Once they get to Mark's house, Kathy asks, "so, what beach do you guys want to go to?" Eddie asks, "do you mean like today's beach or tomorrow's beach?" Mark suggests, "how about tomorrow's beach. The water will be warmer if we pick a day later in the Summer." It will also be farther from the Summer Solstice, so they'll be able to spend more time in the sun, since it won't be as high in the sky, if they pick a date in mid Summer. They ride to the portal, with the girls leading the way.

Once they arrive at the portal, Mark says, "OK, somebody take us there." Kathy tells Mark, "hey, you can make it work too! You take us there." Mark mentions, "I thought it was Eddie's portal." Eddie mentions, "it's not mine. I just found it. It's for all of us." Mark, deciding to give it a try, raises his right hand and says, "about two months from now on a sunny day." The group is immediately transported to a warmer sunny Summer day.

While they are walking their bicycles to the path, Paula asks, "I wonder what would happen if you said, 'beam me up Scotty?'" Kathy then suggests, "hey, we can put Mahoney in the portal, tell him to raise his right hand and say, 'beam me up Scotty!'" Kathy and Paula laugh hysterically, but Eddie and Mark do not. Eddie's and Mark's family never had a television, so they never saw Star Trek. Kathy and Paula will have to explain the joke to them later. Once Kathy and Paula stop laughing, they get on their bicycles and start riding. But, Mahoney will not be beamed up anytime soon. Mahoney is still in the loony bin.

Once they get to the beach, they notice it is not very crowded. Because it is low tide, the beach looks even more sparsely populated. Once the tide comes in and more people arrive, the beach will be more crowded. For some people, their nice place they have staked out in the sand 20 feet from the water will be under water in two or three hours.

After locking their bicycles, they all go to Eddie's favorite spot. This is just beyond the concession area, between the sand dunes and the water. They lay out in the sun for a while, and then go into the ocean to ride some waves.

After everyone comes out of the water and dries off, Kathy and Eddie decide to explore the sand dunes again, in search of a spot where they cannot be seen. Mark and Paula head out in the other direction for a while, searching for their own private getaway location before the afternoon crowd begins to show up.

An hour later, when Eddie and Kathy return to their spot, many people have arrived. Small kids are playing in the sand near the water, while the adults lay out in the sun. There are a few people in the water riding waves or just getting wet. Near the concession stand, which is far back from the water, there is a volleyball game going on. Eddie and Kathy lay out in the sun again for a while. Mark and Paula return a few minutes later and join Eddie and Kathy as they all relax in the sun. They all lay there, dozing off, listening to the waves crash, and the sounds of people talking and radios playing in the background.

All of a sudden, Paula jumps up and screams, "oh no!" She jumps off her towel and heads to where the ocean meets the sand. Mark, Eddie, and Kathy also jump up, wondering what is wrong. Mark chases Paula, who is long gone, and already at the ocean. Paula goes into the water, and, as the waves are going out, pulls a two-year-old girl out of the water. The girl starts crying, which is a dead giveaway she is still alive. Paula holds the child, reassuring her, "its going to be OK." Mark asks, "wow, how did you know about that?" Paula replies, "I don't know. Somehow I just did." Mark asks, "what?" Kathy tells Mark, "just believe her. I'll explain later."

The girl's mother has been searching for her daughter for quite some time. Watching from a distance as Paula pulled the girl out of the ocean, the mother begins running to Paula, skirting around people laying on the beach. Paula's scream did not go unnoticed, and attracted a lot of attention. It only took a minute or two for a crowd to develop. The child's mother, breaking through the crowd, exclaims, "my baby! My baby! Thank God that she's OK!" She tells Paula, "thank you so much! Thank you, thank you!" Paula hands the baby back to her mother, telling her, "here's your little pumpkin." Mark whispers to Eddie, "I want to tell the mother to be more careful next time. That's what all the adults always tell us." Eddie whispers back, "yeah, I know what you mean." The crowd disperses and Eddie, Kathy, Mark and Paula go back to their towels, and sit on the beach.

Mark asks Kathy, "OK, so what were talking about before?" Kathy asks, "when?" Mark replies, "when you said 'just believe her.' You said you'll explain later." Kathy replies, "oh, yeah. I forgot about that. It's Paula's superpower." Paula's eyes light up, and she asks, "what superpower?" Kathy tells Paula, "there's been a lot of times in the past when you knew something was going to happen, and it did." Paula asks Kathy, "like when?" Giving one example, Kathy tells Paula, "right before Mahoney knocked me down, you said something like, 'there's trouble right around the corner.'" Kathy explains, "that was a minute or so before he even arrived." Mark then points out, "hey, right before I ran the 100-yard dash, you told me, 'this is going to work a lot better than you think.'" Paula confesses, "yeah, I did say that! I remember that!" Kathy replies, "see there! That's your superpower."

After thinking about this for a minute, Paula asks Kathy, "so what's your superpower?" Not even a bit hesitant, Kathy replies, "I'm the world's greatest bullshit detector! That's my superpower." Paula replies, "what?" Kathy tells Paula, "somehow I know, and I don't know how I know, when someone lies to me or feeds me bullshit." Kathy also mentions, "I've always been this way for as long as I can remember but, since we've been going through the portal, it's been a lot more apparent." Eddie asks, "really?" Kathy replies, "yeah. I thought I was imagining it but, after what just happened, now I'm sure."

Mark, flexing his biceps, mentions, "I wonder if I have a superpower too." Kathy tells Mark, "sure you do. Your casual comments to your opponents before a race write the future." Mark asks, "how's that?" Paula, catching on quickly, tells Mark, "all that psychological warfare you do before a race. When has that not worked?" After thinking for a while, Mark laughs and replies, "never."

Kathy reminds everyone of what happened during the State invitational meet a few weeks ago, exclaiming, "Mark! When you pulled that limping stunt at State, you left a train wreck behind you after Eddie passed you the baton!" Paula exclaims, "you're right! And, that was so awesomely funny!" Mark mentions, "yeah, I wish I could have seen that." Kathy tells Mark, "see, there's your superpower." Wondering deeply, Kathy asks, "Mark, has that worked better for you since you've been coming through the portal?" Mark and Paula both answer, "yeah!" Kathy mentions, "we might be on to something here."

Mark asks, "then, what's Eddie's superpower, other than running faster than anyone else?" Eddie, as he gives Kathy a kiss, replies, "my superpower is finding someone so special." Kathy smiles, as Paula says, "aw, that's so sweet." After listening to everyone else, Eddie, who thinks that he doesn't have a superpower, says, "I don't have one." Kathy tells Eddie, "oh, yeah! You do!" Eddie asks, "OK then, what is it?" Kathy tells Eddie, "your superpower is knowing who to trust and who not to trust." Eddie asks, "really?" Kathy replies, "yeah. When have you ever been wrong about that?" Thinking for a moment, Eddie replies, "OK, you might be right about that one."

Paula then mentions, "OK, so my superpower is knowing something right before it happens. Mark's is subtly changing the future. Kathy's is detecting bullshit, and Eddie's is knowing who to trust. That sounds like a good set of skills." Eddie remarks, "in the comics, superpowers are like flying and that sort of thing." Kathy tells everyone, "those are make-believe. Our superpowers are real!" Paula, after pulling the baby out or the water a little while ago, says, "I don't need any convincing that mine is real. I just wish I knew about it before Mahoney showed up that day. I could have stopped that from happening." Kathy comments, "well, Mahoney is right where he needs to be, in the loony bin."

Eddie, out of the blue, mentions, "well, Braden's superpower must be kicking ass." Mark laughs, as Kathy replies, "yeah, in a way. But, before a race, Braden sucks the energy out of the opponent with his rants, and that's how he does it." Paula mentions, "and can you believe what he had inscribed on his medal?" Eddie replies, "that is seriously funny! He says he's going to kick ass, and he does it. Then he engraves on his medal that he did it." Mark replies, "he ends up winning before the race starts." Kathy replies, "exactly." Eddie asks, "how about Johnson?" Silence comes over the group. After thinking about it for a moment, Kathy mentions, "you got me on that one. But, we'll figure it out." Everyone then lays back and relaxes for a while before lunch.

After lunch, everyone takes a long walk down the beach together. Kathy mentions, "walking in sand is hard. Now I can see why they put that experimental sand track in at the University." Paula mentions, "I know what you mean. I wonder if it's really hard to carry someone in the sand." It's no secret where this is going. Mark casually mentions, "it sounds like someone wants to be carried." Eddie replies, "either that, or they're telling us we haven't worked out enough." While the girls are smiling, Eddie motions to Mark that they should carry them. Kathy ends up on Eddie's shoulders, and Paula on Mark's.

They walk up the beach for a while, and Mark motions to go toward the water. Kathy exclaims, "hey, where are you guys going?" Mark replies, "for a swim." The guys keep walking to the ocean. Kathy and Paula start to giggle like little kids. Once they get to the water, Eddie and Mark keep walking. When the water is almost up to their heads, Mark and Eddie fall over, landing their girls in the water. Kathy yells out, "hey, that was fun! Let's do it again!"

Eddie tells Kathy, "OK, stand on my shoulders." He drops down and Kathy stands on his shoulders while she is holding on to his hands. Once she is balanced, Eddie yells out, "anybody got a Hula Hoop." Holding Kathy's legs, Eddie carries her into the water, and once the water is up to his waist, he tells her, "OK, dive in." Kathy dives into the water. When she comes up, she says, "that was fun! You make a great diving board!"

Eddie looks at Paula, telling her, "OK, it's your turn." Turning to Mark, Eddie tells him, "we'll each clasp our hands, she'll put one foot in your hands and one in mine. Then we'll make her fly." They go into the water, just about up to their waist. They tell Paula to hold on to them, and put one foot in Eddie's hands, and the other in Mark's. Watching out toward the ocean, Eddie tells Mark, "here comes a big wave. Talk about perfect timing!" Eddie announces, "on three. One two, three." They both hurl Paula into the air, making her airborne, flying high before she lands into the water. When she comes up, Paula exclaims, "wow that was fun!"

Hearing Paula's excitement, Kathy says, "I want a turn, please, please, please!" Mark looks at Eddie, and mentions to him, "this is a good upper body workout." Getting Kathy ready to fly, the guys wait for a good wave to approach. Mark sees a good one coming, and counts, "one, two, three." They then send Kathy airborne. While she is in the air, Kathy spreads her arms like a bird, and dives into the ocean. Coming up, Kathy exclaims, "wow, that was really fun!" Kathy and Paula fly a few more times, and then they all head back to their towels.

After a while, it comes time to go home. Today was a fun day at the beach for everyone. After they dry off and pack up, the group heads to their bicycles. They then begin the long ride up the path, which seems to get easier with each trip. Kathy and Paula are getting in awesome shape just riding to the beach with Eddie and Mark. When they arrive at the portal, they enter through, and return to their time. They left early in the morning, spent the day at the beach, and returned to their time at the same time they left. They realize they have the whole day ahead of them.

Paula mentions, "OK, guys, now what do we do?" Kathy replies, "wow, we still have the whole day!" Eddie jokingly suggests, "we had our workout. You girls should work out now." Kathy replies, "hey, wait! You're on to something!" Mark replies, "like what?" Kathy explains, "you guys can work out while we're in the portal, and come back to our time and work out even more." Kathy adds, "you can get even faster." Mark replies, "us? How about you guys?" Paula replies, "yeah! We can too!" Eddie replies, "I'm going to need to take some more vitamins." They all ride back to Eddie's house, and decide to work out for a while.

Once they get to Eddie's house, they go downstairs to Eddie's home gym to work out. When they are together, they have a tendency to push each other harder. They also know each other's limits. Since they had a good ride to the beach, today they are working on their upper bodies. Next time, they decide to work out their lower bodies, and then go to the pool and swim. In changing up their routine, they can make better gains.

Kathy and Paula rotate through the bench press, raising the weight each set. Paula gets on the bench, attempting to lift a weight that is seemingly heavy for her. She lowers the bar, and does not seem to have the energy to complete the lift. Kathy, standing behind the bench spotting her, tells her, "you can lift it!" Mark looks, telling her, "just lift it. You know you can." Eddie is watching, somehow knowing she can lift the weight. Paula, already fatigued from her first attempt, tries again and manages to lift the weight.

While Paula is getting off the bench, Kathy says the word, "superpowers." Paula replies, "superpowers? How's that?" Kathy replies, "Mark told you that you can lift it, and you did." Mark then tells Kathy, "yeah, and you knew it was bullshit that she couldn't lift it." They all have a good laugh. Kathy, in amazement, realizes and mentions, "yeah, and Eddie knew we were right. He totally trusted our instincts." Paula flexes her biceps, and replies, "yeah, superpowers."

As the Summer gets into full swing, a schedule seems to have appeared. Kathy and Paula are working three days a week at the camp. Their working hours are from 8:00 a.m. until 1:00 p.m. Eddie changes his schedule to cut lawns in the morning so he can have more time with Kathy. Mark also tries to schedule most of his work in the mornings, so he can spend more time with Paula. Eddie buys and sells his gold early in the morning. He then waits until late at night time to hide any gold and the money.

Eddie, Kathy, Paula and Mark often work out together. Tuesday, Thursday, and Saturday seems to be the days they frequently get together to work out. Eddie and Kathy go to the beach several times during the week. On the days they don't go to the beach, they go to the county pool. Mark and Paula also go to the beach frequently. Once or twice a week, the couples join each other, either at the beach or at the local pool.

While Eddie and Mark are off working, Eddie's mother, Nina, runs into Mark's mother, Mariana, at the local farmers market. Having the same shopping schedule, they see each other at the market at least once per the week. They know when the new shipments arrive, so they get there before the food has been picked over.

Nina mentions to Mariana, "Eddie is eating me out of house and home." Mariana replies, "I know what you mean, Mark is doing the same." Nina tells Mariana, "we've even planted a bigger garden this year." Mariana adds, "we planted a larger garden too this year. It's looking pretty good right now." Mariana asks Nina, "is Eddie home anymore?" Nina replies, "no. He's either working, exercising, or he's with Katarina." Preferring the name "Katarina" to "Kathy," Nina is one of the few who calls Kathy by her real name, Katarina. Mariana tells Nina, "Mark is the same way. He's always out with Paula now."

Mariana mentions to Nina, "here comes trouble." Mariana spied Kathryn Black, the mother of Chuckie. Once a month or so, Kathryn feels the need to make her presence known. Kathryn, with her usual sarcastic introduction, announces, "well, well, well, if it isn't Mariana and Nina." Nina returns the serve, replying, "well, and if it isn't the Kathryn Black." Kathryn asks Nina and Mariana, "how are your little boys doing?" Answering Kathryn's sarcasm with a hand grenade, Nina replies, "Eddie is very big and strong now. You should see him! He won a lot of medals in track this year, and he's doing really good!"

Having absolutely no tolerance for Kathryn, Mariana tells her, "I hear your little Chuckie is taking the dope now." This comes as a shock to Kathryn, who replies, "oh no, not Charles. He would never do anything like that." Mariana hits back hard, telling Kathryn, "no, that's right! He's a dope and he's a taking the dope! You might want to check under his bed. That's where all little kids hide things, you know." Kathryn makes herself scarce, feeling once again like she's been beaten to a pulp by Nina and Mariana. Nina mentions to Mariana, "you got rid of her real fast this time." Nina and Mariana continue shopping, hoping not to run into Kathryn anytime soon.

One Saturday morning, Eddie, Kathy, Mark and Paula get together to work out at Eddie's house. Kathy asks Eddie and the group, "can you guys time me?

I want to see how fast I can run." Eddie, thinking this is right up his alley, replies, "sure." Eddie asks, "what do you want to run?" Kathy replies, "maybe 100 yards, or maybe 440 yards. I don't know." Mark mentions, "well, lets head out to the track and decide when we get there."

Paula asks Eddie and Mark, "can you guys time me too?" Eddie asks Mark, "do you have a stopwatch?" Mark replies, "yeah. But, I only have one." Eddie tells Mark, "go and get it. We'll need two of them." Mark asks Eddie, "I thought you had two stopwatches?" Eddie replies, "I do, but one of them only measures to one fifth of a second." Mark, who lives only a half mile from Eddie, rides his bicycle home to get his stopwatch.

When Mark returns, they head to the high school track. When they arrive, they find the football team practicing for the upcoming season. Kathy decides she wants to run Eddie's race, the 100-yard dash. They find the markings on the track for the start and finish for the 100-yard dash, which are engraved on the concrete curb. Kathy asks Paula if she wants to run the 100-yard dash with her, or run a different race. Paula decides she wants to run the 100-yard dash too, so she is happy to join Kathy. Competition breeds better performance, so Kathy is happy to have Paula run with her.

Kathy and Paula get ready to run. They decide that Mark will be the Starter, and Eddie will be the Timekeeper for both runners. Eddie walks to the finish line, as Kathy and Paula stretch and warm up, preparing to run. Mark, making light of some of the interesting stuff Starters sometimes say, jokingly tells them, "I want you to run a fair race, and I don't want any girl fights to break out during the race. And I want no hair pulling. And, please keep your fingernails to yourself." Kathy laughs, and remarks, "don't worry, that ain't happening." Once Eddie arrives at the finish line, Mark tells Kathy and Paula to get ready.

Mark tells Kathy and Paula, "take your marks." Correcting Mark, Kathy tells him, "it's 'on your marks.'" Mark, correcting himself, tells them again, "OK, on your marks." He waits two seconds, and says, "set." Kathy and Paula taught the proper "set" position to Eddie and Mark, so they know this position quite well. Mark yells out, "go." At the other end of the track, Eddie starts both watches. Kathy and Paula are off, doing exactly what they've watched hundreds of times before. Kathy takes an early lead, but Paula's competitive spirit leads her to run faster. Hearing Paula behind her, Kathy runs as fast as she can. The girls can hear Eddie and Mark yelling, "faster, faster," as they run. While Kathy and Paula are running, the football team momentarily stops practicing, and they all turn to watch. Just before the finish line, Kathy is in the lead, but Paula is giving her a good run for her money. Eddie, at the finish line, clicks one stopwatch when Kathy crosses, and the other when Paula crosses.

While the girls were running, Mark has been jogging down the track, following them. He didn't want to be the last to find out Kathy's and Paula's times. Eddie, looking at the stopwatches, shows them to Mark. Mark, almost in disbelief, replies, "wow." Eddie replies, "yeah." Mark and Eddie are thinking the same thing. The girls both ran a very good race.

The girls return from overrunning the finish line, and Eddie hands them the stopwatch with their respective times. They both look, and jump up and down with excitement. Kathy ran a 10.7 and Paula ran a 10.9. Eddie exclaims to Kathy, "do you know how good that is?" Kathy replies, "yeah! Now I wish I had blocks and spikes!" They all celebrate the girl's awesome run. This time it is Eddie who gives Kathy a victory hug and kiss, and Mark giving the same to Paula.

Mark tells Paula, "that was really awesome!" Mark then asks, "so, what race will you be running next?" Kathy looks at Paula, and asks, "how about the 440?" Paula replies, "sure, why not. But, let me rest for a while." While they are standing around the track, a stray football from a lousy kickoff attempt comes in the direction of Mark and Eddie. Mark picks up the football, and throws it 40 yards back to the football team. Mark targeted one of the players accurately, but Mark thought nothing of it. Mark's pass did, however, get the full attention of Mr. Moreno, the football coach. Meanwhile, the girls drink a little water, and decide they are ready for the next race. Eddie and Mark will each work one stopwatch for this event. Mark decided he likes being the Starter, so he will start the race.

They find the starting point for the 440-yard run, or dash, depending on how you see it. Mark instructs the girls again, telling them, "I want a fair race. No hair pulling, no girl fights halfway around the track, and definitely no tripping." Mark then tells Kathy and Paula, "on your marks." The girls get down, in position to run. Mark announces, "set." The girls look like this is going to be fierce competition. Mark announces, "go," and the girls are off. For once, Eddie and Mark get to stand around and observe, as their stopwatches are ticking away the seconds. Kathy and Paula start off quickly, knowing well the strategy in the 440-yard dash.

While Eddie and Mark are watching Kathy and Paula intently, Mr. Moreno, the football coach, walks up to Mark. The coach interrupts Mark, and asks, "are you Mark Svoboda?" Mark replies, "yeah. But, I'm really busy right now." The coach sees the stopwatch in Mark's hand, and backs off. Mark walks away, with his eyes fixed on Paula, who has a little less than 220 yards left to go. Eddie is looking at Kathy, then at his stopwatch, and back to Kathy again. Eddie, who is all excited, tells Mark, "Kathy might break 60!" Kathy and Paula show no signs of fatigue during the last half of the race. As Kathy and Paula approach the finish line, they sprint as hard as they can. Kathy, who is slightly ahead of Paula, crosses the finish line first, with Paula right behind her.

Kathy, temporarily exhausted, utters, "so, that's the kind of crap you guys go through!" Kathy lies face up on the ground, trying to catch her breath. Paula sees Kathy, and thinks laying on the ground is a wonderful idea. In a minute or so, Kathy yells out, "OK, I'm still alive! That's a good sign!" The girls lie there for a while, recovering from the race that, to use Braden's terms, "kicked their ass." Eddie and Mark look at the stopwatches together. Mark whispers, "look. They both broke 60." Eddie whispers back, "wow, they're faster than Mahoney on average."

After the girls somewhat recover, Eddie asks, "well, do you want to know your time?" Kathy, still trying to catch her breath, asks, "I don't know. Do I?" Eddie holds the stopwatch up, and Kathy stands up abruptly. She takes the stopwatch out of Eddie's hand, and looks at it as if she is in shock. Kathy yells out, "57!" She somehow finds the energy to jump up and down, still yelling, "57, 57, 57! Awesome!" After hearing Kathy's time, Paula jumps up and takes her stopwatch from Mark. Paula knows that if Kathy ran a 57, her time is very close to that. Paula looks at it and yells out, "60 seconds!" Mark, who looked at the stopwatch closely, tells Paula, "actually, it's a 59.8." Paula, all excited, yells out, "I broke 60!" Eddie tells Mark, "it looks like we're finally going to have some competition." Kathy says, "yeah, you see that! We're catching up! You guys are going to have to carry us more!" Paula whispers to Kathy, "shh, they're going to make us carry them."

Eddie asks, "well, what event is next?" Kathy, who is very happy with her performance, replies, "the discus, yeah the discus. But, since we don't have a discus, we'll have to get a pizza. Yeah, that's it! A pizza. A pizza looks like a discus, so that's close enough. Once I eat the pizza, I can throw the pan like a discus." Paula replies, "yeah, pizza, discus, what's the difference?" Eddie replies, "for one, you can't eat a discus." Paula asks, "then what good is a discus?" Kathy tells everyone, "I'm going to order a discus with shot-puts on it." Mark mentions, "it sounds like we're getting pizza with meatballs." Kathy tells Mark, "yeah, buddy! You got it! Meatballs, shot-put, they're both round!" Everyone breaks out laughing at Kathy's silliness. They all then head off to get pizza.

Over lunch, Eddie asks, "so, when are we going to work out?" Kathy replies, "work out? Are you crazy? I'm worn out." Paula agrees, working out is no longer on their list of activities for today. Eddie asks Kathy, "how could you be worn out? You only ran 540 yards today." Kathy replies, "somehow I knew that was on the horizon." Paula laughs and replies, "well, you did set yourself up really good for that one." Eddie then suggests, "why don't we just go to the pool and hang out." Everyone agrees to an afternoon at the pool. Eddie and Mark can swim laps, while Kathy and Paula lie in the sun, celebrating their awesome runs.

At the pool, Kathy and Paula talk about their 100-yard dash and 440-yard dash times while Eddie and Mark both swim laps. Paula mentions, "we should be on the track team. We're faster than some of the guys." Kathy replies, "Barbara tried out two years ago when she was a freshman, and they told her she couldn't join the boys' team." Paula comments, "she seems like she's a really good distance runner." Kathy replies, "I think she's faster in the mile than everyone on the team, except for Mitchell." Paula then concedes, "I guess we're destined to play badminton." Kathy replies, "well, there's also a girls' volleyball team." Paula ends the discussion by saying, "well, I'd rather watch Mark run." Kathy replies, "yeah, being with Eddie. That's where I'd rather be." Kathy and Paula turn over to sun their other side, and doze off.

After Eddie and Mark finish swimming their laps, they find the girls asleep. Not wanting them to get too much sun, Eddie and Mark wake them up with gentle kisses on their necks. Eddie gives Kathy, who is still half asleep, a kiss on her lips. Paula, waking up a lot faster, lands quickly onto Mark's lap. Kathy, who wakes up very slowly, does not even remember where she is. Eddie whispers to Kathy, "good morning." Before she even opens up her eyes, she puts her arms around Eddie, and gives him a good morning embrace. Kathy sits up and stretches, and lands on Eddie's lap with her arms around him, whispering to him, "that's the first time you ever woke me up." They embrace each other again, as Kathy finally wakes up.

They hang around the pool for a while until the sun sets. Kathy mentions to everyone, "hey, please don't tell anyone about my times." Paula asks, "why not?" Kathy tells everyone, "I want to keep it as a surprise." Eddie asks, "how's that?" Kathy explains, "I don't know. But, somewhere, someday, I want someone to watch me run those times, not just hear about it." Paula agrees, "yeah, that would definitely be better." Eddie and Mark agree to keep Kathy's and Paula's times a secret. Mark and Paula head out together, and Eddie and Kathy head out together.

Later in the Summer, Eddie decides to go through the portal in order to find another place to hide the money and gold he is accumulating. Eddie decides to go into the future, specifically sometime in the Summer after he graduates high school. His plan is to make sure his parents are still living in the same house, and to find an undisturbed area of the yard where he can hide his money and gold. Putting the money in the bank, or storing the gold and money in his room, might attract the wrong kind of attention.

Eddie wakes up early on a Wednesday, and prepares to make the trip. Before he goes into the portal, Eddie looks all around the yard. He knows the yard very well, for he cuts the lawn and does all the yard maintenance. There are two or three locations in the back yard that look promising, but none in the front yard. One good location is behind a bird bath in the corner of the yard that has been there since Eddie can remember. The bird bath is surrounded by large pieces of slate, which haven't been moved in years. Another good place is anywhere between the garden and the back fence. This area serves more as a walking path, and not suitable for planting. Eddie identifies a few other areas, and will check them out when he arrives in the future.

Eddie gets a flashlight, and heads to the portal. He is planning to look at the yard at night, lest anyone sees Eddie and his future counterpart together. At the portal, Eddie raises his right arm, and declares a time in mid-Summer after he graduates, adding a specific time, which is 3:00 a.m. No one is usually around this time of night. It suddenly becomes dark, and Eddie is off to his house.

Once he is at his house, Eddie hides his bicycle behind a bush. The first thing he notices is his father's truck is parked on the cement pad next to the driveway. This is good news. Eddie still lives here. He enters the backyard, and sees that a lot has changed. Since it is a full moon, there is not much need for the flashlight. The garden has been expanded to occupy nearly the entire back yard. Eddie, seeing the larger garden, thinks to himself, "well, it looks like I'll be expanding the garden sometime." The bird bath is still in the same place, and appears undisturbed. The area between the fence and the garden is the same. Eddie returns to the portal, and now has a plan.

Arriving back at the present, Eddie takes another look at the backyard. The place around the birdbath looks like the most promising hiding spot. No one ever goes there, and it will be undisturbed in the future. Eddie then gets ready to go to work. Today, Eddie has three lawns to cut, and a pool to clean. This will be enough to keep Eddie busy until Kathy gets off work. After work, it's anybody's guess where the day will lead.

Later that day, Eddie meets up with Kathy. It doesn't take Eddie a minute to notice that Kathy is not her usual self today. Eddie asks Kathy, "what's wrong?" Kathy tells Eddie, "bad news. Mahoney is out." Eddie asks, "how do you know?" Kathy explains, "his prick of a father called my father and begged him not to press charges against that asshole." Eddie comments, "I thought your dad dropped the charges." Kathy replies, "he did. I guess Mahoney's father never got the memo. It shows how suckky of an attorney he is anyway. My father told him that if Paul comes anywhere close to me, he will press the charges again." Eddie replies, "well, that sounds OK. He won't bother you." Kathy tells Eddie, "it's just knowing that he's out there."

Eddie explains to Kathy, "well, to start, he's been sitting on his ass for a few months in a loony bin, so he's way out of shape." Kathy replies, "yeah, but." Before Kathy could finish, Eddie points out, "you can outrun him now! He couldn't catch you to save his life!" A smile comes across Kathy's face, and she exclaims, "yeah, you're right!" Eddie reminds Kathy, "your times now are better than his were at the end of the season!" Eddie also explains, "besides, all you have to do is look at him and say, 'we are Katarina Karakova,' and he'll land himself back in the hospital in no time." Kathy, who is suddenly in a better mood, replies, "yeah, I could do that!" Kathy gives Eddie a big hug, telling him, "you just made my day!"

Eddie tells Kathy, "hey, I have a plan." Kathy asks, "what's that?" Eddie, explaining his plan, tells Kathy, "we'll just call everyone, Braden, Johnson, Mark, and everybody else, and tell them that if they see Mahoney, they are to tell him there are now four of you." Kathy laughs, and says, "yeah, he'll be back in that place so fast." Kathy asks, "what did they used to call those places, a sanitarium or something?" Eddie replies, "yeah. I think so." Kathy replies, "yeah, a sanitarium, that's what they were called. From now on, we're calling it a sanitarium, no more hospital or looney bin." Trying out the new word, Kathy says, "Mahoney's out of the sanitarium. Mahoney is back in the sanitarium. Mahoney has moved back into the sanitarium." Eddie admits, "yeah, that definitely makes him sound a lot more crazy."

Now that Kathy is in a better mood, they go and work out at Eddie's house. Working out will help Kathy get rid of a lot of adrenaline that built up after finding out that Mahoney is out of the sanitarium. Kathy has an awesome workout, which puts her in even a better mood. While they are working out, Kathy suggests, "hey, let's see if Paula and Mark want to go to the beach or pool." Eddie agrees, "yeah, that would be a good afternoon." They call Mark first, who is with Paula working out at his house. Mark and Paula agree to meet Eddie and Kathy at the pool afterwards, since it is late and the pool is a lot closer.

When Eddie and Kathy arrive at the pool, they find Mark and Paula are already there. Since it is a little later in the day, the pool is sparsely populated. They join Mark and Paula, who are just standing around in the water cooling off. Mark asks everyone, "so, does anyone want to swim some laps?" Kathy replies, "yeah. I'm swimming laps today." Everyone begins swimming laps, each having their own lane, which is unusual on a sunny day.

Kathy, watching Eddie do flip turns, realizes how artistic they are. Kathy waits for Eddie to get to the end of his lane. When he gets there, she asks him, "will you show me how to do a flip turn?" Eddie replies, "sure. I'll do one in slow motion, so you can watch." Backing up a bit, Eddie swims toward the wall and approaches the wall in slow motion. Right before the wall, he does a somersault in the water, and kicks off the wall. Eddie asks Kathy, "could you see how it's done?" Kathy replies, "yeah. I got it. Give me the strategy." When it comes to athletic stuff, Kathy learns quickly.

Paula and Mark are now standing around, also wanting to learn how to do a flip turn. Eddie tells Kathy, "when you are about an arms length from the wall, that is when you want to begin your flip turn. A flip turn is nothing more than a half somersault in the water. You'll still have some forward motion but, once you're flipped, just kick and you're off. Then, once you've kicked off the wall, you will be upside down. Just turn in the water to get face down again." Eddie also tells Kathy, "that black lane marker, the 'T' at the end of the lane, is a guide to tell you when to flip." Mark replies, "oh, so that's what it's for. I never knew that." Mark is not alone. Not a lot of people know why there is a "T" at the end of the lane in a pool.

Kathy backs up and gives it a try. She approaches the wall, and when she thinks she is in position, she does her somersault. Kathy kicks, but there is no wall to push off. Eddie tells her, "try again, but go a little farther this time." Kathy backs up and tries it again. Getting a little closer to the wall this time, she does the somersault, kicks, and is off. She does a flip turn at the other end of the pool, and comes back to Eddie. Kathy exclaims, "this is fun!" Being very athletic, Kathy learns the technique very quickly.

Mark and Paula then give it a try. Eddie mentions, "the faster you are swimming, the sooner you want to start the somersault, because you have more forward motion." After a few attempts, it seems like everyone is now an expert at flip turns. Eddie gets out of the pool and watches a few of their turns. Everyone appears to have the technique mastered in no time, so Eddie gets back into the pool and continues his laps.

The mother of a young girl watched as Eddie explained the flip turn to Kathy, Mark and Paula. The mother approaches Eddie, asking him, "will you please show my daughter how to turn like that? She's always wanted to be able do that, but she can't figure it out." Eddie replies, "sure. Go and get her." At the end of her lap, Kathy sees Eddie standing at the end of the lane, and asks, "what's up?" Eddie replies, "I'm teaching swimming lessons now." Kathy asks, "what?" Eddie explains, "the lady wanted me to show her daughter how to do a flip turn." Kathy says, "how can you say no to that."

The woman's daughter, in the lane next to Eddie, stops at the wall where Eddie is waiting. The mother returns, introducing her daughter, "this is my daughter, Tessa Klement." Eddie replies, "hi. I'm Eddie, and this is Kathy." Tessa is a very athletic looking girl. This is obviously not her first time in the water. Kathy, the future gym teacher, asks Tessa, "so, your mom says you want to do a flip turn." Tessa replies, "yeah. But, I keep messing it up." Kathy tells Tessa, "OK, Eddie's going to do one in slow motion. You just watch first." Eddie backs up about ten yards and swims toward the wall. Approaching the wall, Eddie does the somersault, kicks off the wall, and turns 180 degrees in the water, continuing his stroke. Eddie returns, explaining to Tessa in detail how he did the flip turn.

Kathy tells Tessa, "OK, it's your turn." Tessa backs up, swims, and approaches the wall. After doing the somersault, she kicks, but the wall is too far away. This is a common problem when learning a flip turn. But, it's better that the other problem, which is hitting the wall with your head. Kathy tells her, "try again, and I'll tap you on your back when you should flip." Kathy then tells Tessa, "OK, let's try again." As Tessa approaches the wall, Kathy taps her on her back when she is close enough. Tessa then does the somersault, kicks, and is now off in the other direction. She goes off a bit of an angle, but quickly straightens up. She takes a few strokes, and stops. Eddie tells her, "OK, try

272   Eddie – The Freshman Year

it again, but this time Kathy is not going to tap you." Tessa swims toward the wall, but this time she swims a little faster. When she gets within an arms length, she flips, kicks off the wall, and swims straight in the lane this time. Tessa tries a few more times, getting better with her timing after each attempt.

While Tessa is practicing, Kathy asks Mrs. Klement, "how old is Tessa?" Mrs. Klement tells Kathy, "she's fourteen. She's always been very athletic, but this flip turn thing has really got her." Kathy replies, "looks like she's got it down now," as she watches Tessa do another turn. Watching as Tessa does another flip turn, Mrs. Klement exclaims, "wow! That one looked really good!" Kathy asks, "so, Tessa will be in high school next year?" Mrs. Klement replies, "yeah. And, she's really nervous." Kathy asks, "Northside?" Mrs. Klement replies, "yeah. We just moved here in the beginning of the Summer, and she doesn't really know too many people." Kathy tells her, "well, I guess we'll see her in high school next year."

When Tessa returns to the end of the pool, she tells Eddie and Kathy, "hey, thanks so much for showing me how to do that!" Eddie tells her, "no problem." Eddie tells Tessa, "if you want to just practice your flip turns, swim the short dimension of the pool." Kathy gives Tessa a high-five, and Eddie, Kathy, and Tessa go back to swimming laps.

After a while Tessa gets out of the pool, and dries off. Tessa tells her mother, "I'm so excited! I can do a flip turn!" Tessa's mother tells her, "some of your turns looked really great! Oh, and they go to Northside. I guess you'll see them there when school starts." Tessa tells her mother, "they seem really nice." Tessa's mother replies, "see, there's nothing to be worried about."

Mark and Paula get out of the pool, followed by Eddie and Kathy. They have had enough for today, and dry off. Mark asks everyone, "OK, are we taking on the swimming team next year?" Eddie replies, "you can't be serious." Mark replies, "no, but it's a thought." Kathy asks, "is there a pizza team? We can take them on. That won't be a problem." Paula replies, "they won't stand a chance." Mark mentions, "yeah, I can see it now. A discus with shot-put toppings." Kathy asks, "how about the javelin? Where does that fit in?" Paula reveals the mystery, telling Kathy, "the javelin is just cut into little pieces, and they call them bread sticks." Kathy then comes to the conclusion, "yeah, I guess no one can eat a whole javelin on their own." Eddie mentions, "don't forget about those drill bits on the salad." Kathy thinks for a while, and yells out, "yeah, that spiral shaped pasta! Drill bits! I knew it! I knew it!" Paula adds, "yeah, and the ziti are really water pipes, and spaghetti is electrical wires." Kathy adds, "spaghetti is electrical wires only after it's cooked!" Mark tells everyone, "well, it looks like Joe is in for a surprise next time we go for pizza." Kathy says, "well, let's go and surprise him now." They get on their bicycles and head to the pizzeria.

While Eddie, Kathy, Mark and Paula were drying off, Tessa looked over and noticed not only how big and strong the high school guys look, but the girls too. She also noticed that they were all were having fun together. Something happened to Tessa today at that moment. Today, Tessa learned how to do a flip turn. What is more important, today Tessa was filled with the motivation and drive to be a great athlete. Tessa decided that she is going to be athletic like Kathy and Paula. Tessa knows what she wants and has set her goals. Nothing can stop Tessa now.

When they get to the pizzeria, Joe yells out, "hey, look at who's here!" Joe is always happy to see happy people. The whole group walks up to the counter, and place their order. With a straight face, Kathy tells Joe, "I would like a discus with shot-put toppings. Oh, and we want a javelin, all cut up, please." Paula, also acting very serious, tells Joe, "we'd also like a large salad, but please don't put any drill bits on it." Joe starts laughing. Looking at Eddie, Joe tells him, "it's no wonder why you guys always come up and place the order!" Kathy and Paula laugh at what they just said. Kathy exclaims, "I can't even believe I said that!" Mark explains to Joe, "a pizza looks like a discus, and the meatballs are the shot-puts." Joe begins to catch on. Joe asks, "what's this about drill bits?" Mark explains, "that's the spiral pasta on the salads." Joe laughs, telling them, "you guys are so much fun!" They place their real order, and find a seat.

After dinner, they head out. Mark asks, "how about the beach this weekend?" Everyone agrees the beach is a good idea. Eddie suggests, "maybe, we can get the whole tribe together for pizza sometime." Paula is quick to respond, telling everyone, "I'm in." Kathy suggests, "yeah, and we'll see who's brave enough to eat drill bits." Paula has suggestion too, mentioning, "I want to see Bobby B. eat a shot-put." Kathy says, "yeah, we're crazy." Paula remarks, "when we all get together, it's really going to be something." Mark and Paula then head out together. Kathy suggests to Eddie, "lets go to my house and just hang out in the pool." Eddie replies, "that sounds great." Eddie and Kathy then head out to Kathy's house.

For the next few weeks, the workouts continue. Eddie and Kathy are both getting stronger and faster. Mark and Paula are also working out together.

They are keeping pace with Eddie and Kathy. Eddie improves his nutrition, taking more amino acids to build muscle. Eddie also notices that, because he is taking the methylfolate, the heat does not bother him as much as it has in previous years.

Eddie's bicycle is holding up well. He does notice, however, that Kathy's bicycle can use a little work. Kathy's bicycle is a quality bicycle. It is a top of the line Motobecane touring bicycle with Campagnolo components. A squeak somewhere, however, suggests it's time for service. One day, Eddie asks Kathy, "hey, do you want to tune up your bicycle?" Kathy replies, "sure, if you think it needs it." Eddie tells Kathy, "it needs it. Let's ride over to Vito's and get some parts." Riding over to Vito's, Eddie and Kathy pick up some brake shoes, new cables, handlebar tape, and a few other items. Kathy also buys a small handlebar bag, so she can carry more stuff to the beach. They then ride back to Eddie's house to tune up Kathy's bicycle. Eddie brings the bicycle into his father's shop in the basement, where they begin to work on it.

In no time, Eddie has Kathy's entire bicycle disassembled. Kathy is amazed, seeing the parts from her bicycle spread all around. Eddie tells Kathy, "if you want to, you can clean the frame." Kathy cleans up the frame, and anything else that looks dirty. The first thing Eddie does is to disassemble the front hub, clean and repack the bearings, and reassemble the hub. He then removes the freewheel from the rear wheel, rebuilds the rear hub in the same way he did the front hub. After replacing the freewheel, he lubricates it, and moves on to the cranks. Removing the cranks, he cleans and repacks the bearings, and reinstalls the crank set. He tells Kathy to remove the old brake shoes. After showing her how to remove one, she quickly catches on and removes the others.

Kathy mentions, "wow, I didn't know there are so many parts." Eddie replies, "yeah, there are lots of little ones, but I know where they all go." Eddie removes the derailleurs, cleans and lubricates them, and reinstalls them. They then install the new brake shoes. Eddie tells Kathy, "we're almost done." Removing the old cables, Eddie replaces them with better cables that have Teflon sleeves. Flipping the bicycle upside down, Eddie adjusts the gears and the brakes. They then check all the bolts, making sure they are tight. The last thing is to replace the plastic handlebar tape with leather tape. This will afford a better and more comfortable grip.

The bicycle is now done. The effort to rebuild the bicycle took a little more than two hours, including the trip to Vito's. Eddie takes Kathy's bicycle outside, and gives it a short test ride. It seems to ride perfectly, so he lets Kathy give it a try. Kathy gets on her bicycle, and takes it for a test ride. As Kathy rides, she exclaims, "wow, is this really my bicycle?" Kathy rides up the street, and back to Eddie's house. She stops, and tells Eddie, "I can't believe how good it rides!" Eddie replies, telling her, "it's back to factory specs again." Kathy exclaims, "it never rode this good before! You're not going to be able to keep up with me anymore!" Eddie replies, "then I'll guess I'll have to carry you more." Eddie and Kathy go for a short ride together to give the bicycle a good test.

During the next few rides, Kathy is able to keep up a better pace. On the way to the beach one day, Paula tries Kathy's bicycle. After seeing how well it rides, she asks Eddie if he can tune hers up someday too. Paula's bicycle, like Kathy's, is a quality machine. Machines do require periodic maintenance. Eddie gives Paula's bicycle a test ride, and agrees that it definitely needs some work.

When they are all together later that week, Eddie tunes up Paula's bicycle. As Eddie disassembles each bearing set, Paula cleans the parts. Eddie, with Mark's help, lubricates and reassembles the bearings. Mark and Kathy, in the mean time, clean the frame and wheels. The difference after the tune-up is remarkable. They can all now enjoy an easier ride to the beach.

With Summer vacation coming to an end, Kathy and Paula plan for the tribe to get together at the pool, and pizza afterwards. They choose the last Friday afternoon before school starts. This will give everyone a chance to meet up before the school year begins, in a more relaxed atmosphere. Kathy and Paula did not set any specific time to show up at the pool. They rule their life like a bird in flight, so plans are not set in stone. They decide to tell everyone to show up at the pool in the afternoon. Afterwards, when they are hungry, they will all go out and get pizza.

Before the end of the Summer celebration, the schedules arrive in the mail. Eddie tells everyone to spread the word to bring their schedules to the pool party, so they all can compare. With any luck, they will be in some of the same classes. Eddie talks with Mark, and they discover they are again in the same section, so most of their classes overlap. Eddie, now a sophomore, is eligible to take auto shop. Mark, however, signed up for woodworking and metal shop, which will be an easy A for him. Last year, Eddie's and Kathy's path did not cross during the school day. Eddie's big hope for this year is that he has the same lunch period as Kathy.

The day of the party arrives, and Eddie and Kathy ride to the pool together. When they arrive, they find Braden and Wendy sitting at a table under an umbrella. Kathy and Eddie put their stuff on a nearby table, and join Braden and Wendy. Eddie compares schedules with Braden, and notice they are in the same section as well. Eddie tells Braden that Mark is also in the same section, which is good news. Braden mentions, "the best part is gym class is right before lunch." Eddie replies, "yeah, and not right after." Gym class right after lunch is never too much fun. While Eddie and Braden are comparing schedules, Kathy announces, "I'll be right back."

Kathy walks over to the pool, where she sees Tessa swimming laps. What caught Kathy's eye was the flip turn Tessa did. Kathy sits at the edge of the lane waiting for Tessa. Seeing Kathy, Tessa stops and says, "Kathy! Hey there!" Kathy tells Tessa, "you've gotten really good!" Tessa replies, "I've been practicing almost every day since you guys showed be how to do a flip turn." Giving Tessa some encouragement, Kathy tells her, "well, your turns look awesome!" Tessa tells Kathy, "it's my favorite part of swimming laps now." Kathy asks, "is your mom here?" Tessa replies, "no. She got tired of taking me every day, so she lets me ride my bicycle here now. She just makes me call her when I get here and when I leave. But, sometimes I come here with a friend, so she knows that I'm safe." Kathy tells Tessa, "hey, when you're done, come and join us. We're over there," pointing to the tables where they dropped their stuff.

Kathy returns to the group, noticing that Mark and Paula have arrived. Eddie asks Kathy, "isn't that Tessa?" Kathy replies, "yeah. And her turns have gotten really good." Eddie replies, "so, she's been practicing." Kathy tells Eddie, "she said almost every day." Paula remarks, "yeah, she definitely has what it takes." Kathy tells the group, "I told her she can come and join us when she's done."

Bobby B. arrives, two inches taller and with twenty more pounds of muscle. The shot-doc, who was highly motivated after the last regular meet of the Spring season, has been working out all Summer. The shot-doc drops his stuff on the table. Mark jokingly says to him, "hey, did you take the Summer off, bro?" Bobby B. replies, "yeah. I only worked out five days a week over the Summer." Bobby B. exchanges a fist bump with his friends, and takes a seat. Eddie announces, "I'm going to swim a few laps before it gets crowded," and heads to the pool. Everyone else sits back and relaxes for a while.

Eddie gets into the water, and notices Tessa is swimming like a machine. She apparently now has the flip turn down to a science. Eddie starts swimming, and is in the lane next to Tessa. While Eddie is doing his laps, he notices Tessa in still keeping her same pace, and is not slowing a bit. Eddie and Tessa, otherwise, do not pay much attention to each other. They are too focused on their workouts. After a while, Mark gets in the pool, and also starts swimming laps.

Johnson and Barbara arrive. They put their stuff down, say a quick hello, and head right for the water. Kathy mentions to Paula, "Barbara looks like she's been working out a lot too." Kathy remarks, "I wonder what everyone else does over the Summer." Bobby B. answers, telling everyone, "they sit in their houses, getting a head start on next years school work." Bobby B., who lives near Kathy, is in a neighborhood where are a lot of kids, but they are rarely seen outside. It's not hard to see why Bobby B. came to that conclusion. Paula mentions, "well, there were a lot of kids in the camp this year. Maybe everyone goes to camps." Kathy points out, "Tessa has been swimming all Summer."

Eddie and Mark get out of the pool, and take a seat. Mitchell walks up, telling everyone, "hey, it's great to see everyone!" They all talk for a while and catch up on what they did this Summer. As they are talking, Hoffer, the sprinter who will be a freshman this year, notices Mark and Eddie sitting with a group of people. Looking a little closer, Hoffer also recognizes Johnson, Bobby B., and Mitchell. Hoffer, who hasn't seen them in a year, comes over to say hello. Mark introduces Hoffer to Kathy, Paula, and Barbara. They all talk about track for a while, filling Hoffer in on last year's indoor and Spring track seasons.

Tessa finishes her laps, and gets out of the pool. Tessa gets her towel, and dries off. Looking around, she walks over to the table where Eddie and his tribe are sitting. As Tessa is walking up, Kathy mentions to her, "it looks like you had a great workout!" Tessa replies, "yeah, I'm exhausted." This is the first time any of them have seen Tessa out of the water. Paula whispers to Mark, "she's got lats the size of angel wings."

Tessa sees Hoffer sitting with the group. All excited, Tessa asks Hoffer, "hey, do you know these guys?" Hoffer replies, "yeah. I ran with them in middle school a while ago." It is obvious to everyone that Hoffer and Tessa have met before. Kathy tells Tessa, "come and sit with us." Kathy introduces Tessa to everyone. Tessa tells everyone, "my family just moved here in the beginning of the Summer. I met Jimmy here at the pool during our first week here. We've been hanging out together." Tessa is as happy as she can be right now. She'll be in high school next week, and has already been accepted by the upperclassmen.

Mitchell asks, "did anybody bring their schedules?" In no time, everyone takes out their schedules. Everyone compares their schedules and, to everyone's amazement, all the sophomores are all in the same section. This means everyone in the group is all in the same core classes. Braden exclaims, "hey look, we're all in the same gym class!" Mark replies, "I wonder how we all got the same classes together." Barbara tells everyone, "I know how." Eddie asks Barbara, "tell us." Barbara explains, "Mr. Frazier or Mr. Zunde probably pulled some strings to get you guys in the same class. They've done that before for other teams. It boosts team morale."

Braden then exclaims, "since we're in the same gym class, we're kicking ass during that football game! We're gonna be kicking ass all year long!" While Braden is on his rant, Kathy whispers to Tessa, "Braden is the team's chief ass kicker. He gets like this, especially during track meets." Tessa replies, "he sounds really confident." Kathy replies, "oh, yeah! He is, and then some!" Tessa asks, "what's this about a football game?" Barbara explains to Tessa and Hoffer, "in gym class, Mr. Frazier arranges the first football game of the freshmen versus the sophomores." Eddie adds, "it's like some sort of initiation rite." Braden is quick to point out, "we kicked a lot of sophomore ass last year."

For the next hour or so, Hoffer and Tessa talk with the group. People go in and out of the pool to cool off. As the afternoon winds down, the decision is made to get pizza. Kathy asks Tessa and Hoffer, "we're getting pizza. Do you guys want to join us?" Tessa tells Kathy, "let me call my mom and make sure it's OK first." Hoffer and Tessa go off to make the phone call.

As they are packing up their stuff, Eddie asks Kathy, "when's your lunch period?" Kathy replies, "fifth period." Eddie pulls out his schedule, and Kathy rips it right out of his hands before he could take a look at it. She looks down the list, seeing Eddie also has lunch during fifth period. Kathy screams, "awesome! Yes!" She gives Eddie a big hug. Mark asks, "what was that all about?" Eddie replies, "we have lunch together." Paula asks, "what period?" Eddie replies, "fifth." Paula looks at Mark, telling him, "awesome, we have lunch together too!" Barbara, overhearing all of this, looks at Johnson, and says, "me too."

Barbara mentions to Paula, "someone had to have pulled a lot of strings to get all this to happen." Paula curiously asks, "who do you think it was?" Barbara tells her, "Mr. Frazier probably suggested it, but one thing is for sure. If Mr. Zunde wants something, he gets it." Paula replies, "really?" Barbara informs Paula, "Mr. Zunde doesn't even need his job. The rumor is that no one messes with him, not even the principal." Paula, having a revelation, mentions, "yeah, he seems to do whatever he wants."

Barbara whispers to Paula, "I know a secret about Mr. Zunde." Paula, whispering back, asks, "what's that?" Barbara tells Paula, "well, it's not really a secret. A few people know. Mr. Zunde is actually Dr. Zunde, but he doesn't want to be called Dr. Zunde. He has a Ph.D. in Exercise Science and a Ph.D. in Nutrition." Barbara also tells Paula, "Kathy knows about it, only because Mr. Zunde knows her father." Barbara explains, "he can walk into any university or high school and get a job that he doesn't even need." Paula remarks, "this is beginning to make a lot of sense."

Many years ago, the high school principal, Mr. Crum, suspended John Davies, the school's star football quarterback. Davies was on target to get a scholarship to a major university. Many college scouts were present at the regional semifinals, with the team being a strong contender for a State championship. Davies was so good, the team retired his number, number 7. No other student before or has since had that honor. A few days before the game, Davies was caught drinking a beer on school grounds. Even though he was of legal age[5], and school was not in session, Mr. Crum suspended him anyway. Davies was therefore not allowed to play in the divisional semifinals. The team got beat, 63-6, clearly proving that Davies was a key player. His father, Mr. Davies, took the issue to the school board, which lead to the hiring of Dr. Zunde. Davies, a walk-on in college, eventually got the scholarship he was due.

Mr. Maurice Crum, the principal, is quite afraid of Dr. Gerhard Zunde. Dr. Zunde was appointed by the school board years ago to beef up the failing athletic program. Before Dr. Zunde arrived, many of the Northside teams occupied the basement, courtesy of Mr. Crum. After Mr. Zunde began working with the teams, championships, State invitational meets, and subsequently scholarships for the students have been commonplace. Dr. Zunde is also the

---

[5] At the time of Davies suspension, the legal drinking age was eighteen years of age.

Eddie – The Freshman Year

highest paid teacher in the school district, earning more than three times what Mr. Crum makes. Of special interest is Dr. Zunde does not report to the principal. He was appointed by, and reports directly to, the school board, which annoys Mr. Crum. Dr. Zunde drives to school in his Porsche 911, and parks it next to Mr. Crum's dilapidated Volkswagen Beetle. Mr. Zunde also often mispronounces Mr. Crum's name, calling him Mr. Crumb.

Hoffer and Tessa return with good news. Tessa announces, "I can go! Well, as long as Jimmy goes with me." Kathy tells her, "awesome!" Once they are all packed up, they all head out to the pizzeria. On the way, Kathy yells out, "wow, my bicycle rides really good!" Eddie yells back, "yeah, I'm having trouble keeping up with you!" On the way, they pass through Bobby B. and Kathy's neighborhood. As they drive down the street, Tessa points to her house and yells out, "hey Kathy! There's my house!" Kathy yells back, "wow! We live in the same neighborhood!" Kathy takes the lead, and makes a turn so they can ride by her house. When they pass by Kathy's house, Kathy yells out to Tessa, "there's my house!"

When they arrive at the Pizzeria, Joe yells out from behind the counter, "hey, look who's here!" Mark yells back, "hey Joe, we're really hungry today!" Joe yells back, "hey Kathy, what will it be? A discus or a shot-put today? Oh, and we're having a special on drill bits!" Tessa is now really beginning to feel special. Tessa has found her tribe.

They all take a seat near the window, spreading over a few tables. Since it is a large group, Joe comes over to take their order. Kathy, pointing at Bobby B. tells Joe, "he's having a shot-put. Yeah, make sure he gets a shot-put." Bobby B. asks, "what?" Joe turns to Bobby B., asking him, "do want a javelin to go with your shot-put?" Kathy starts laughing, and explains to Bobby B., "a meatball is a shot-put, a pizza is a discus, and bread sticks are a javelin that is cut up into small pieces." Everyone laughs, as Paula remarks, "this is never going to end, I can see it."

Once they have all placed their order, Tessa asks, "what's this about drill bits?" Kathy explains, "drill bits are those little spiral pasta things they put in salads." Tessa starts laughing, and says, "you guys are so funny!" Eddie says, "just wait until we get back to school. Kathy's going to have a special name for everything they serve in the school cafeteria." Paula remarks, "I can't wait to hear what she comes up with."

During dinner, Paula whispers to Kathy, "uh oh! Trouble is coming." Kathy whispers to Paula, "like in your superpowers?" Paula replies, "yeah." Paula looks out the window, and sees Mahoney drive into the parking lot in his Corvette. Paula tells everyone, "hey, Mahoney just drove up." Kathy, who is not afraid in the least bit, tells everyone, "if he comes anywhere near here, I'll take care of him." Eddie reassures Kathy, "don't worry about him at all." Braden adds, "yeah, he's about due for another ass kicking anyway. He's got to get through us to get to you." Tessa asks, "what's this all about?" Kathy explains, "Paul Mahoney. He's an escaped crack pot from the sanitarium." They continue to eat, and Mahoney walks through the door.

Mahoney, seeing the group together, spies Kathy and freezes for a moment. Mahoney walks to the counter to place an order, and looks again at Kathy. Eddie turns around to look at Mahoney, and turns back around. Paula whispers to Kathy, "this is not good." Kathy tells everyone, "don't ask questions now but, if he comes over here, whatever I say, say exactly the same thing." Everyone agrees to Kathy's request. Mahoney looks again in the direction of Kathy. Kathy is ready. She no longer has any fear in confronting Mahoney.

Mahoney places his order, and walks in the direction of Kathy's table. Eddie turns around, but Mahoney stares right through him looking at Kathy. Kathy stands up, looks at Mahoney, and says in a monotone voice, "we are Katarina Karakova." Everyone repeats in unison what Kathy said, "we are Katarina Karakova." Mahoney panics, puts his hands over his ears, and screams out, "nooooo!" All the patrons turn to look to see what happened. Mahoney runs to the door, and is barely able to get it open. When he finally opens the door, he runs down the street in the opposite direction of his car, screaming out words that make no sense.

Hoffer asks, "wow! Is that guy crazy, or what?" Kathy replies, "yeah. He is. I guess it's back to the good old sanitarium for him." Tessa asks, "what's up with that guy?" Paula interjects, "he's a real mental case. His elevator is stuck between floors. Apparently, they let him out of the sanitarium way too early." Kathy reassures Tessa, "don't worry about him. He's pretty much harmless now." Mitchell mentions, "Mahoney is what you would call an entitled brat. His parents kept telling him that he's so special when he was younger." They resume their dinner, not giving Mahoney any further attention.

With dinner over, they all get up and head out. While they are unlocking their bicycles, a police car with flashing lights drives up the road slowly. The officer, whose name is Richard, asks the group, "did any of you see a guy screaming and running around here?" Kathy, taking control of the situation, tells Richard, "yeah, his name is Paul Mahoney. He must have escaped from the sanitarium." Understanding that Kathy has some valuable information, the police officer pulls over, parks his car, and gets out.

The officer tells Kathy, "Paul Mahoney. We know all about him." The officer then asks Kathy, "how do you know him?" Kathy replies, "he was supposed to graduate high school last year, but they had to put him in a sanitarium." Kathy, pointing to the parking lot, tells the officer, "his car is over there." Kathy and the officer go over to take a look. The officer writes down Mahoney's license plate number. Kathy tells the officer, "Mahoney is seriously crazy. You need to get him off the streets." The officer replies, "I agree. He allegedly almost caused an accident up the street. The complainant states that he was screaming as he was running down the middle of the street." Getting back into his car, the officer radios to the precinct information regarding Mahoney. The officer asks Kathy for her name and phone number, which she is quick to give him. The officer thanks Kathy for her help, and tells her she can go.

When Kathy returns to the group, Eddie tells her, "you handled that really well." Kathy replies, "I'm not afraid of that jerk anymore." They all say goodbye, and will meet again in a few days at school. Hoffer mentions to Eddie, "I have to hear about this one sometime." Eddie tells Hoffer, "well, if you're riding home with Tessa, we'll explain when we get to Kathy's." Mark and Paula then head out together. Johnson and Barbara head in another direction. Eddie, Kathy, Bobby B., Mitchell, Hoffer, and Tessa all head in the direction of Kathy's house.

When they arrive at Kathy's house, they all sit on the front lawn. Kathy and Eddie explain to Hoffer and Tessa what happened at the end of the last school year regarding Mahoney. Eddie tells Hoffer, "Mahoney was supposed to be the star of the track team last year but, as the year went on, he kept getting slower and slower." Hoffer mentions to Eddie, "he looked kind of weak for a senior." Kathy points out, "that's what a few months in a sanitarium will do to you. His muscles wasted away, and now he's Mahoney baloney."

Tessa asks, "what was that name that you said to get rid of him?" Kathy tells Tessa, "oh, that's my real name, 'Katarina Karakova.'" Tessa tells Kathy, "that's a really beautiful name." Kathy replies, "thank you." Tessa mentions, "my real name is Tessa. But, everyone thinks it's short for something, like Contessa, Theresa, or Quintessa."

After a while, Hoffer and Tessa ride their bicycles to Tessa's house. Bobby B. and Mitchell head home. Eddie and Kathy have what's left of the evening to spend with each other. Eddie tells Kathy, "today was fun." Kathy replies, "yeah, and I'm doing really good." Kathy whispers Eddie, "thank you for a wonderful Summer." Eddie whispers back, "this was my best Summer ever. I loved our time together." Kathy sighs, and says, "yeah, and next week it's back to school." Eddie tells Kathy, "we'll just make it the best school year together." Kathy tells Eddie, "take me home." Eddie reminds Kathy, "you are home." Kathy says, "no, silly. Take me home the long way." Kathy and Eddie walk to the schoolyard behind Kathy's house, and take the long way home.

Where Are They Now

Once you've read the entire series, you might be wondering where some of the characters landed. This chapter tells where the characters who will not return for Eddie - The Sophomore Year are now. It also gives you an idea who will return for Eddie - The Sophomore Year.

Matt Wood

After graduating, the shot-put star went to college. He did not make the track and field team at college. He did, however, try out for the university football team. Making the team as a walk-on, he developed a skill that he never knew he had. Matt averaged 1.7 sacks per game. Matt often blew through the offensive line as if it wasn't there. He was eventually drafted into the NFL.

Steven Wagner

After graduating, Steven Wagner, the guy who let the air out of Ralph's tires, is now working in a tire shop. Every day, the words, "pump," and, "start pumping, pinion head," resonate through his mind, reminding him of his nasty deed. Fortunately, Wagner no longer has to use a bicycle pump to pump up tires.

Appendix I
Track Meet Officials

This section describes the officials found in the typical track meet. Not all meets have officials assigned to the positions described below. In smaller meets, many of the positions described below may overlap. For example, the Head Timekeeper may also fill the position of Meet Director. As another example, Timekeepers may also fulfil the role of a Lane Judge or Starter.

Meet Director

>The Meet Director is responsible for the overall smooth running of the track and field meet. The Meet Director is an administrative position, and is responsible for directing the other officials and volunteers. If there is any conflict, the Meet Director is consulted for a resolution.

Meet Announcer

>The Meet Announcer does exactly that, announces whatever needs to be announced. The Meet Announcer typically opens the meet and offers the opening prayer. During the meet, the Meet Announcer makes the call for contestants to prepare for their events. The initial call is usually 15 minutes before the event, and the final call 5 minutes before the event. In some meets, the Meet Announcer announces the winners of each event at the end of the meet.

Starter

>The Starter issues the start commands. The first command, "on your marks," is only for races in which starting blocks are utilized. Once the runners appear to be ready, the Starter announces, "set," or, "get set." After the runners are set, usually one to three seconds, the Starter fires the gun or sounds the buzzer. In any given meet, there may be multiple Starters for each event. If so, the second Starter, aided by the Lane Judges, issues the signal for any false start.

Meet Clerk

The Meet Clerk compiles and maintains statistics. Based upon these statistics, the Meet Clerk assigns the lanes to the runners. Higher seeded runners are awarded what is considered to be the more desirable lanes.

Head Timekeeper

The Head Timekeeper starts the clock when the start device, either a gun or buzzer, sounds. In smaller meets, the Head Timekeeper could also take the role of the Meet Clerk.

Timekeepers

Timekeepers time each runner. One Timekeeper is usually assigned for each lane. This, however, is not practical in middle school and high school. After the event has completed, the Timekeepers report the times to the Head Timekeeper or the Meet Clerk. In larger meets, Timekeepers may be aided by automated electronic devices. In modern day meets, such as the Olympics, the Timekeeper is completely replaced by electronic devices.

Lane Judge

The Lane Judge is responsible for reporting any infractions during a race. This includes, but not limited to, infractions such as leaving a lane, interfering with another runner, or handing off a baton outside the transition zone during a relay race. Wearing a watch during a race, incidently, is an infraction.

Field Judge

Field Judges manage the field events. Field Judges may have specific titles which more accurately describe what they do. The various responsibilities of a Field Judge may include measuring distances (javelin, discus, shot-put, etc.), watching for fouls, or setting the height of the bar (high jump, pole vault).

The Next Time Around

Eddie has proven himself to be a competitive athlete. There is no longer doubt that Eddie will make the high school track team. In fact, Eddie, Mark, Braden, Johnson, and Mitchell now set the standard that others must live up to. With Kathy now in Eddie's life, and Paula in Mark's, big changes are ahead.

In the next book, Eddie - The Sophomore Year, Mark and Eddie are no longer the bottom of the food chain in high school. In the next book, we will find out:

How well does Eddie perform in the 100-yard dash this next year?

Who was faster during tryouts this year, Eddie or Mark?

Eddie, Mark, Braden, and Johnson, and Bobby B. are recruited by the football coach. Do they decide to be big man on campus and play football?

Anthony Ambrosini had to be carried off the football field during football practice. What exactly happened to him?

Kathy will no longer be helping the track team train, during either indoor or the outdoor season. What happened to cause Mr. Frazier to remove her from her position?

Why do Barbara and Paula stand solidly behind Mr. Frazier's decision to no longer let Kathy help the team train?

Will Paula and Barbara also be removed from their positions as team assistants? Just what is it that these girls are doing that Mr. Frazier must consider dismissing them from their duties?

Does Hoffer have what it takes to make the high school track team?

Will Tessa be helping out with the track team this next year?

Do Mark and Paula stay together?

Eddie gets in serious trouble and may not be able to run track for a while. What exactly did Eddie do? What happens when the school principal tries to suspend him?

What happens with Johnson and Barbara? Do they stay together, or was their interest in each other like a fleeting mist?

Mahoney is back, and makes a huge scene at the end of the Summer. What ultimately happened to Mahoney?

The truth about Mahoney finally comes out. What is it that is causing him to go crazy all the time?

Kathy, Paula, Barbara, and Tessa plan and carry out quite a controversy at the State invitational meet. What exactly is the controversy that irritates so many of the coaches.

Eddie and Kathy find out something amazingly new about the portal. What is their discovery?

Kathy gets her driver's license and wants to buy a car. She obtains one on impulse, without telling her parents. What is her parent's reaction?

What kind of car did Kathy buy?